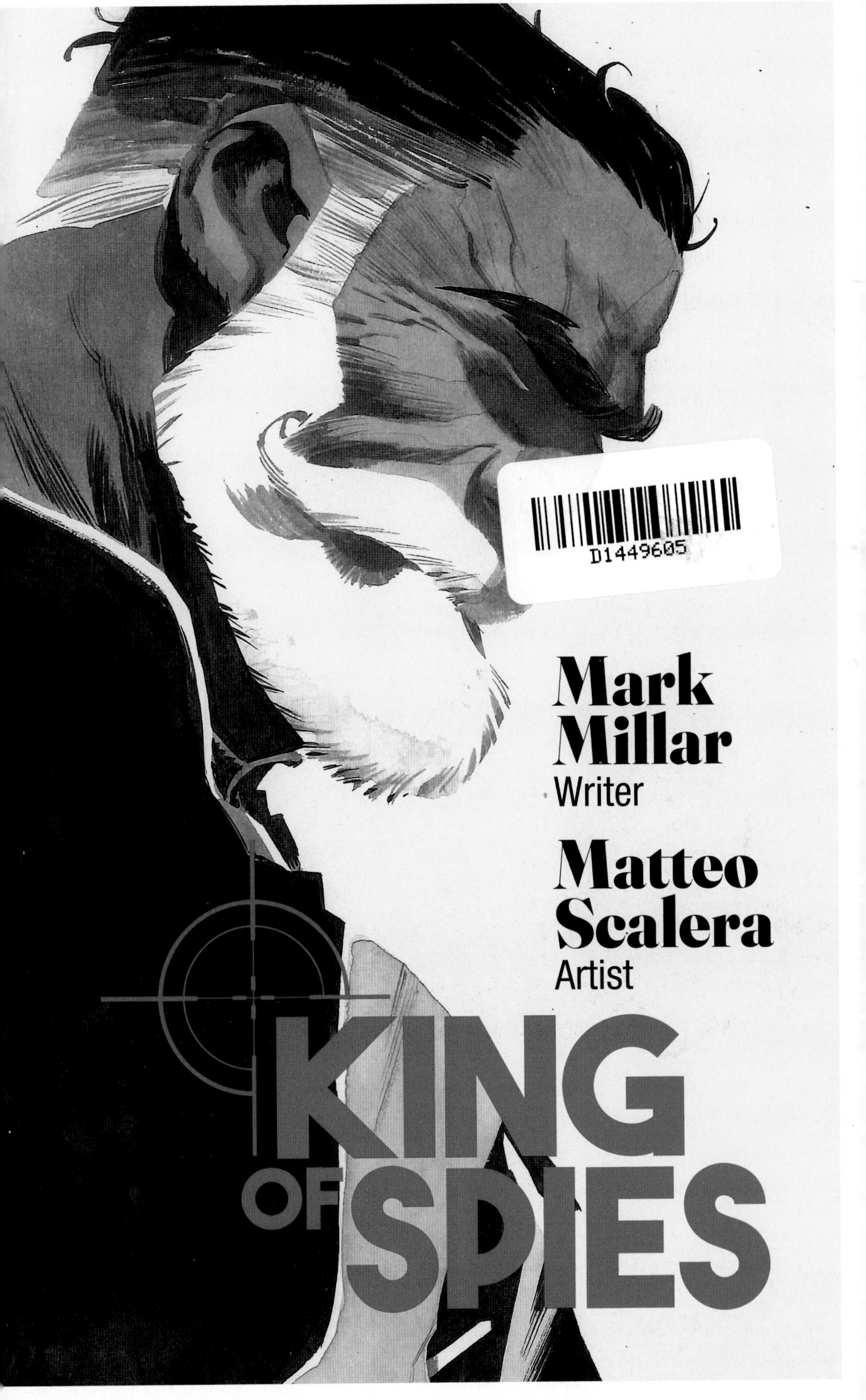

Mark Millar
Writer
Matteo Scalera
Artist
KING OF SPIES

Giovanna Niro
Colourist

Clem Robins
Letterer

Melina Mikulic
Design and Production

Frances Mullen
Sarah Unwin
Editorial Production Managers

Lucy Millar
CEO

Design Team
Ozgur Yildirim
Eddie Thornton

KING OF SPIES

Created by Mark Millar at Netflix

IMAGE COMICS, INC. · Robert Kirkman: Chief Operating Officer · Erik Larsen: Chief Financial Officer · Todd McFarlane: President · Marc Silvestri: Chief Executive Officer · Jim Valentino: Vice President · Eric Stephenson: Publisher / Chief Creative Officer · Nicole Lapalme: Controller · Leanna Caunter: Accounting Analyst · Su Korpela: Accounting & HR Manager · Marla Eizik: Talent Liaison · Jeff Boison: Director of Sales & Publishing Planning · Lorelei Bunjes: Director of Digital Services · Dir Wood: Director of International Sales & Licensing · Alex Cox: Director of Direct Market Sales · Chloe Ramos: Book Market & Library Sales Manager · Emilio Bautista Digital Sales Coordinator · Jon Schlaffman: Specialty Sales Coordinator · Kat Salazar: Director of PR & Marketing · Monica Garcia: Marketing Design Manager · Drew Fitzgerald: Marketing Content Associate · Heather Doornink: Production Director · Drew Gill: Art Director · Hilary DiLoreto: Print Manager · Tricia Ramos: Traffic Manager · Melissa Gifford: Content Manager · Erika Schnatz: Senior Production Artist · Ryan Brewer: Production Artist · Deanna Phelps: Production Artist · **IMAGECOMICS.COM**

KING OF SPIES TP. First printing. May 2022. Published by Image Comics, Inc. Office of publication: PO BOX 14457, Portland, OR 97293. Copyright © 2022 Netflix Entertainment, LLC. All rights reserved. Contains material originally published in single magazine form as KING OF SPIES #1-4. "King of Spies" its logos, and the likenesses of all characters herein are trademarks of Netflix Entertainment, LLC unless otherwise noted. "Image" and the Image Comics logos are registered trademarks of Image Comics, Inc. No part of this publication may be reproduced or transmitted, in any form or by any means (except for short excerpts for journalistic or review purposes), without the express written permission of Netflix Entertainment, LLC or Image Comics, Inc. All names, characters, events, and locales in this publication are entirely fictional. Any resemblance to actual persons (living or dead), events, or places, without satiric intent, is coincidental. Printed in Canada. For international rights, contact: lucy@netflixmw.com. ISBN: 978-1-5343-2212-7

One

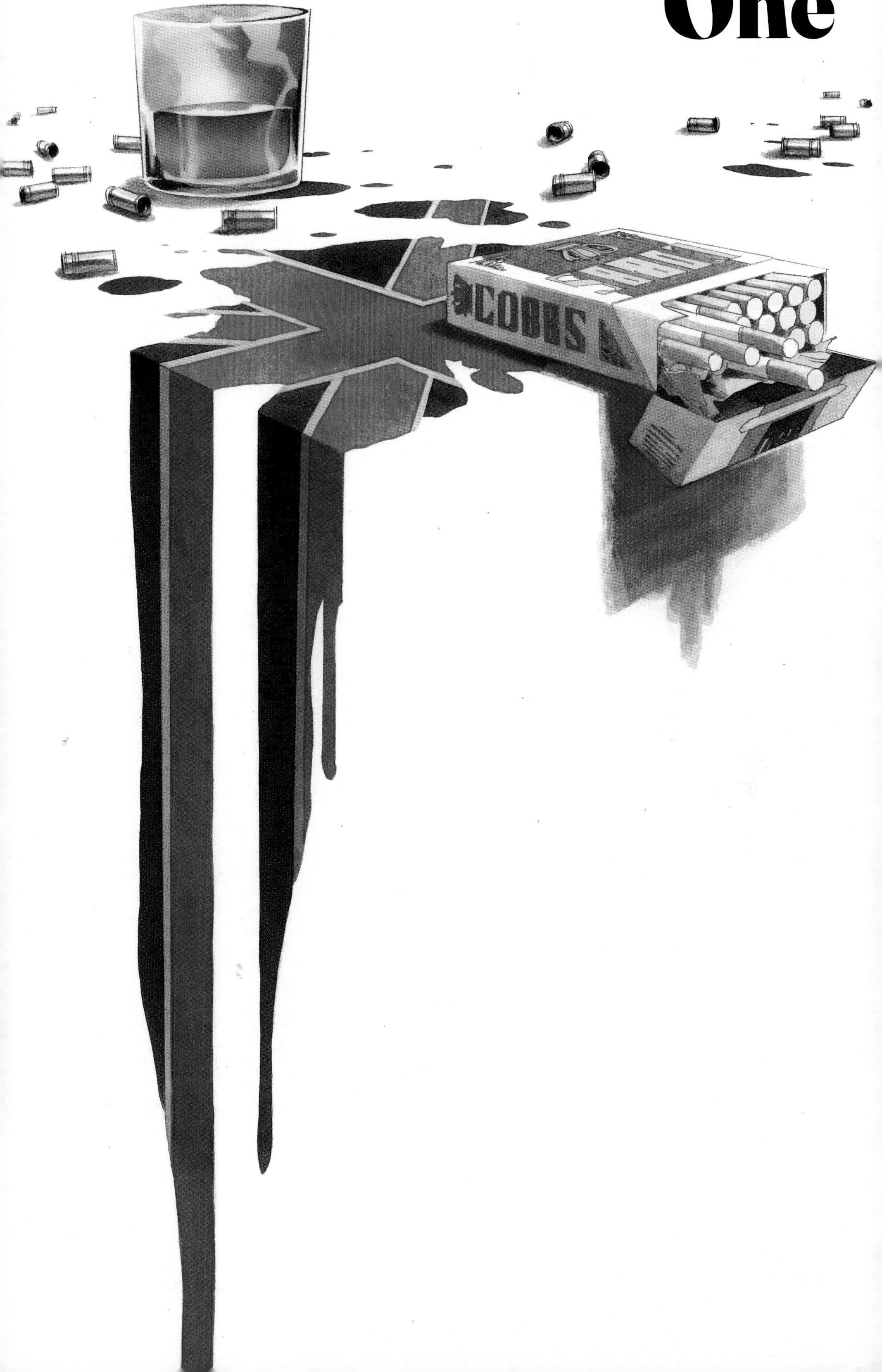
COBBS

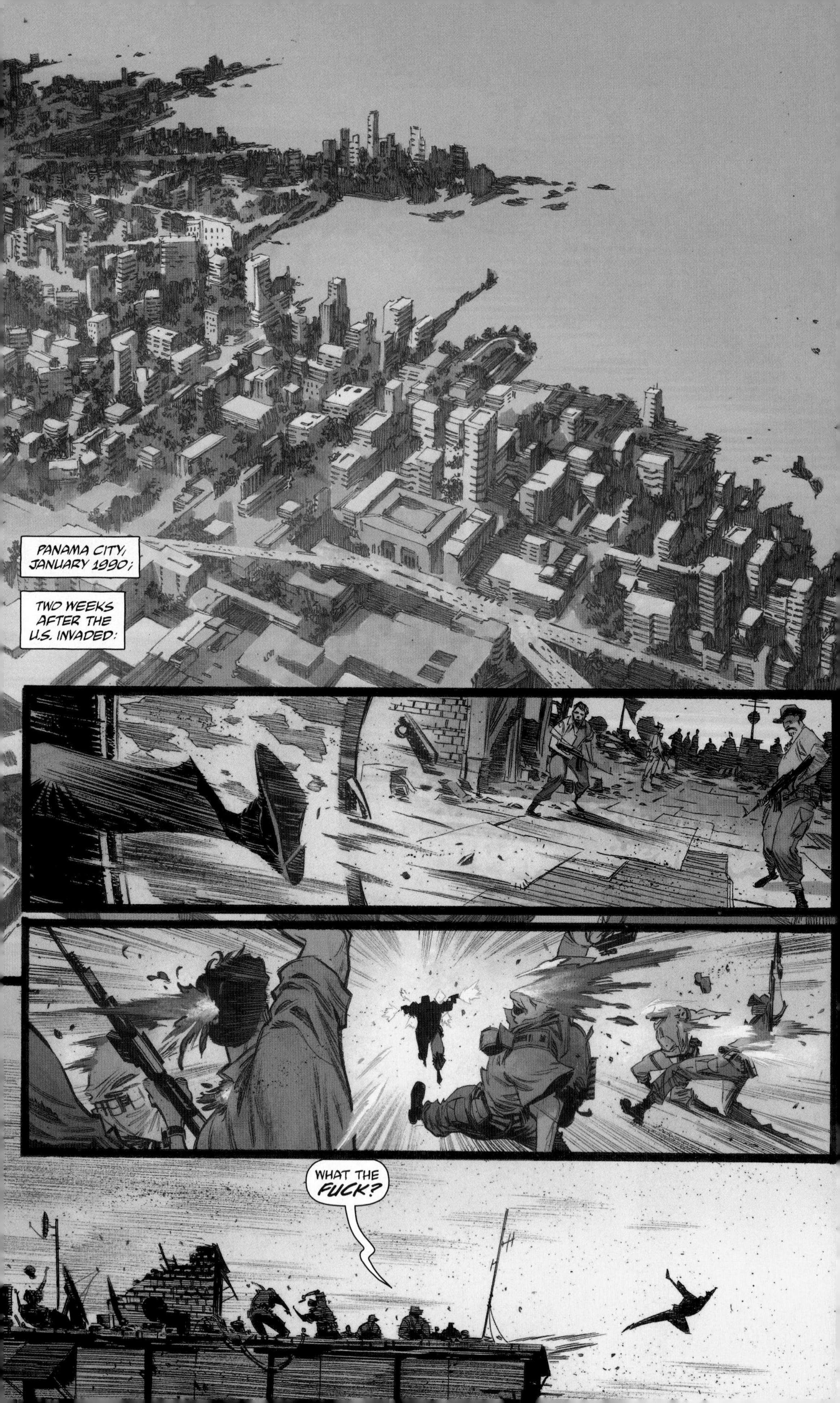
PANAMA CITY, JANUARY 1990;
TWO WEEKS AFTER THE U.S. INVADED:
WHAT THE FUCK?

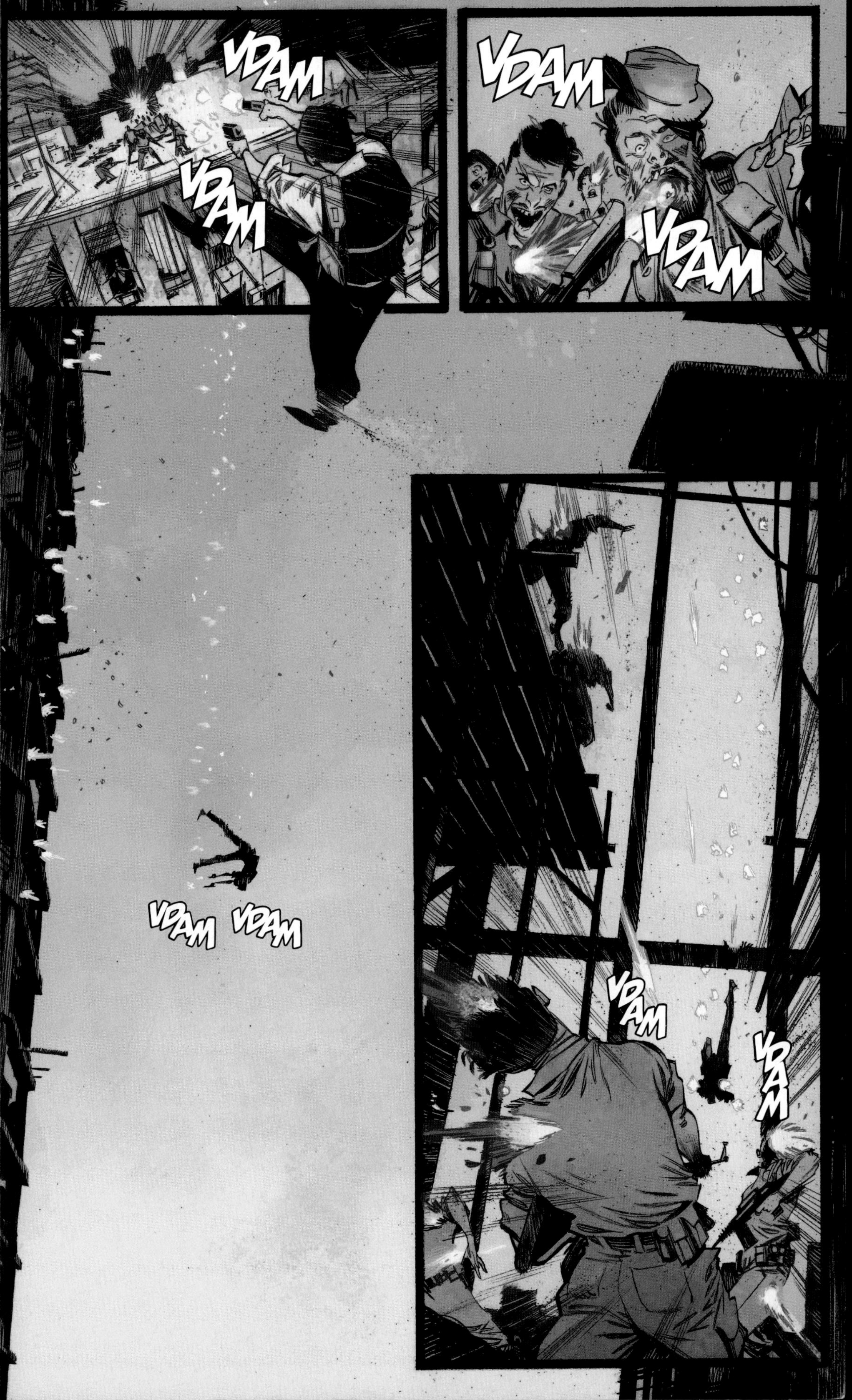
VDAM
VDAM
VDAM
VDAM
VDAM
VDAM
VDAM
VDAM

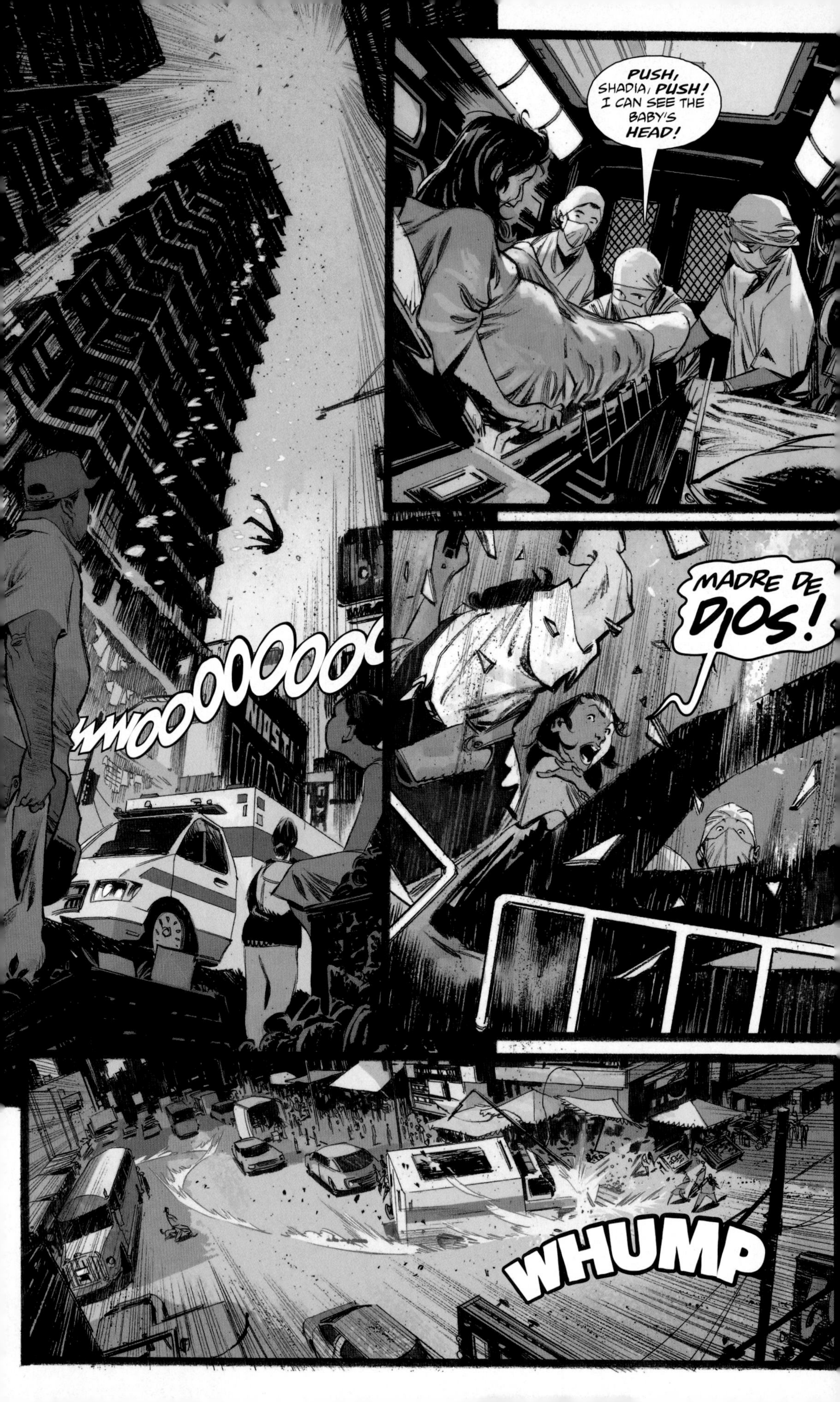
PUSH, SHADIA, PUSH! I CAN SEE THE BABY'S HEAD!
WWOOOOOOOOO
MADRE DE DIOS!
WHUMP

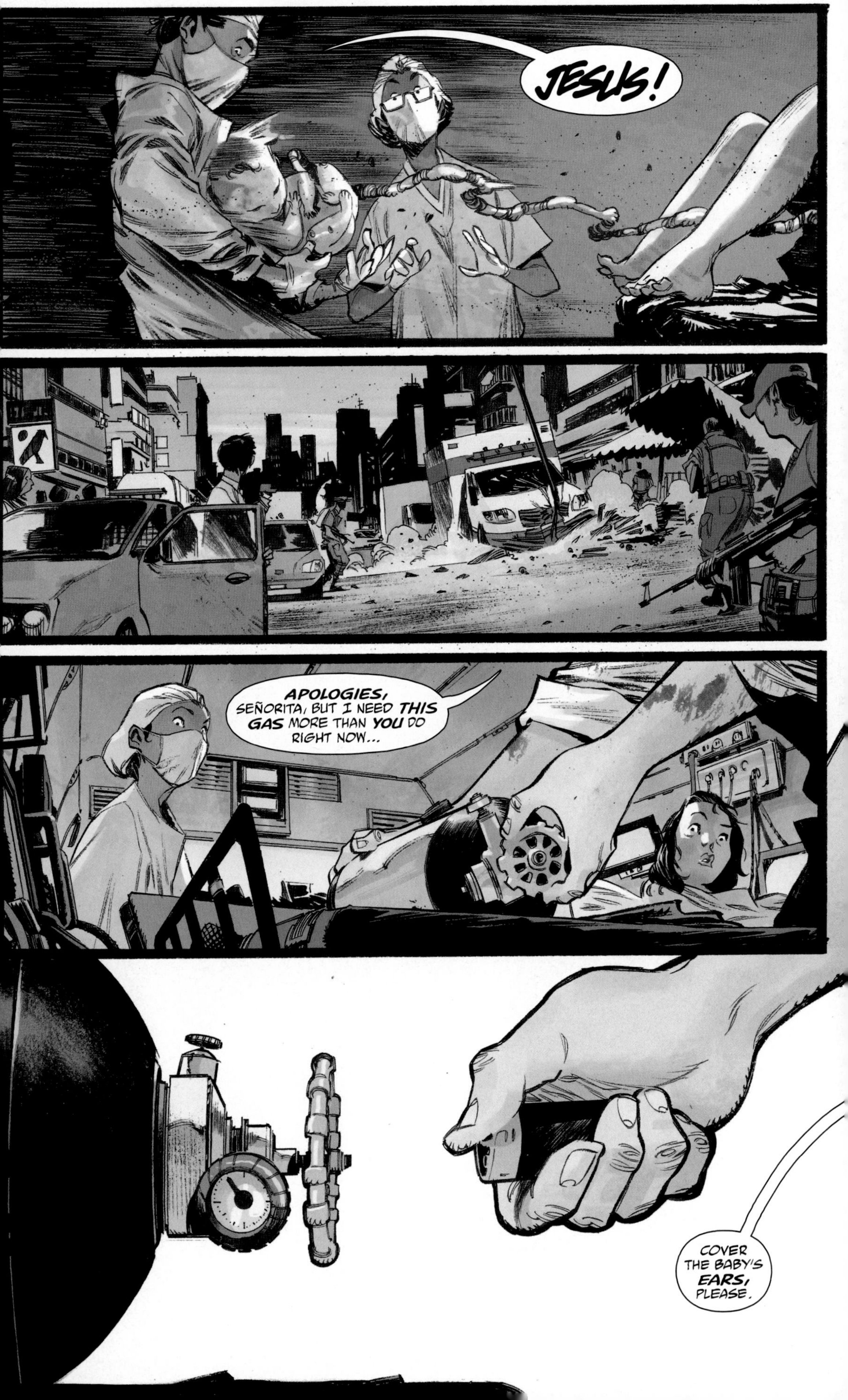
JESUS!
APOLOGIES, SEÑORITA, BUT I NEED THIS GAS MORE THAN YOU DO RIGHT NOW...
COVER THE BABY'S EARS, PLEASE.

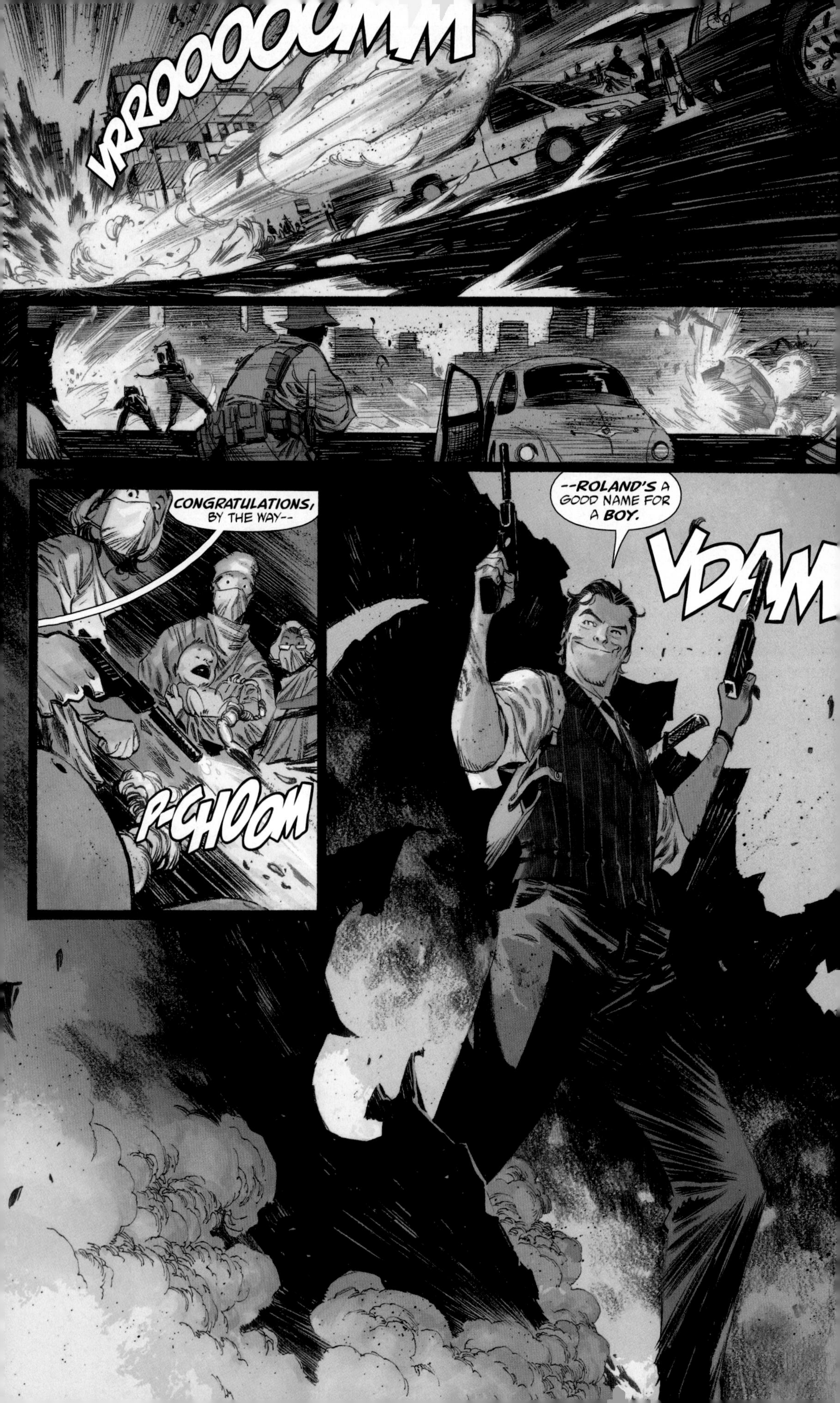
VRROOOOOMM
CONGRATULATIONS, BY THE WAY--
P-CHOOM
--ROLAND'S A GOOD NAME FOR A BOY.
VDAM

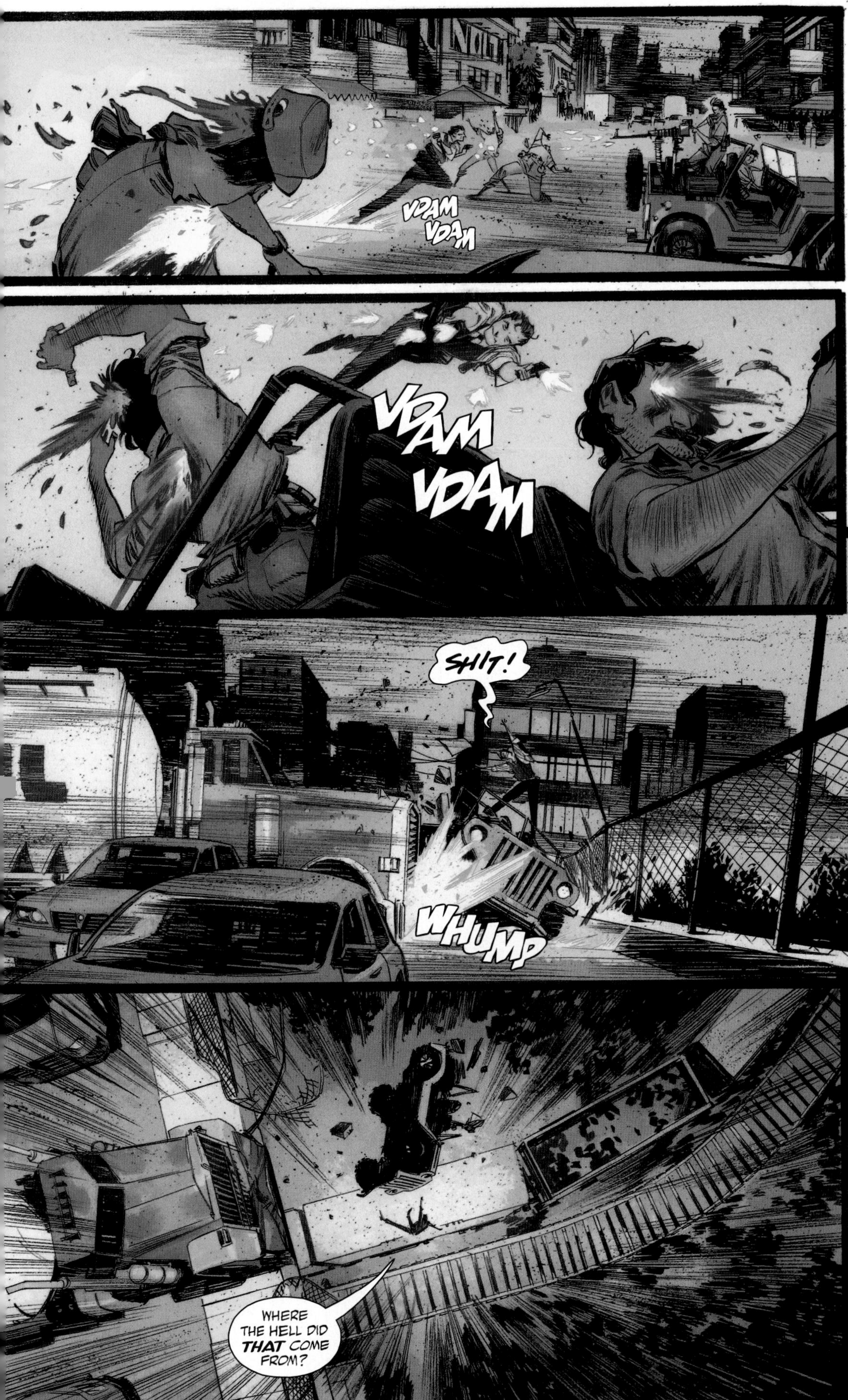
VDAM
VDAM
VDAM
VDAM
SHIT!
WHUMP
WHERE THE HELL DID **THAT** COME FROM?

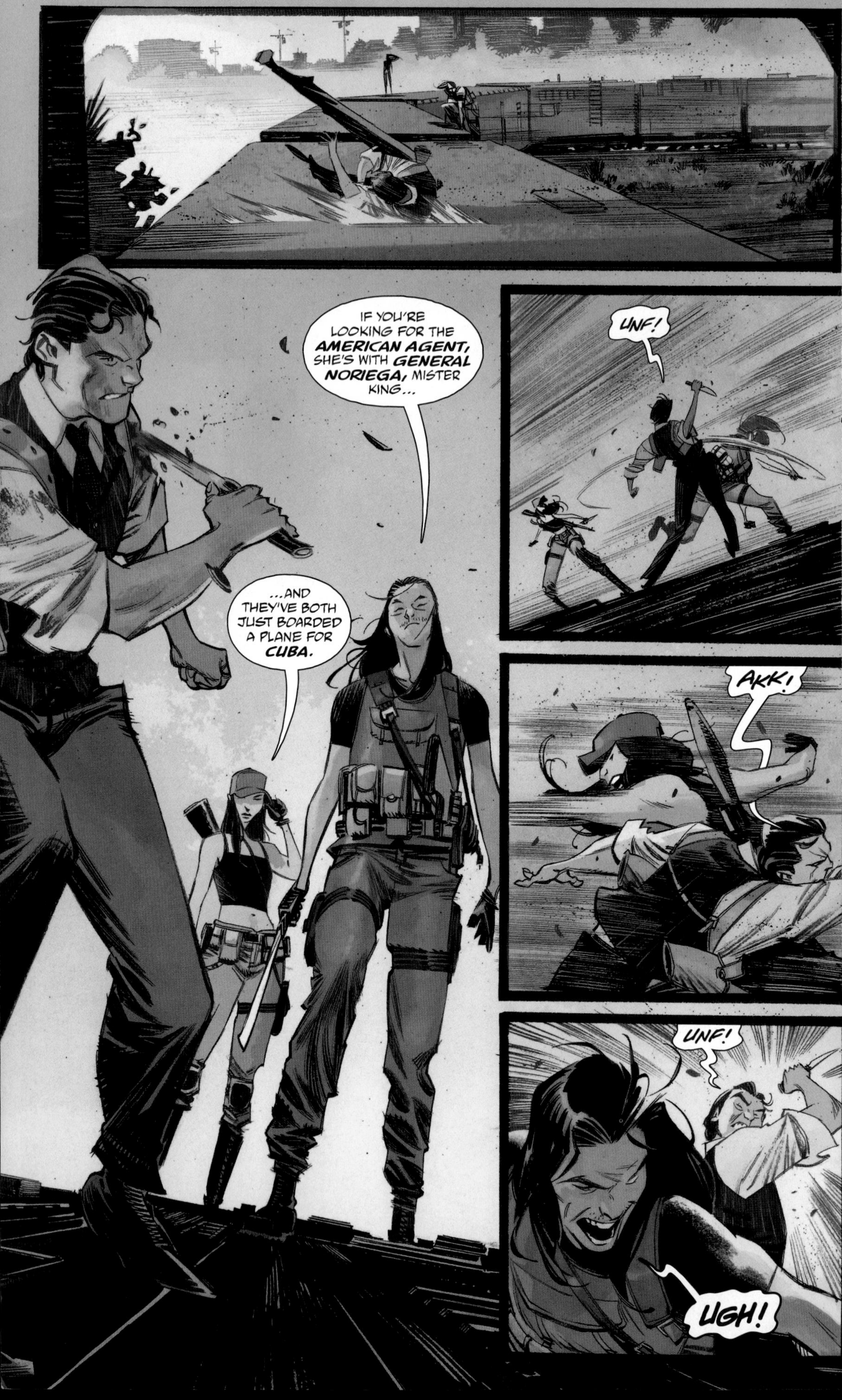
IF YOU'RE LOOKING FOR THE AMERICAN AGENT, SHE'S WITH GENERAL NORIEGA, MISTER KING...
...AND THEY'VE BOTH JUST BOARDED A PLANE FOR CUBA.
UNF!
AKK!
UNF!
UGH!

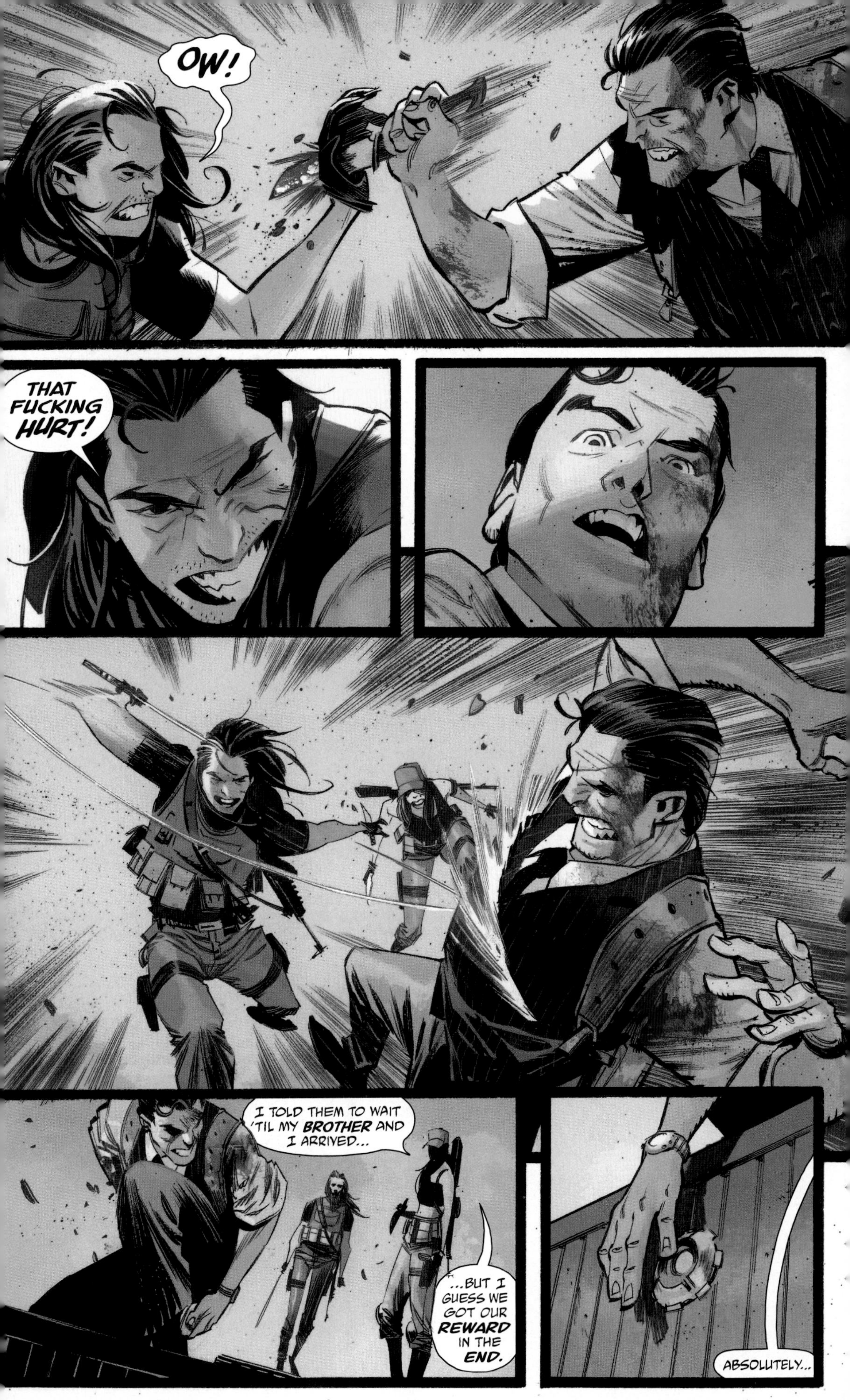
OW!
THAT FUCKING HURT!
I TOLD THEM TO WAIT 'TIL MY BROTHER AND I ARRIVED...
...BUT I GUESS WE GOT OUR REWARD IN THE END.
ABSOLUTELY...

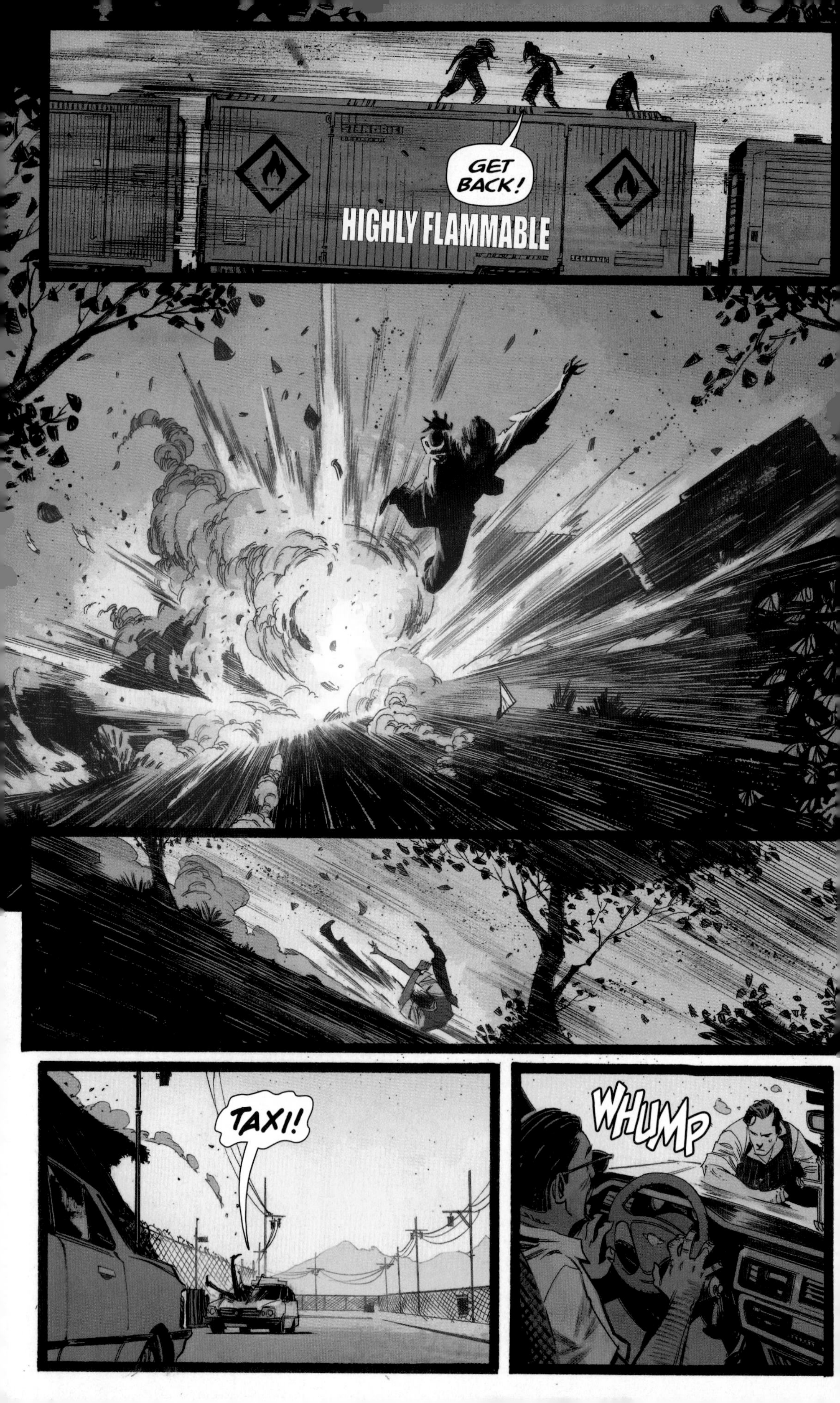
GET BACK!
HIGHLY FLAMMABLE
TAXI!
WHUMP

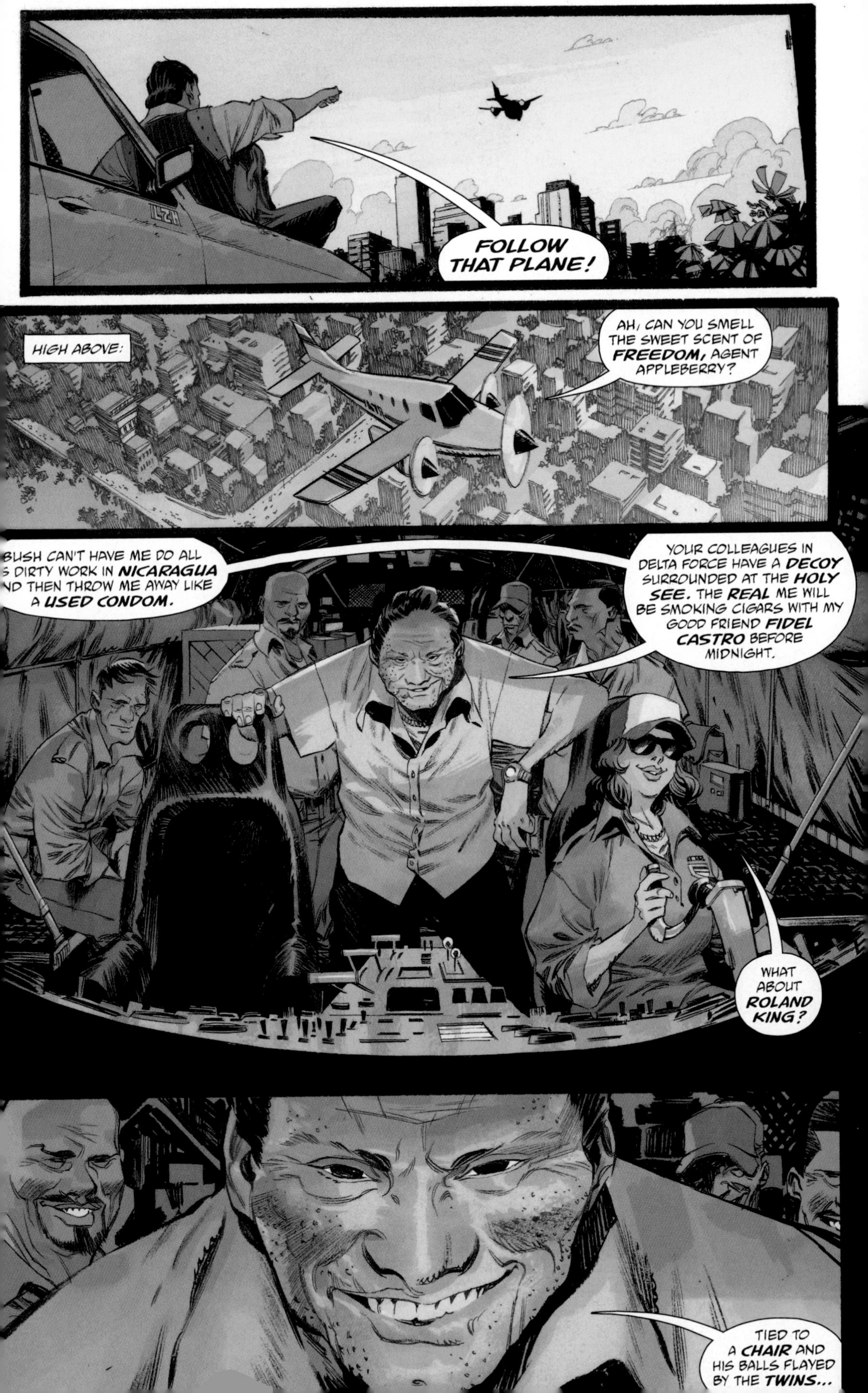
FOLLOW THAT PLANE!
HIGH ABOVE:
AH, CAN YOU SMELL THE SWEET SCENT OF FREEDOM, AGENT APPLEBERRY?
BUSH CAN'T HAVE ME DO ALL
S DIRTY WORK IN NICARAGUA
ND THEN THROW ME AWAY LIKE
A USED CONDOM.
YOUR COLLEAGUES IN DELTA FORCE HAVE A DECOY SURROUNDED AT THE HOLY SEE. THE REAL ME WILL BE SMOKING CIGARS WITH MY GOOD FRIEND FIDEL CASTRO BEFORE MIDNIGHT.
WHAT ABOUT ROLAND KING?
TIED TO A CHAIR AND HIS BALLS FLAYED BY THE TWINS...

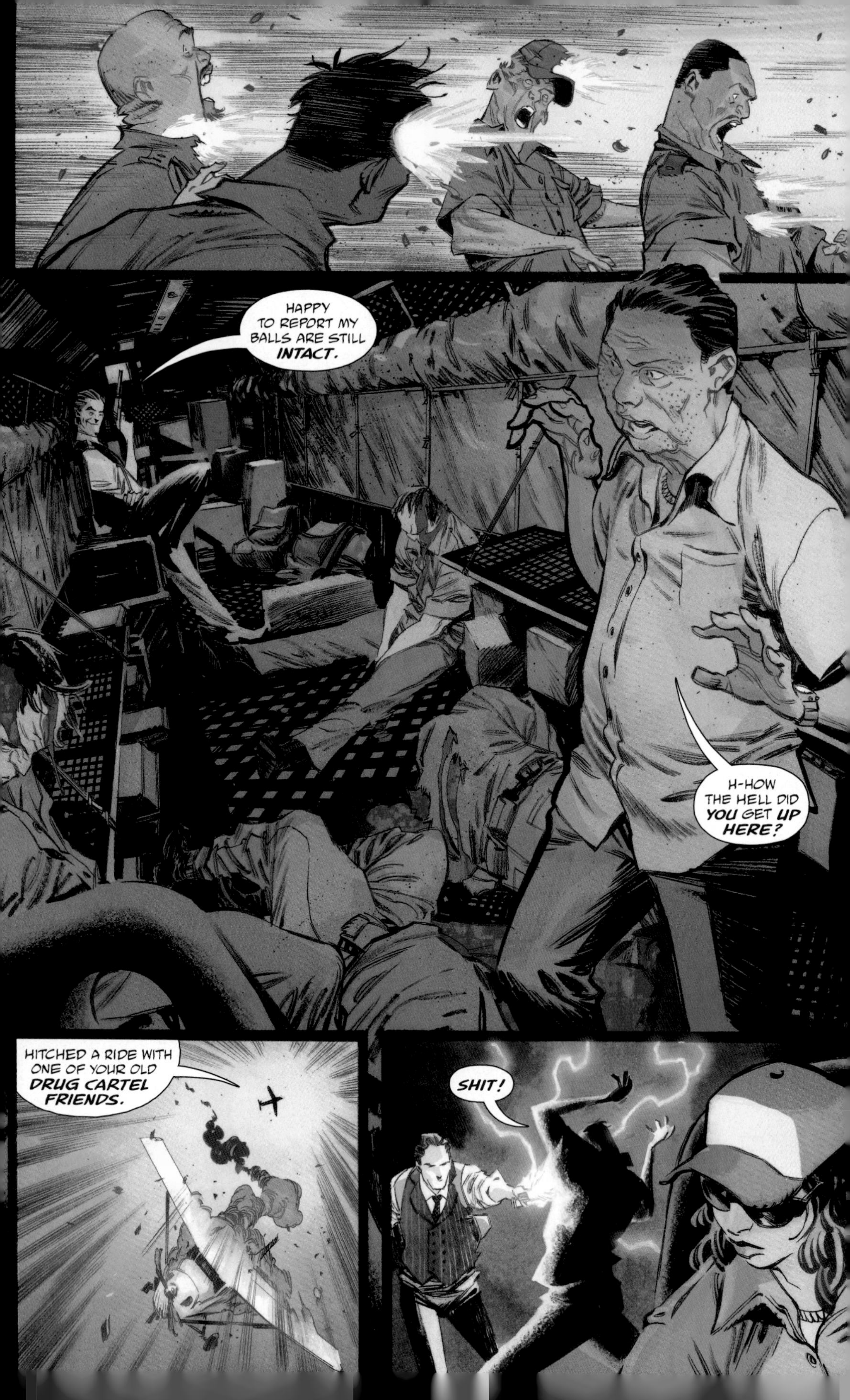
HAPPY TO REPORT MY BALLS ARE STILL **INTACT.**
H-HOW THE HELL DID **YOU** GET **UP HERE?**
HITCHED A RIDE WITH ONE OF YOUR OLD **DRUG CARTEL FRIENDS.**
SHIT!

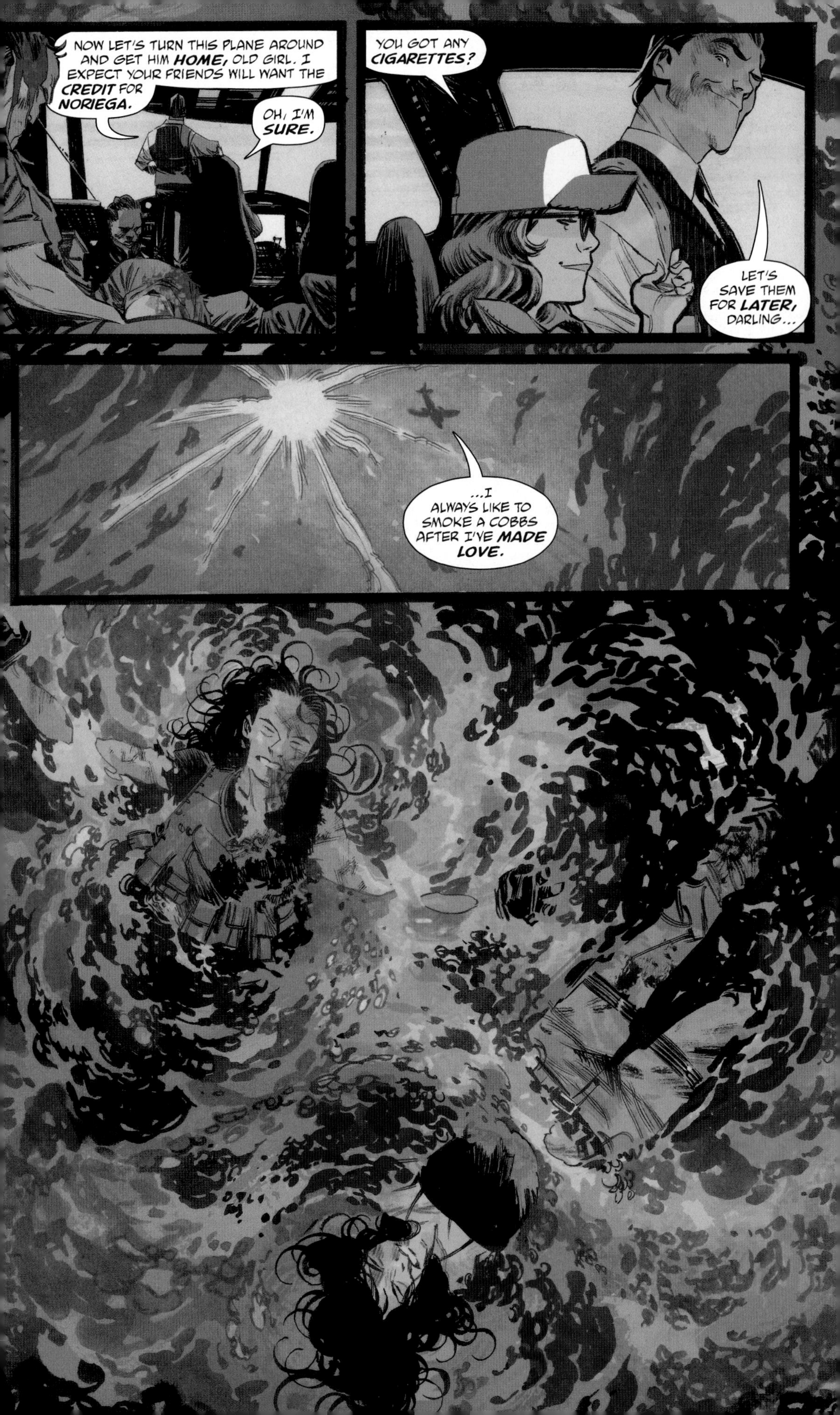
NOW LET'S TURN THIS PLANE AROUND AND GET HIM HOME, OLD GIRL. I EXPECT YOUR FRIENDS WILL WANT THE CREDIT FOR NORIEGA.
OH, I'M SURE.
YOU GOT ANY CIGARETTES?
LET'S SAVE THEM FOR LATER, DARLING...
...I ALWAYS LIKE TO SMOKE A COBBS AFTER I'VE MADE LOVE.

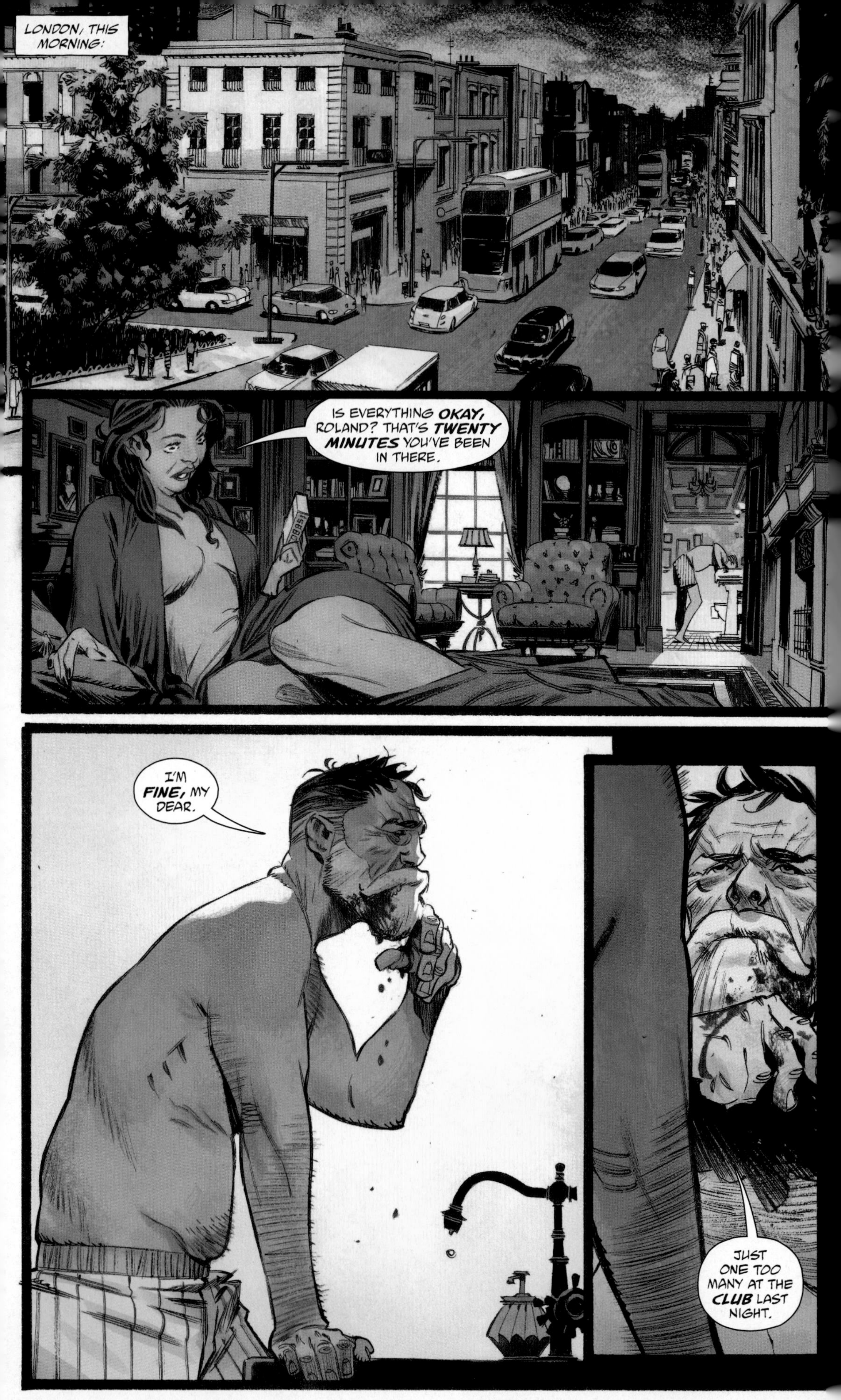
LONDON, THIS MORNING:
IS EVERYTHING OKAY, ROLAND? THAT'S TWENTY MINUTES YOU'VE BEEN IN THERE.
I'M FINE, MY DEAR.
JUST ONE TOO MANY AT THE CLUB LAST NIGHT.

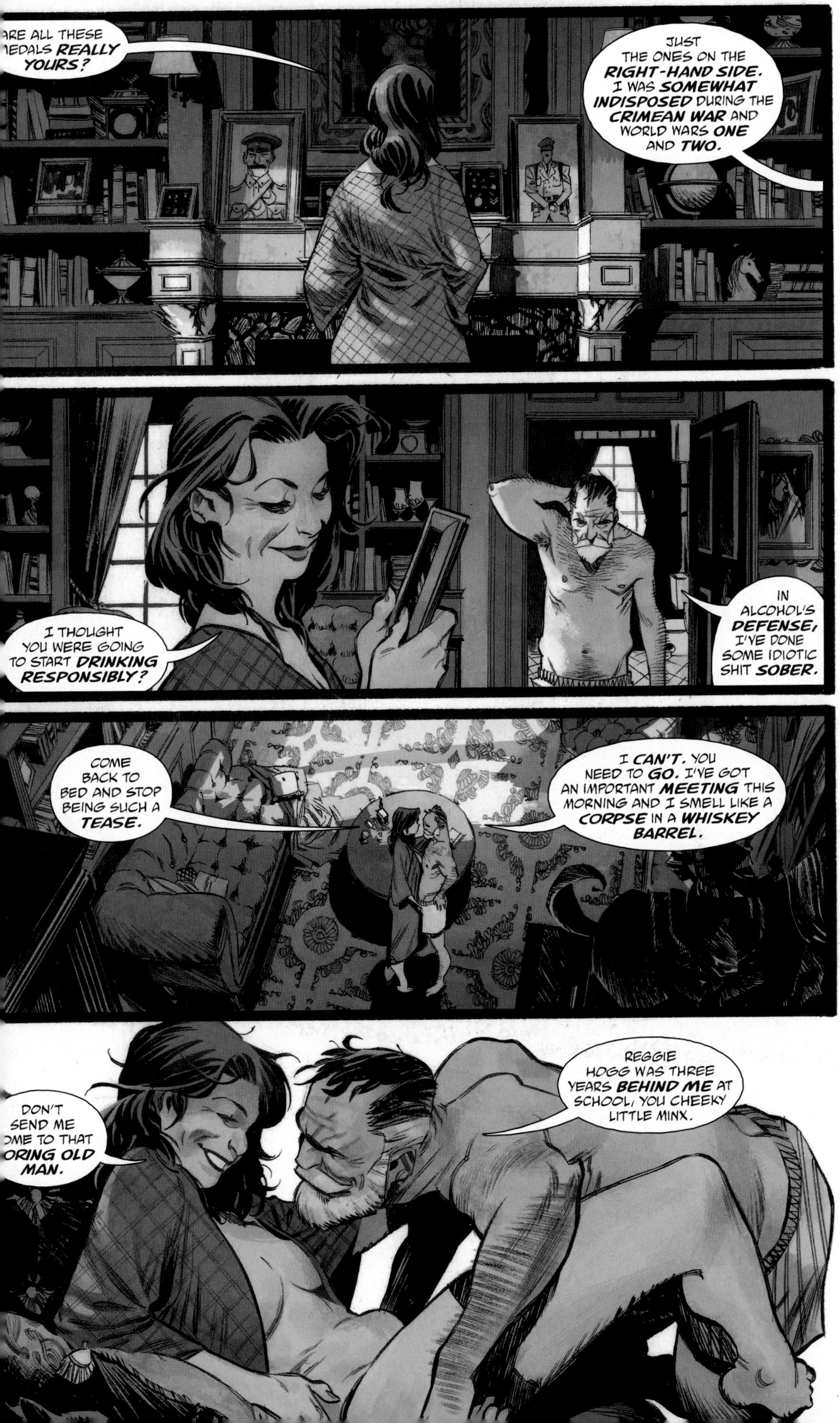

ARE ALL THESE MEDALS REALLY YOURS?
JUST THE ONES ON THE RIGHT-HAND SIDE. I WAS SOMEWHAT INDISPOSED DURING THE CRIMEAN WAR AND WORLD WARS ONE AND TWO.
I THOUGHT YOU WERE GOING TO START DRINKING RESPONSIBLY?
IN ALCOHOL'S DEFENSE, I'VE DONE SOME IDIOTIC SHIT SOBER.
COME BACK TO BED AND STOP BEING SUCH A TEASE.
I CAN'T. YOU NEED TO GO. I'VE GOT AN IMPORTANT MEETING THIS MORNING AND I SMELL LIKE A CORPSE IN A WHISKEY BARREL.
DON'T SEND ME OME TO THAT ORING OLD MAN.
REGGIE HOGG WAS THREE YEARS BEHIND ME AT SCHOOL, YOU CHEEKY LITTLE MINX.

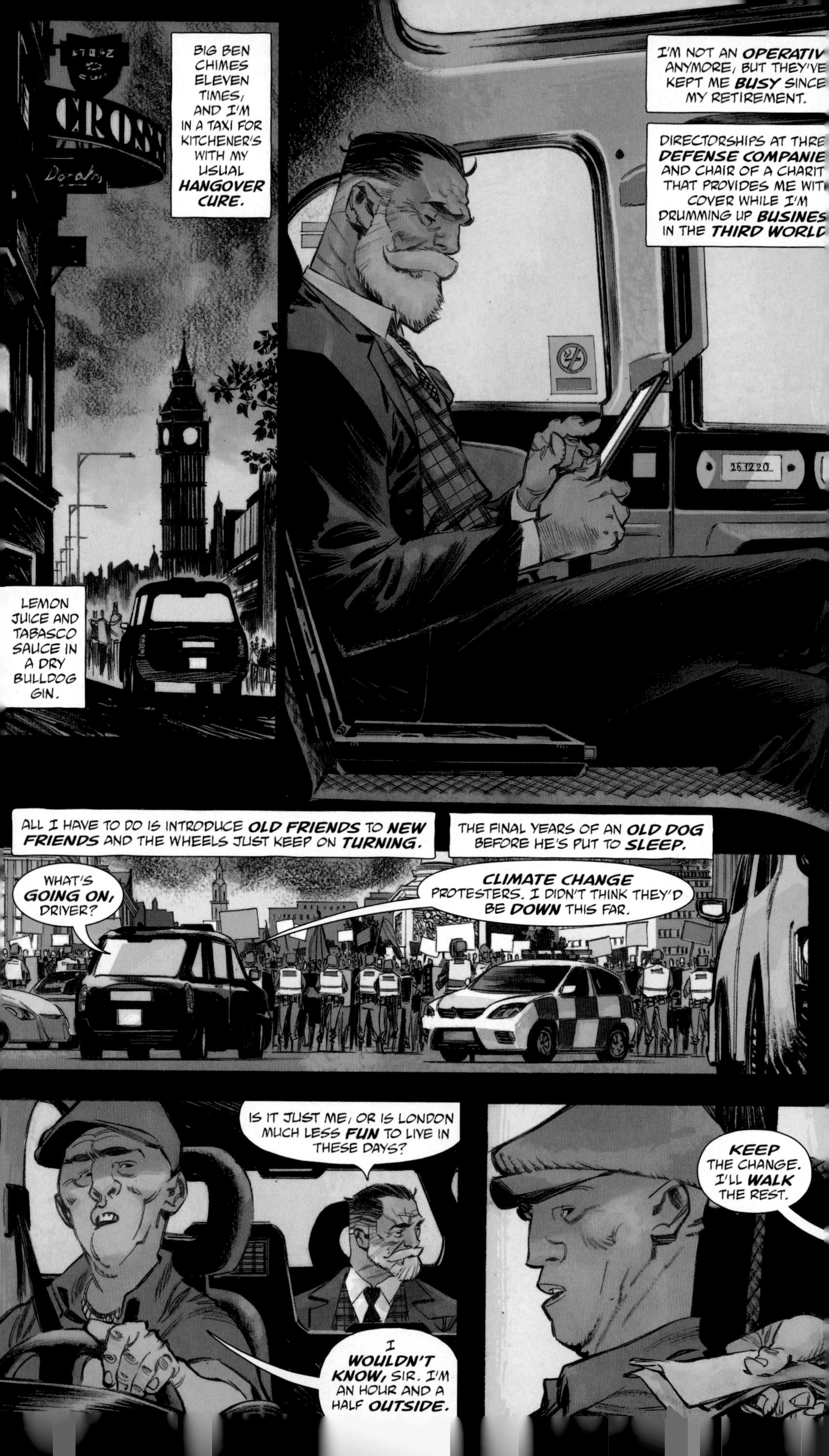

BIG BEN CHIMES ELEVEN TIMES, AND I'M IN A TAXI FOR KITCHENER'S WITH MY USUAL HANGOVER CURE.
LEMON JUICE AND TABASCO SAUCE IN A DRY BULLDOG GIN.
I'M NOT AN OPERATIV ANYMORE, BUT THEY'VE KEPT ME BUSY SINCE MY RETIREMENT.
DIRECTORSHIPS AT THRE DEFENSE COMPANIE AND CHAIR OF A CHARIT THAT PROVIDES ME WIT COVER WHILE I'M DRUMMING UP BUSINES IN THE THIRD WORLD
ALL I HAVE TO DO IS INTRODUCE OLD FRIENDS TO NEW FRIENDS AND THE WHEELS JUST KEEP ON TURNING.
THE FINAL YEARS OF AN OLD DOG BEFORE HE'S PUT TO SLEEP.
WHAT'S GOING ON, DRIVER?
CLIMATE CHANGE PROTESTERS. I DIDN'T THINK THEY'D BE DOWN THIS FAR.
IS IT JUST ME, OR IS LONDON MUCH LESS FUN TO LIVE IN THESE DAYS?
I WOULDN'T KNOW, SIR. I'M AN HOUR AND A HALF OUTSIDE.
KEEP THE CHANGE. I'LL WALK THE REST.

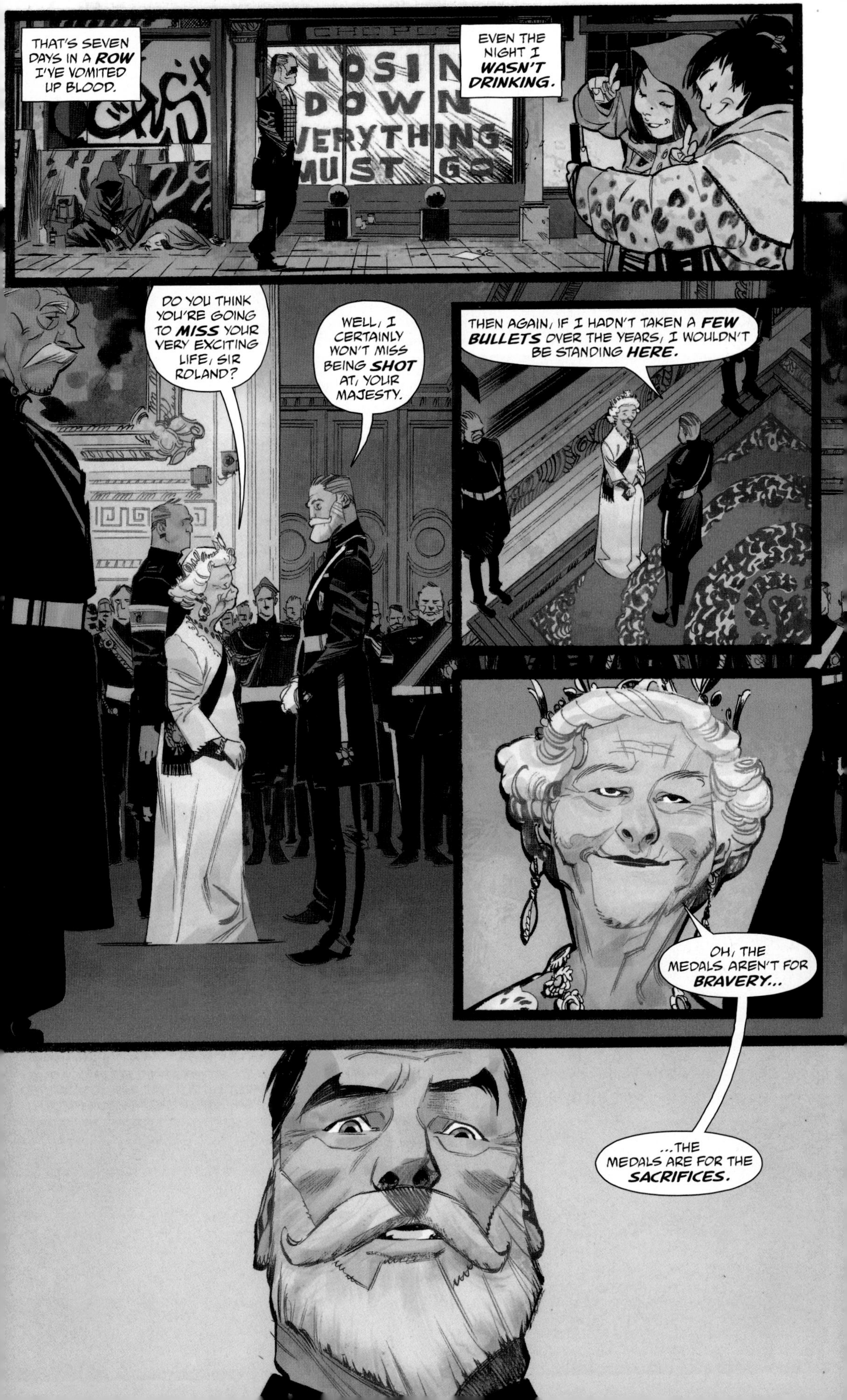
THAT'S SEVEN DAYS IN A ROW I'VE VOMITED UP BLOOD.
LOSIN DOWN VERYTHING MUST GO
EVEN THE NIGHT I WASN'T DRINKING.
DO YOU THINK YOU'RE GOING TO MISS YOUR VERY EXCITING LIFE, SIR ROLAND?
WELL, I CERTAINLY WON'T MISS BEING SHOT AT, YOUR MAJESTY.
THEN AGAIN, IF I HADN'T TAKEN A FEW BULLETS OVER THE YEARS, I WOULDN'T BE STANDING HERE.
OH, THE MEDALS AREN'T FOR BRAVERY...
...THE MEDALS ARE FOR THE SACRIFICES.

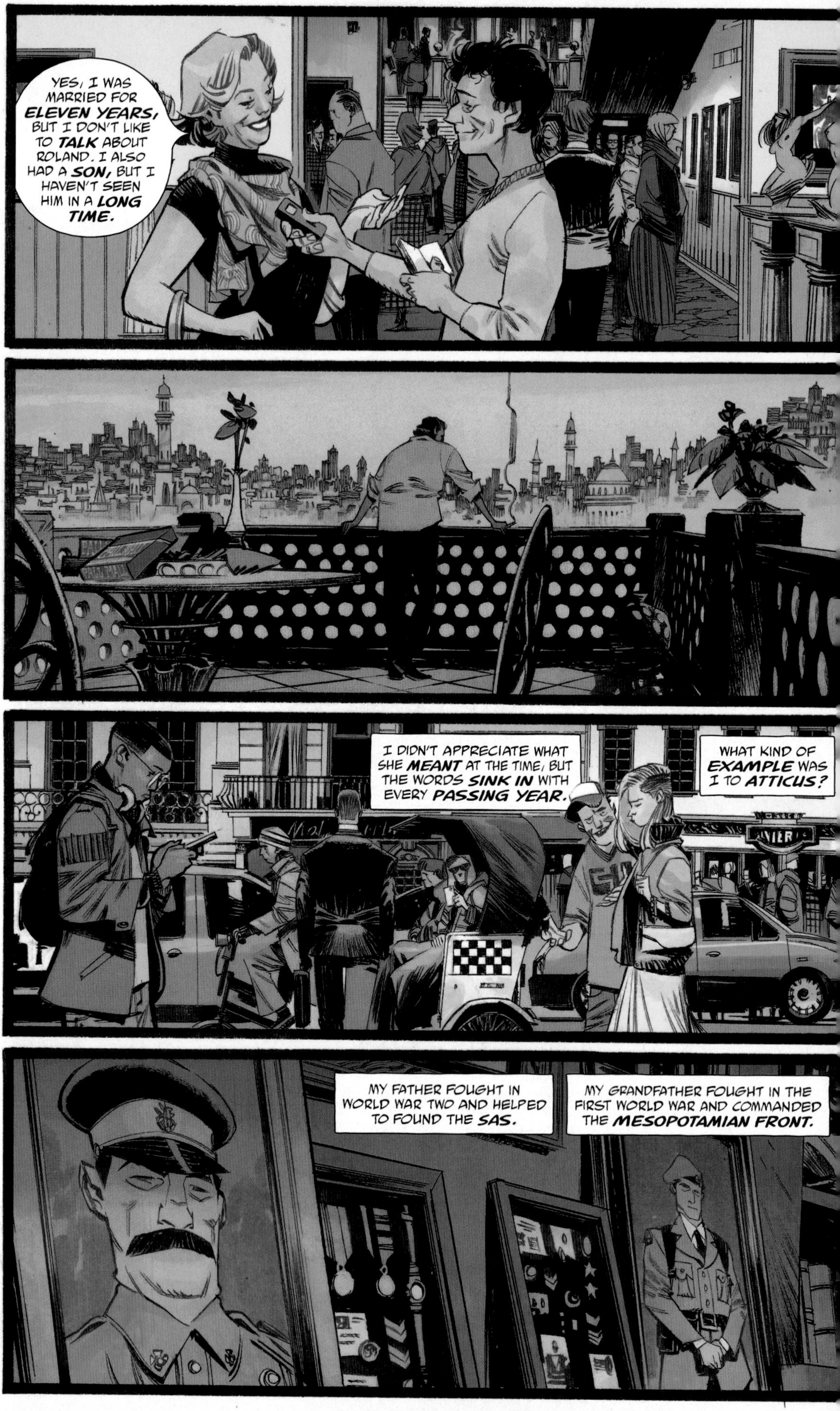
YES, I WAS MARRIED FOR ELEVEN YEARS, BUT I DON'T LIKE TO TALK ABOUT ROLAND. I ALSO HAD A SON, BUT I HAVEN'T SEEN HIM IN A LONG TIME.
I DIDN'T APPRECIATE WHAT SHE MEANT AT THE TIME, BUT THE WORDS SINK IN WITH EVERY PASSING YEAR.
WHAT KIND OF EXAMPLE WAS I TO ATTICUS?
MY FATHER FOUGHT IN WORLD WAR TWO AND HELPED TO FOUND THE SAS.
MY GRANDFATHER FOUGHT IN THE FIRST WORLD WAR AND COMMANDED THE MESOPOTAMIAN FRONT.

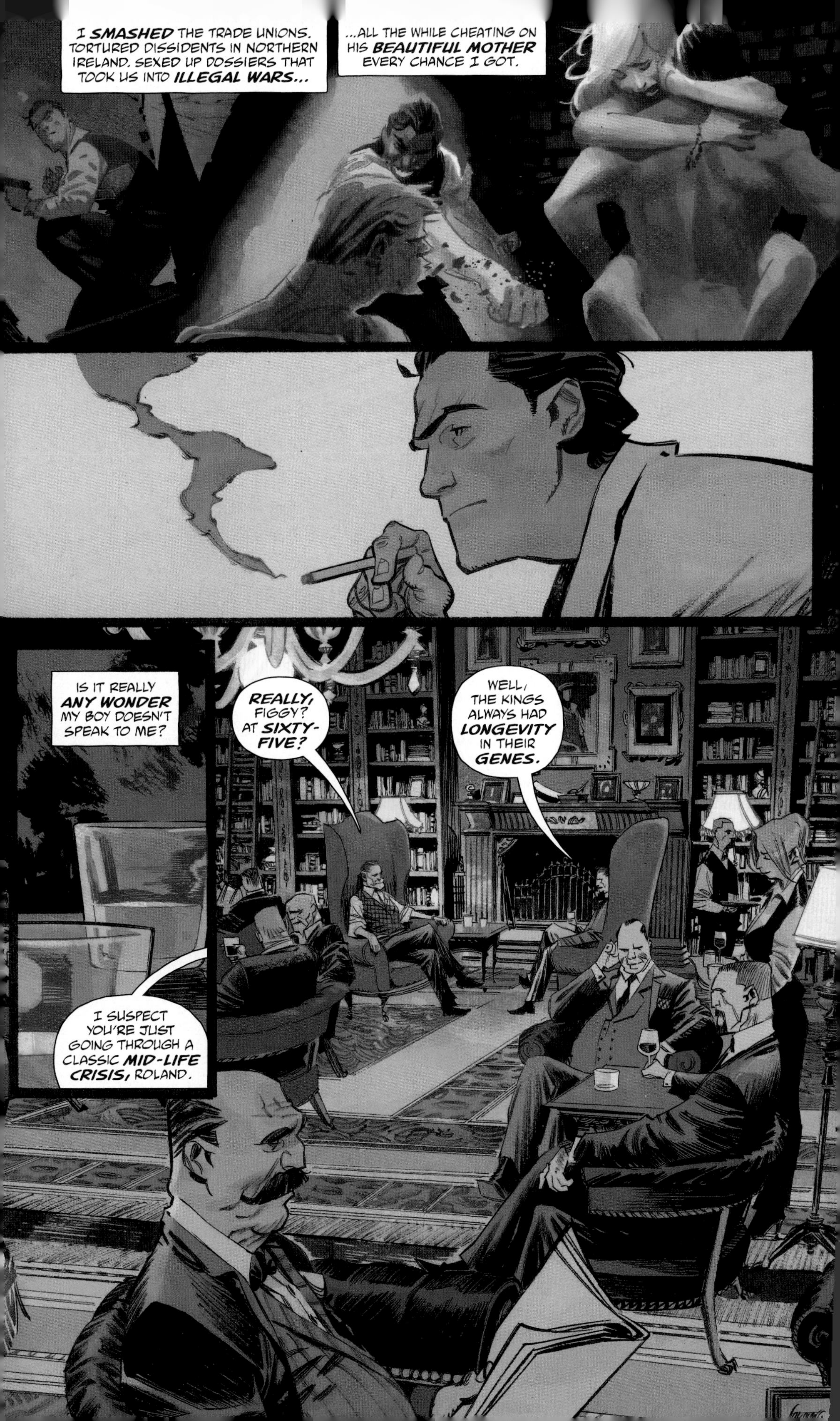
I SMASHED THE TRADE UNIONS. TORTURED DISSIDENTS IN NORTHERN IRELAND. SEXED UP DOSSIERS THAT TOOK US INTO ILLEGAL WARS...
...ALL THE WHILE CHEATING ON HIS BEAUTIFUL MOTHER EVERY CHANCE I GOT.
IS IT REALLY ANY WONDER MY BOY DOESN'T SPEAK TO ME?
REALLY, FIGGY? AT SIXTY-FIVE?
WELL, THE KINGS ALWAYS HAD LONGEVITY IN THEIR GENES.
I SUSPECT YOU'RE JUST GOING THROUGH A CLASSIC MID-LIFE CRISIS, ROLAND.

I JUST WORRY SOMETIMES WE MADE A **MESS** OF THINGS. ALL THOSE YEARS WE WERE OUT IN THE FIELD. DID WE EVER MAKE A **DIFFERENCE?**

WE'RE NOT **SUPPOSED** TO MAKE A DIFFERENCE. THE JOB IS DEFENDING A **WORKING SYSTEM.** WE'VE BOTH SEEN WHAT HAPPENS WHEN **EMPIRES FALL.**

SOMETIMES I THINK IT'S FALLEN **ALREADY.**

MORE DRINK!

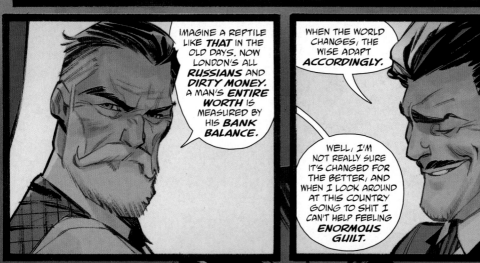

IMAGINE A REPTILE LIKE **THAT** IN THE OLD DAYS. NOW LONDON'S ALL **RUSSIANS** AND **DIRTY MONEY.** A MAN'S **ENTIRE WORTH** IS MEASURED BY HIS **BANK BALANCE.**

WHEN THE WORLD CHANGES, THE WISE ADAPT **ACCORDINGLY.**

WELL, I'M NOT REALLY SURE IT'S CHANGED FOR THE BETTER, AND WHEN I LOOK AROUND AT THIS COUNTRY GOING TO SHIT I CAN'T HELP FEELING **ENORMOUS GUILT.**

WHY?

BECAUSE THIS IS THE WORLD WE FORGED FOR OUR **CHILDREN.** WE **ALWAYS KNEW** WHO THE REAL CROOKS WERE, BUT WE WERE ALL TOO BUSY **FEATHERING** OUR **OWN NESTS.**

MEN LIKE US COULD HAVE **CHANGED THE WORLD,** BUT WE TURNED A BLIND EYE FOR THE **MONEY** AND THE **LITTLE TRINKETS.**

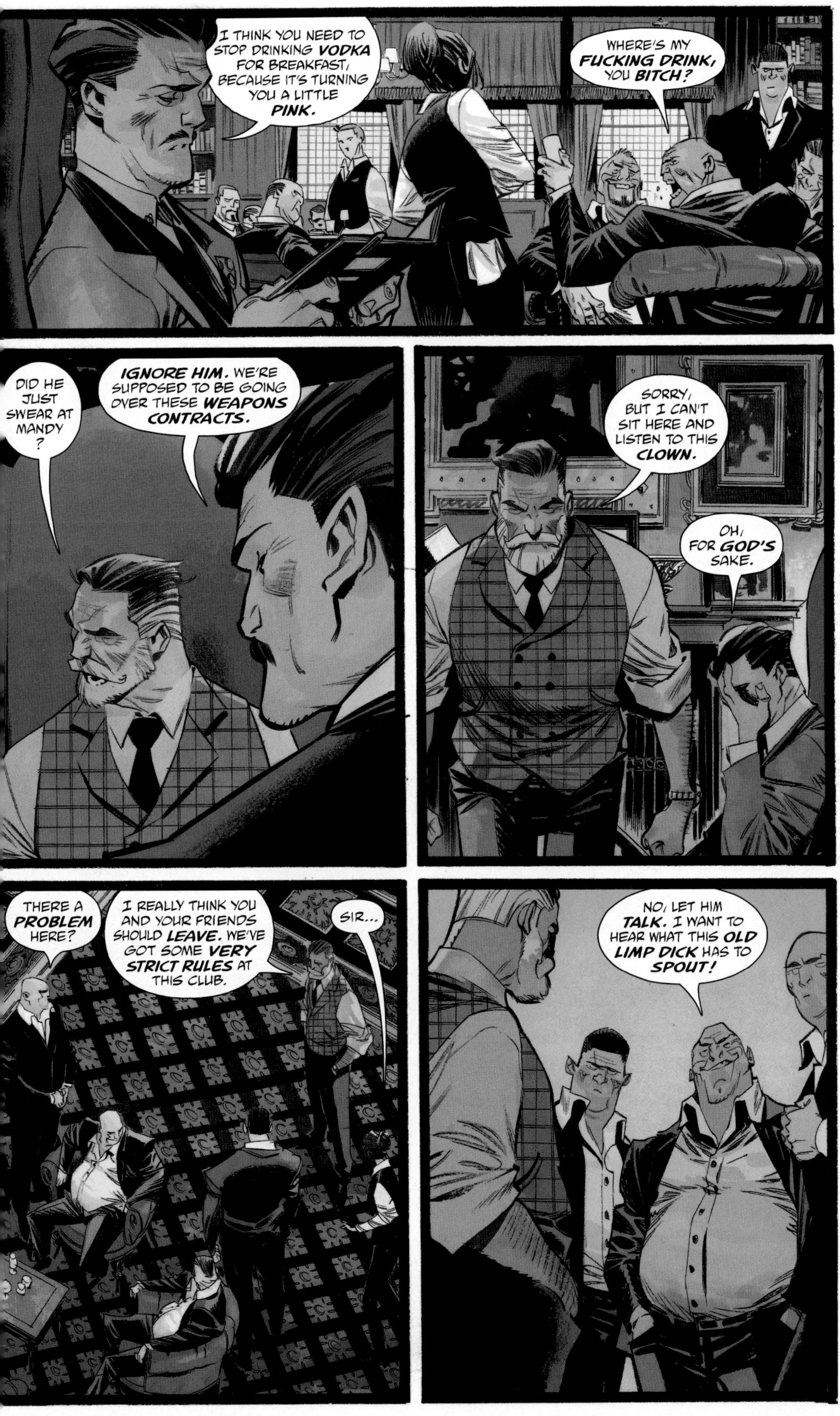
I THINK YOU NEED TO STOP DRINKING VODKA FOR BREAKFAST, BECAUSE IT'S TURNING YOU A LITTLE PINK.
WHERE'S MY FUCKING DRINK, YOU BITCH?
DID HE JUST SWEAR AT MANDY?
IGNORE HIM. WE'RE SUPPOSED TO BE GOING OVER THESE WEAPONS CONTRACTS.
SORRY, BUT I CAN'T SIT HERE AND LISTEN TO THIS CLOWN.
OH, FOR GOD'S SAKE.
THERE A PROBLEM HERE?
I REALLY THINK YOU AND YOUR FRIENDS SHOULD LEAVE. WE'VE GOT SOME VERY STRICT RULES AT THIS CLUB.
SIR...
NO, LET HIM TALK. I WANT TO HEAR WHAT THIS OLD LIMP DICK HAS TO SPOUT!

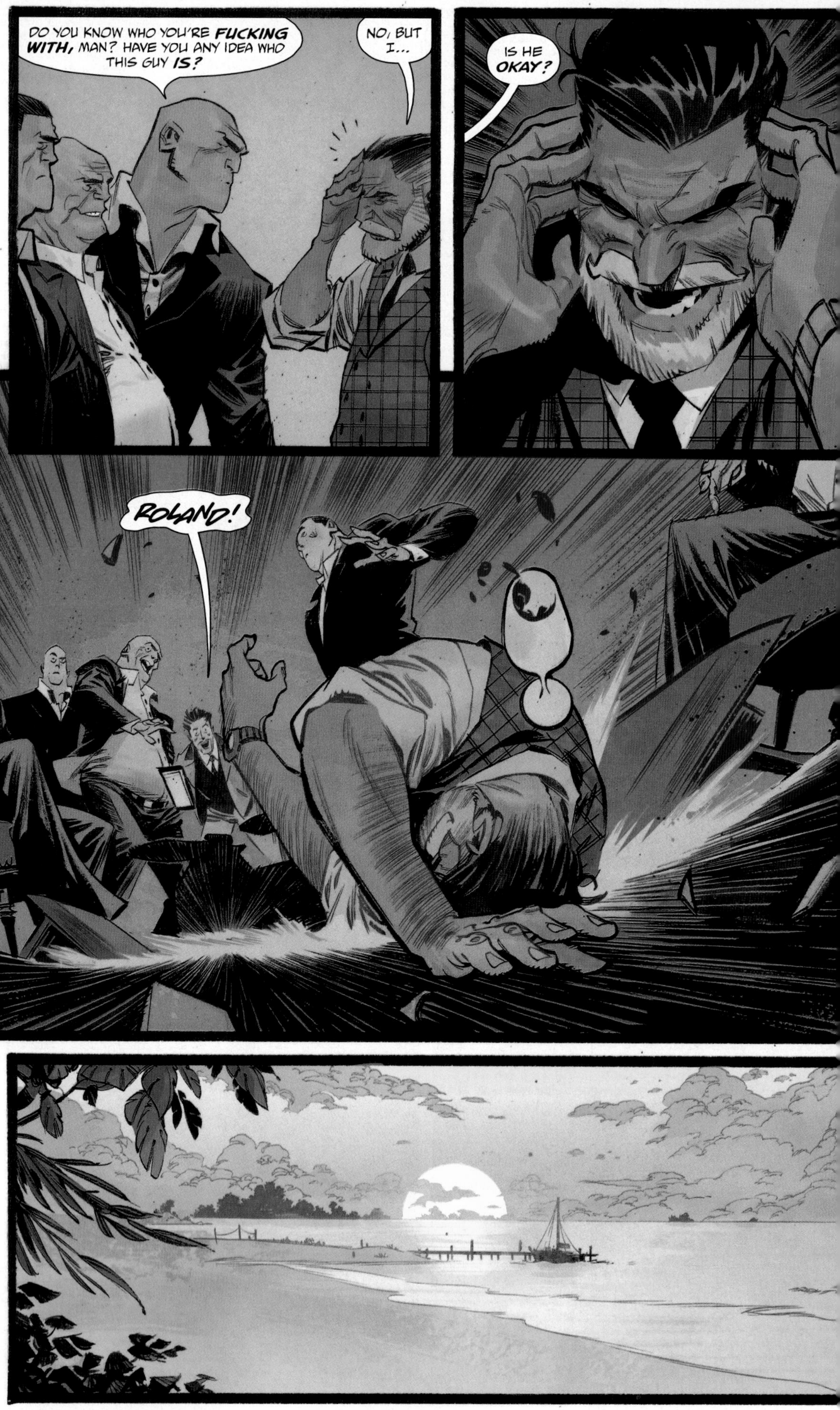
DO YOU KNOW WHO YOU'RE FUCKING WITH, MAN? HAVE YOU ANY IDEA WHO THIS GUY IS?
NO, BUT I...
IS HE OKAY?
ROLAND!

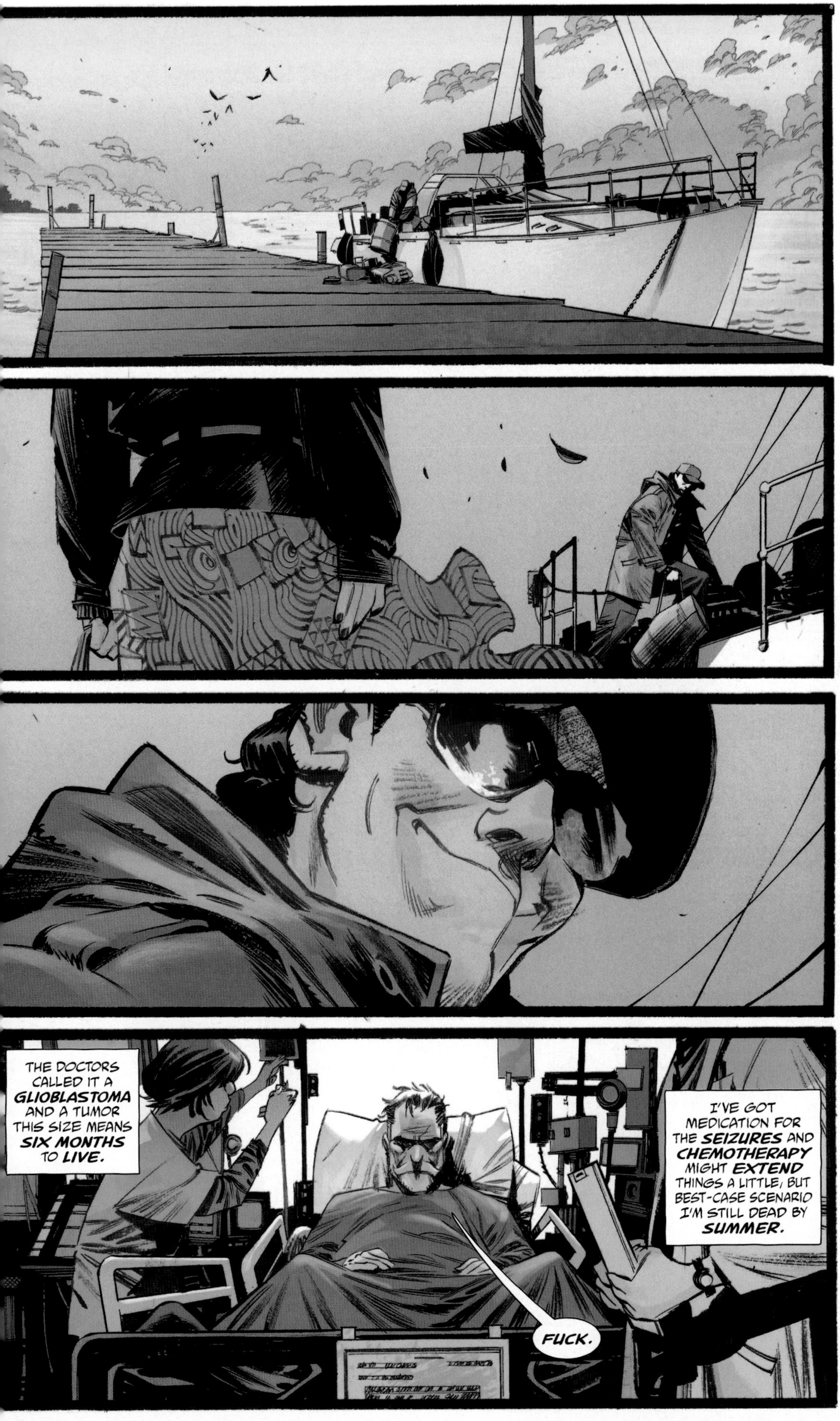
THE DOCTORS CALLED IT A GLIOBLASTOMA AND A TUMOR THIS SIZE MEANS SIX MONTHS TO LIVE.
I'VE GOT MEDICATION FOR THE SEIZURES AND CHEMOTHERAPY MIGHT EXTEND THINGS A LITTLE, BUT BEST-CASE SCENARIO I'M STILL DEAD BY SUMMER.
FUCK.

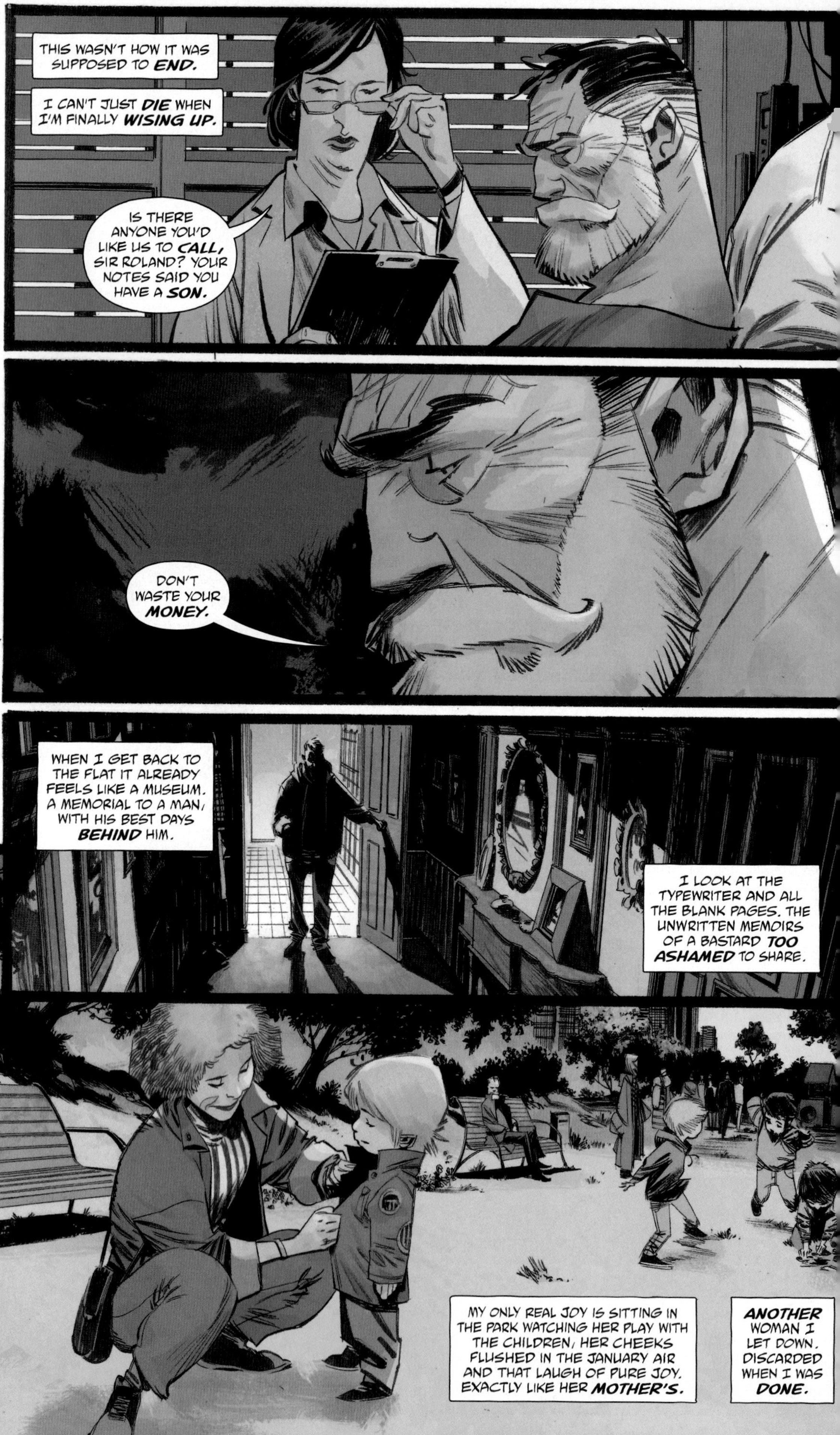

THIS WASN'T HOW IT WAS SUPPOSED TO END.
I CAN'T JUST DIE WHEN I'M FINALLY WISING UP.
IS THERE ANYONE YOU'D LIKE US TO CALL, SIR ROLAND? YOUR NOTES SAID YOU HAVE A SON.
DON'T WASTE YOUR MONEY.
WHEN I GET BACK TO THE FLAT IT ALREADY FEELS LIKE A MUSEUM. A MEMORIAL TO A MAN, WITH HIS BEST DAYS BEHIND HIM.
I LOOK AT THE TYPEWRITER AND ALL THE BLANK PAGES. THE UNWRITTEN MEMOIRS OF A BASTARD TOO ASHAMED TO SHARE.
MY ONLY REAL JOY IS SITTING IN THE PARK WATCHING HER PLAY WITH THE CHILDREN, HER CHEEKS FLUSHED IN THE JANUARY AIR AND THAT LAUGH OF PURE JOY. EXACTLY LIKE HER MOTHER'S.
ANOTHER WOMAN I LET DOWN. DISCARDED WHEN I WAS DONE.

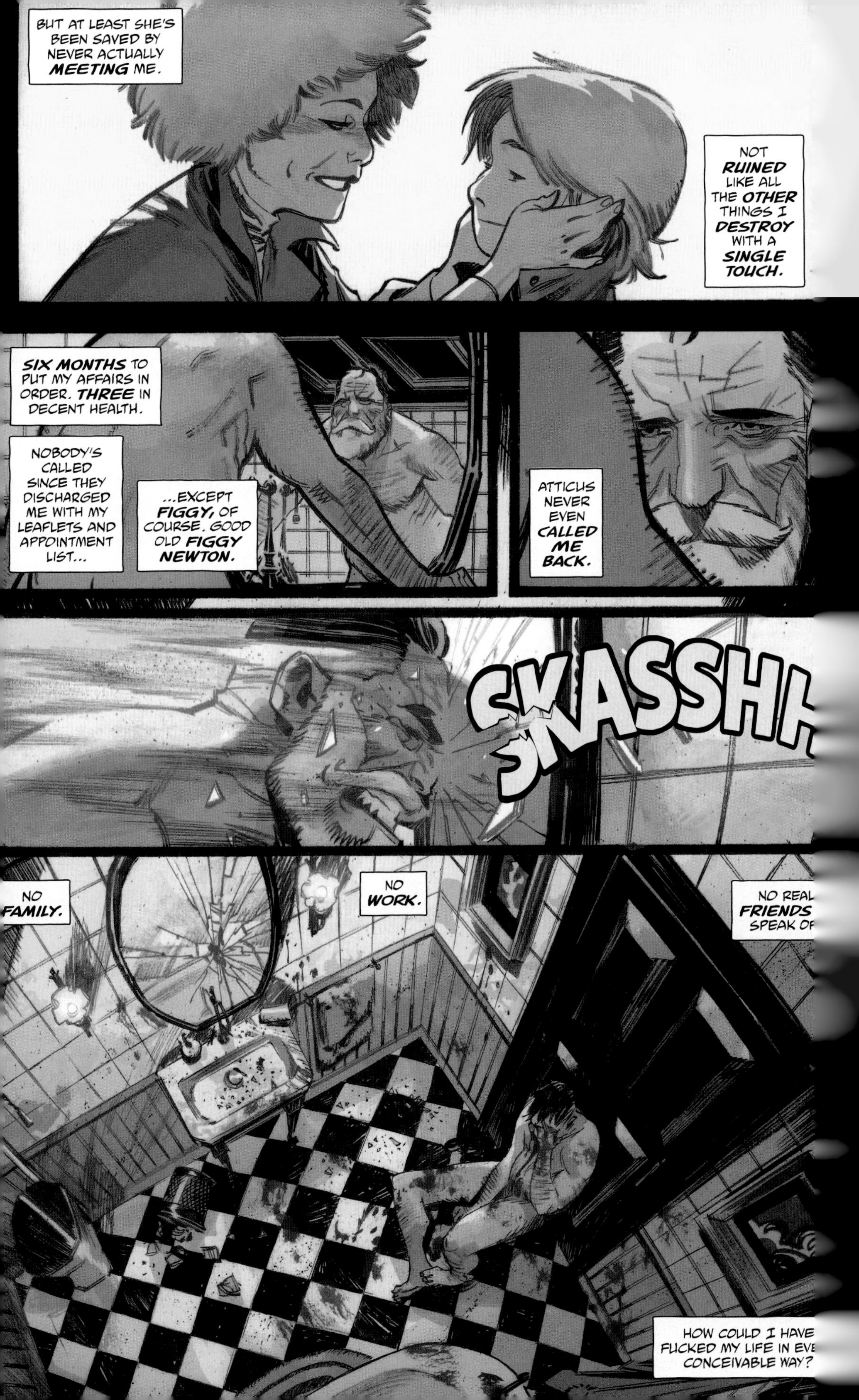
BUT AT LEAST SHE'S BEEN SAVED BY NEVER ACTUALLY MEETING ME.
NOT RUINED LIKE ALL THE OTHER THINGS I DESTROY WITH A SINGLE TOUCH.
SIX MONTHS TO PUT MY AFFAIRS IN ORDER. THREE IN DECENT HEALTH.
NOBODY'S CALLED SINCE THEY DISCHARGED ME WITH MY LEAFLETS AND APPOINTMENT LIST...
...EXCEPT FIGGY, OF COURSE. GOOD OLD FIGGY NEWTON.
ATTICUS NEVER EVEN CALLED ME BACK.
SKASSHH
NO FAMILY.
NO WORK.
NO REAL FRIENDS SPEAK OF
HOW COULD I HAVE FUCKED MY LIFE IN EVE CONCEIVABLE WAY?

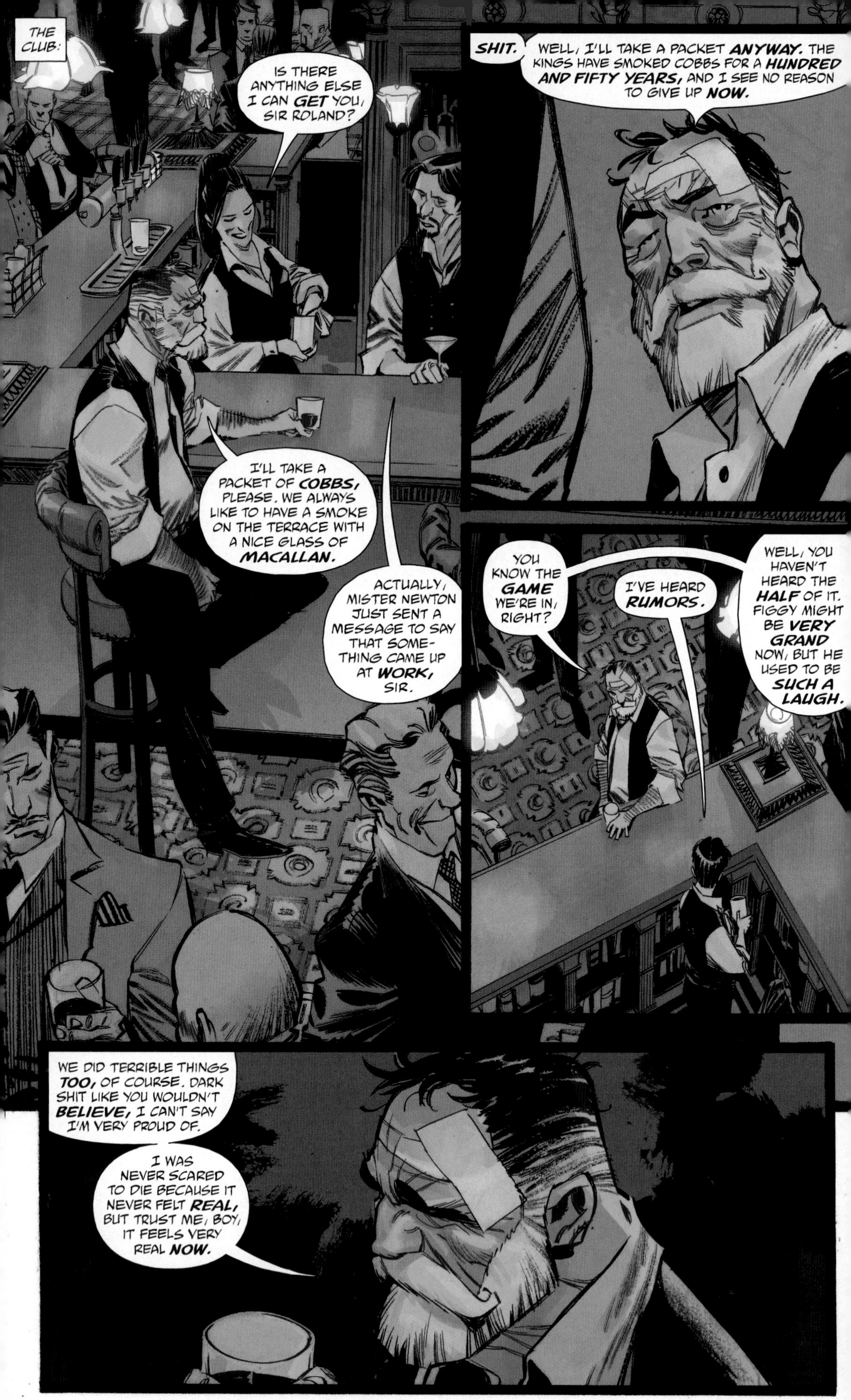
THE CLUB:
IS THERE ANYTHING ELSE I CAN GET YOU, SIR ROLAND?
I'LL TAKE A PACKET OF COBBS, PLEASE. WE ALWAYS LIKE TO HAVE A SMOKE ON THE TERRACE WITH A NICE GLASS OF MACALLAN.
ACTUALLY, MISTER NEWTON JUST SENT A MESSAGE TO SAY THAT SOME-THING CAME UP AT WORK, SIR.
SHIT.
WELL, I'LL TAKE A PACKET ANYWAY. THE KINGS HAVE SMOKED COBBS FOR A HUNDRED AND FIFTY YEARS, AND I SEE NO REASON TO GIVE UP NOW.
YOU KNOW THE GAME WE'RE IN, RIGHT?
I'VE HEARD RUMORS.
WELL, YOU HAVEN'T HEARD THE HALF OF IT. FIGGY MIGHT BE VERY GRAND NOW, BUT HE USED TO BE SUCH A LAUGH.
WE DID TERRIBLE THINGS TOO, OF COURSE. DARK SHIT LIKE YOU WOULDN'T BELIEVE, I CAN'T SAY I'M VERY PROUD OF.
I WAS NEVER SCARED TO DIE BECAUSE IT NEVER FELT REAL, BUT TRUST ME, BOY, IT FEELS VERY REAL NOW.

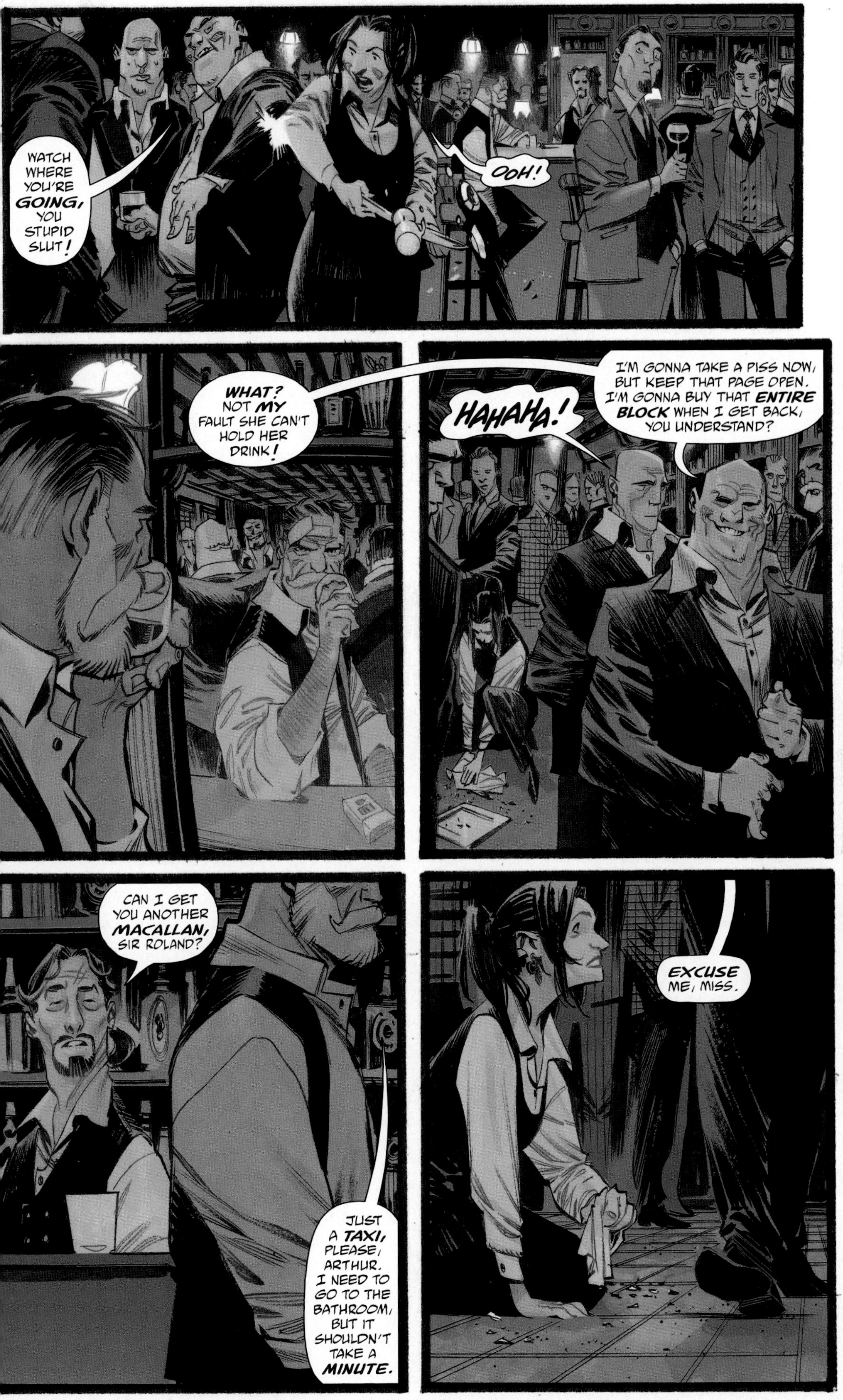
WATCH WHERE YOU'RE GOING, YOU STUPID SLUT!
OOH!
WHAT? NOT MY FAULT SHE CAN'T HOLD HER DRINK!
HAHAHA!
I'M GONNA TAKE A PISS NOW, BUT KEEP THAT PAGE OPEN. I'M GONNA BUY THAT ENTIRE BLOCK WHEN I GET BACK, YOU UNDERSTAND?
CAN I GET YOU ANOTHER MACALLAN, SIR ROLAND?
JUST A TAXI, PLEASE, ARTHUR. I NEED TO GO TO THE BATHROOM, BUT IT SHOULDN'T TAKE A MINUTE.
EXCUSE ME, MISS.

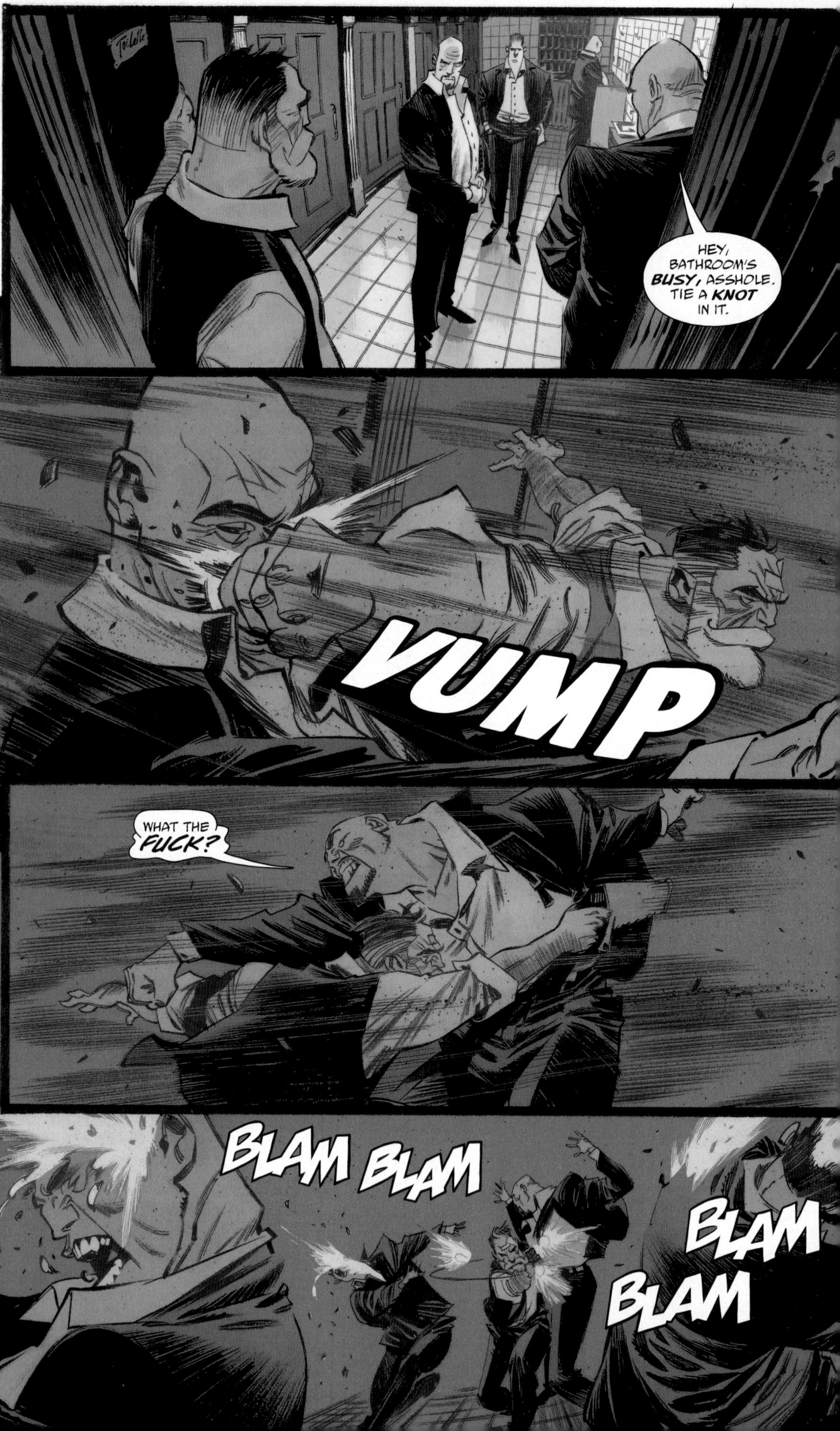
HEY, BATHROOM'S BUSY, ASSHOLE. TIE A KNOT IN IT.
VUMP
WHAT THE FUCK?
BLAM BLAM
BLAM
BLAM

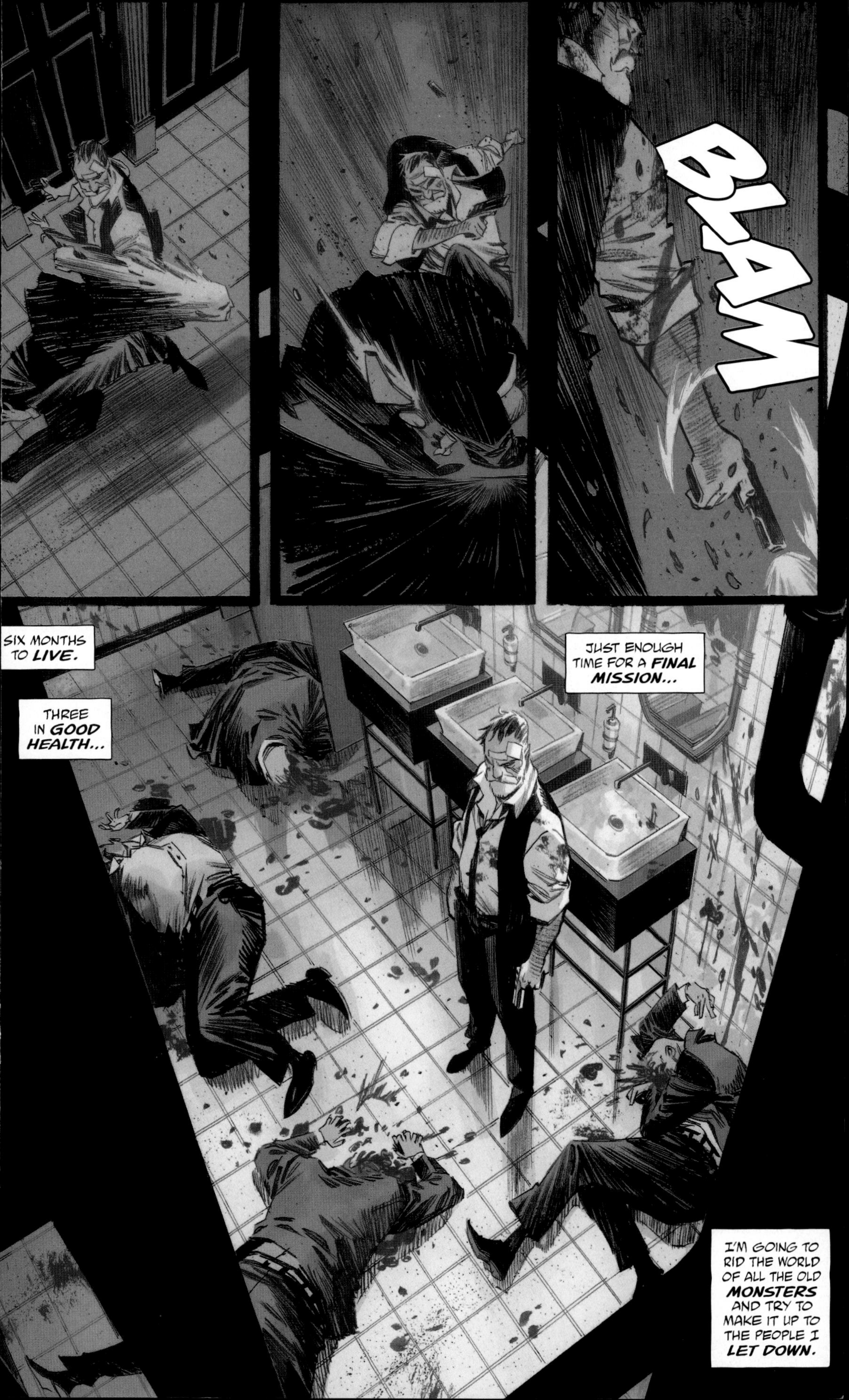
BLAM
SIX MONTHS TO LIVE.
THREE IN GOOD HEALTH...
JUST ENOUGH TIME FOR A FINAL MISSION...
I'M GOING TO RID THE WORLD OF ALL THE OLD MONSTERS AND TRY TO MAKE IT UP TO THE PEOPLE I LET DOWN.

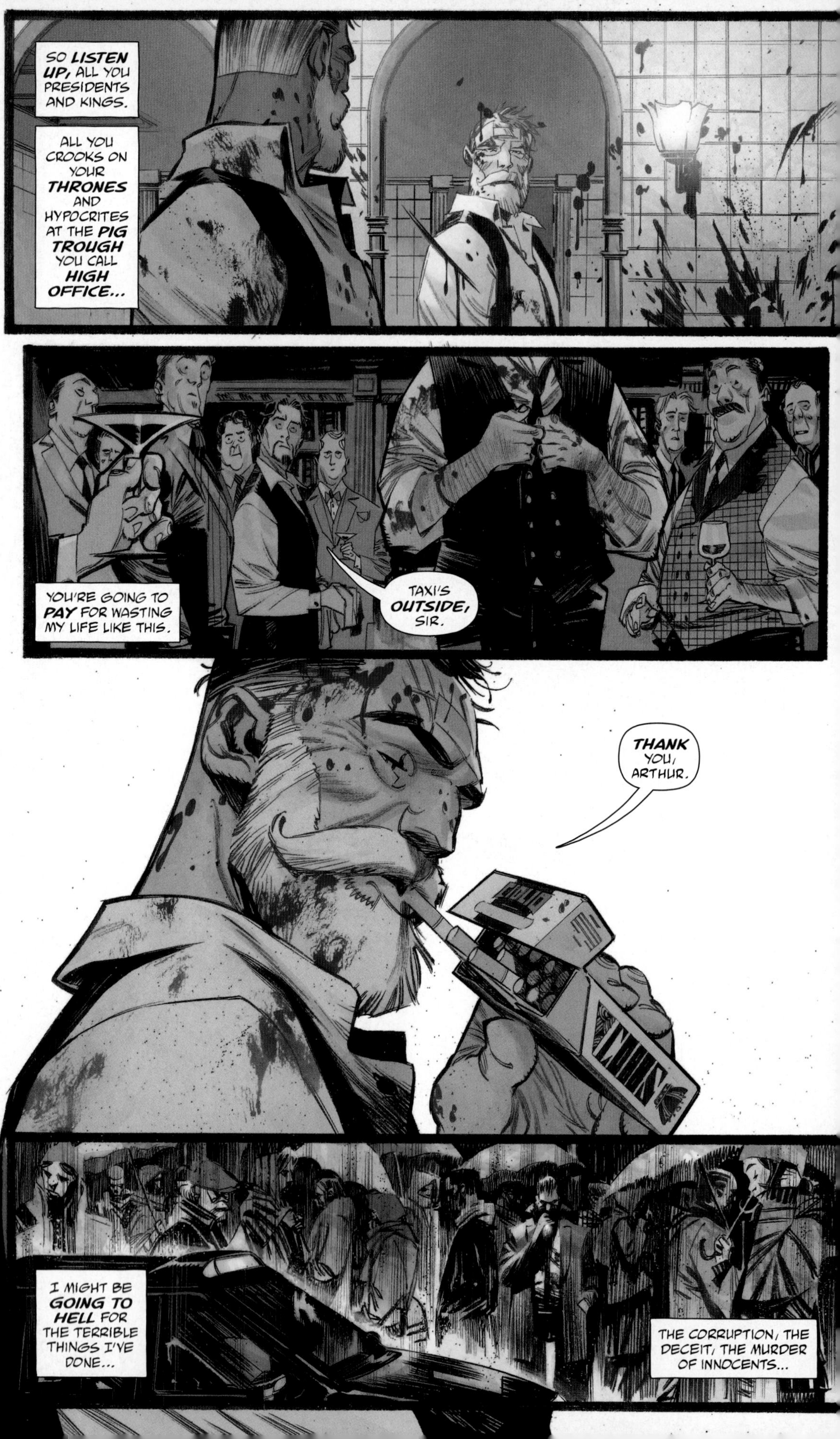

SO LISTEN UP, ALL YOU PRESIDENTS AND KINGS.
ALL YOU CROOKS ON YOUR THRONES AND HYPOCRITES AT THE PIG TROUGH YOU CALL HIGH OFFICE...
YOU'RE GOING TO PAY FOR WASTING MY LIFE LIKE THIS.
TAXI'S OUTSIDE, SIR.
THANK YOU, ARTHUR.
I MIGHT BE GOING TO HELL FOR THE TERRIBLE THINGS I'VE DONE...
THE CORRUPTION, THE DECEIT, THE MURDER OF INNOCENTS...

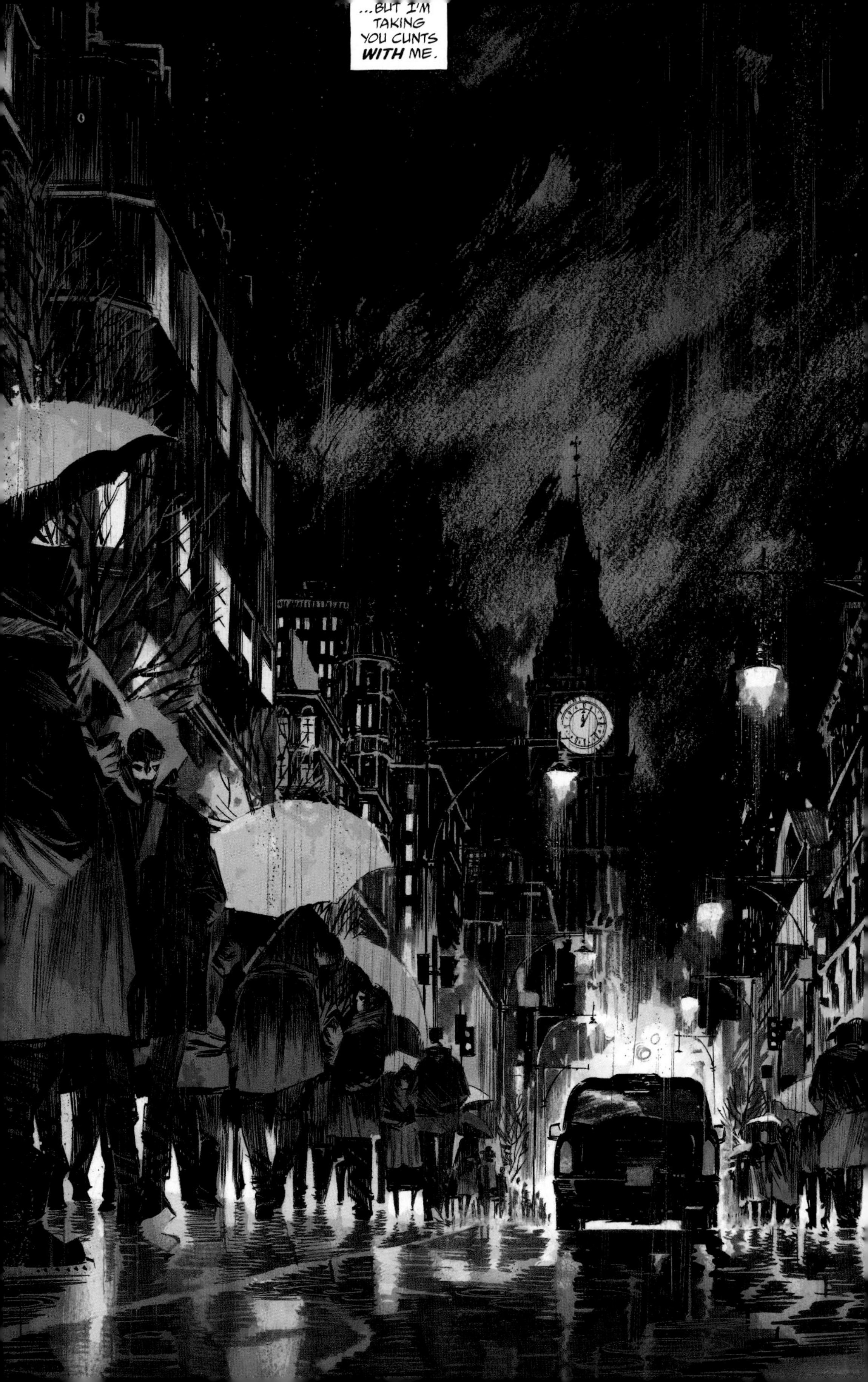
...BUT I'M TAKING YOU CUNTS WITH ME.

Two

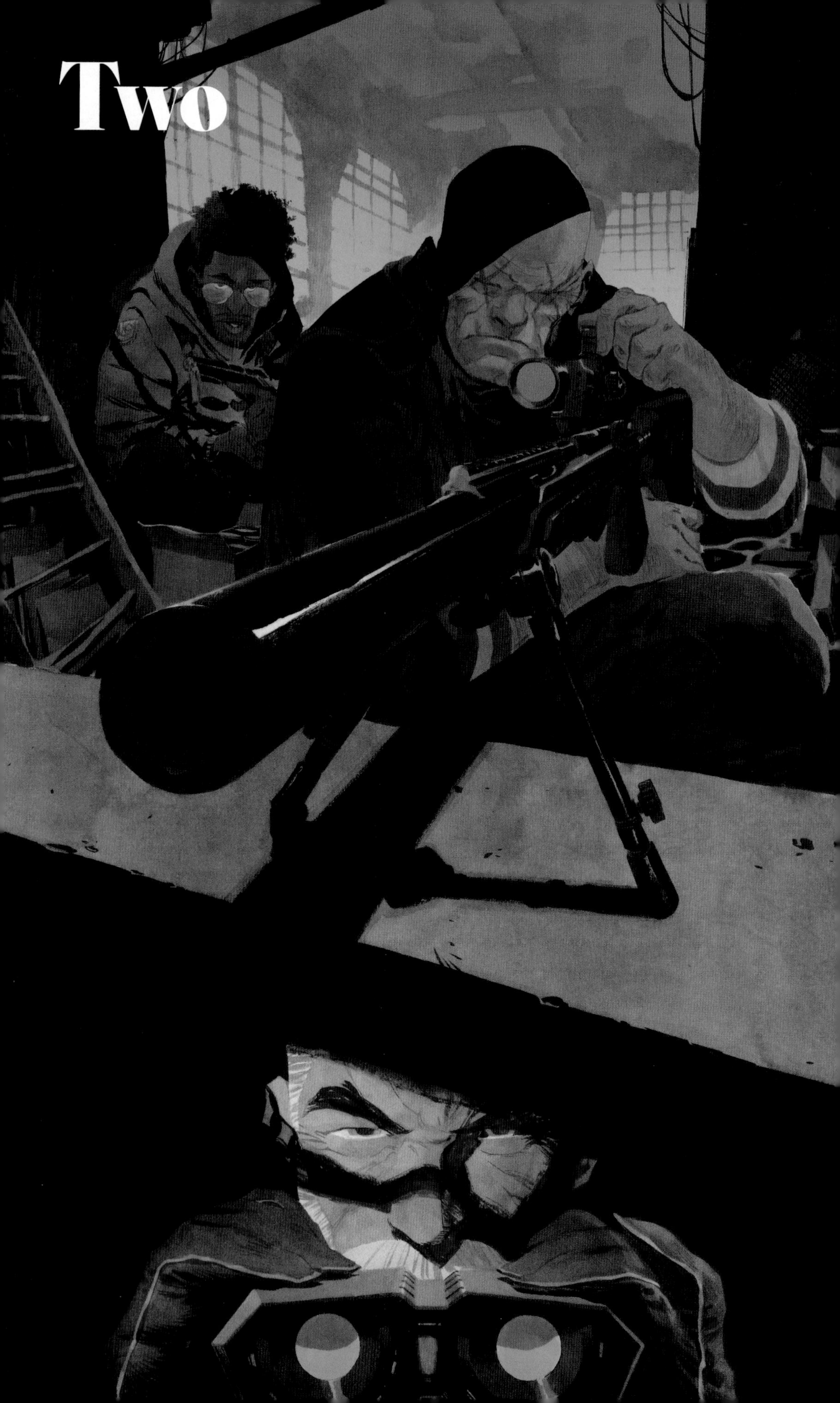

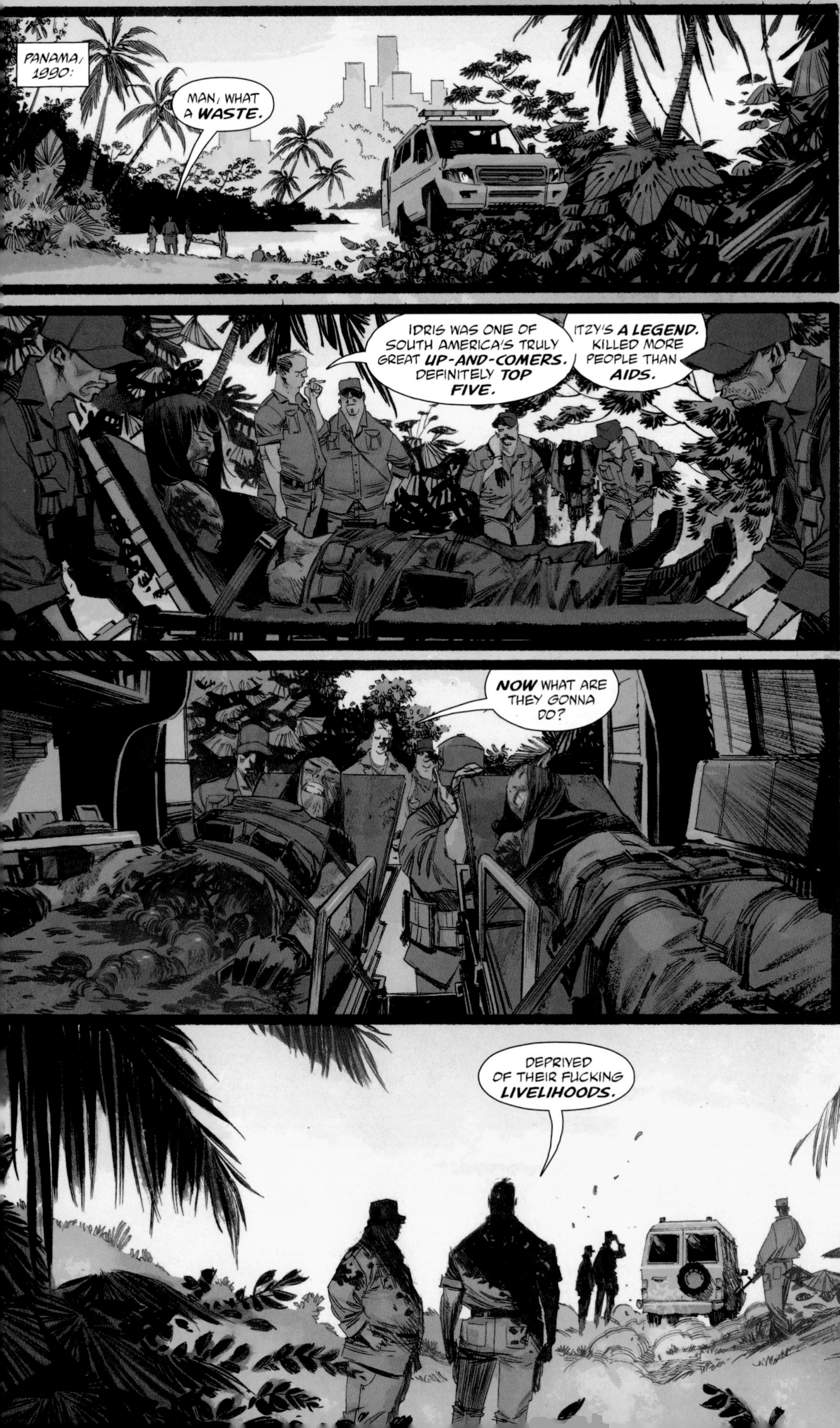
PANAMA, 1990:
MAN, WHAT A WASTE.
IDRIS WAS ONE OF SOUTH AMERICA'S TRULY GREAT UP-AND-COMERS. DEFINITELY TOP FIVE.
ITZY'S A LEGEND. KILLED MORE PEOPLE THAN AIDS.
NOW WHAT ARE THEY GONNA DO?
DEPRIVED OF THEIR FUCKING LIVELIHOODS.

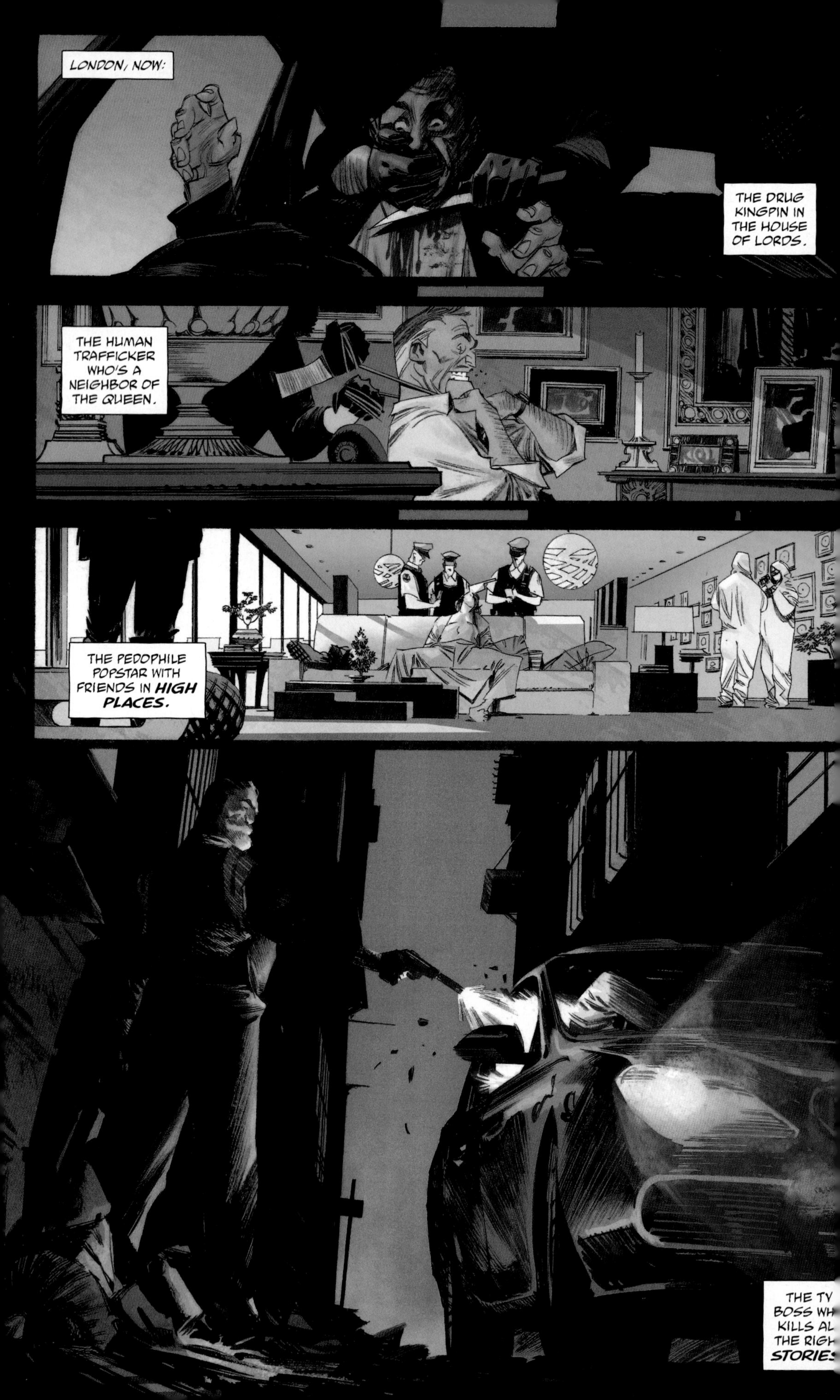
LONDON, NOW:
THE DRUG KINGPIN IN THE HOUSE OF LORDS.
THE HUMAN TRAFFICKER WHO'S A NEIGHBOR OF THE QUEEN.
THE PEDOPHILE POPSTAR WITH FRIENDS IN HIGH PLACES.
THE TV BOSS WH KILLS AL THE RIGH STORIES

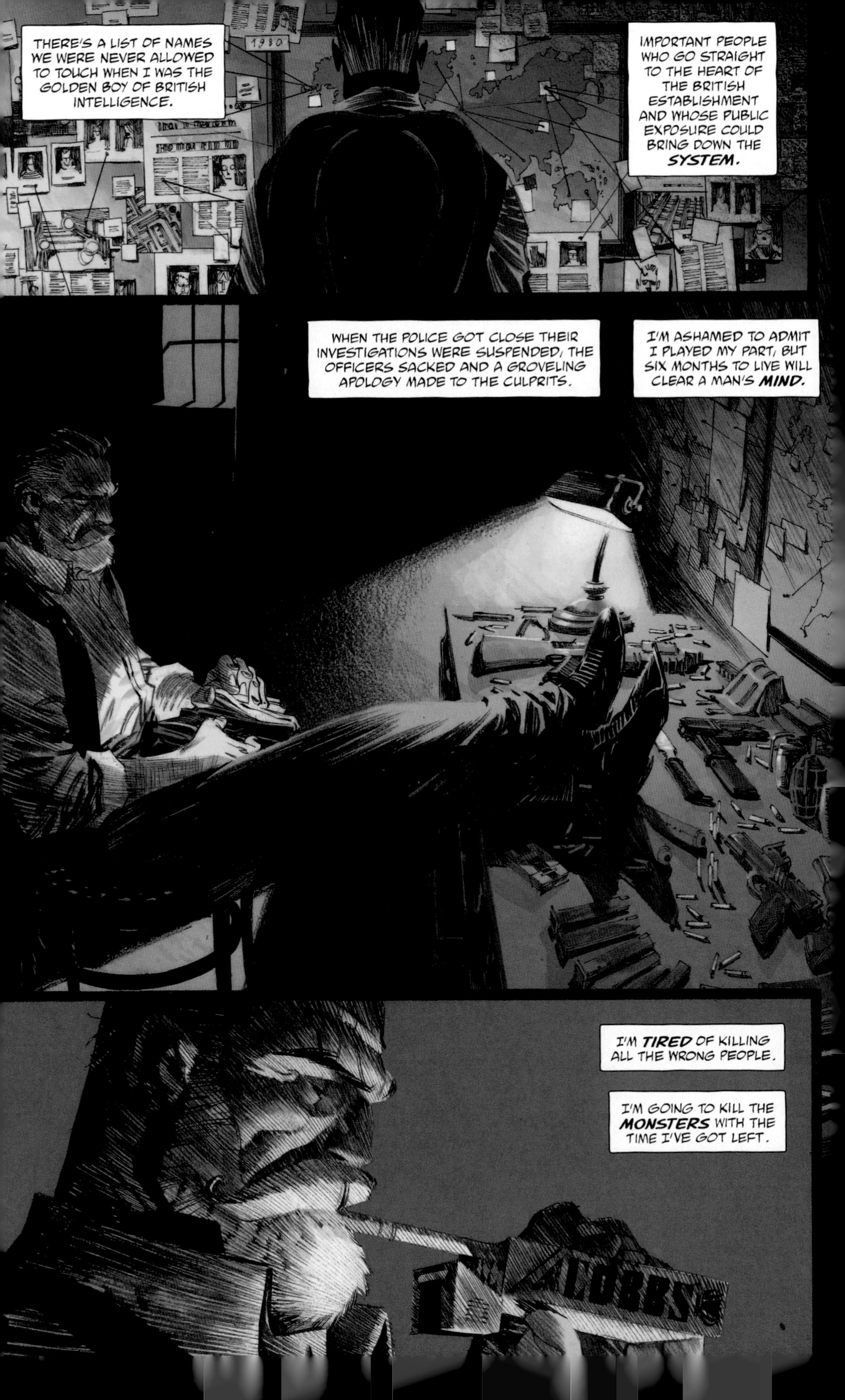
THERE'S A LIST OF NAMES WE WERE NEVER ALLOWED TO TOUCH WHEN I WAS THE GOLDEN BOY OF BRITISH INTELLIGENCE.
IMPORTANT PEOPLE WHO GO STRAIGHT TO THE HEART OF THE BRITISH ESTABLISHMENT AND WHOSE PUBLIC EXPOSURE COULD BRING DOWN THE ***SYSTEM.***
WHEN THE POLICE GOT CLOSE THEIR INVESTIGATIONS WERE SUSPENDED, THE OFFICERS SACKED AND A GROVELING APOLOGY MADE TO THE CULPRITS.
I'M ASHAMED TO ADMIT I PLAYED MY PART, BUT SIX MONTHS TO LIVE WILL CLEAR A MAN'S ***MIND.***
I'M ***TIRED*** OF KILLING ALL THE WRONG PEOPLE.
I'M GOING TO KILL THE ***MONSTERS*** WITH THE TIME I'VE GOT LEFT.
LOBBS

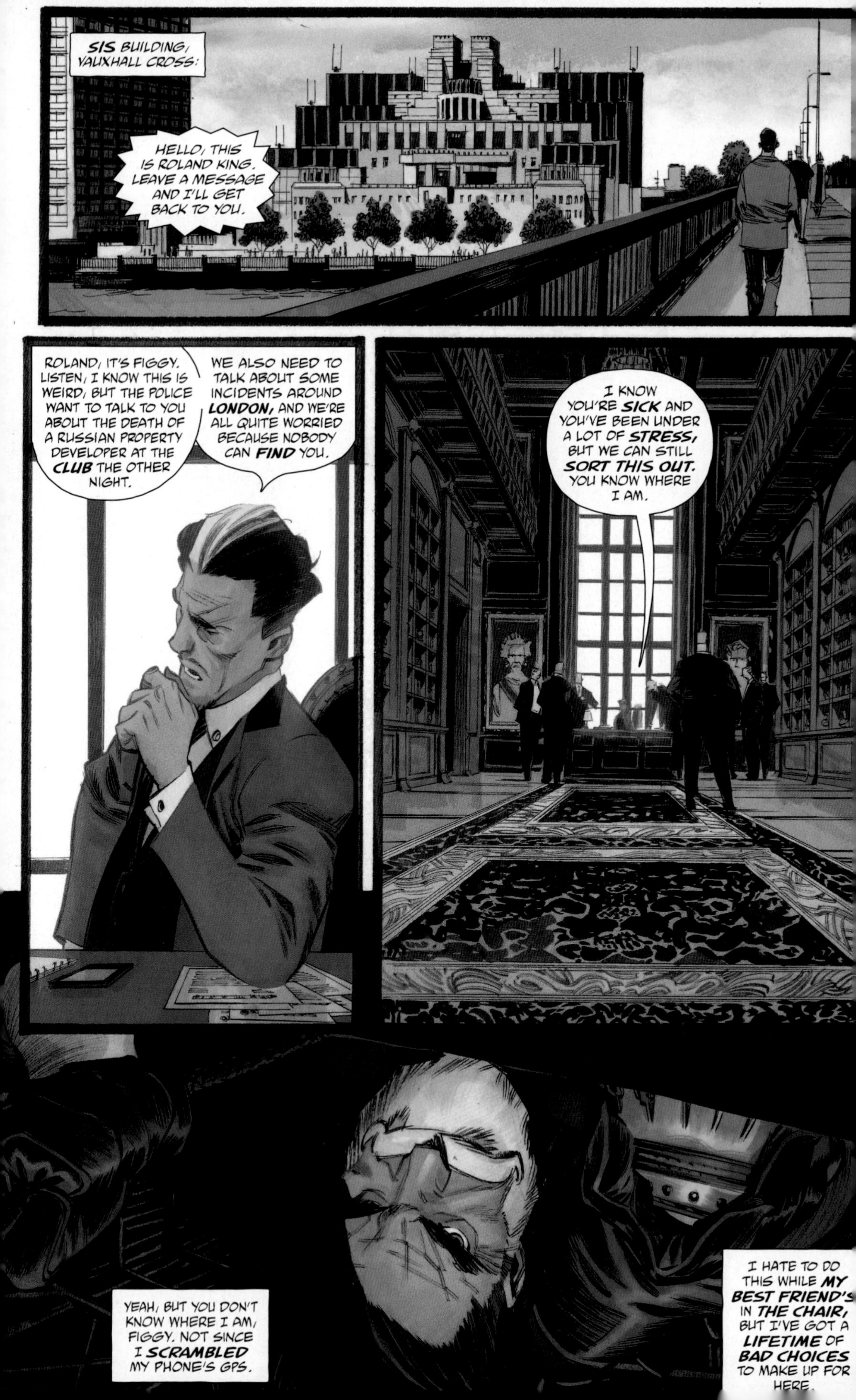
SIS BUILDING, VAUXHALL CROSS:
HELLO, THIS IS ROLAND KING. LEAVE A MESSAGE AND I'LL GET BACK TO YOU.
ROLAND, IT'S FIGGY. LISTEN, I KNOW THIS IS WEIRD, BUT THE POLICE WANT TO TALK TO YOU ABOUT THE DEATH OF A RUSSIAN PROPERTY DEVELOPER AT THE CLUB THE OTHER NIGHT.
WE ALSO NEED TO TALK ABOUT SOME INCIDENTS AROUND LONDON, AND WE'RE ALL QUITE WORRIED BECAUSE NOBODY CAN FIND YOU.
I KNOW YOU'RE SICK AND YOU'VE BEEN UNDER A LOT OF STRESS, BUT WE CAN STILL SORT THIS OUT. YOU KNOW WHERE I AM.
YEAH, BUT YOU DON'T KNOW WHERE I AM, FIGGY. NOT SINCE I SCRAMBLED MY PHONE'S GPS.
I HATE TO DO THIS WHILE MY BEST FRIEND'S IN THE CHAIR, BUT I'VE GOT A LIFETIME OF BAD CHOICES TO MAKE UP FOR HERE.

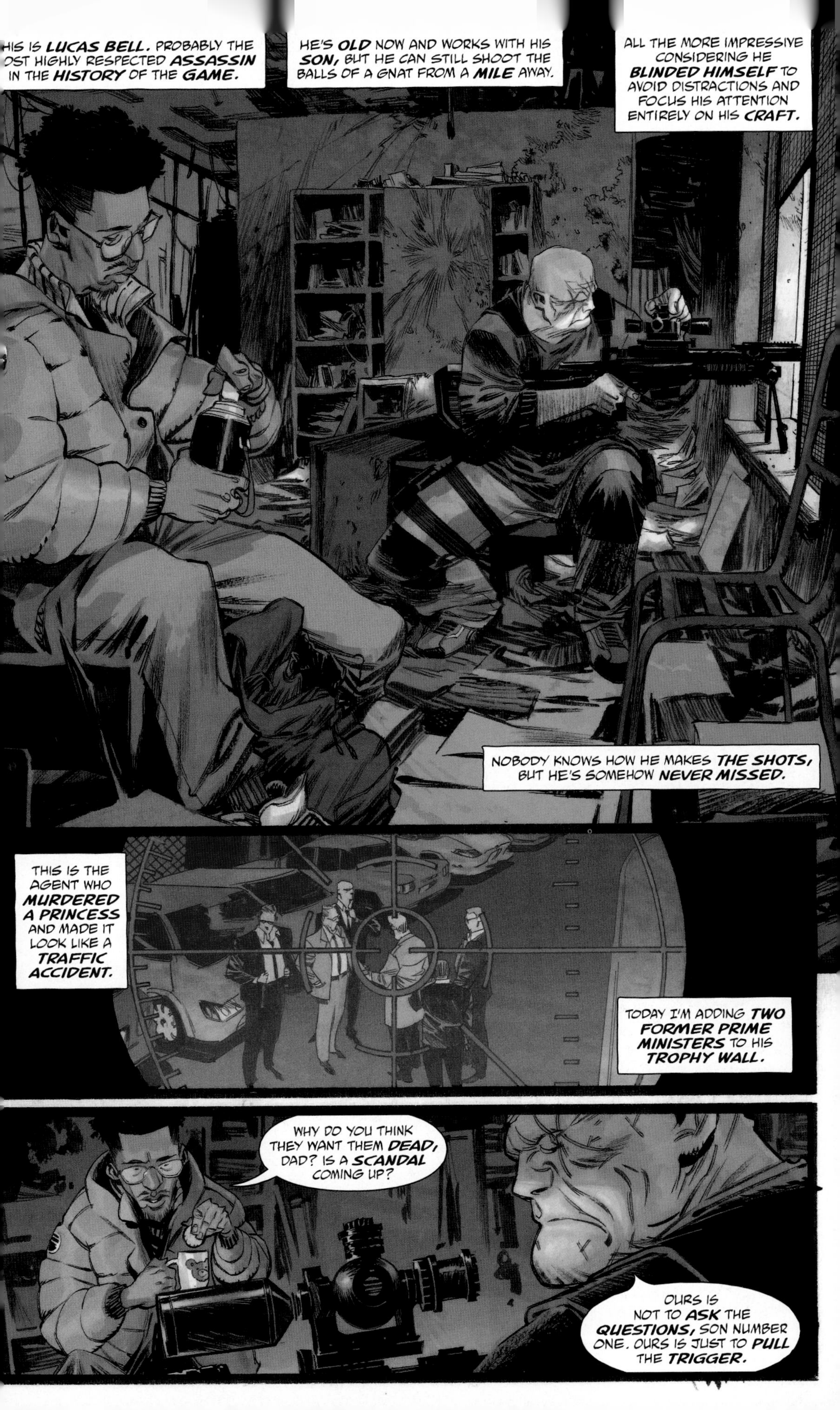
HIS IS LUCAS BELL. PROBABLY THE OST HIGHLY RESPECTED ASSASSIN IN THE HISTORY OF THE GAME.
HE'S OLD NOW AND WORKS WITH HIS SON, BUT HE CAN STILL SHOOT THE BALLS OF A GNAT FROM A MILE AWAY.
ALL THE MORE IMPRESSIVE CONSIDERING HE BLINDED HIMSELF TO AVOID DISTRACTIONS AND FOCUS HIS ATTENTION ENTIRELY ON HIS CRAFT.
NOBODY KNOWS HOW HE MAKES THE SHOTS, BUT HE'S SOMEHOW NEVER MISSED.
THIS IS THE AGENT WHO MURDERED A PRINCESS AND MADE IT LOOK LIKE A TRAFFIC ACCIDENT.
TODAY I'M ADDING TWO FORMER PRIME MINISTERS TO HIS TROPHY WALL.
WHY DO YOU THINK THEY WANT THEM DEAD, DAD? IS A SCANDAL COMING UP?
OURS IS NOT TO ASK THE QUESTIONS, SON NUMBER ONE. OURS IS JUST TO PULL THE TRIGGER.

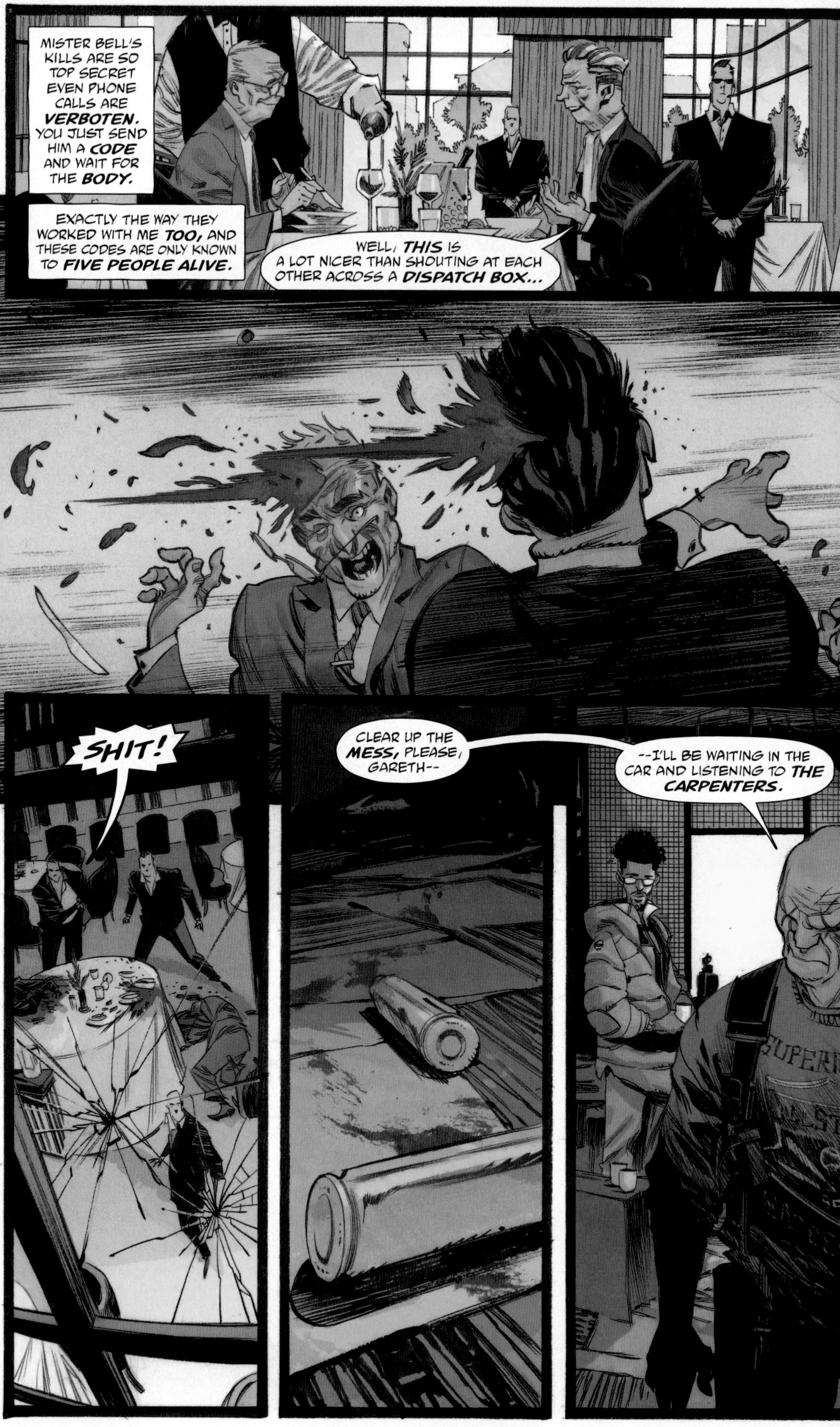
MISTER BELL'S KILLS ARE SO TOP SECRET EVEN PHONE CALLS ARE VERBOTEN. YOU JUST SEND HIM A CODE AND WAIT FOR THE BODY.
EXACTLY THE WAY THEY WORKED WITH ME TOO, AND THESE CODES ARE ONLY KNOWN TO FIVE PEOPLE ALIVE.
WELL, THIS IS A LOT NICER THAN SHOUTING AT EACH OTHER ACROSS A DISPATCH BOX...
SHIT!
CLEAR UP THE MESS, PLEASE, GARETH--
--I'LL BE WAITING IN THE CAR AND LISTENING TO THE CARPENTERS.

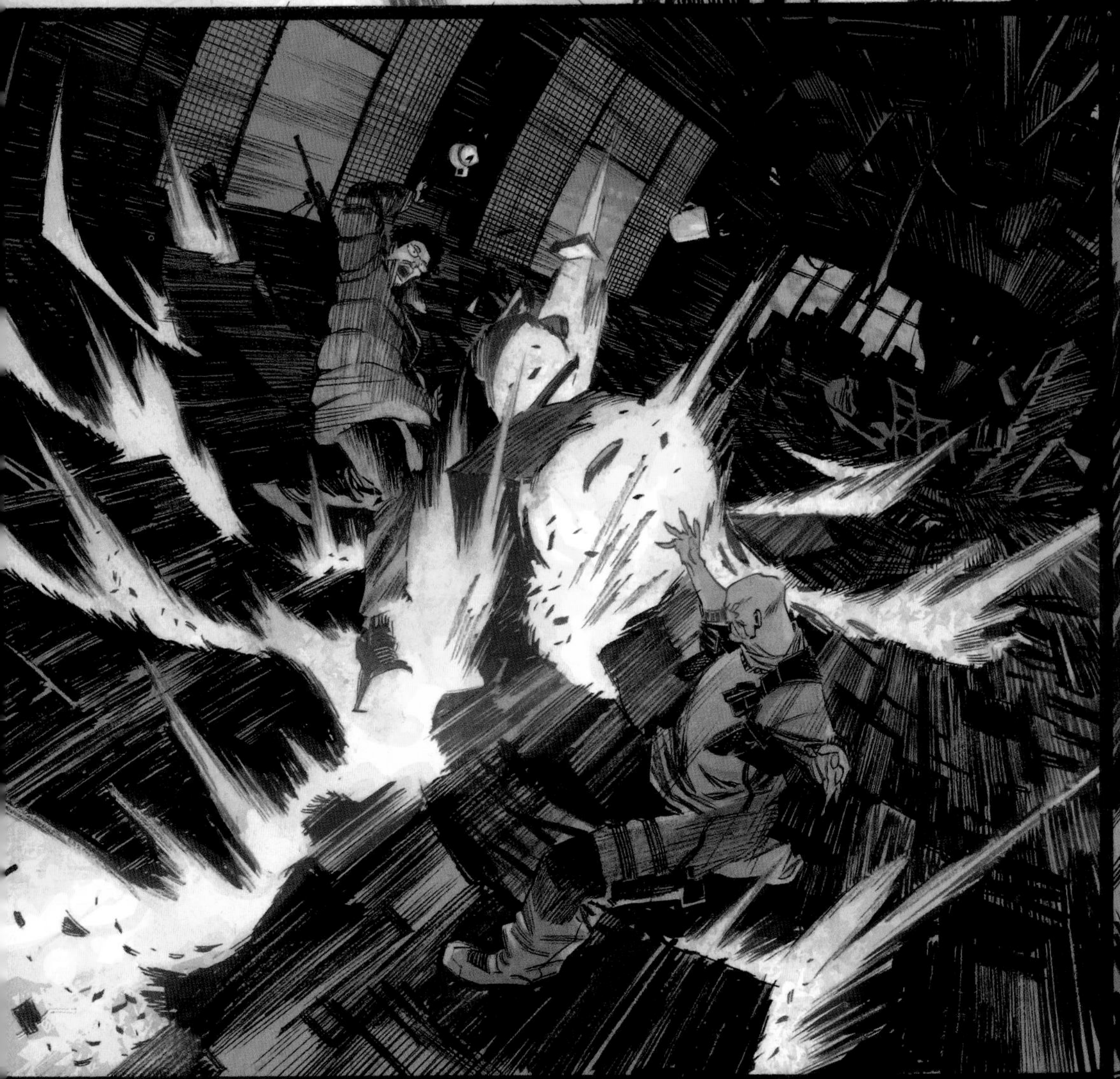

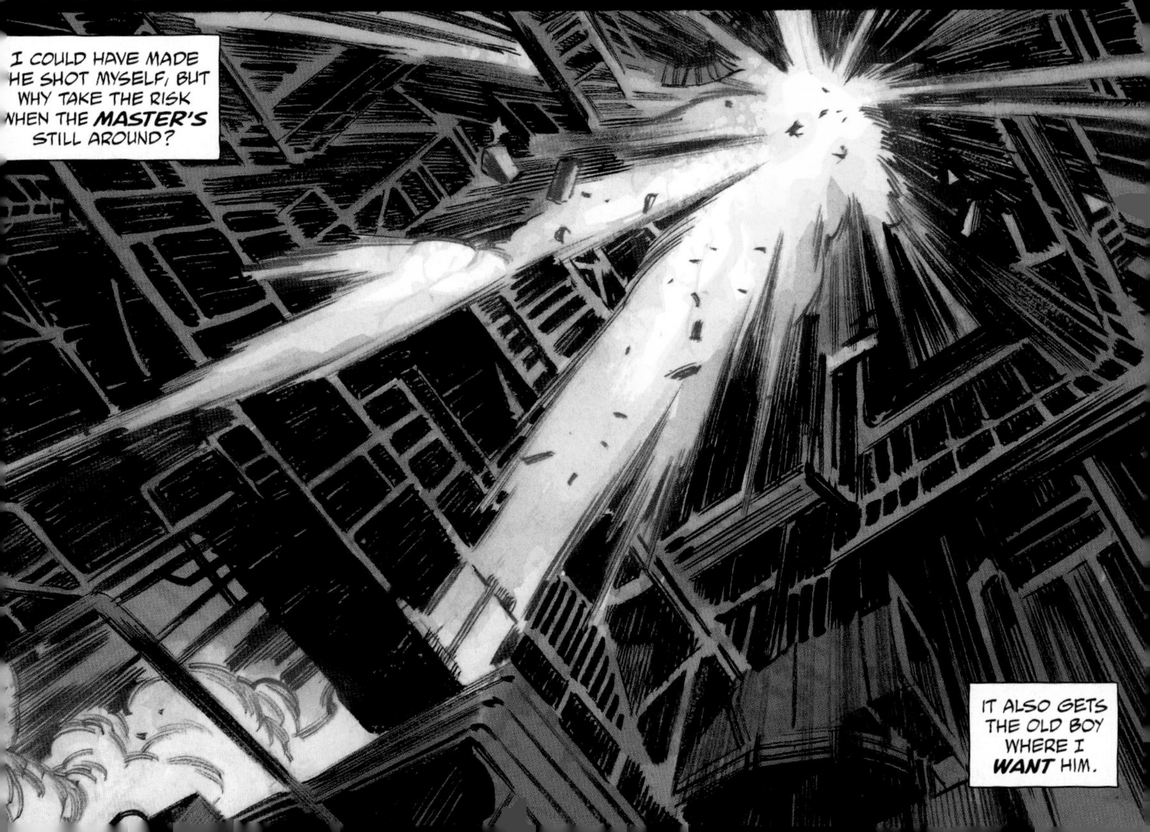
I COULD HAVE MADE HE SHOT MYSELF, BUT WHY TAKE THE RISK WHEN THE MASTER'S STILL AROUND?
IT ALSO GETS THE OLD BOY WHERE I WANT HIM.

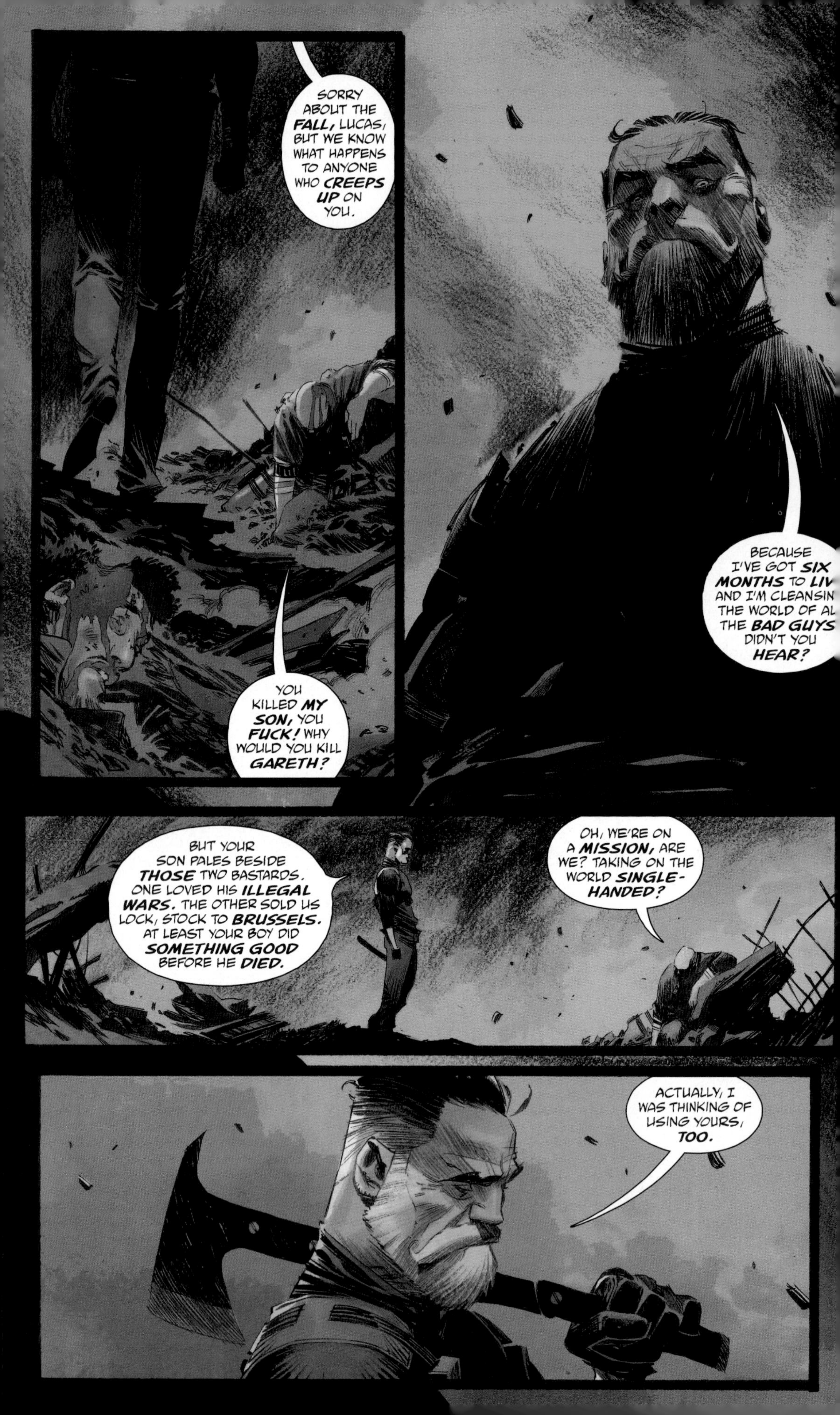
SORRY ABOUT THE FALL, LUCAS, BUT WE KNOW WHAT HAPPENS TO ANYONE WHO CREEPS UP ON YOU.
YOU KILLED MY SON, YOU FUCK! WHY WOULD YOU KILL GARETH?
BECAUSE I'VE GOT SIX MONTHS TO LIV AND I'M CLEANSIN THE WORLD OF AL THE BAD GUYS DIDN'T YOU HEAR?
BUT YOUR SON PALES BESIDE THOSE TWO BASTARDS. ONE LOVED HIS ILLEGAL WARS. THE OTHER SOLD US LOCK, STOCK TO BRUSSELS. AT LEAST YOUR BOY DID SOMETHING GOOD BEFORE HE DIED.
OH, WE'RE ON A MISSION, ARE WE? TAKING ON THE WORLD SINGLE-HANDED?
ACTUALLY, I WAS THINKING OF USING YOURS, TOO.

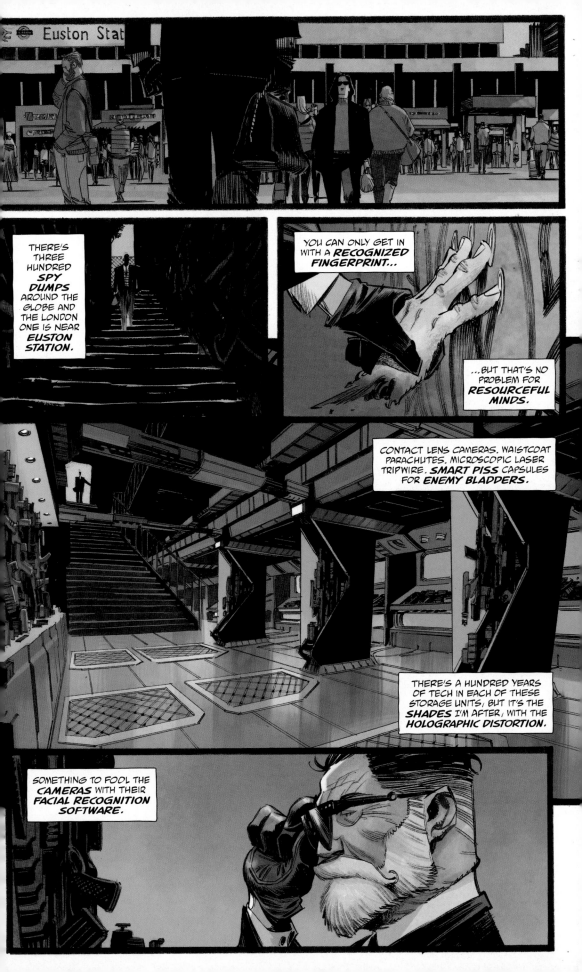

Euston Stat[ion]

THERE'S THREE HUNDRED **SPY DUMPS** AROUND THE GLOBE AND THE LONDON ONE IS NEAR **EUSTON STATION.**

YOU CAN ONLY GET IN WITH A **RECOGNIZED FINGERPRINT...**

...BUT THAT'S NO PROBLEM FOR **RESOURCEFUL MINDS.**

CONTACT LENS CAMERAS. WAISTCOAT PARACHUTES. MICROSCOPIC LASER TRIPWIRE. **SMART PISS** CAPSULES FOR **ENEMY BLADDERS.**

THERE'S A HUNDRED YEARS OF TECH IN EACH OF THESE STORAGE UNITS, BUT IT'S THE **SHADES** I'M AFTER, WITH THE **HOLOGRAPHIC DISTORTION.**

SOMETHING TO FOOL THE **CAMERAS** WITH THEIR **FACIAL RECOGNITION SOFTWARE.**

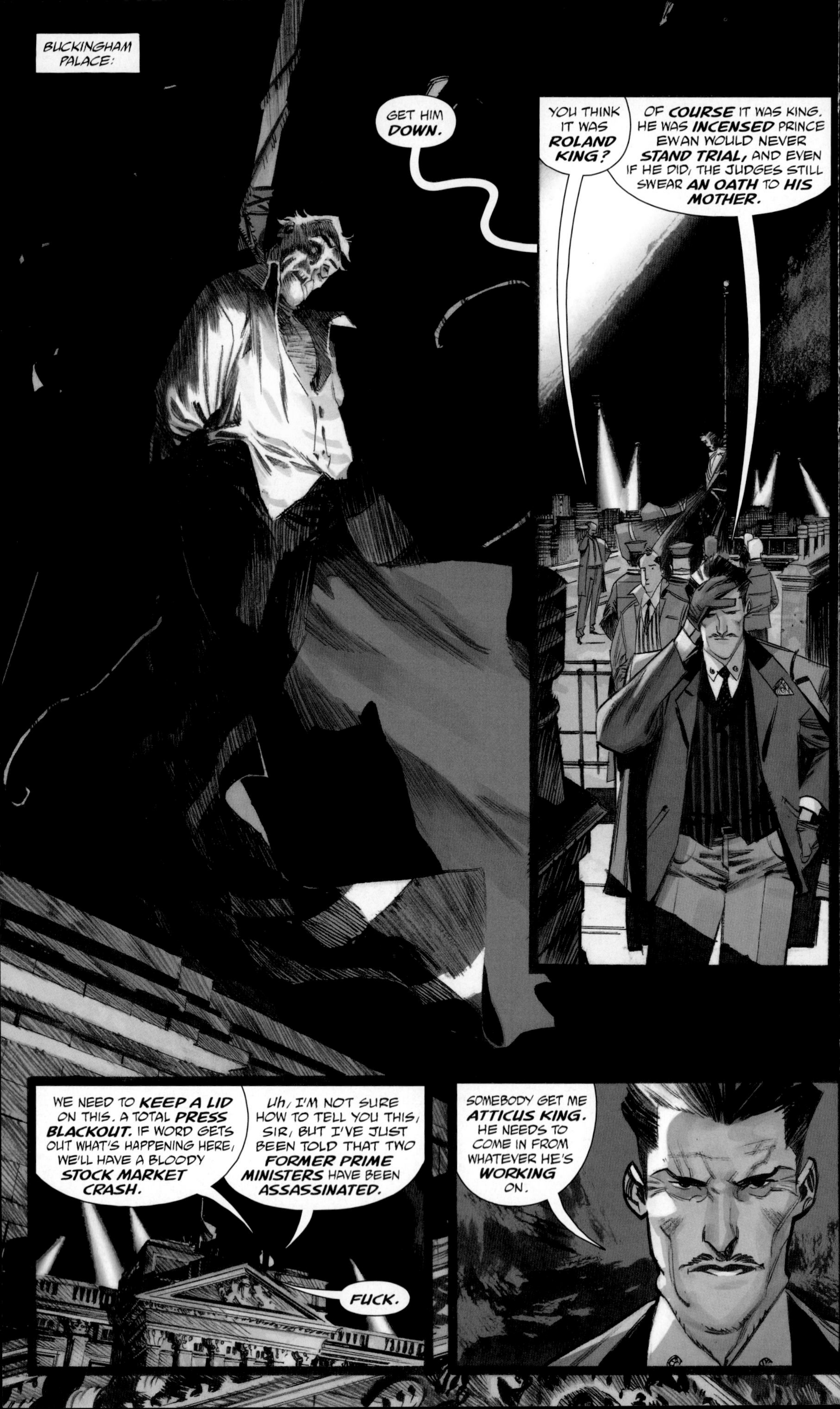
BUCKINGHAM PALACE:
GET HIM DOWN.
YOU THINK IT WAS ROLAND KING?
OF COURSE IT WAS KING. HE WAS INCENSED PRINCE EWAN WOULD NEVER STAND TRIAL, AND EVEN IF HE DID, THE JUDGES STILL SWEAR AN OATH TO HIS MOTHER.
WE NEED TO KEEP A LID ON THIS. A TOTAL PRESS BLACKOUT. IF WORD GETS OUT WHAT'S HAPPENING HERE, WE'LL HAVE A BLOODY STOCK MARKET CRASH.
UH, I'M NOT SURE HOW TO TELL YOU THIS, SIR, BUT I'VE JUST BEEN TOLD THAT TWO FORMER PRIME MINISTERS HAVE BEEN ASSASSINATED.
FUCK.
SOMEBODY GET ME ATTICUS KING. HE NEEDS TO COME IN FROM WHATEVER HE'S WORKING ON.

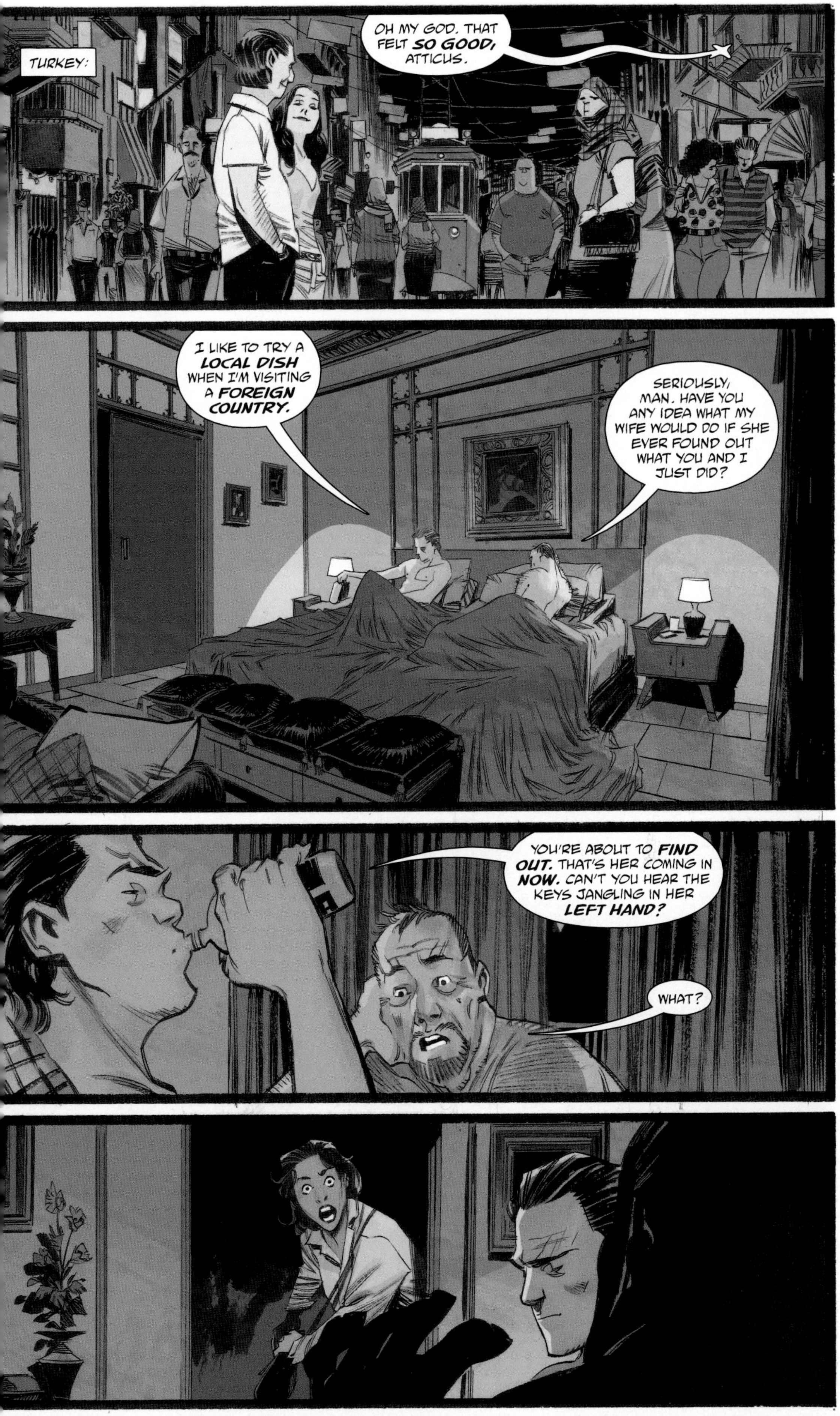
TURKEY:
OH MY GOD. THAT FELT **SO GOOD,** ATTICUS.
I LIKE TO TRY A **LOCAL DISH** WHEN I'M VISITING A **FOREIGN COUNTRY.**
SERIOUSLY, MAN. HAVE YOU ANY IDEA WHAT MY WIFE WOULD DO IF SHE EVER FOUND OUT WHAT YOU AND I JUST DID?
YOU'RE ABOUT TO **FIND OUT.** THAT'S HER COMING IN **NOW.** CAN'T YOU HEAR THE KEYS JANGLING IN HER **LEFT HAND?**
WHAT?

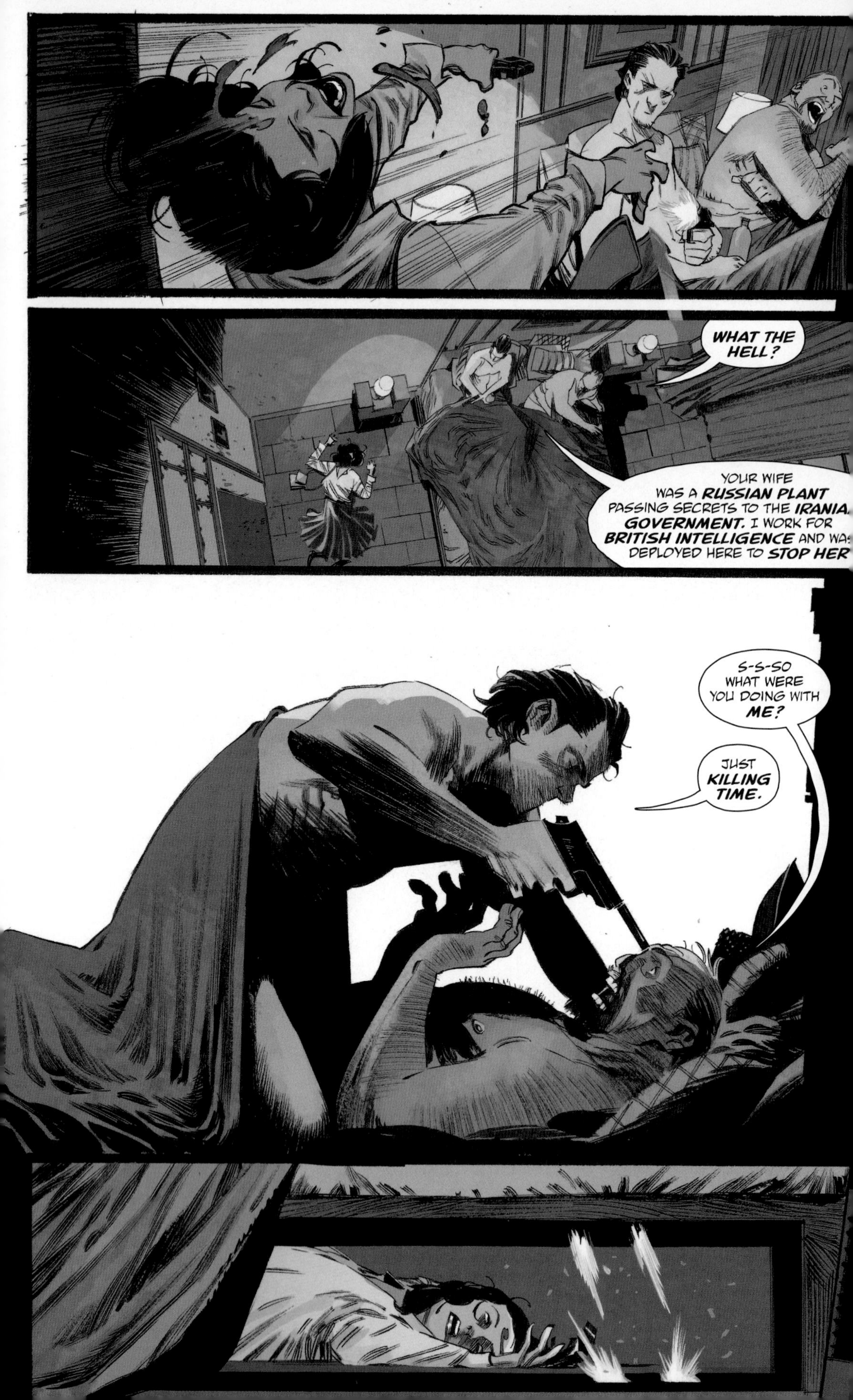
WHAT THE HELL?
YOUR WIFE WAS A RUSSIAN PLANT PASSING SECRETS TO THE IRANIAN GOVERNMENT. I WORK FOR BRITISH INTELLIGENCE AND WAS DEPLOYED HERE TO STOP HER
S-S-SO WHAT WERE YOU DOING WITH ME?
JUST KILLING TIME.

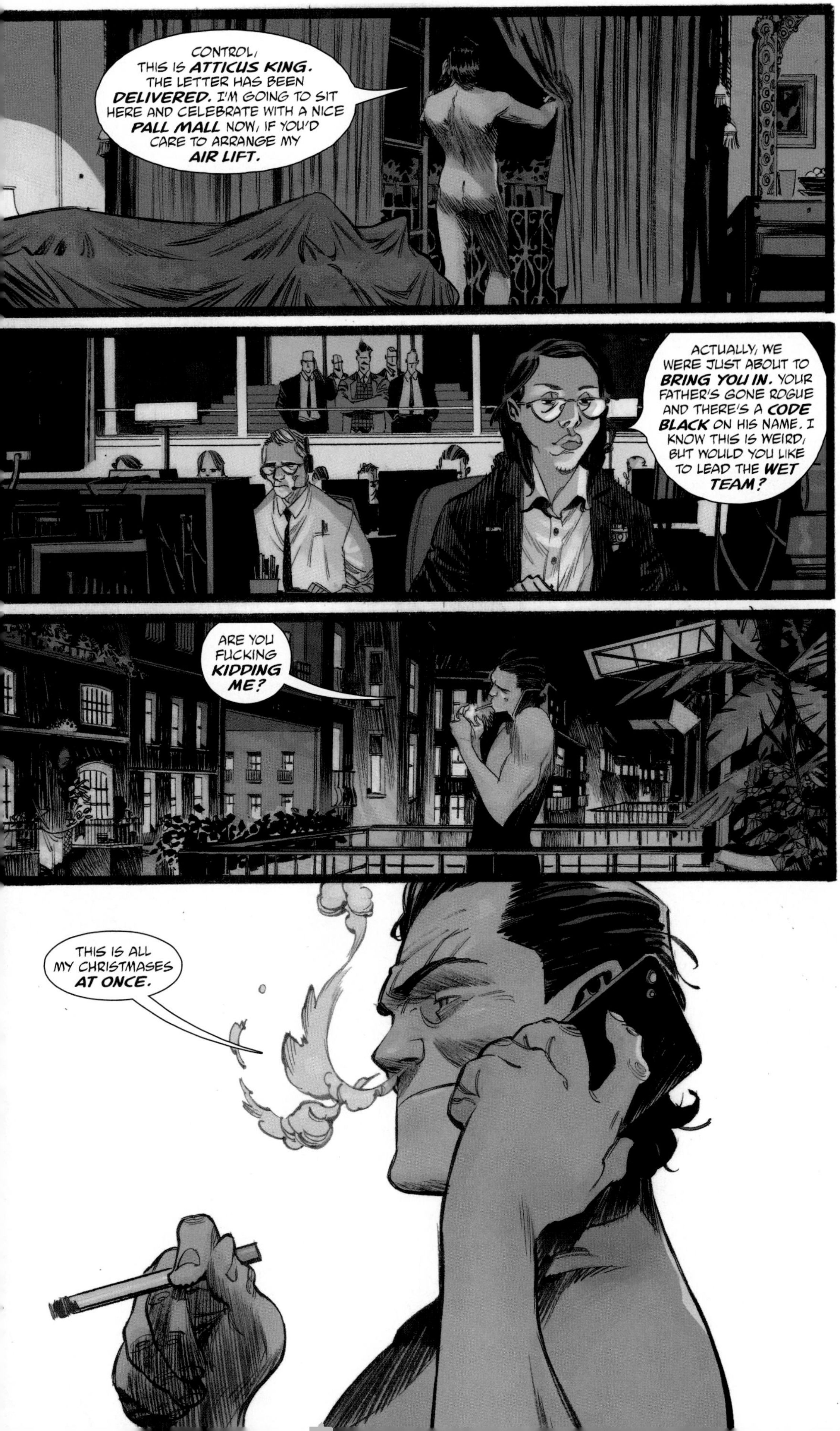
CONTROL, THIS IS **ATTICUS KING.** THE LETTER HAS BEEN **DELIVERED.** I'M GOING TO SIT HERE AND CELEBRATE WITH A NICE **PALL MALL** NOW, IF YOU'D CARE TO ARRANGE MY **AIR LIFT.**
ACTUALLY, WE WERE JUST ABOUT TO **BRING YOU IN.** YOUR FATHER'S GONE ROGUE AND THERE'S A **CODE BLACK** ON HIS NAME. I KNOW THIS IS WEIRD, BUT WOULD YOU LIKE TO LEAD THE **WET TEAM?**
ARE YOU FUCKING **KIDDING ME?**
THIS IS ALL MY CHRISTMASES **AT ONCE.**

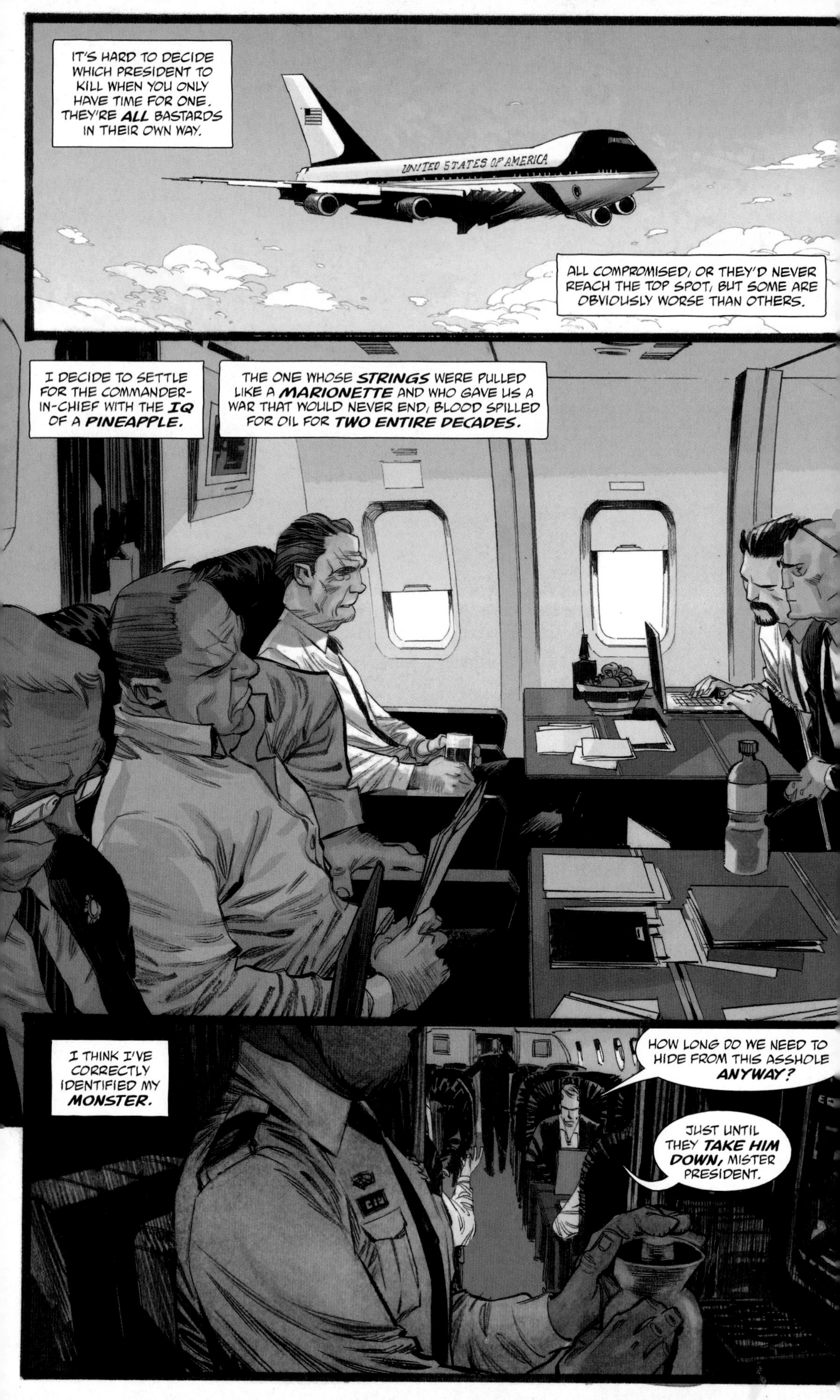
IT'S HARD TO DECIDE WHICH PRESIDENT TO KILL WHEN YOU ONLY HAVE TIME FOR ONE. THEY'RE ALL BASTARDS IN THEIR OWN WAY.
UNITED STATES OF AMERICA
ALL COMPROMISED, OR THEY'D NEVER REACH THE TOP SPOT, BUT SOME ARE OBVIOUSLY WORSE THAN OTHERS.
I DECIDE TO SETTLE FOR THE COMMANDER-IN-CHIEF WITH THE IQ OF A PINEAPPLE.
THE ONE WHOSE STRINGS WERE PULLED LIKE A MARIONETTE AND WHO GAVE US A WAR THAT WOULD NEVER END, BLOOD SPILLED FOR OIL FOR TWO ENTIRE DECADES.
I THINK I'VE CORRECTLY IDENTIFIED MY MONSTER.
HOW LONG DO WE NEED TO HIDE FROM THIS ASSHOLE ANYWAY?
JUST UNTIL THEY TAKE HIM DOWN, MISTER PRESIDENT.

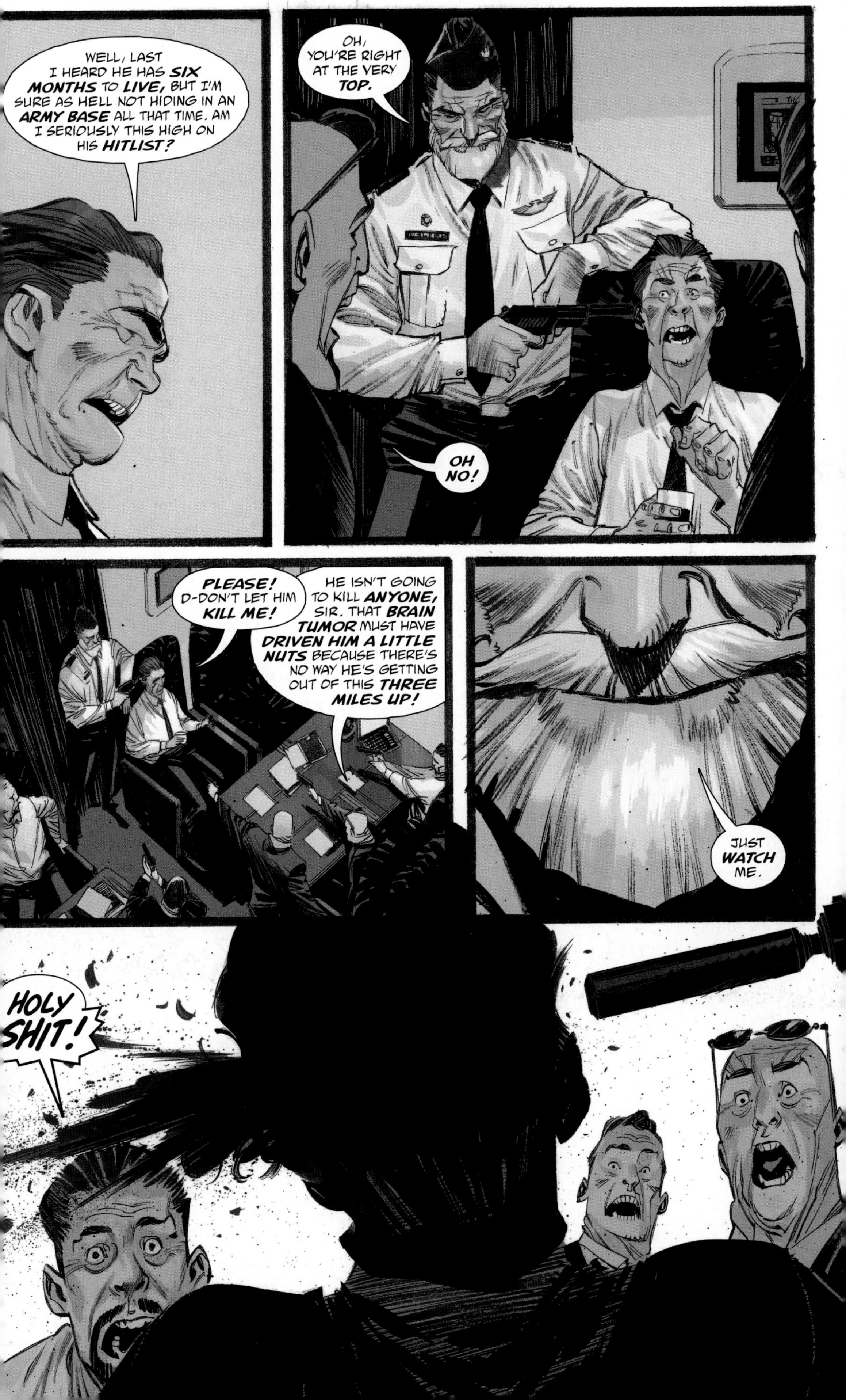

WELL, LAST I HEARD HE HAS SIX MONTHS TO LIVE, BUT I'M SURE AS HELL NOT HIDING IN AN ARMY BASE ALL THAT TIME. AM I SERIOUSLY THIS HIGH ON HIS HITLIST?
OH, YOU'RE RIGHT AT THE VERY TOP.
OH NO!
PLEASE! D-DON'T LET HIM KILL ME!
HE ISN'T GOING TO KILL ANYONE, SIR. THAT BRAIN TUMOR MUST HAVE DRIVEN HIM A LITTLE NUTS BECAUSE THERE'S NO WAY HE'S GETTING OUT OF THIS THREE MILES UP!
JUST WATCH ME.
HOLY SHIT!

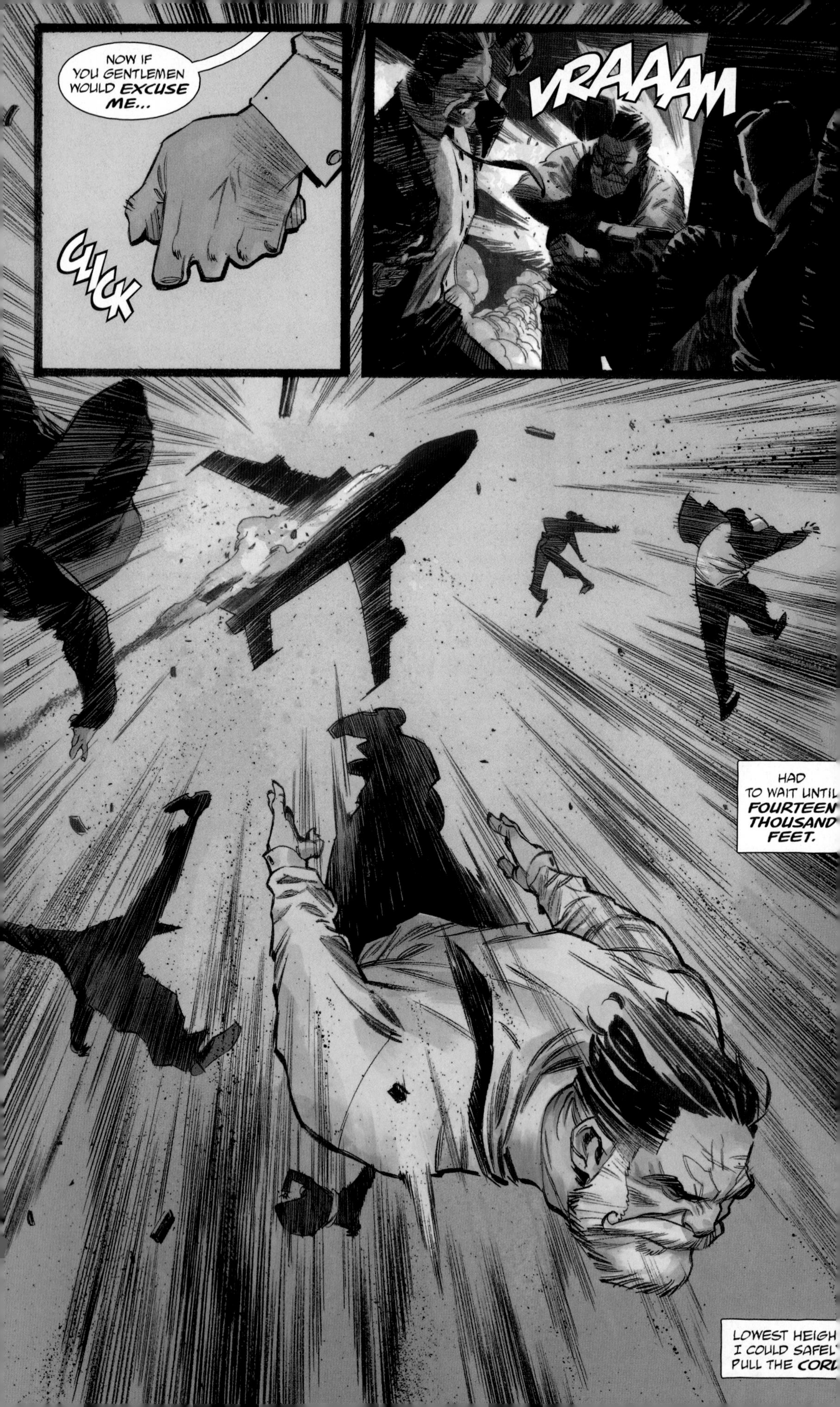
NOW IF YOU GENTLEMEN WOULD EXCUSE ME...
CLICK
VRAAAM
HAD TO WAIT UNTIL FOURTEEN THOUSAND FEET.
LOWEST HEIGH I COULD SAFEL PULL THE CORI

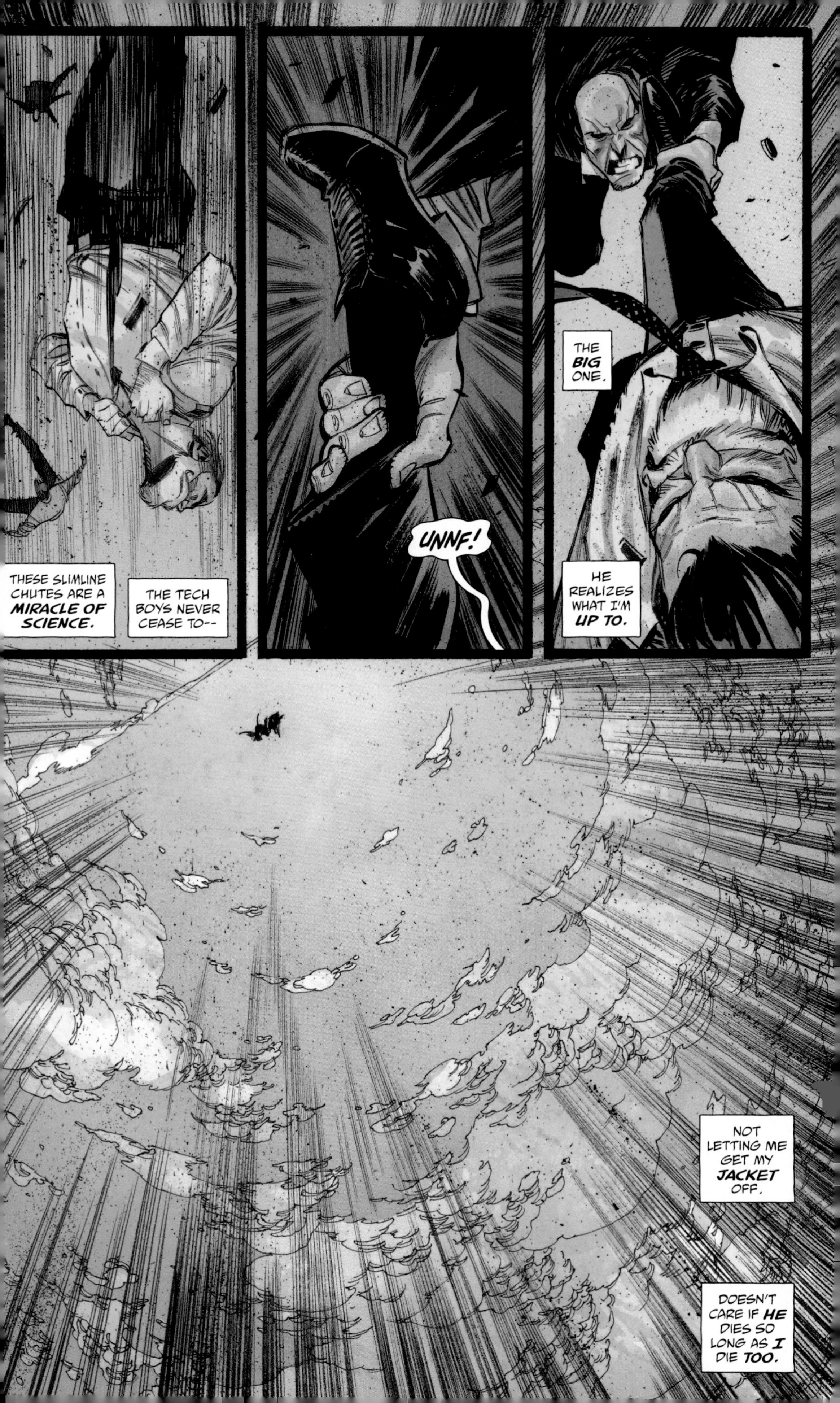

THESE SLIMLINE CHUTES ARE A MIRACLE OF SCIENCE.
THE TECH BOYS NEVER CEASE TO--
UNNF!
THE BIG ONE.
HE REALIZES WHAT I'M UP TO.
NOT LETTING ME GET MY JACKET OFF.
DOESN'T CARE IF HE DIES SO LONG AS I DIE TOO.

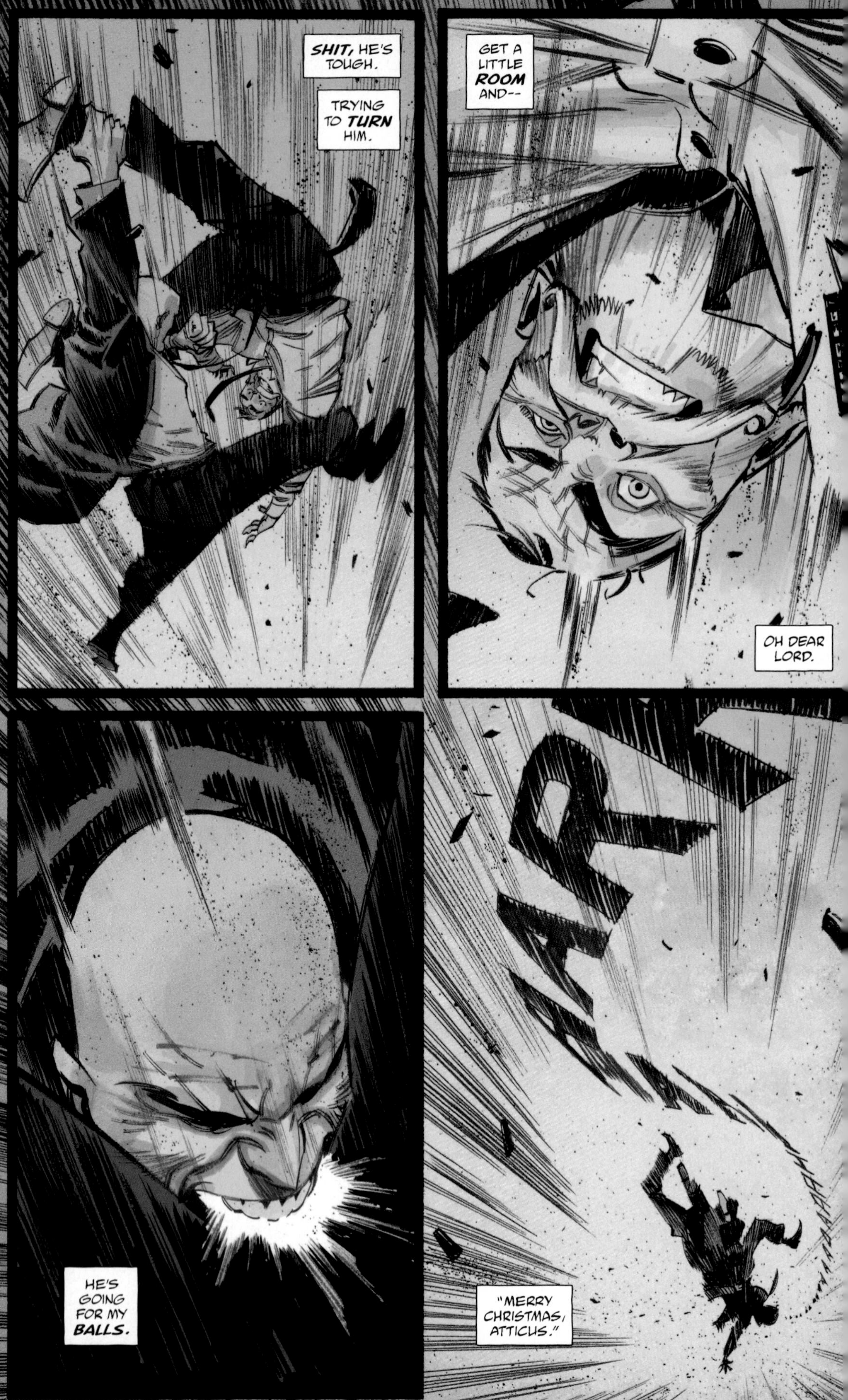
SHIT, HE'S TOUGH.
TRYING TO TURN HIM.
GET A LITTLE ROOM AND--
OH DEAR LORD.
HE'S GOING FOR MY BALLS.
"MERRY CHRISTMAS, ATTICUS."

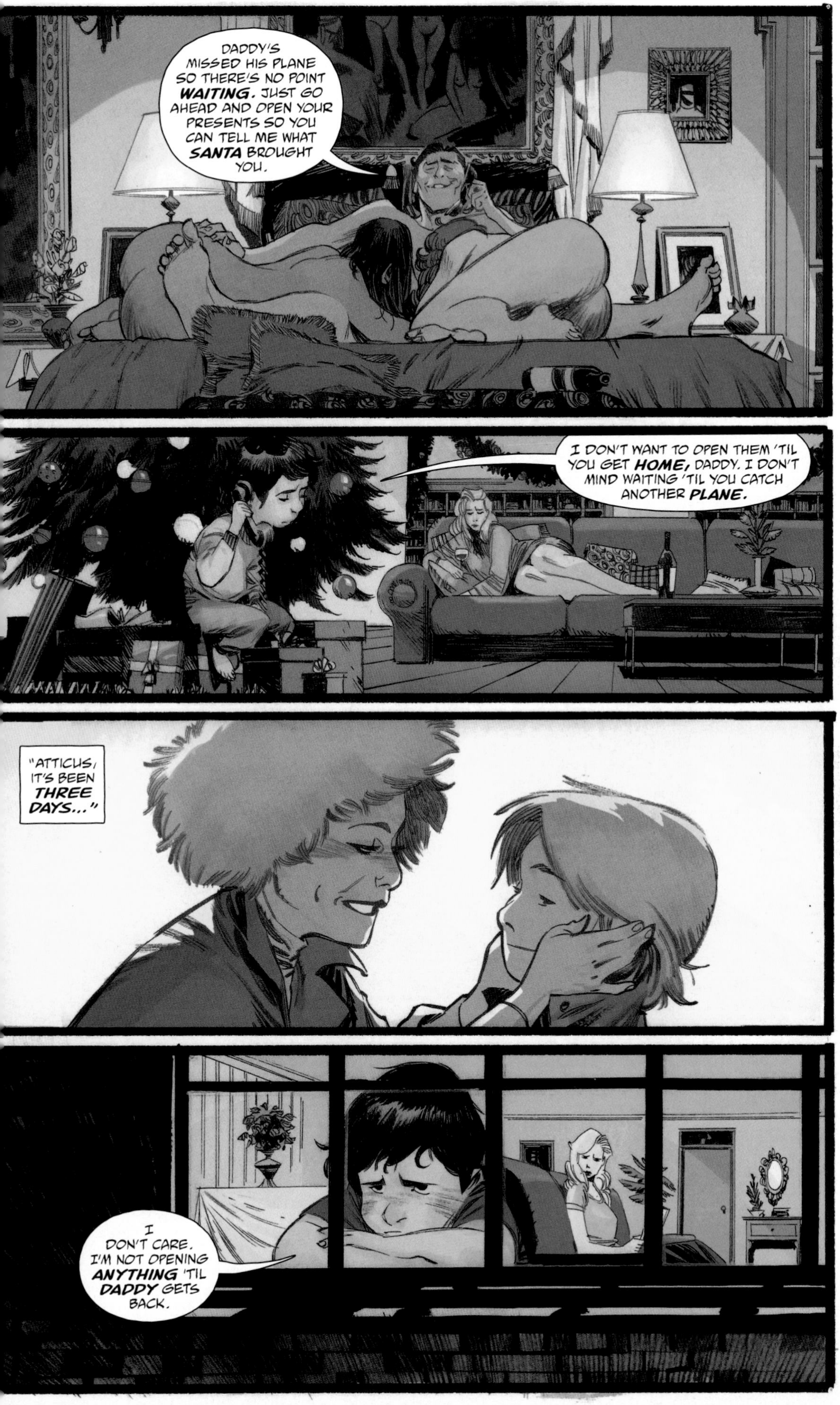
DADDY'S MISSED HIS PLANE SO THERE'S NO POINT **WAITING.** JUST GO AHEAD AND OPEN YOUR PRESENTS SO YOU CAN TELL ME WHAT **SANTA** BROUGHT YOU.
I DON'T WANT TO OPEN THEM 'TIL YOU GET **HOME,** DADDY. I DON'T MIND WAITING 'TIL YOU CATCH ANOTHER **PLANE.**
"ATTICUS, IT'S BEEN **THREE DAYS...**"
I DON'T CARE. I'M NOT OPENING **ANYTHING** 'TIL **DADDY** GETS BACK.

THE **ANTI-SEIZURE PILLS** ARE **VERY EFFECTIVE,** BUT YOU'LL STILL GET A SENSE OF **DÉJÀ-VU.** THINGS MIGHT NOT FEEL **REAL.**

"I WOULDN'T RECOMMEND **DRIVING** FOR THE MOMENT..."

"...AND THOSE **FORTY COBBS A DAY** ARE JUST **OUT OF THE QUESTION...**"

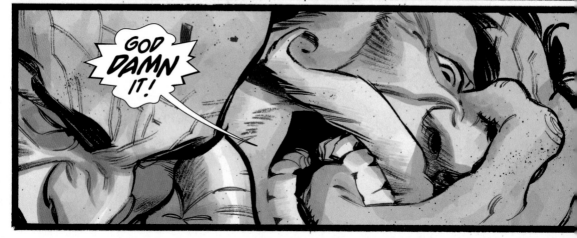

GOD DAMN IT!

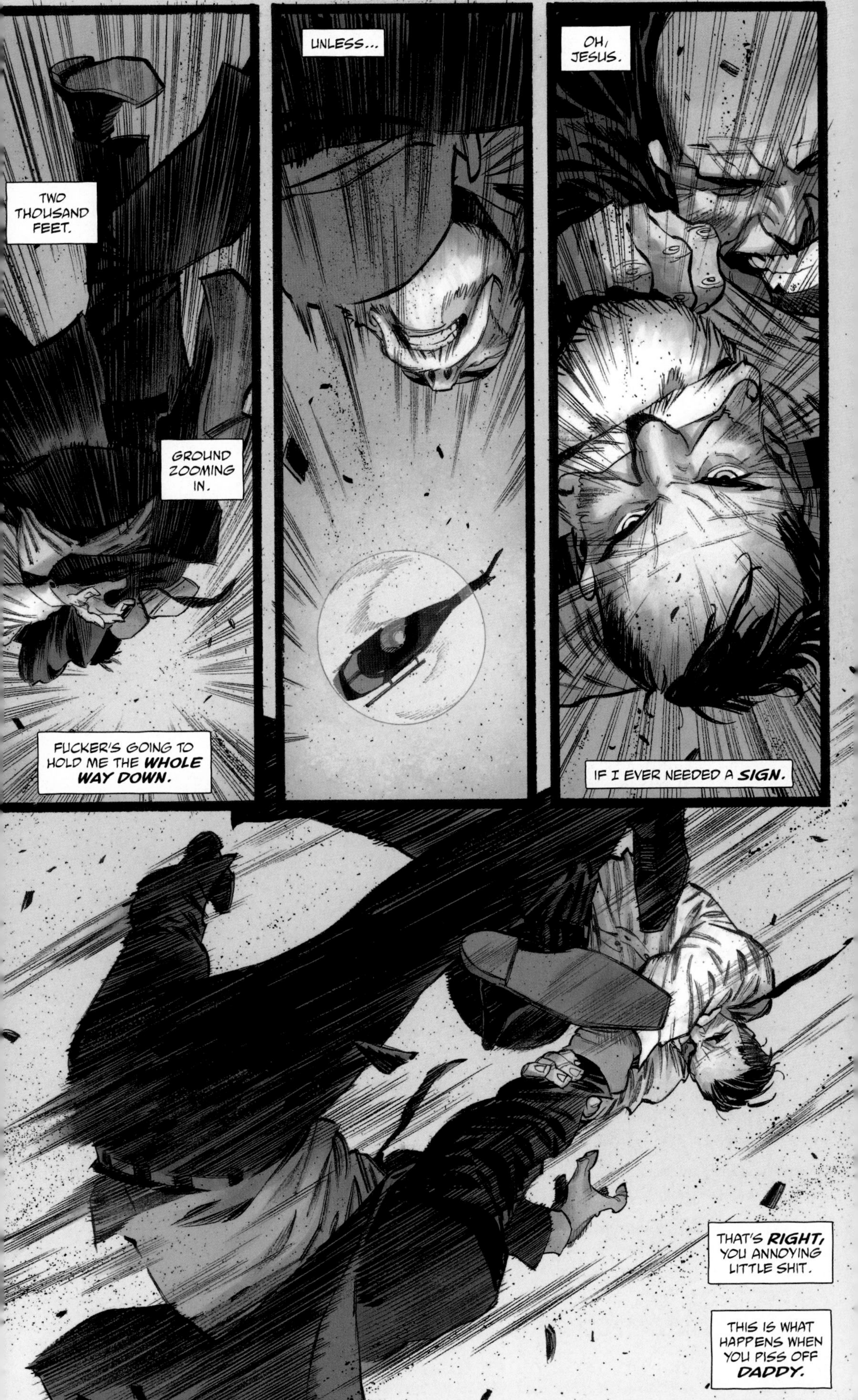
TWO THOUSAND FEET.
GROUND ZOOMING IN.
FUCKER'S GOING TO HOLD ME THE WHOLE WAY DOWN.
UNLESS...
OH, JESUS.
IF I EVER NEEDED A SIGN.
THAT'S RIGHT, YOU ANNOYING LITTLE SHIT.
THIS IS WHAT HAPPENS WHEN YOU PISS OFF DADDY.

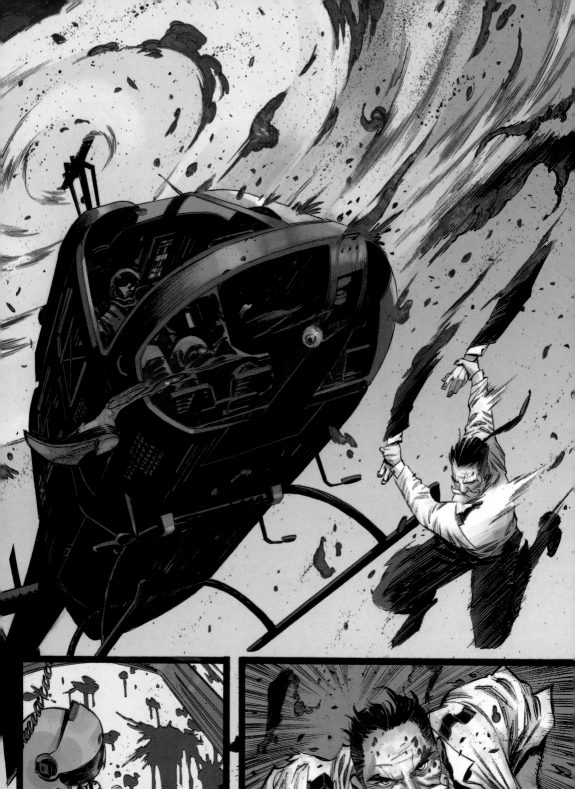

AT
BLOODY
LAST.

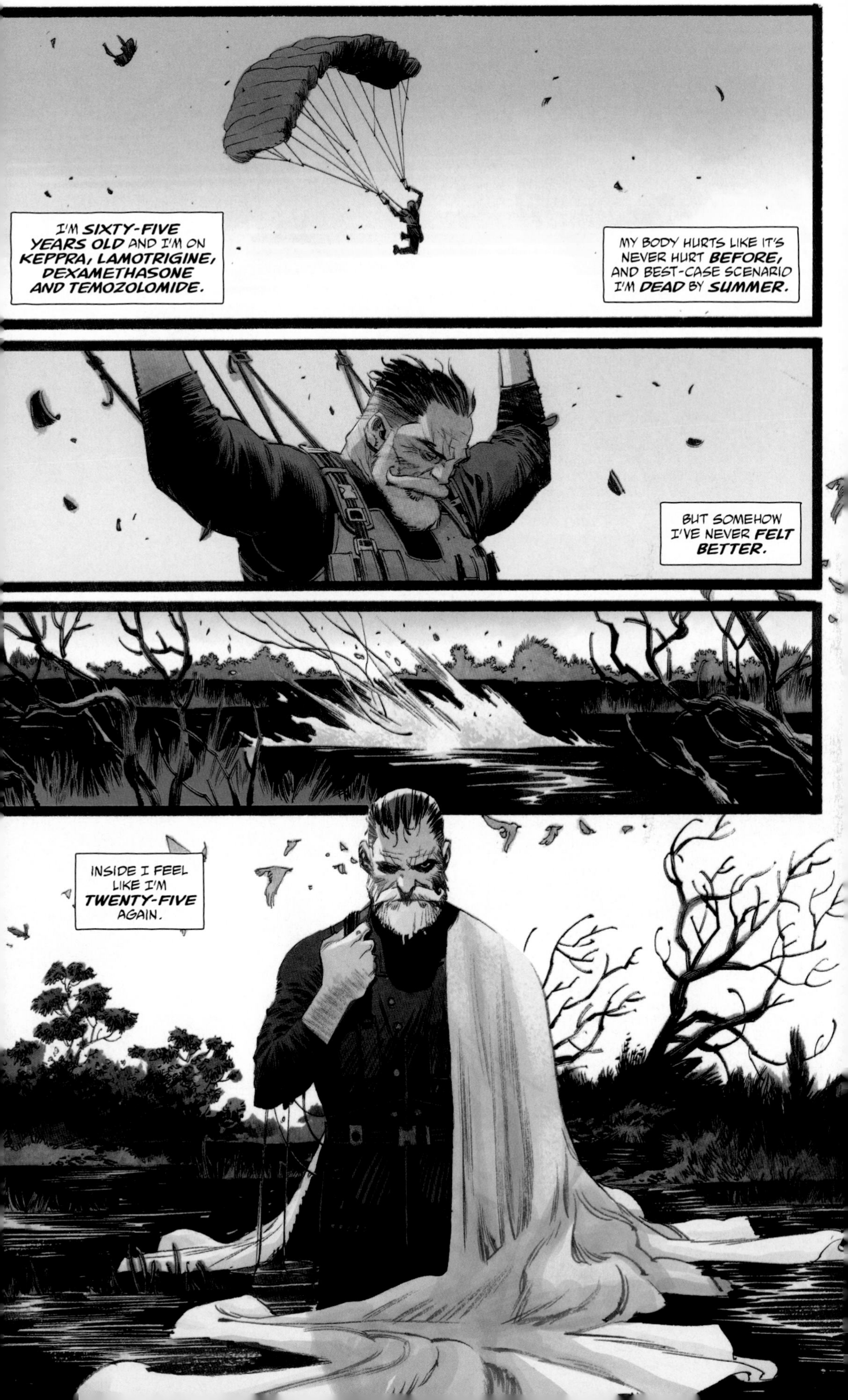
I'M SIXTY-FIVE YEARS OLD AND I'M ON KEPPRA, LAMOTRIGINE, DEXAMETHASONE AND TEMOZOLOMIDE.
MY BODY HURTS LIKE IT'S NEVER HURT BEFORE, AND BEST-CASE SCENARIO I'M DEAD BY SUMMER.
BUT SOMEHOW I'VE NEVER FELT BETTER.
INSIDE I FEEL LIKE I'M TWENTY-FIVE AGAIN.

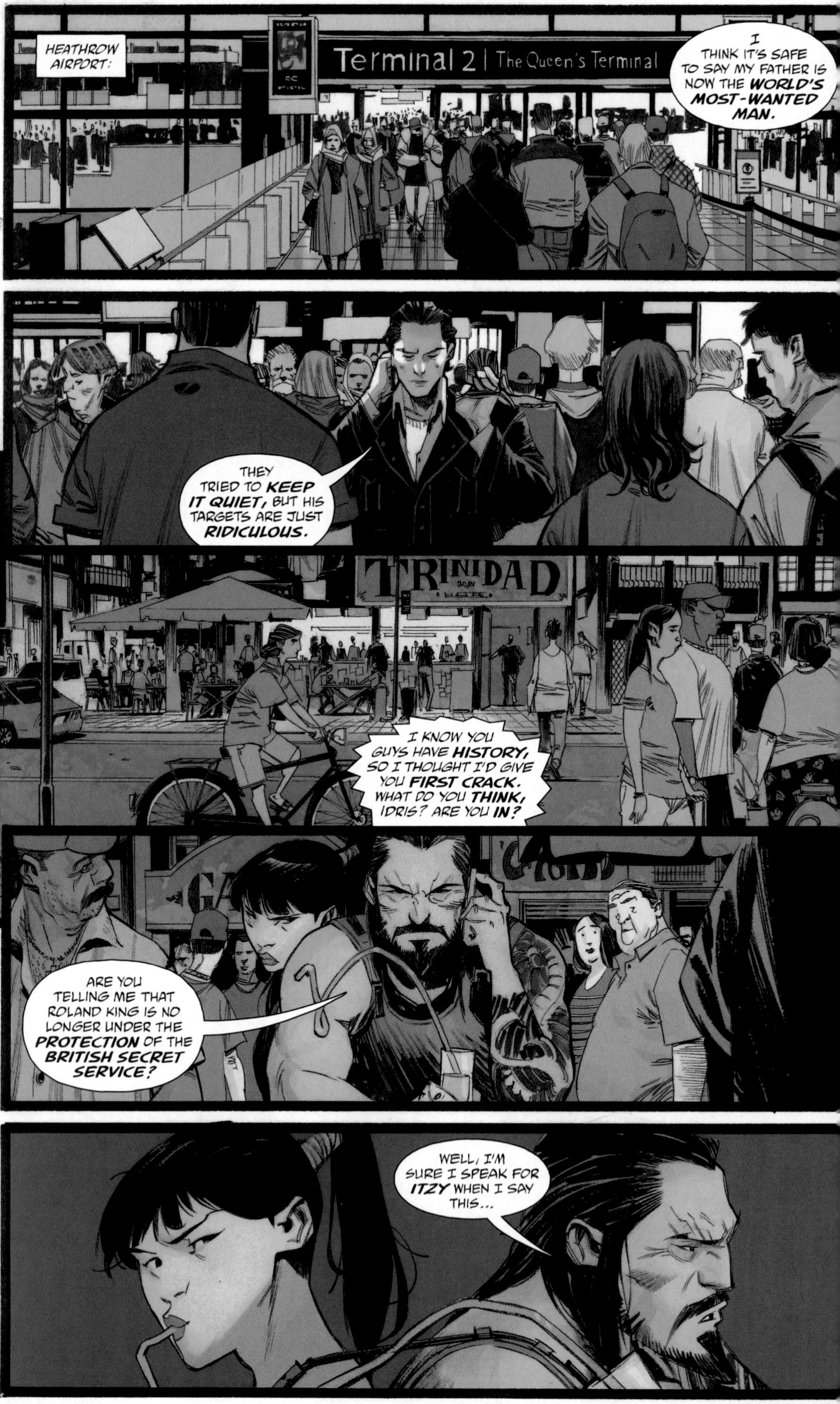
HEATHROW AIRPORT:
Terminal 2 | The Queen's Terminal
I THINK IT'S SAFE TO SAY MY FATHER IS NOW THE WORLD'S MOST-WANTED MAN.
THEY TRIED TO KEEP IT QUIET, BUT HIS TARGETS ARE JUST RIDICULOUS.
TRINIDAD
I KNOW YOU GUYS HAVE HISTORY, SO I THOUGHT I'D GIVE YOU FIRST CRACK. WHAT DO YOU THINK, IDRIS? ARE YOU IN?
ARE YOU TELLING ME THAT ROLAND KING IS NO LONGER UNDER THE PROTECTION OF THE BRITISH SECRET SERVICE?
WELL, I'M SURE I SPEAK FOR ITZY WHEN I SAY THIS...

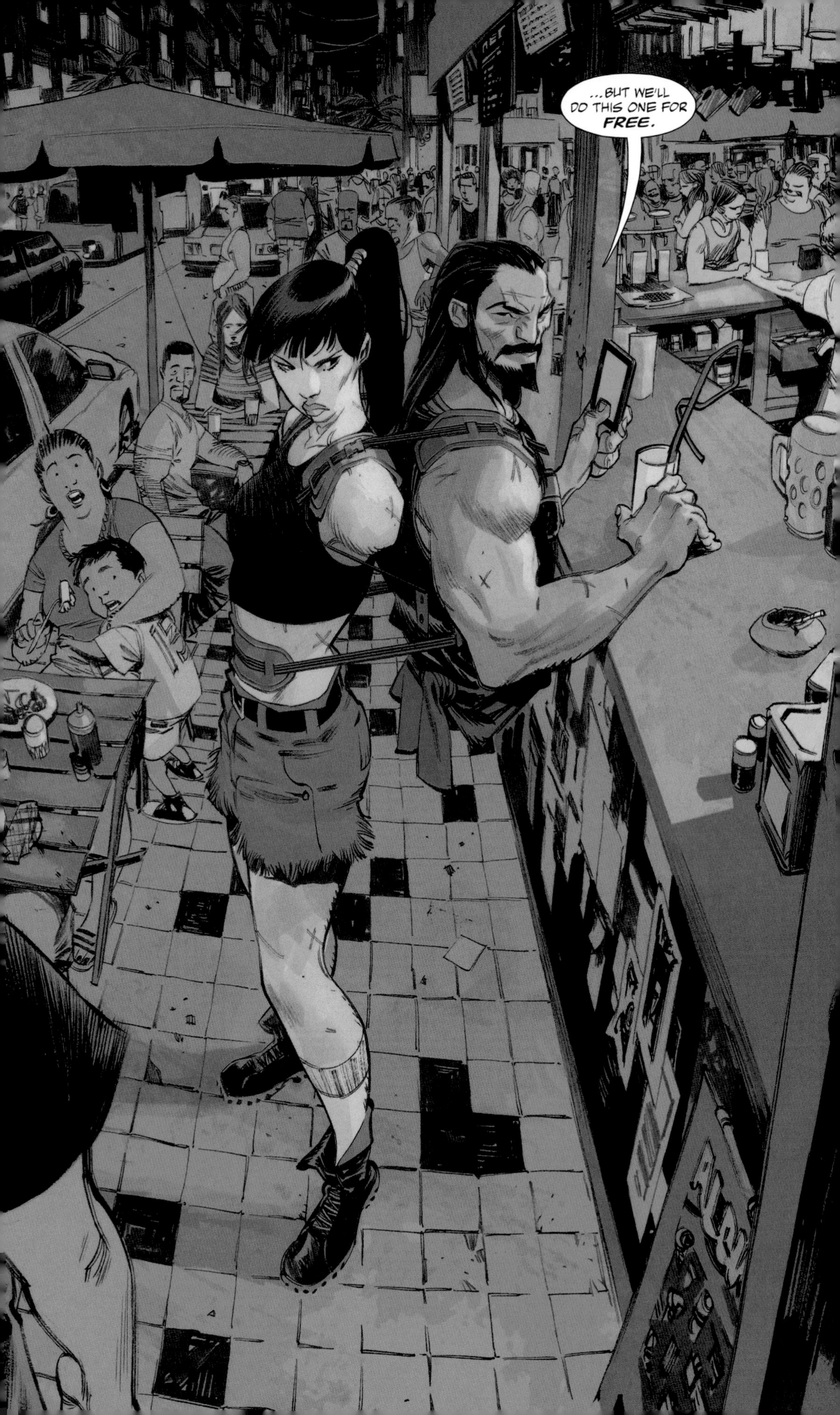
...BUT WE'LL DO THIS ONE FOR **FREE.**

Three

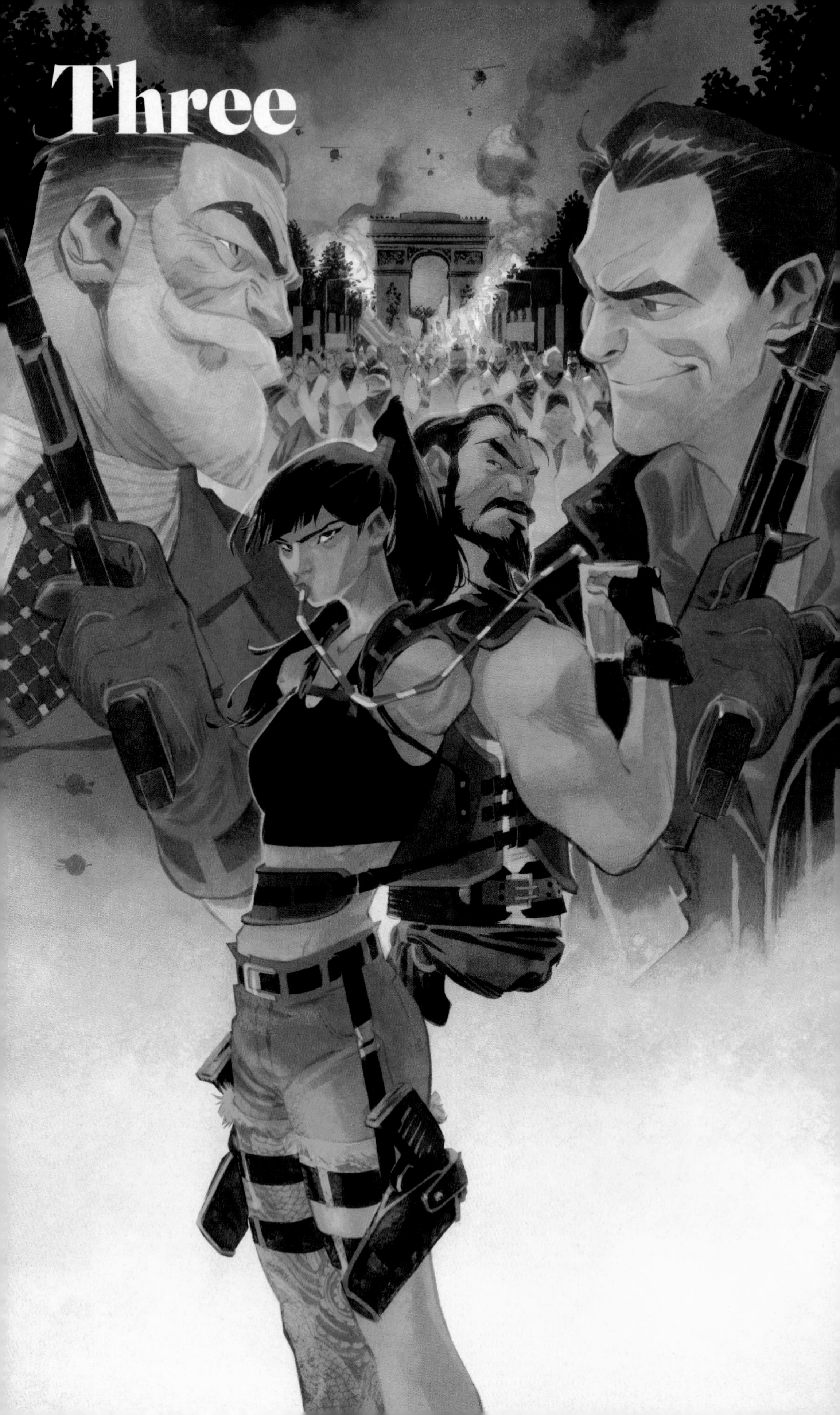

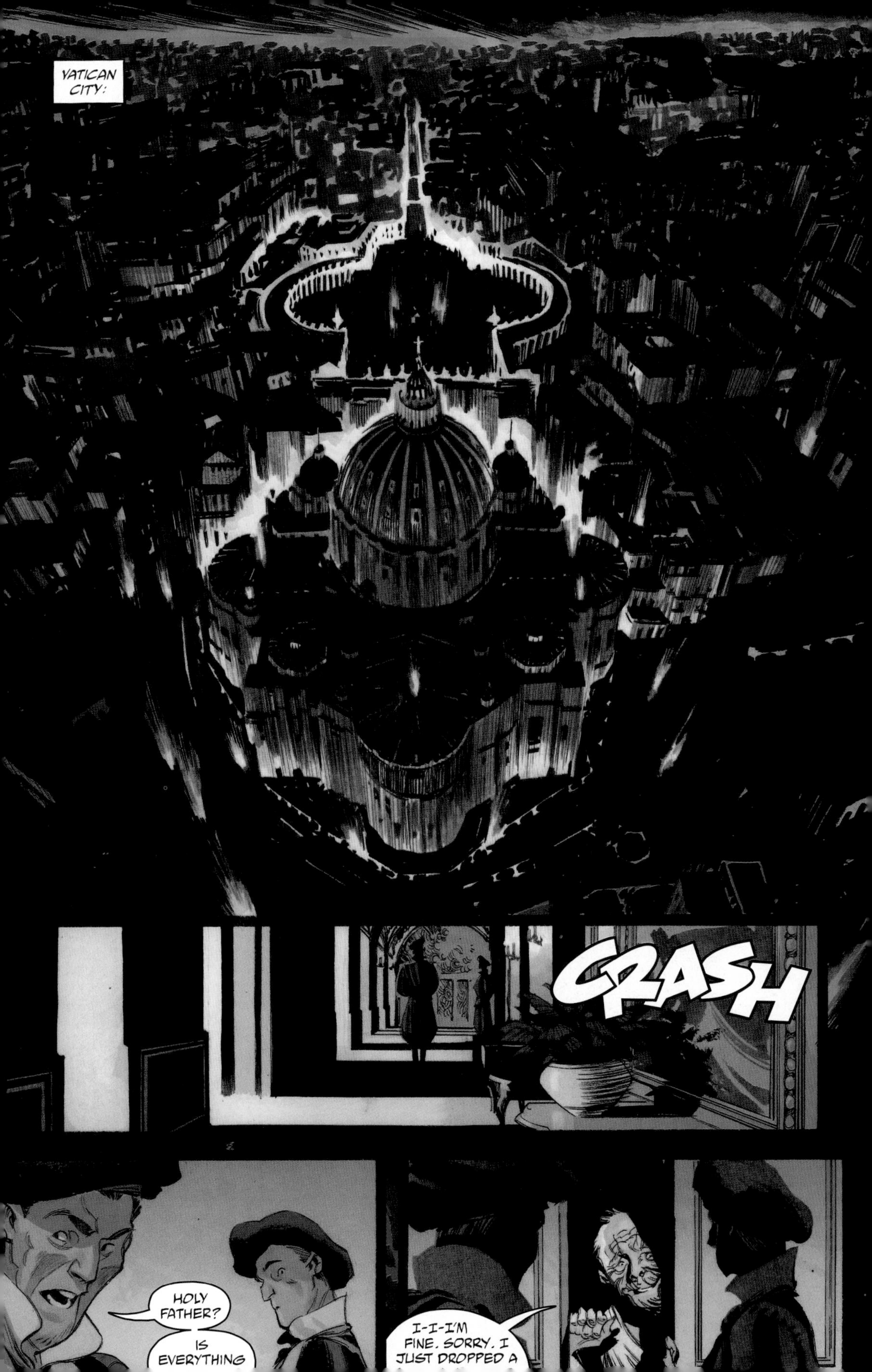
VATICAN CITY:
CRASH
HOLY FATHER?
IS EVERYTHING
I-I-I'M FINE. SORRY. I JUST DROPPED A

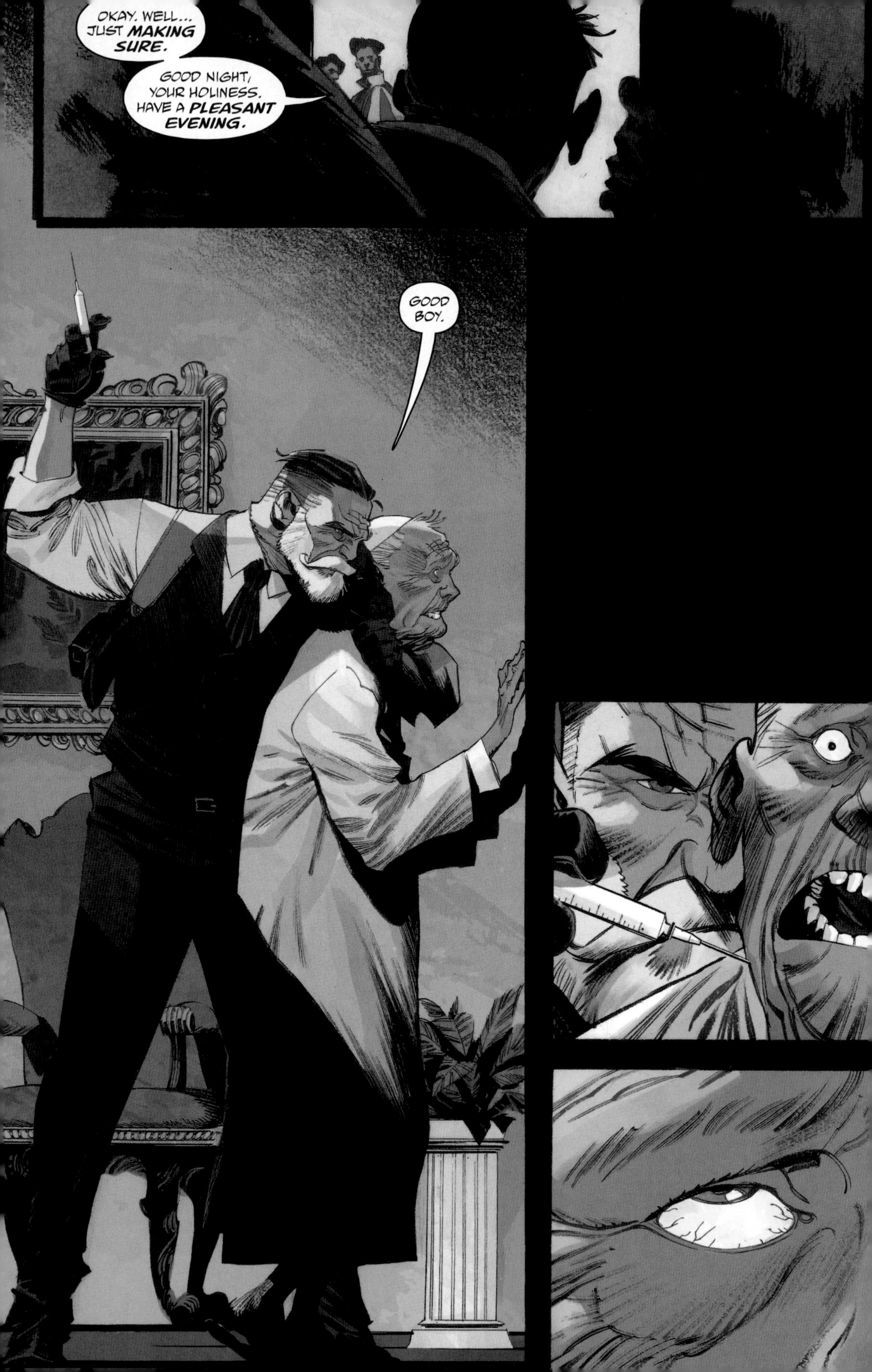
OKAY. WELL... JUST **MAKING SURE.**
GOOD NIGHT, YOUR HOLINESS. HAVE A **PLEASANT EVENING.**
GOOD BOY.

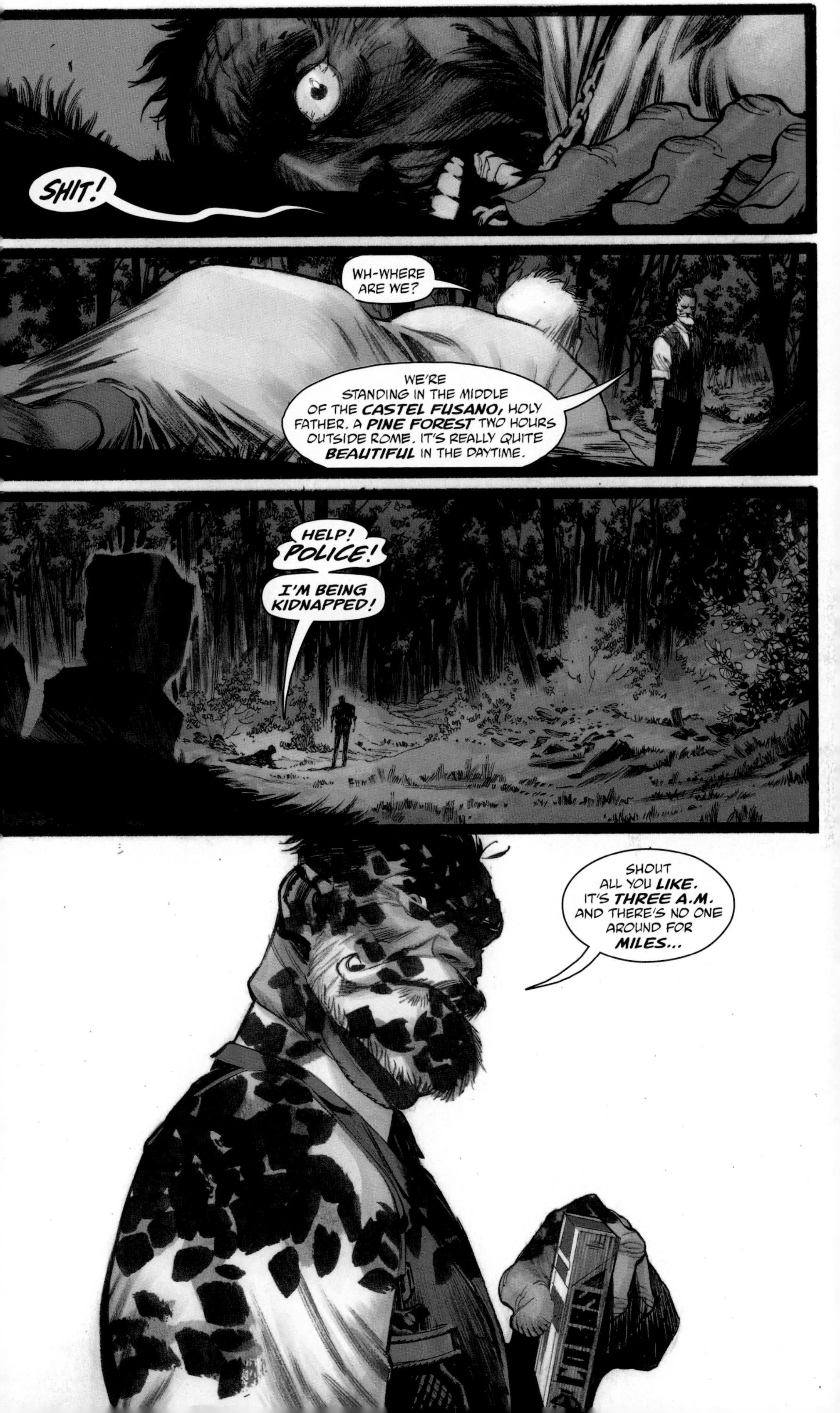
SHIT!
WH-WHERE ARE WE?
WE'RE STANDING IN THE MIDDLE OF THE CASTEL FUSANO, HOLY FATHER. A PINE FOREST TWO HOURS OUTSIDE ROME. IT'S REALLY QUITE BEAUTIFUL IN THE DAYTIME.
HELP! POLICE!
I'M BEING KIDNAPPED!
SHOUT ALL YOU LIKE. IT'S THREE A.M. AND THERE'S NO ONE AROUND FOR MILES...

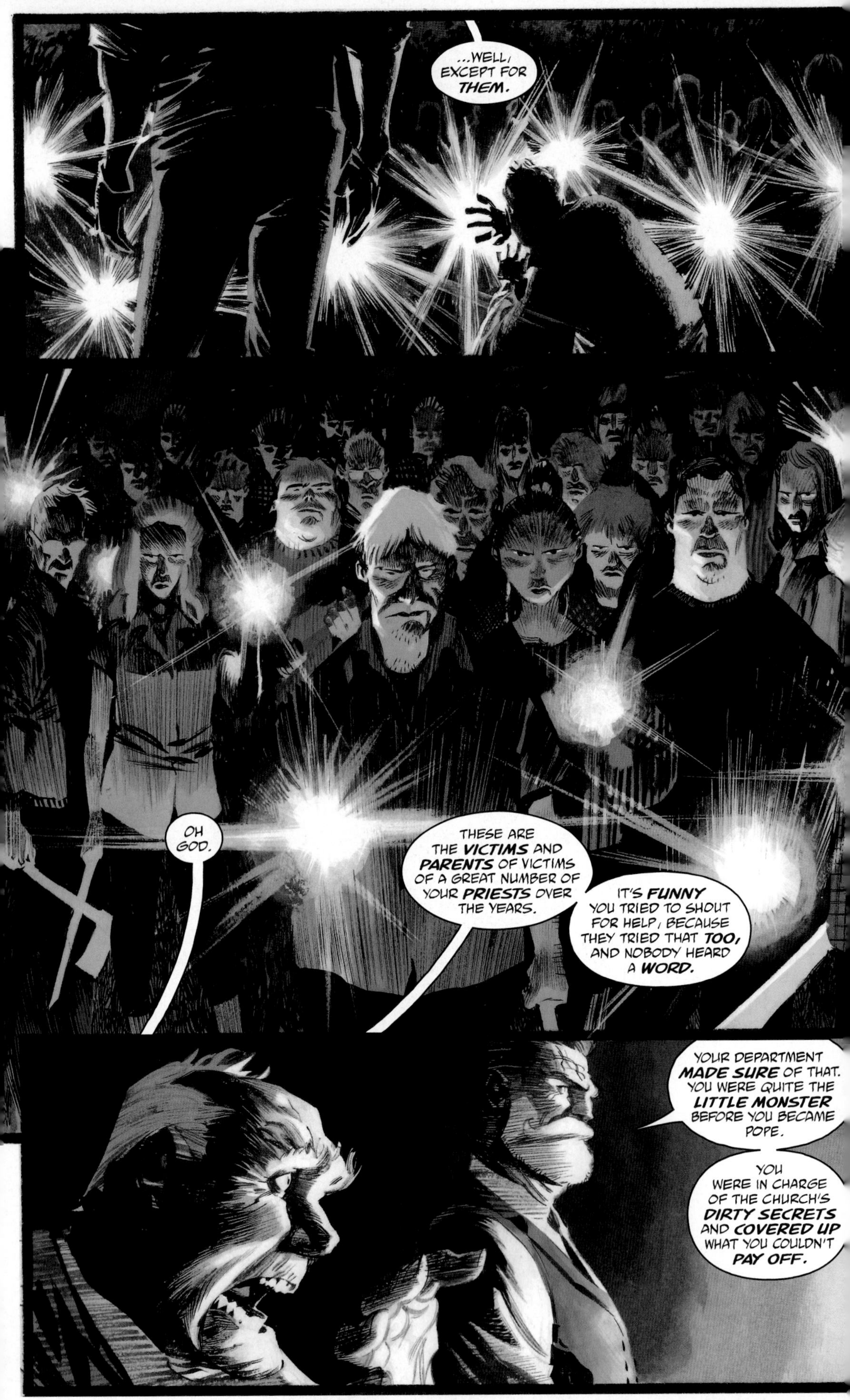
...WELL, EXCEPT FOR THEM.
OH GOD.
THESE ARE THE VICTIMS AND PARENTS OF VICTIMS OF A GREAT NUMBER OF YOUR PRIESTS OVER THE YEARS.
IT'S FUNNY YOU TRIED TO SHOUT FOR HELP, BECAUSE THEY TRIED THAT TOO, AND NOBODY HEARD A WORD.
YOUR DEPARTMENT MADE SURE OF THAT. YOU WERE QUITE THE LITTLE MONSTER BEFORE YOU BECAME POPE.
YOU WERE IN CHARGE OF THE CHURCH'S DIRTY SECRETS AND COVERED UP WHAT YOU COULDN'T PAY OFF.

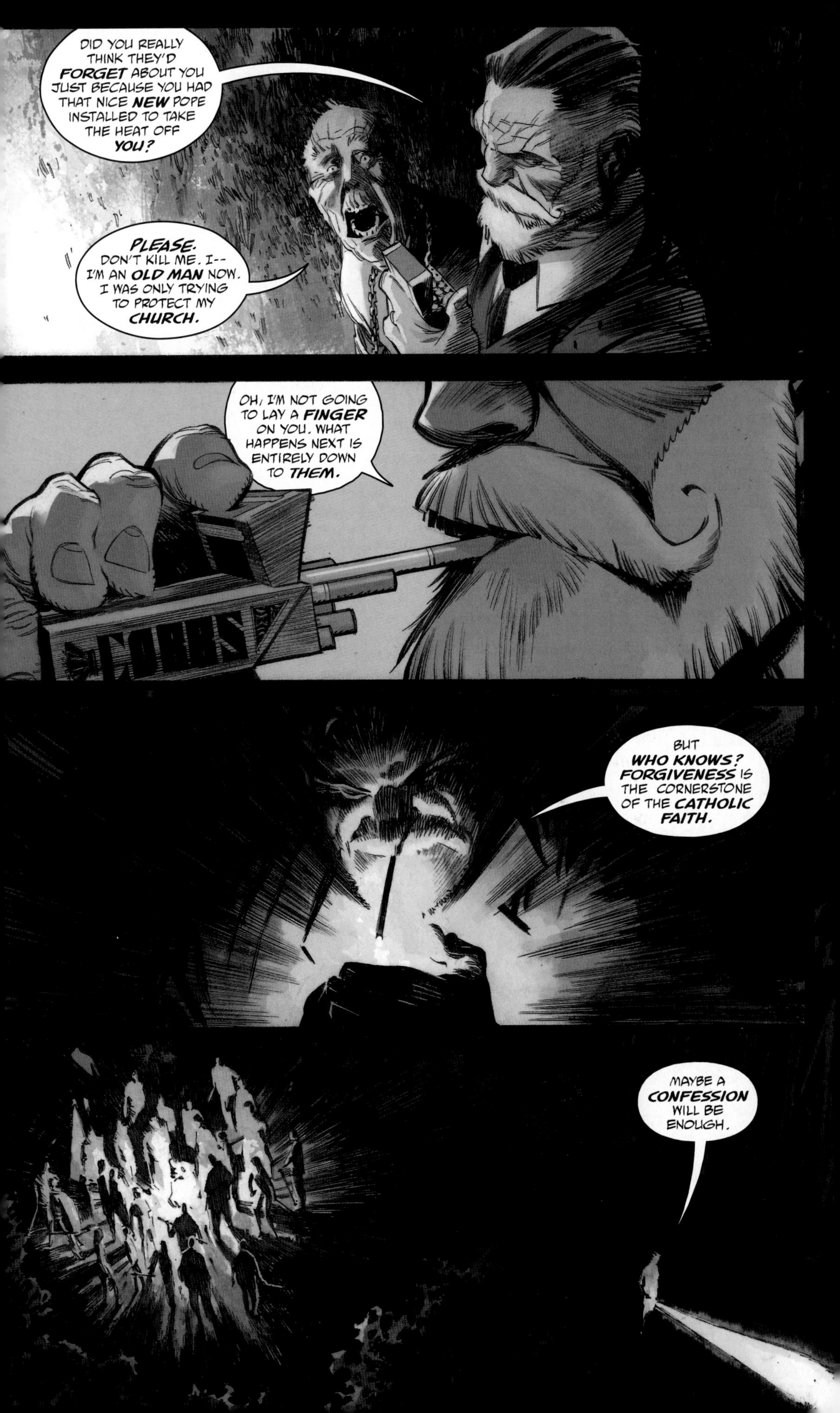
DID YOU REALLY THINK THEY'D FORGET ABOUT YOU JUST BECAUSE YOU HAD THAT NICE NEW POPE INSTALLED TO TAKE THE HEAT OFF YOU?
PLEASE. DON'T KILL ME. I-- I'M AN OLD MAN NOW. I WAS ONLY TRYING TO PROTECT MY CHURCH.
OH, I'M NOT GOING TO LAY A FINGER ON YOU. WHAT HAPPENS NEXT IS ENTIRELY DOWN TO THEM.
BUT WHO KNOWS? FORGIVENESS IS THE CORNERSTONE OF THE CATHOLIC FAITH.
MAYBE A CONFESSION WILL BE ENOUGH.

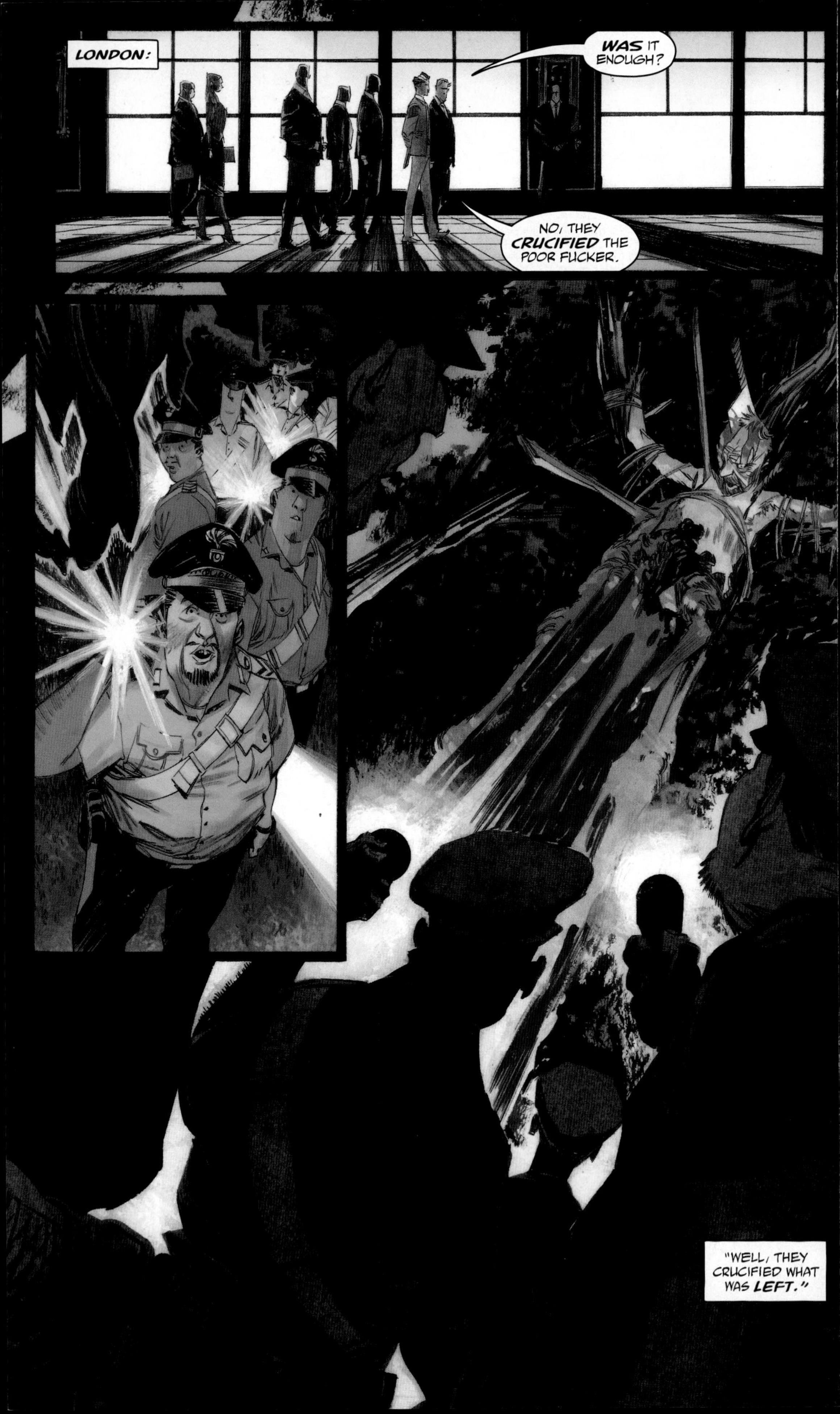
LONDON:
WAS IT ENOUGH?
NO, THEY CRUCIFIED THE POOR FUCKER.
"WELL, THEY CRUCIFIED WHAT WAS LEFT."

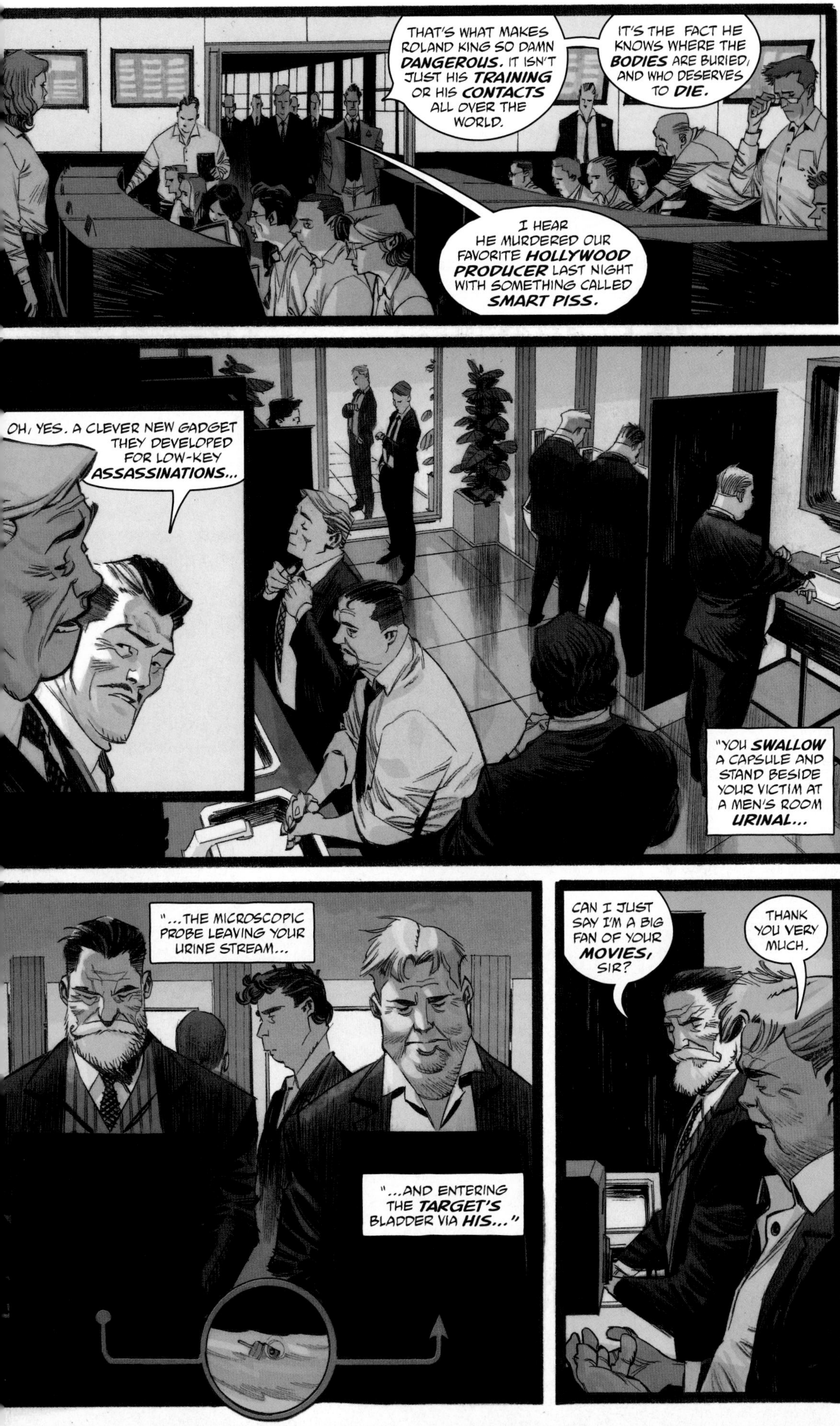
THAT'S WHAT MAKES ROLAND KING SO DAMN **DANGEROUS.** IT ISN'T JUST HIS **TRAINING** OR HIS **CONTACTS** ALL OVER THE WORLD.
IT'S THE FACT HE KNOWS WHERE THE **BODIES** ARE BURIED, AND WHO DESERVES TO **DIE.**
I HEAR HE MURDERED OUR FAVORITE **HOLLYWOOD PRODUCER** LAST NIGHT WITH SOMETHING CALLED **SMART PISS.**
OH, YES. A CLEVER NEW GADGET THEY DEVELOPED FOR LOW-KEY **ASSASSINATIONS...**
"YOU **SWALLOW** A CAPSULE AND STAND BESIDE YOUR VICTIM AT A MEN'S ROOM **URINAL...**
"...THE MICROSCOPIC PROBE LEAVING YOUR URINE STREAM...
"...AND ENTERING THE **TARGET'S** BLADDER VIA **HIS...**"
CAN I JUST SAY I'M A BIG FAN OF YOUR **MOVIES,** SIR?
THANK YOU VERY MUCH.

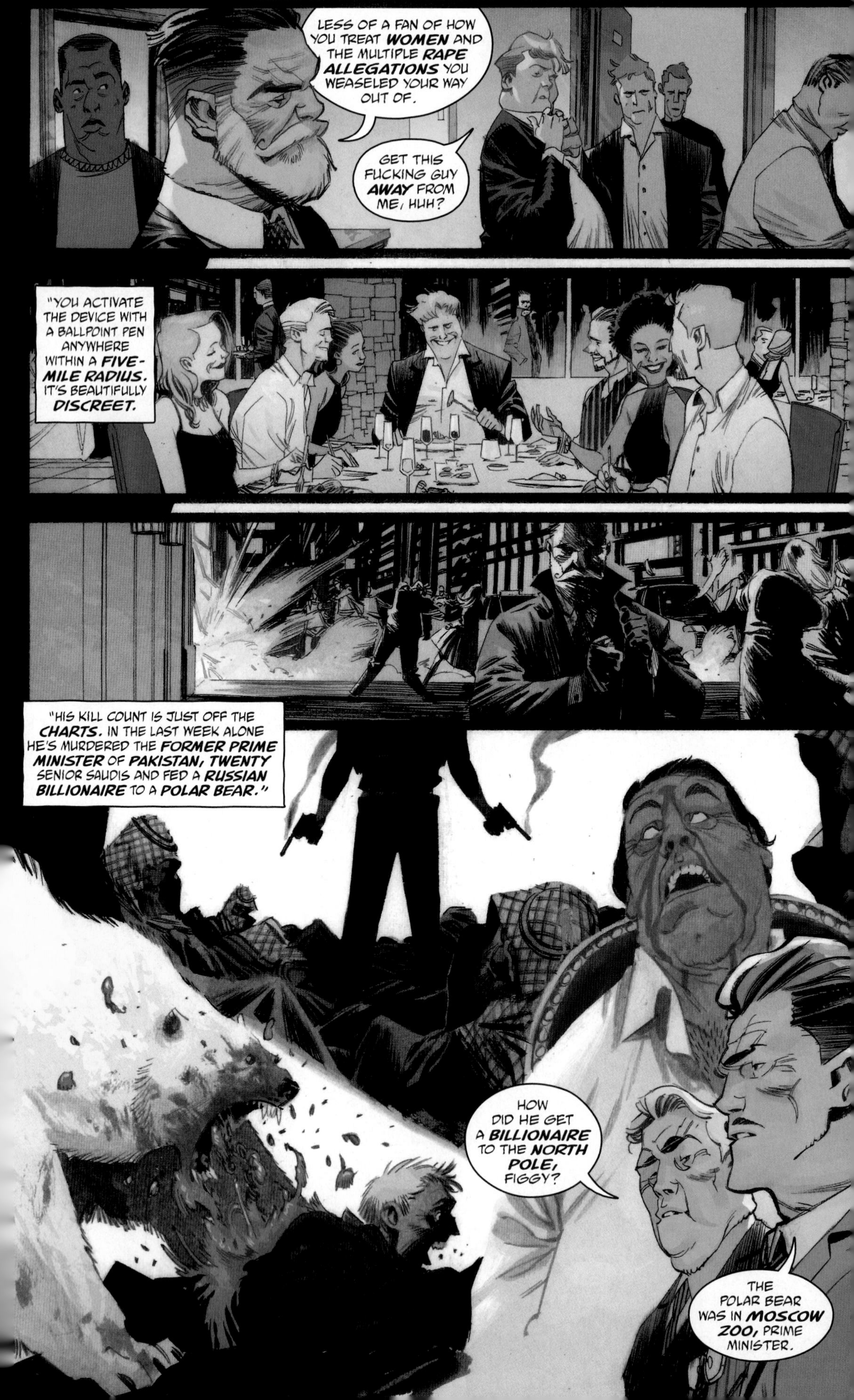

LESS OF A FAN OF HOW YOU TREAT WOMEN AND THE MULTIPLE RAPE ALLEGATIONS YOU WEASELED YOUR WAY OUT OF.
GET THIS FUCKING GUY AWAY FROM ME, HUH?
"YOU ACTIVATE THE DEVICE WITH A BALLPOINT PEN ANYWHERE WITHIN A FIVE-MILE RADIUS. IT'S BEAUTIFULLY DISCREET.
"HIS KILL COUNT IS JUST OFF THE CHARTS. IN THE LAST WEEK ALONE HE'S MURDERED THE FORMER PRIME MINISTER OF PAKISTAN, TWENTY SENIOR SAUDIS AND FED A RUSSIAN BILLIONAIRE TO A POLAR BEAR."
HOW DID HE GET A BILLIONAIRE TO THE NORTH POLE, FIGGY?
THE POLAR BEAR WAS IN MOSCOW ZOO, PRIME MINISTER.

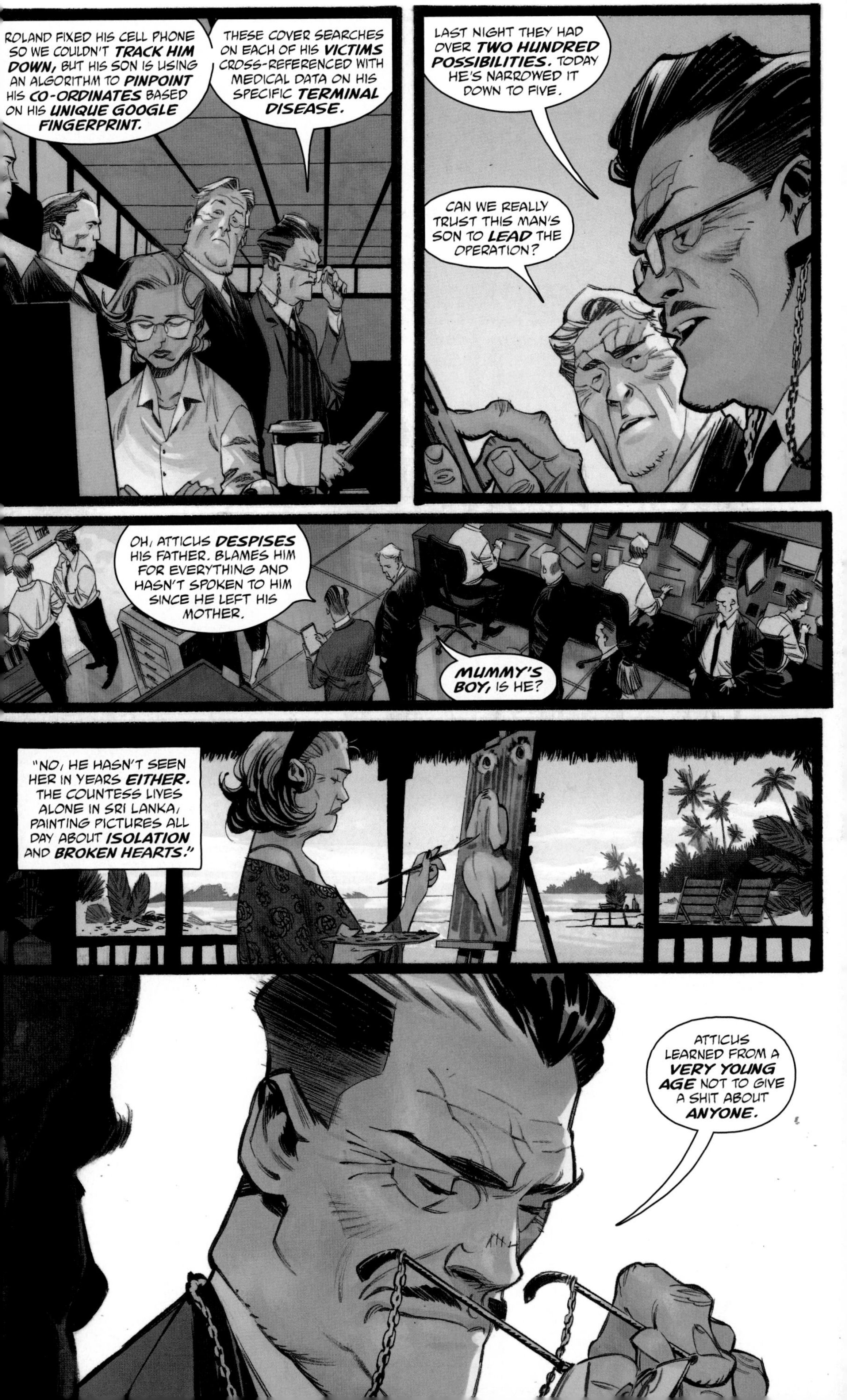
ROLAND FIXED HIS CELL PHONE SO WE COULDN'T TRACK HIM DOWN, BUT HIS SON IS USING AN ALGORITHM TO PINPOINT HIS CO-ORDINATES BASED ON HIS UNIQUE GOOGLE FINGERPRINT.
THESE COVER SEARCHES ON EACH OF HIS VICTIMS CROSS-REFERENCED WITH MEDICAL DATA ON HIS SPECIFIC TERMINAL DISEASE.
LAST NIGHT THEY HAD OVER TWO HUNDRED POSSIBILITIES. TODAY HE'S NARROWED IT DOWN TO FIVE.
CAN WE REALLY TRUST THIS MAN'S SON TO LEAD THE OPERATION?
OH, ATTICUS DESPISES HIS FATHER. BLAMES HIM FOR EVERYTHING AND HASN'T SPOKEN TO HIM SINCE HE LEFT HIS MOTHER.
MUMMY'S BOY, IS HE?
"NO, HE HASN'T SEEN HER IN YEARS EITHER. THE COUNTESS LIVES ALONE IN SRI LANKA, PAINTING PICTURES ALL DAY ABOUT ISOLATION AND BROKEN HEARTS."
ATTICUS LEARNED FROM A VERY YOUNG AGE NOT TO GIVE A SHIT ABOUT ANYONE.

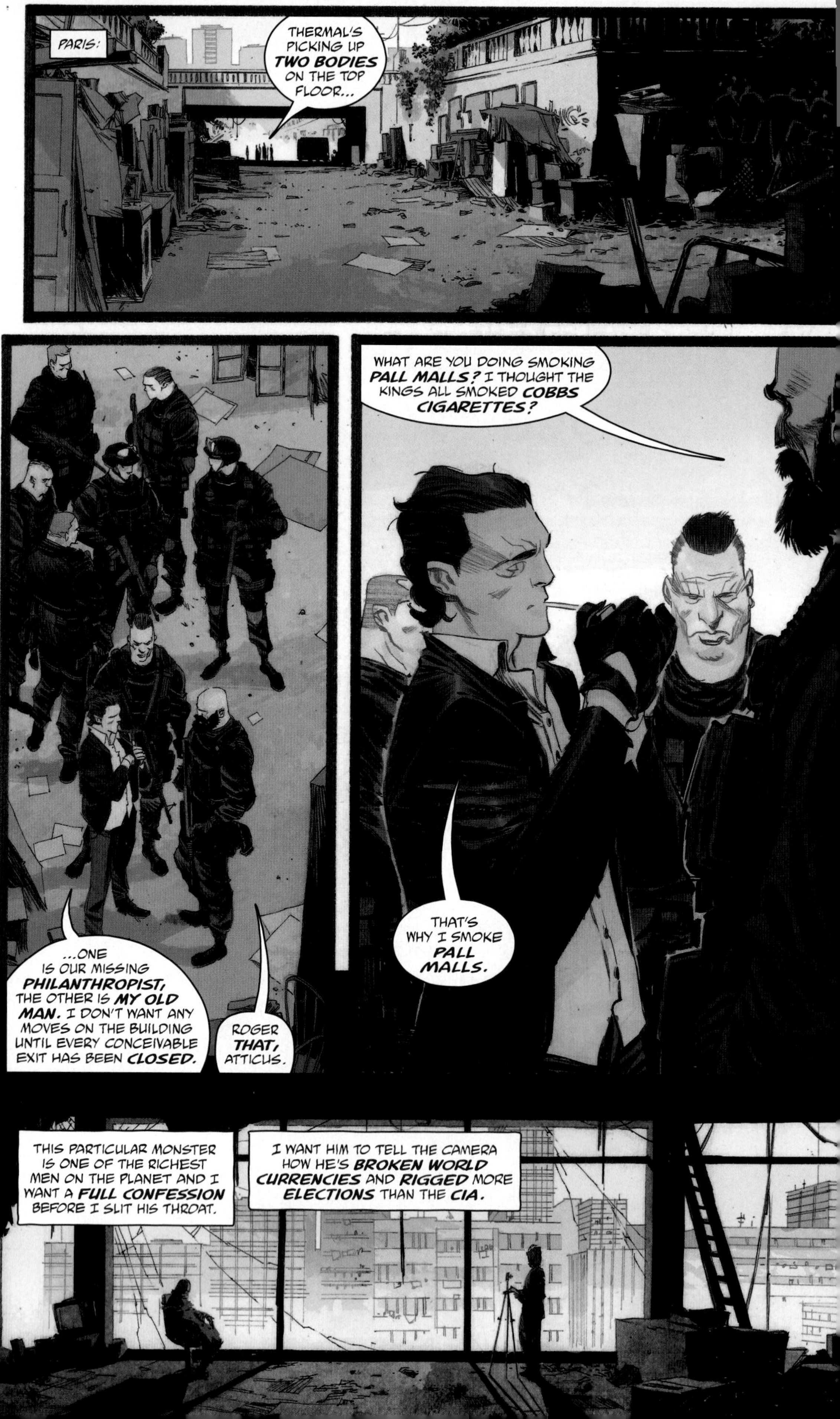
PARIS:
THERMAL'S PICKING UP TWO BODIES ON THE TOP FLOOR...
...ONE IS OUR MISSING PHILANTHROPIST, THE OTHER IS MY OLD MAN. I DON'T WANT ANY MOVES ON THE BUILDING UNTIL EVERY CONCEIVABLE EXIT HAS BEEN CLOSED.
ROGER THAT, ATTICUS.
WHAT ARE YOU DOING SMOKING PALL MALLS? I THOUGHT THE KINGS ALL SMOKED COBBS CIGARETTES?
THAT'S WHY I SMOKE PALL MALLS.
THIS PARTICULAR MONSTER IS ONE OF THE RICHEST MEN ON THE PLANET AND I WANT A FULL CONFESSION BEFORE I SLIT HIS THROAT.
I WANT HIM TO TELL THE CAMERA HOW HE'S BROKEN WORLD CURRENCIES AND RIGGED MORE ELECTIONS THAN THE CIA.

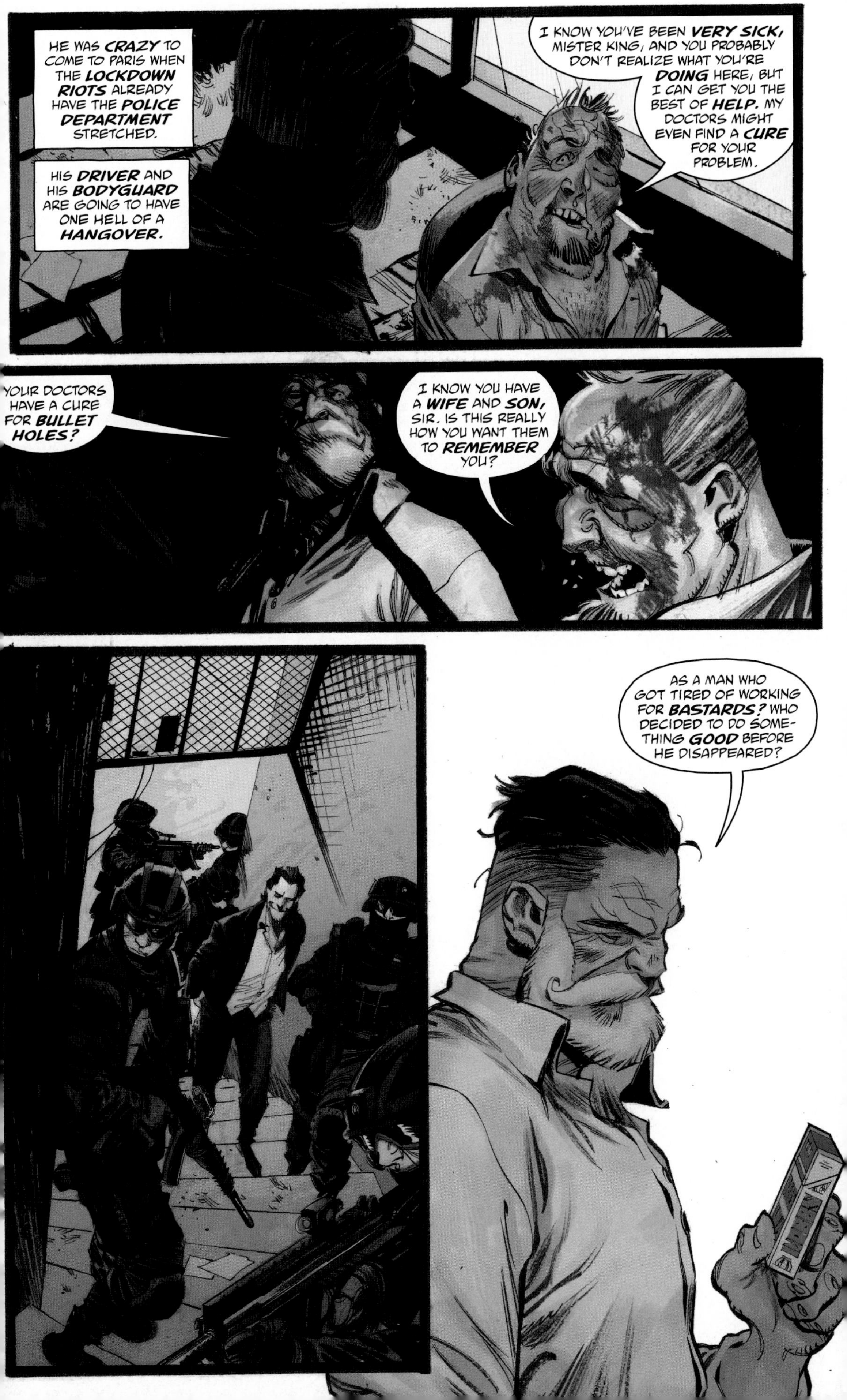
HE WAS CRAZY TO COME TO PARIS WHEN THE LOCKDOWN RIOTS ALREADY HAVE THE POLICE DEPARTMENT STRETCHED.
HIS DRIVER AND HIS BODYGUARD ARE GOING TO HAVE ONE HELL OF A HANGOVER.
I KNOW YOU'VE BEEN VERY SICK, MISTER KING, AND YOU PROBABLY DON'T REALIZE WHAT YOU'RE DOING HERE, BUT I CAN GET YOU THE BEST OF HELP. MY DOCTORS MIGHT EVEN FIND A CURE FOR YOUR PROBLEM.
YOUR DOCTORS HAVE A CURE FOR BULLET HOLES?
I KNOW YOU HAVE A WIFE AND SON, SIR. IS THIS REALLY HOW YOU WANT THEM TO REMEMBER YOU?
AS A MAN WHO GOT TIRED OF WORKING FOR BASTARDS? WHO DECIDED TO DO SOME-THING GOOD BEFORE HE DISAPPEARED?

"ACTUALLY, THAT'S *EXACTLY* HOW I'D LIKE TO BE REMEMBERED."

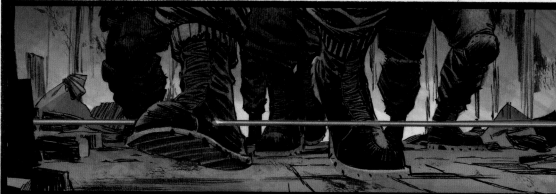

NOW!

SHOOT THE MOTHERFUCKER!

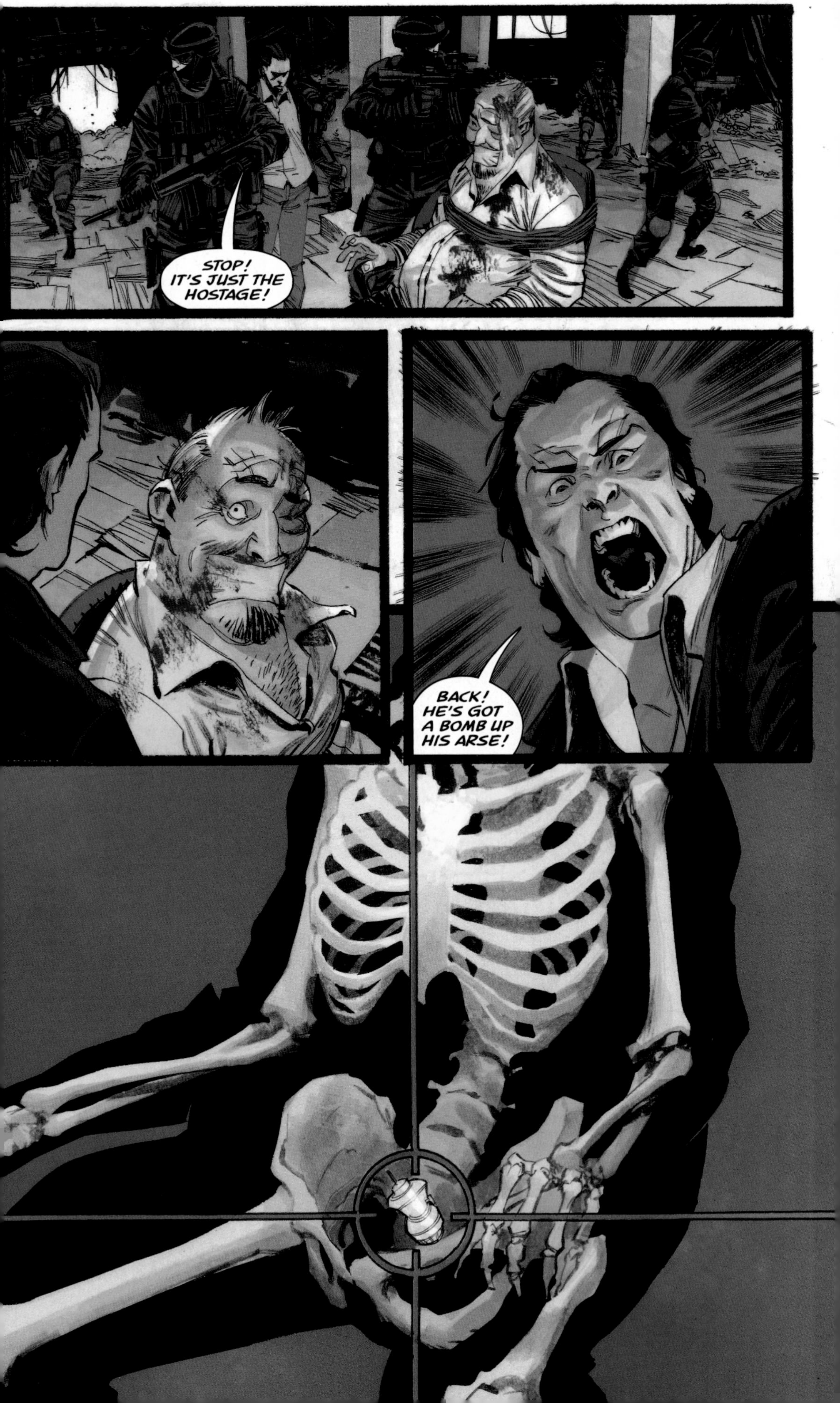
STOP! IT'S JUST THE HOSTAGE!
BACK! HE'S GOT A BOMB UP HIS ARSE!

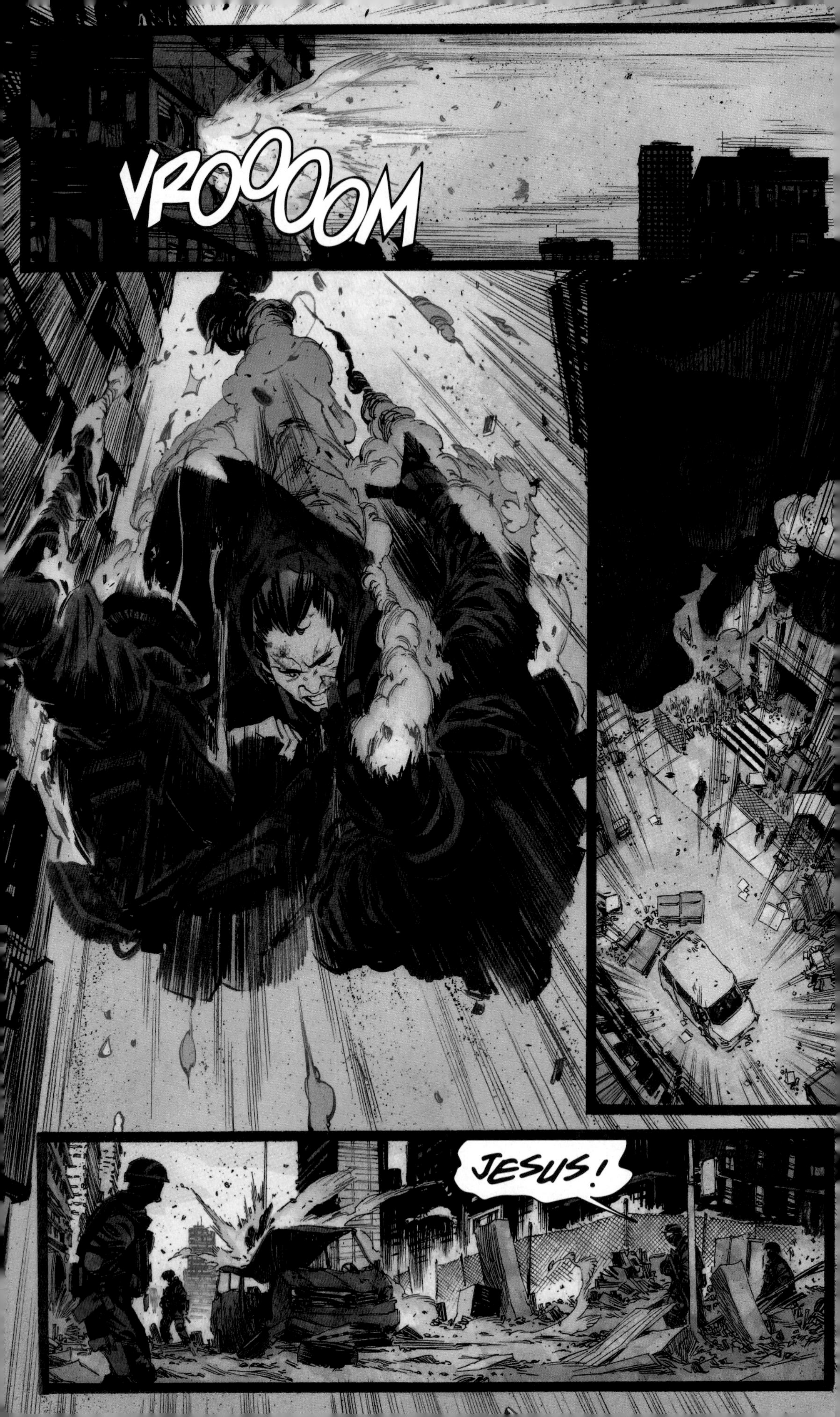
VROOOOOM
JESUS!

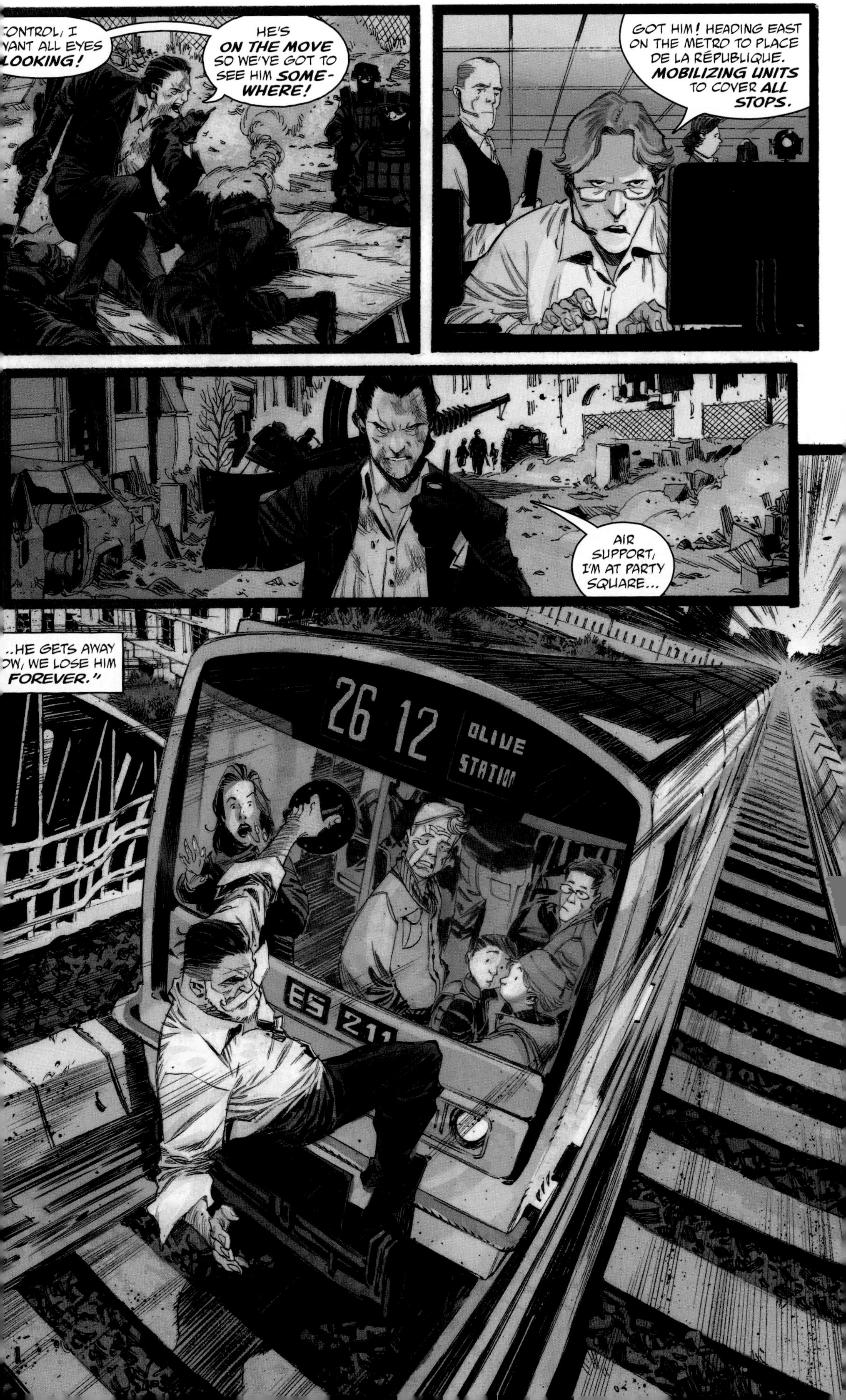

CONTROL, I
WANT ALL EYES
LOOKING!
HE'S ON THE MOVE SO WE'VE GOT TO SEE HIM SOME-WHERE!
GOT HIM! HEADING EAST ON THE METRO TO PLACE DE LA RÉPUBLIQUE. MOBILIZING UNITS TO COVER ALL STOPS.
AIR SUPPORT, I'M AT PARTY SQUARE...
..HE GETS AWAY
OW, WE LOSE HIM
FOREVER."
26 12
OLIVE STATION
ES 211

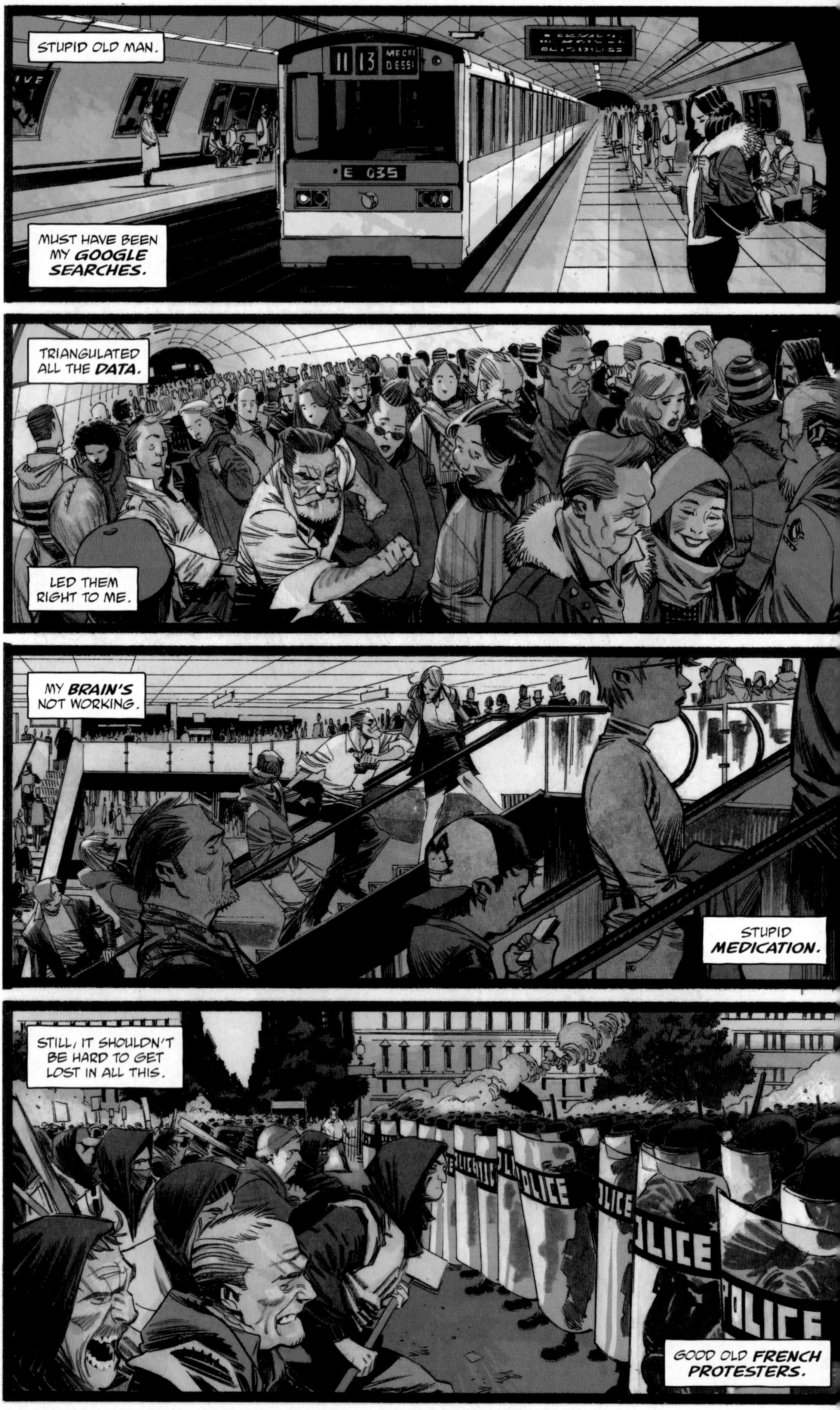
STUPID OLD MAN.
MUST HAVE BEEN MY GOOGLE SEARCHES.
TRIANGULATED ALL THE DATA.
LED THEM RIGHT TO ME.
MY BRAIN'S NOT WORKING.
STUPID MEDICATION.
STILL, IT SHOULDN'T BE HARD TO GET LOST IN ALL THIS.
GOOD OLD FRENCH PROTESTERS.
POLICE

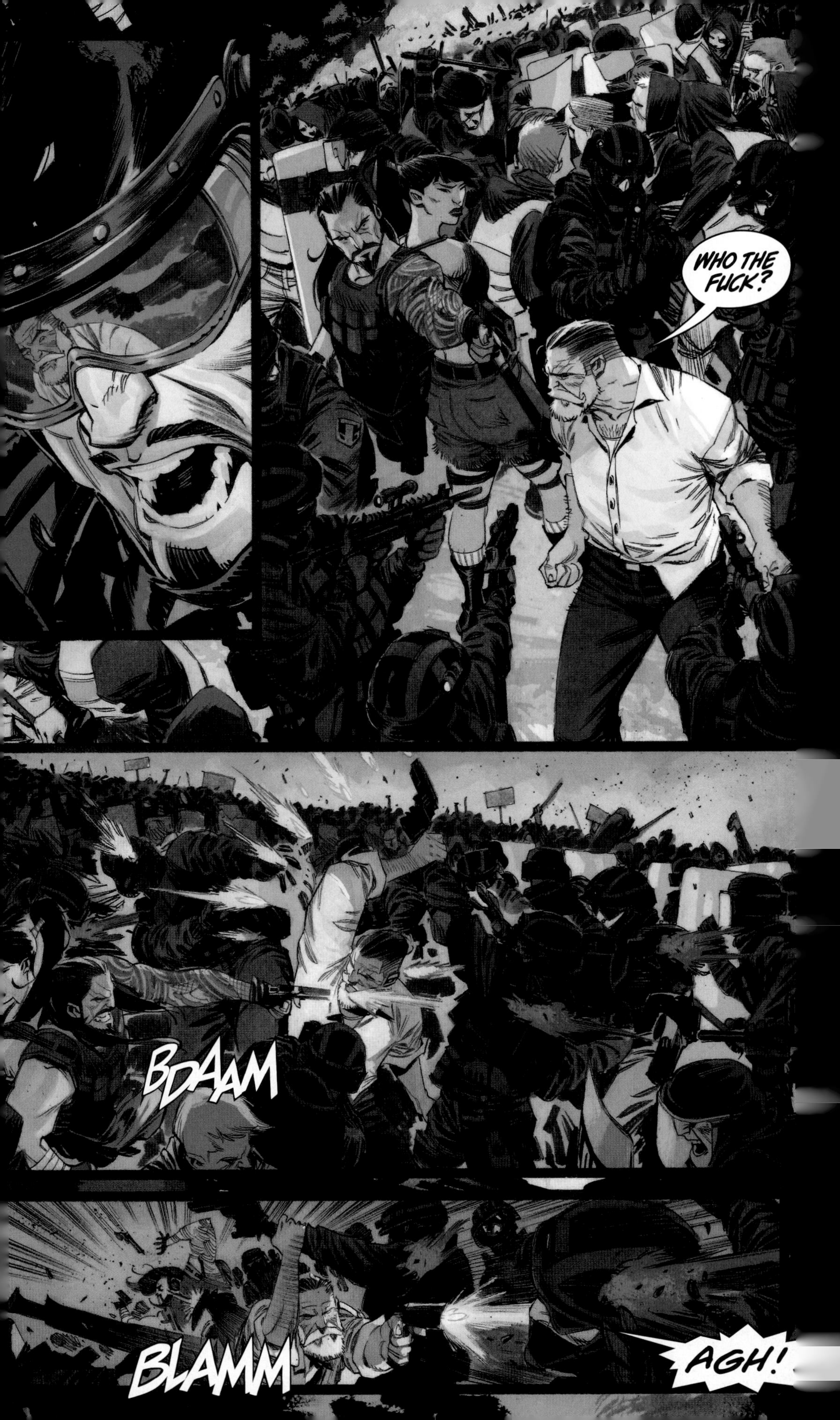
WHO THE FUCK?
BDAAM
BLAMM
AGH!

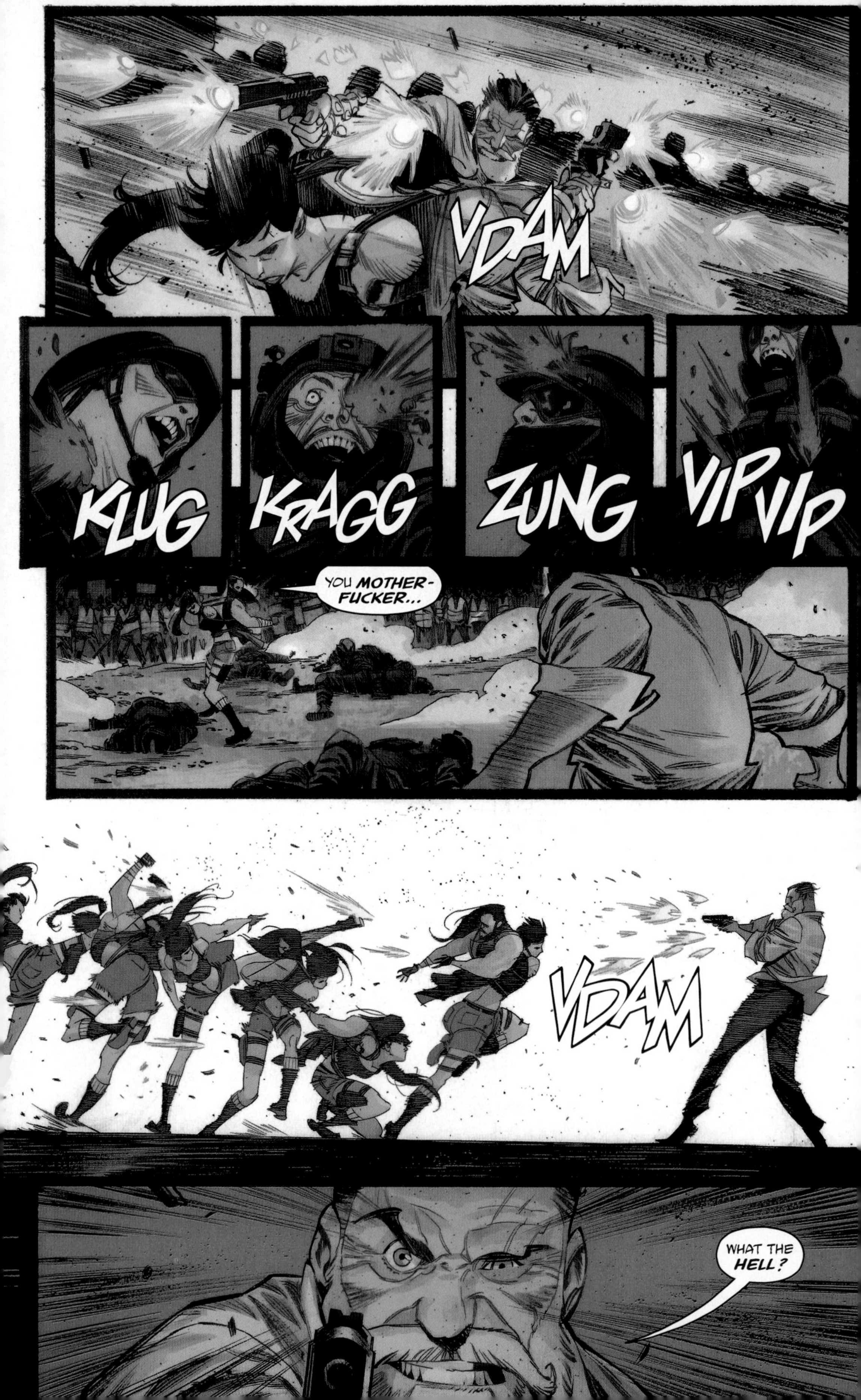
VDAM
KLUG
KRAGG
ZUNG
VIP VIP
YOU MOTHER-FUCKER...
VDAM
WHAT THE HELL?

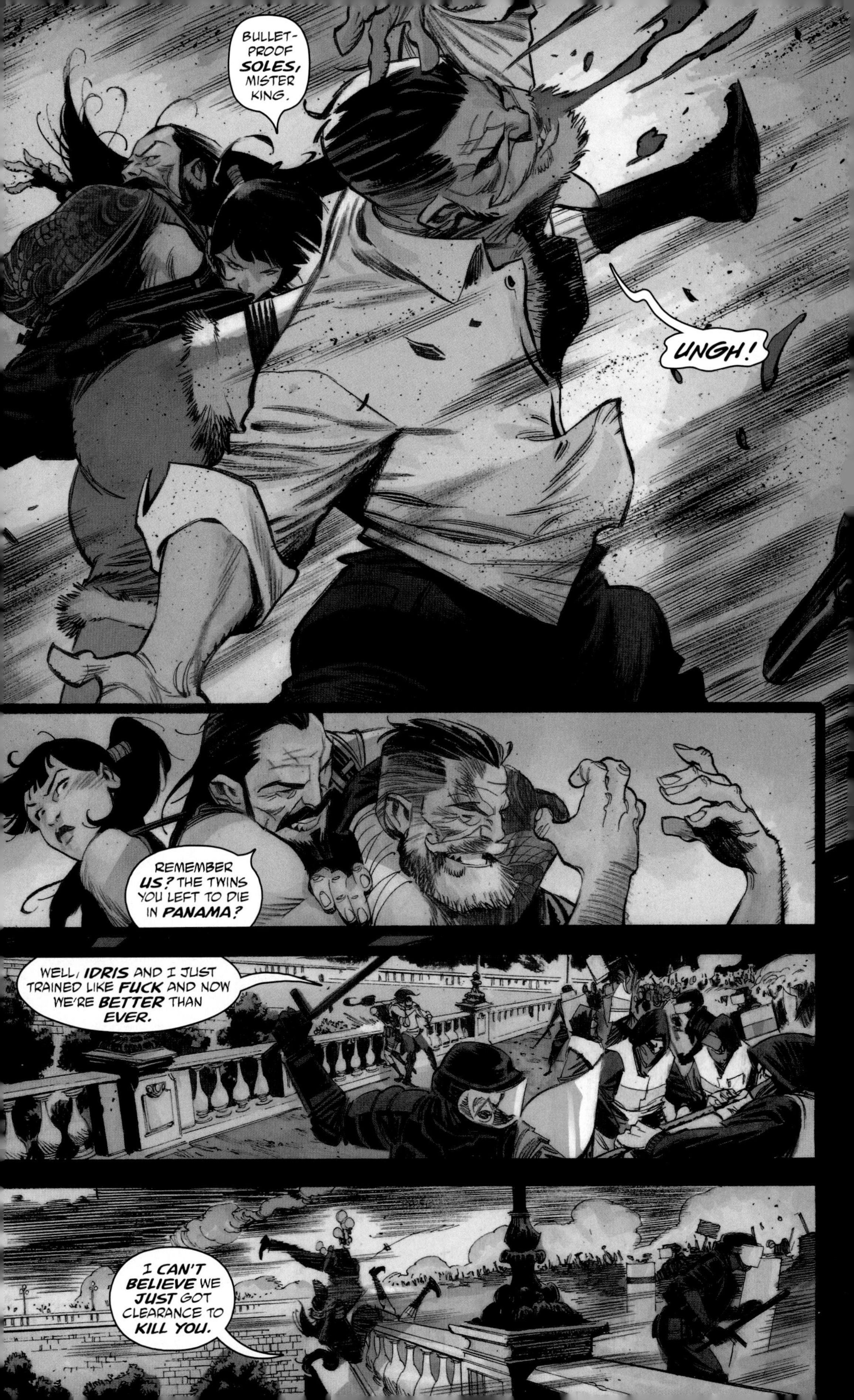
BULLET-PROOF SOLES, MISTER KING.
UNGH!
REMEMBER US? THE TWINS YOU LEFT TO DIE IN PANAMA?
WELL, IDRIS AND I JUST TRAINED LIKE FUCK AND NOW WE'RE BETTER THAN EVER.
I CAN'T BELIEVE WE JUST GOT CLEARANCE TO KILL YOU.

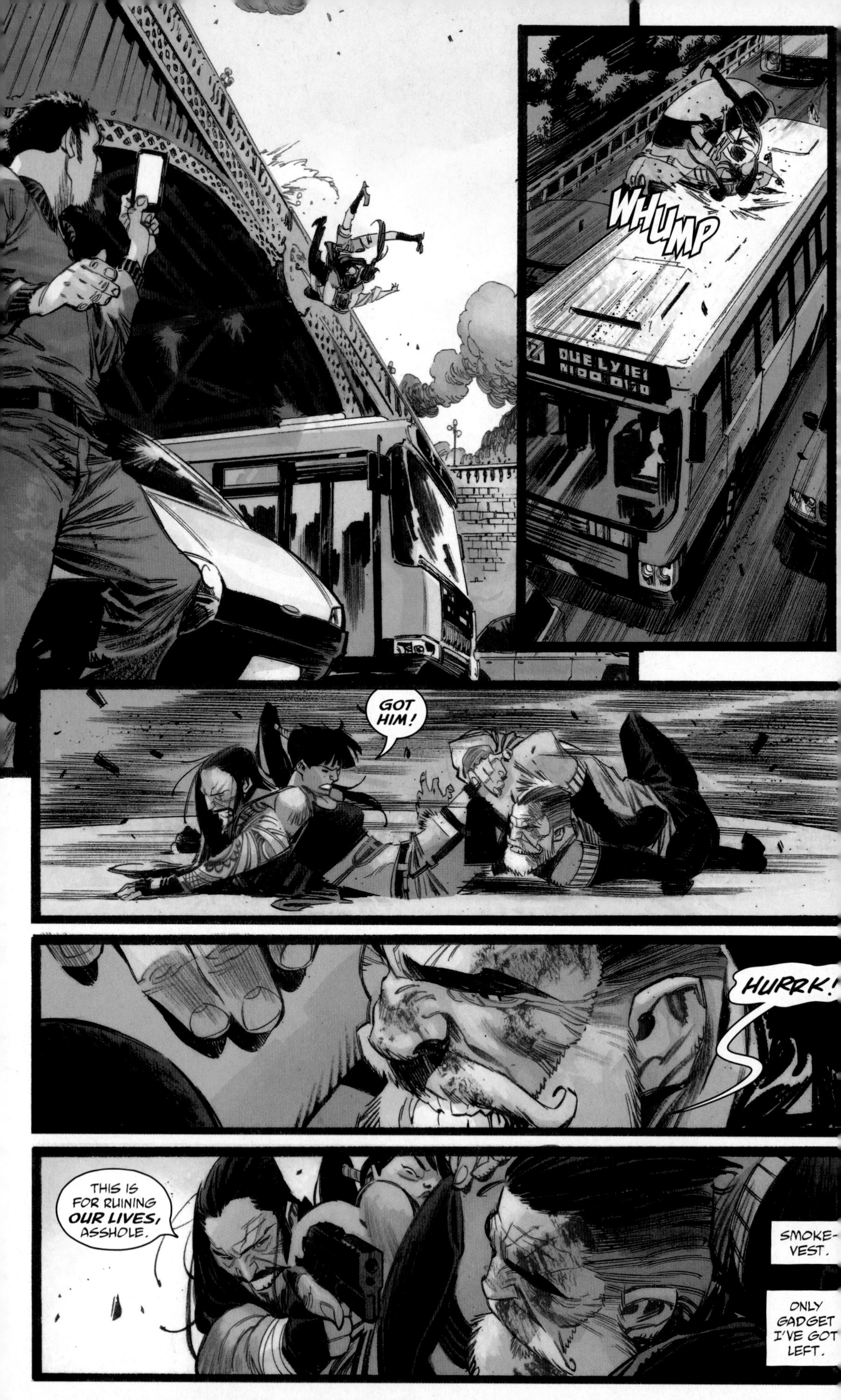
WHUMP
GOT HIM!
HURRK!
THIS IS FOR RUINING OUR LIVES, ASSHOLE.
SMOKE-VEST.
ONLY GADGET I'VE GOT LEFT.

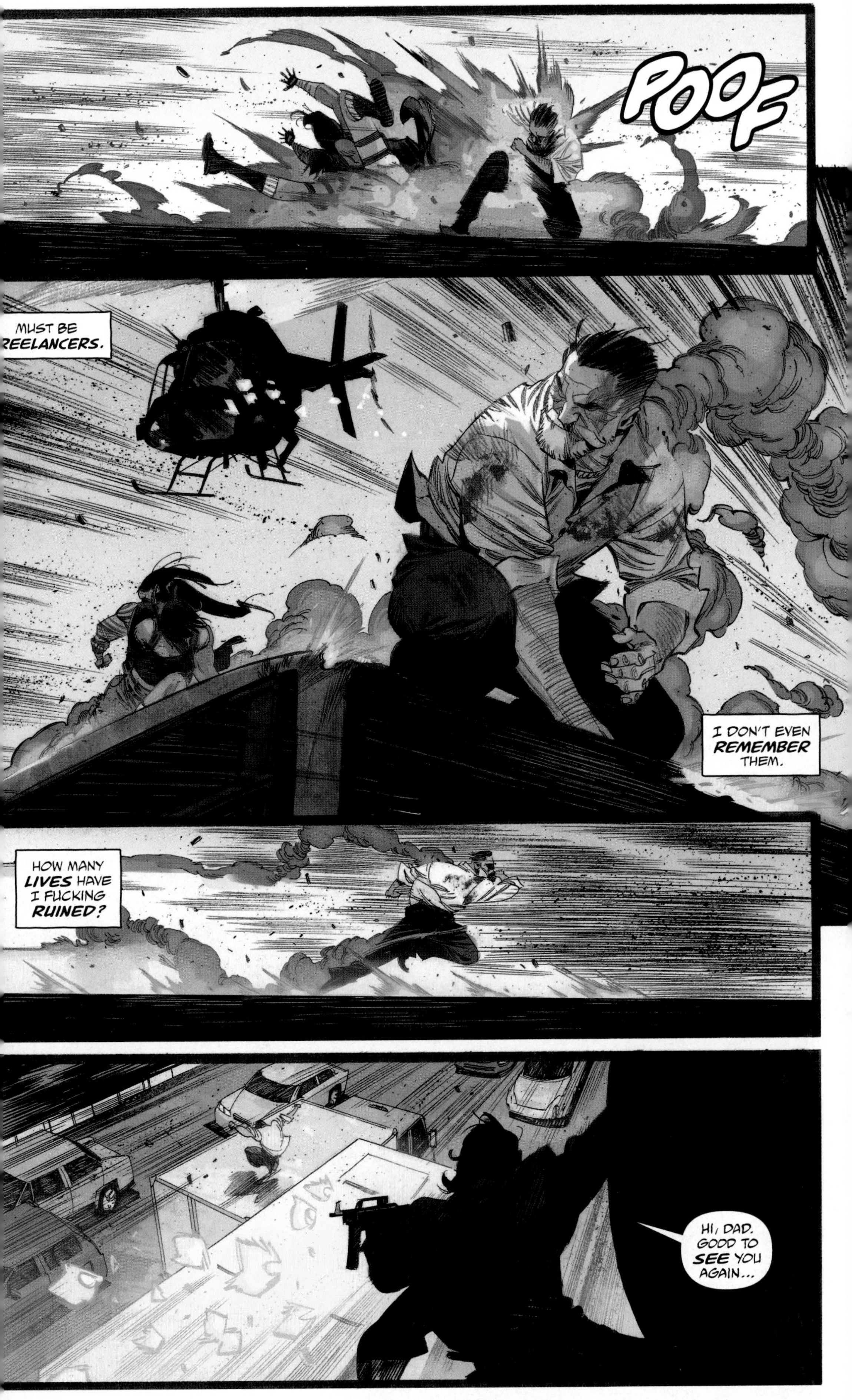
POOF
MUST BE FREELANCERS.
I DON'T EVEN REMEMBER THEM.
HOW MANY LIVES HAVE I FUCKING RUINED?
HI, DAD. GOOD TO SEE YOU AGAIN...

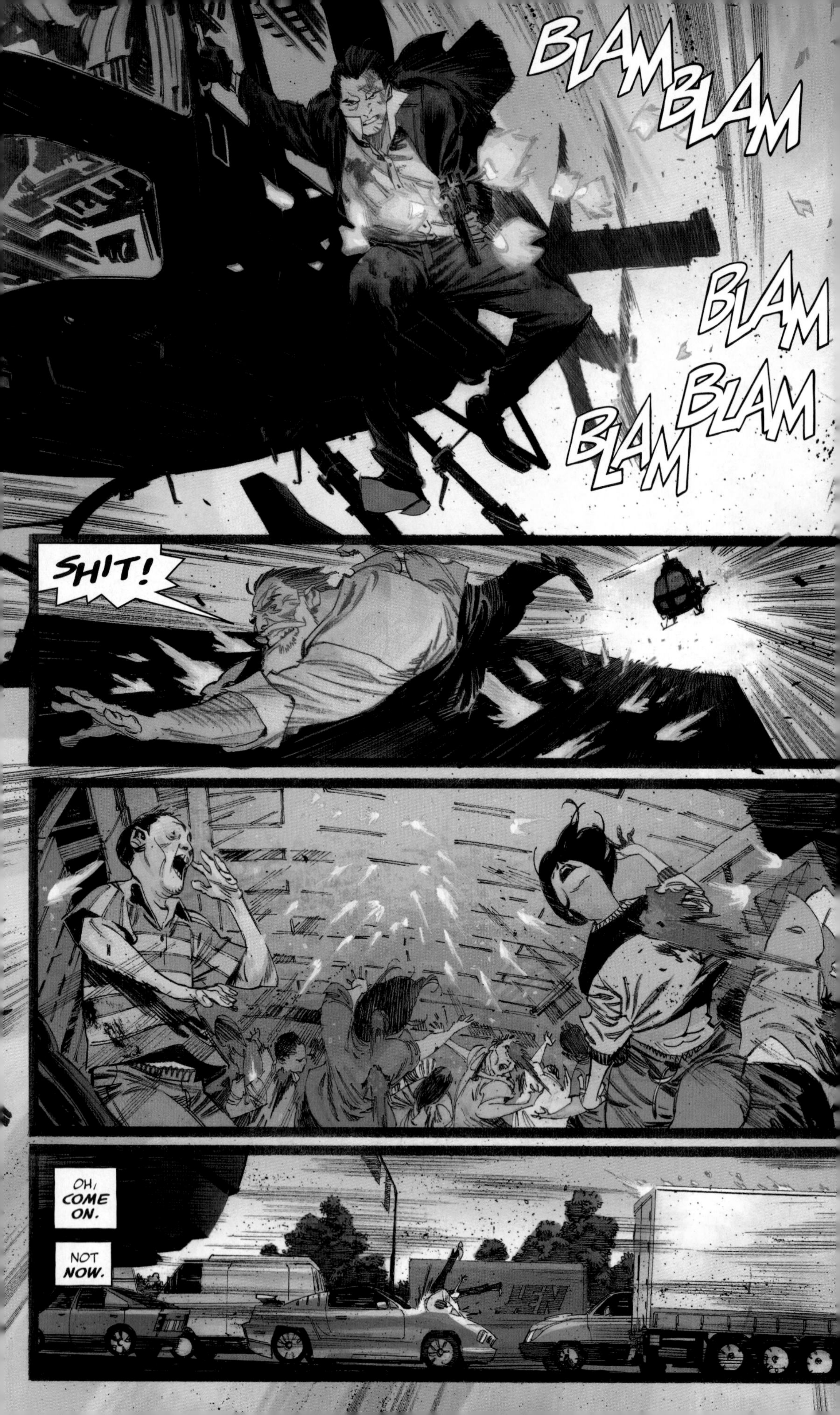
BLAM BLAM
BLAM
BLAM
BLAM BLAM
SHIT!
OH, COME ON.
NOT NOW.

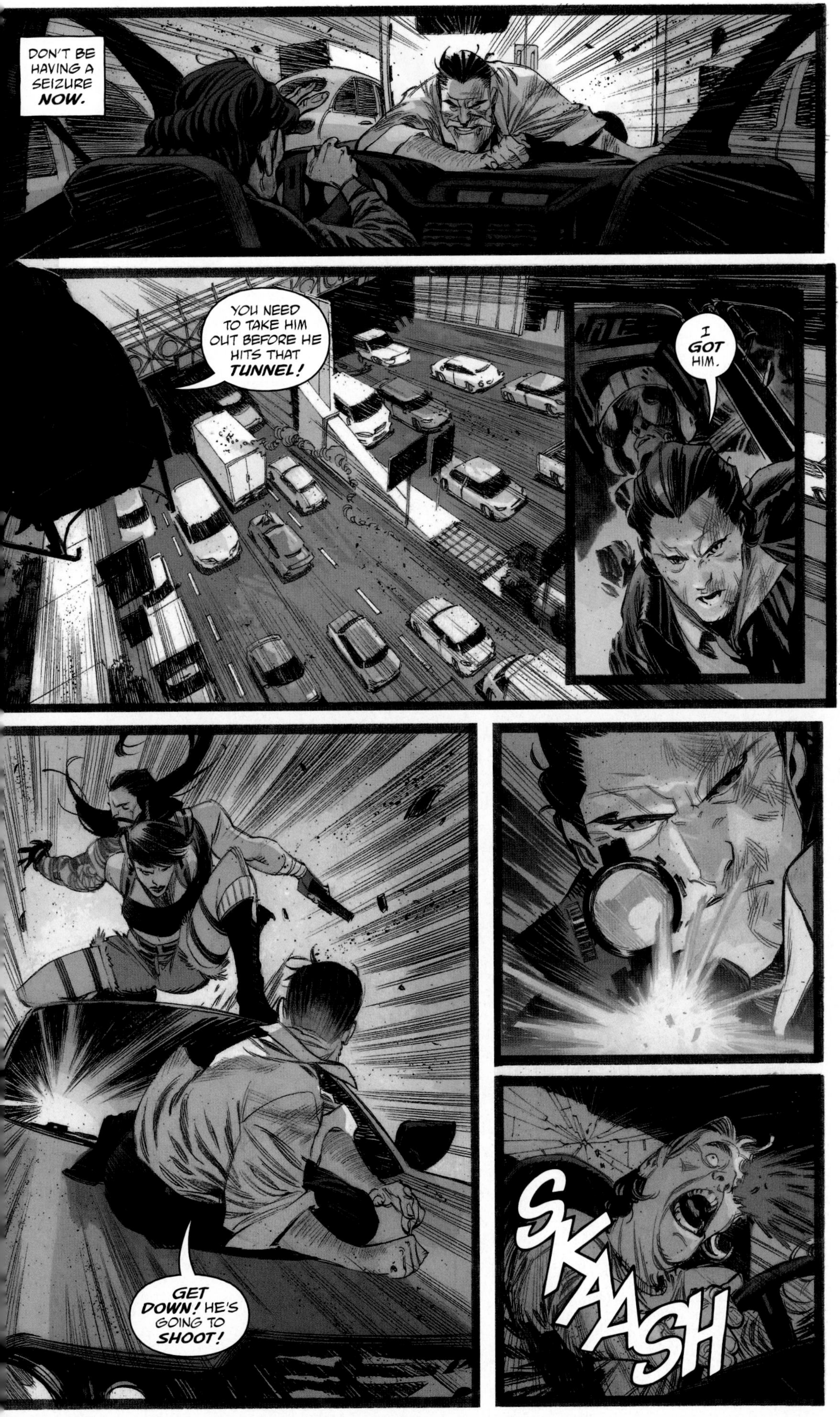
DON'T BE HAVING A SEIZURE NOW.
YOU NEED TO TAKE HIM OUT BEFORE HE HITS THAT TUNNEL!
I GOT HIM.
GET DOWN! HE'S GOING TO SHOOT!
SKAASH

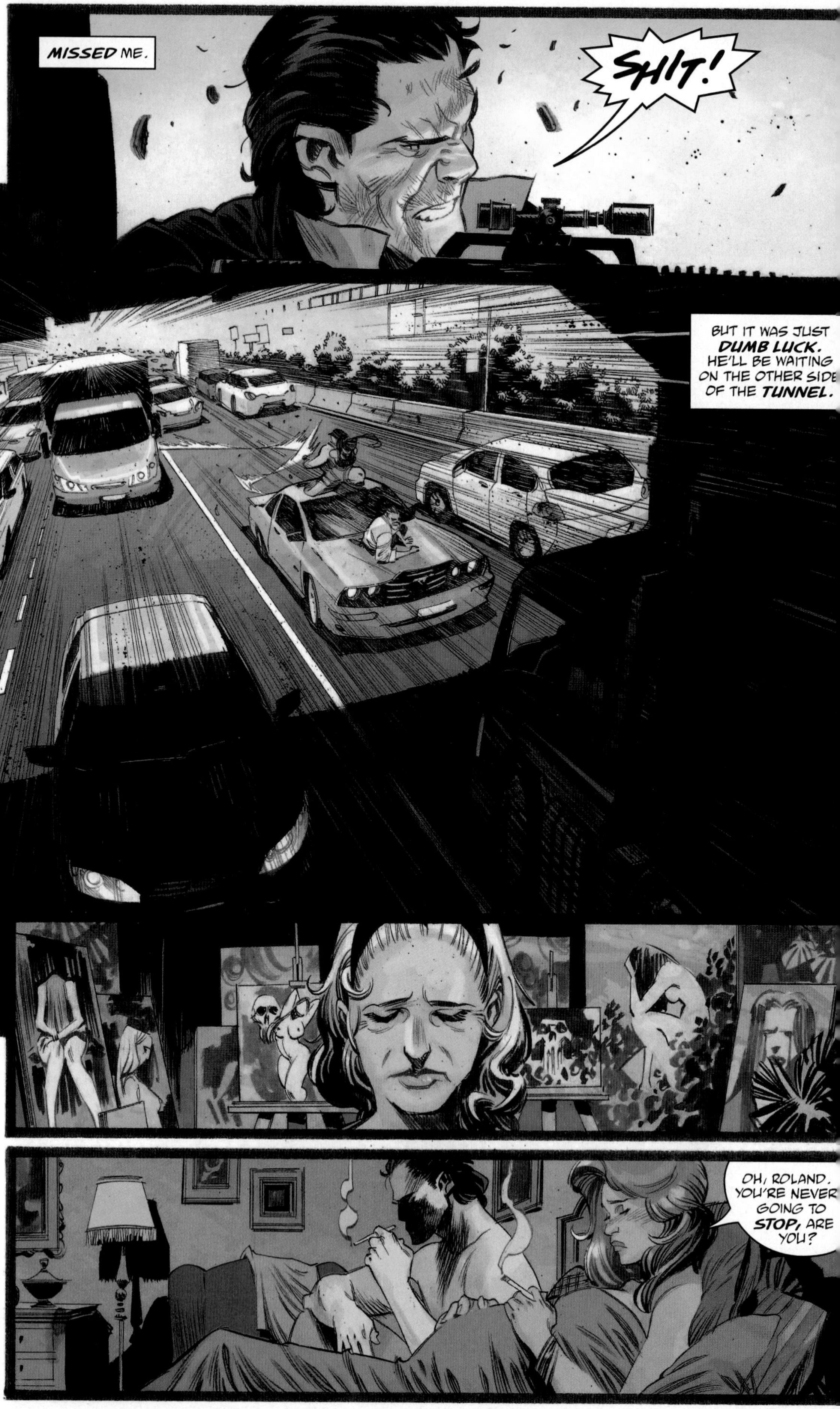
MISSED ME.
SHIT!
BUT IT WAS JUST DUMB LUCK. HE'LL BE WAITING ON THE OTHER SIDE OF THE TUNNEL.
OH, ROLAND. YOU'RE NEVER GOING TO STOP, ARE YOU?

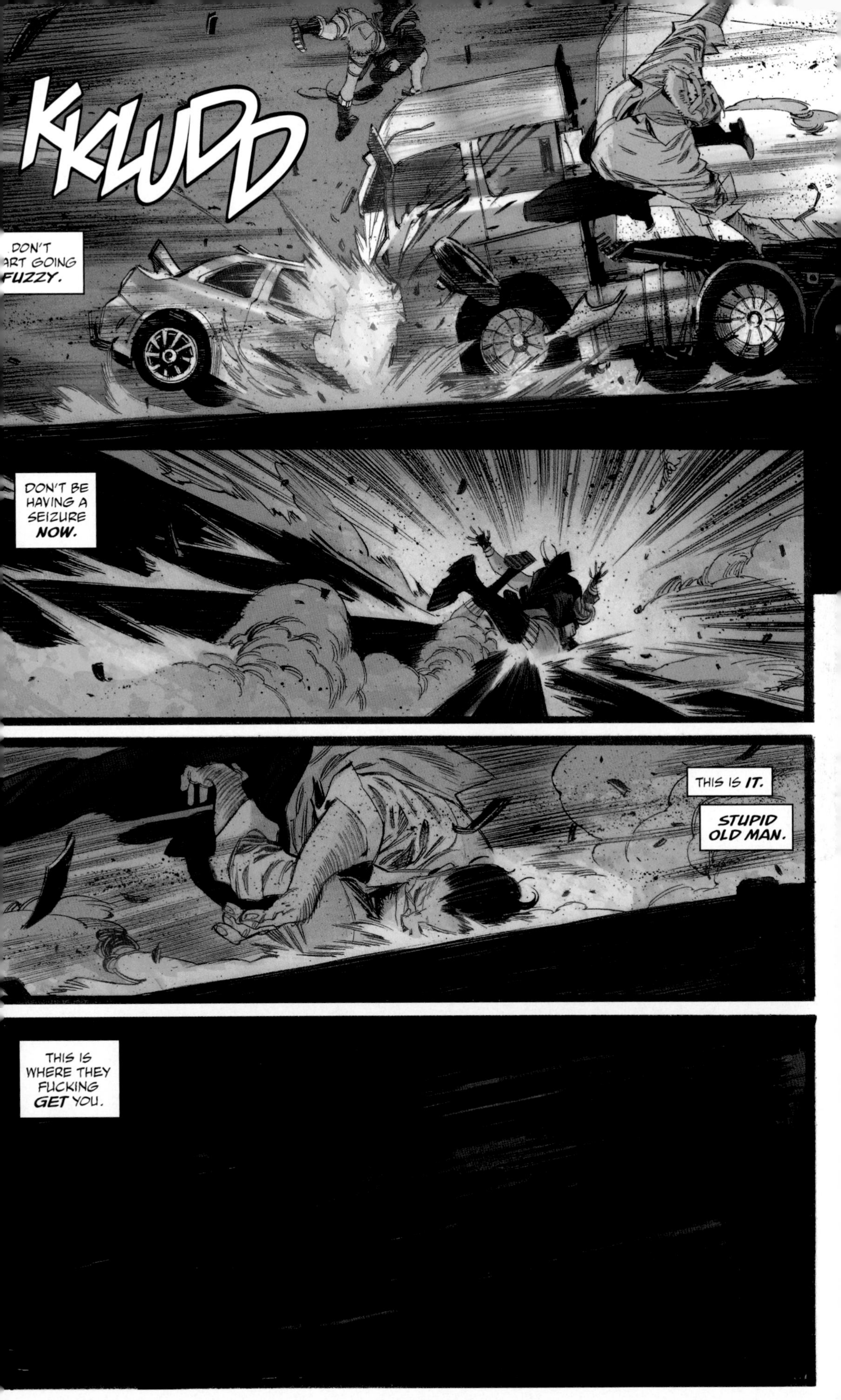
KKLUDD
DON'T ...ART GOING FUZZY.
DON'T BE HAVING A SEIZURE NOW.
THIS IS IT.
STUPID OLD MAN.
THIS IS WHERE THEY FUCKING GET YOU.

Four

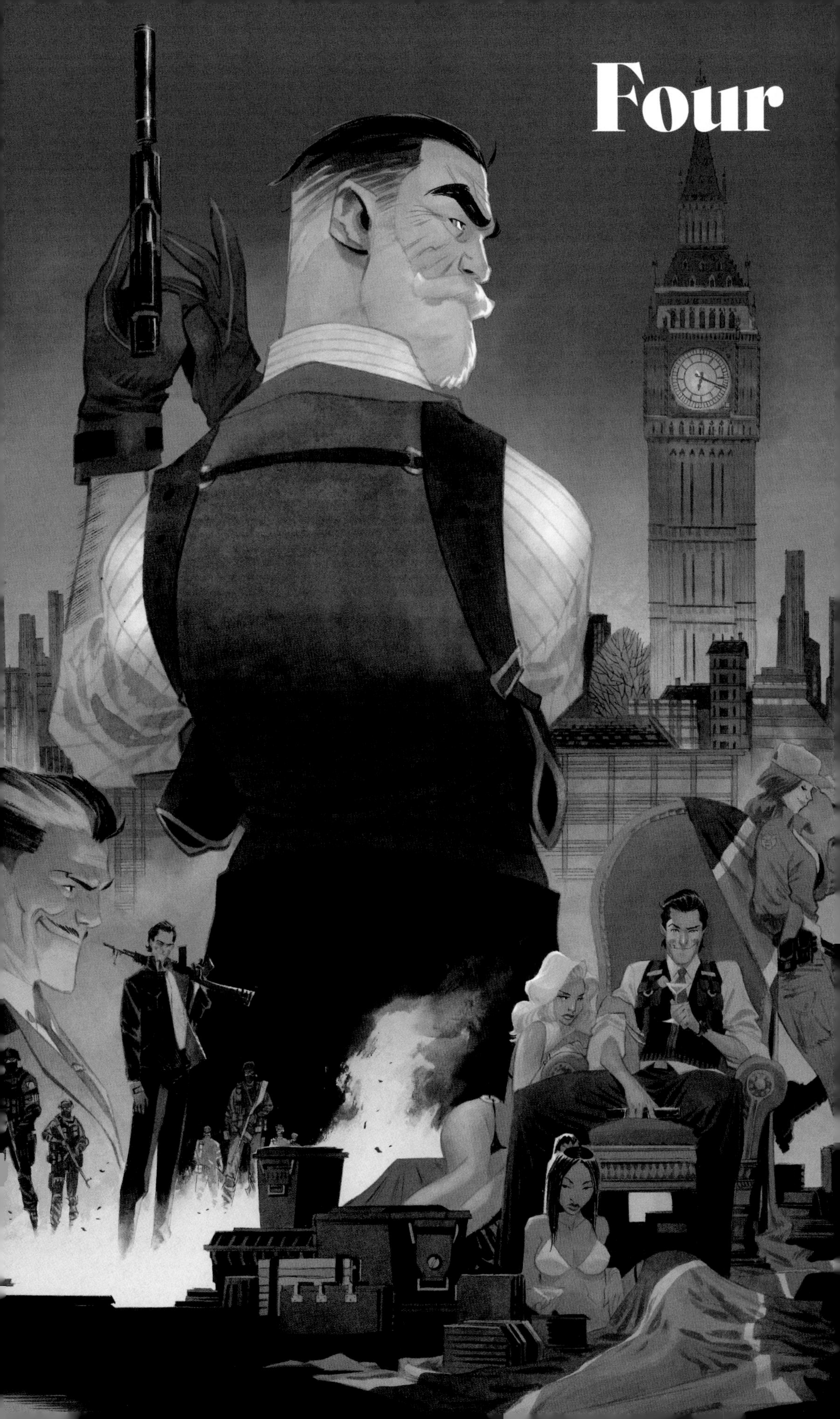

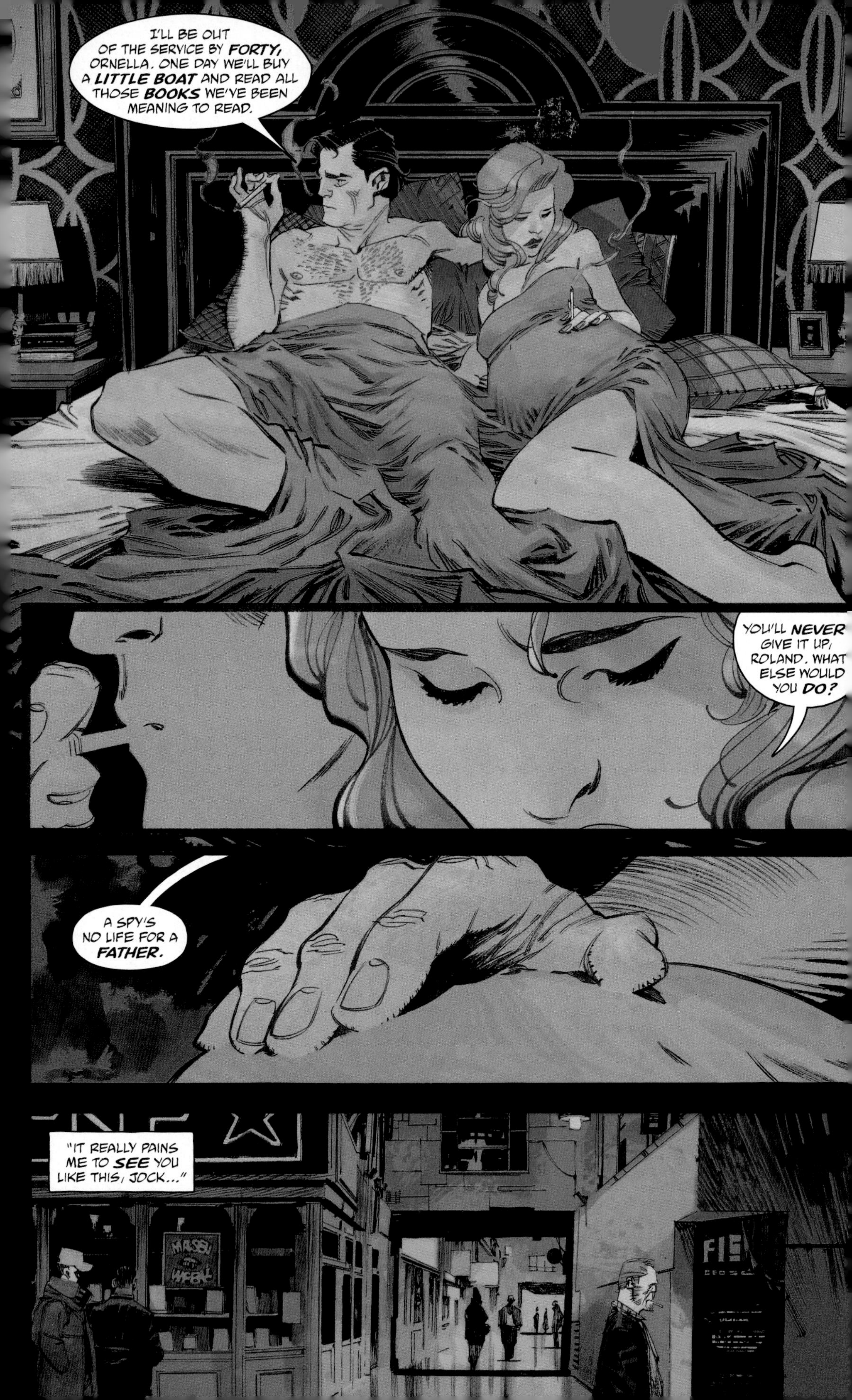
I'LL BE OUT OF THE SERVICE BY FORTY, ORNELLA. ONE DAY WE'LL BUY A LITTLE BOAT AND READ ALL THOSE BOOKS WE'VE BEEN MEANING TO READ.
YOU'LL NEVER GIVE IT UP, ROLAND. WHAT ELSE WOULD YOU DO?
A SPY'S NO LIFE FOR A FATHER.
"IT REALLY PAINS ME TO SEE YOU LIKE THIS, JOCK..."

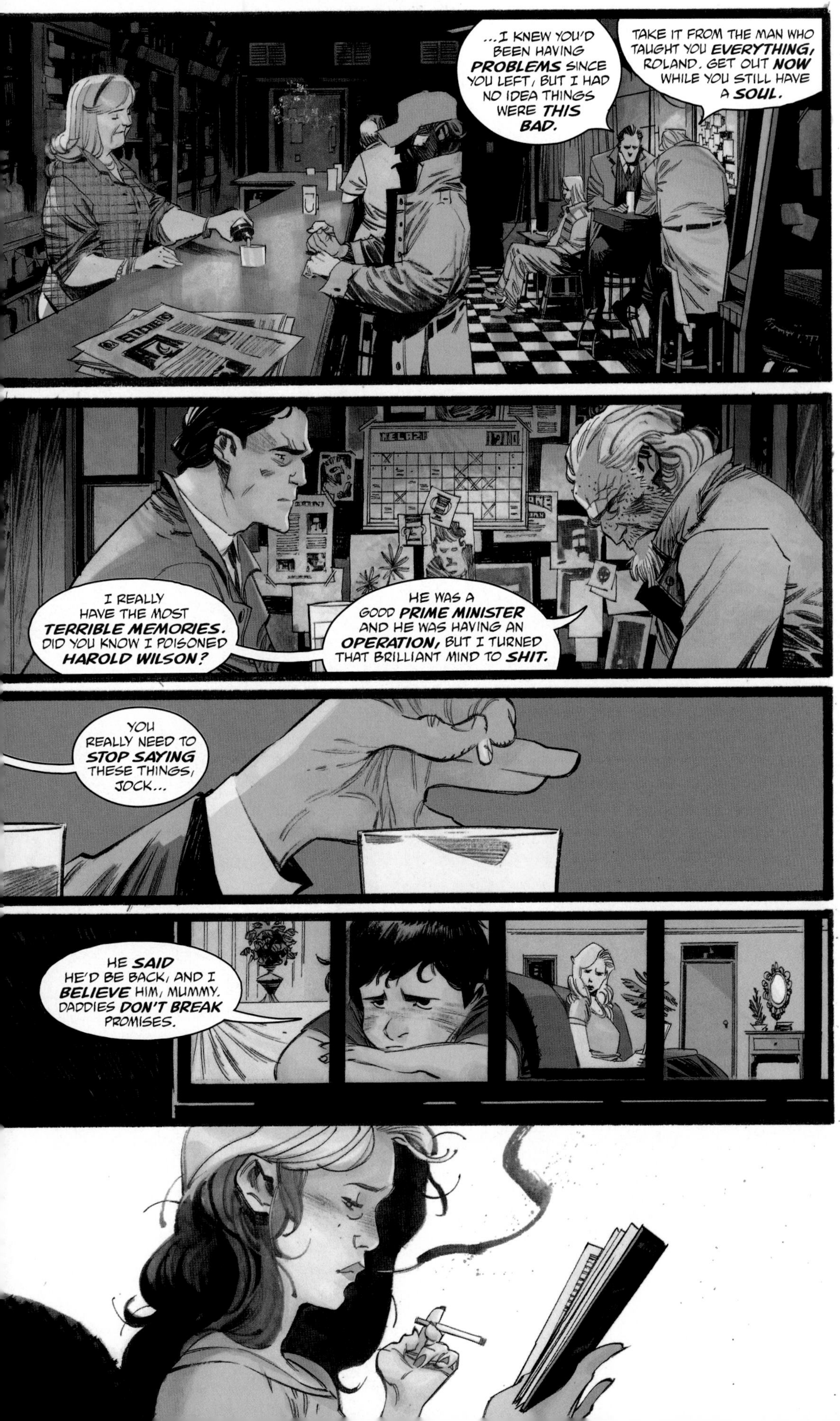
...I KNEW YOU'D BEEN HAVING PROBLEMS SINCE YOU LEFT, BUT I HAD NO IDEA THINGS WERE THIS BAD.
TAKE IT FROM THE MAN WHO TAUGHT YOU EVERYTHING, ROLAND. GET OUT NOW WHILE YOU STILL HAVE A SOUL.
I REALLY HAVE THE MOST TERRIBLE MEMORIES. DID YOU KNOW I POISONED HAROLD WILSON?
HE WAS A GOOD PRIME MINISTER AND HE WAS HAVING AN OPERATION, BUT I TURNED THAT BRILLIANT MIND TO SHIT.
YOU REALLY NEED TO STOP SAYING THESE THINGS, JOCK...
HE SAID HE'D BE BACK, AND I BELIEVE HIM, MUMMY. DADDIES DON'T BREAK PROMISES.

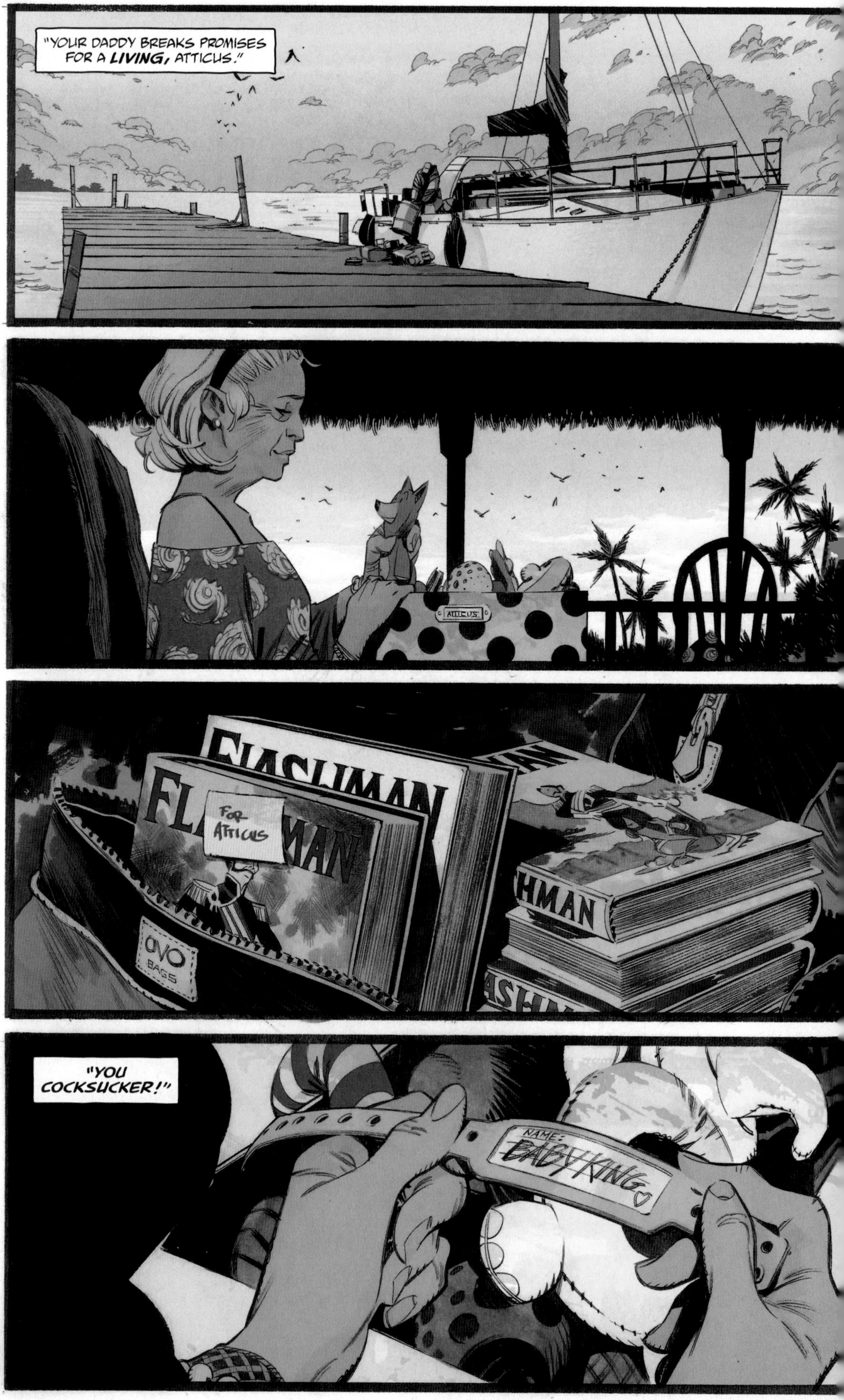
"YOUR DADDY BREAKS PROMISES FOR A LIVING, ATTICUS."
ATTICUS
FLASHMAN
FLASHMAN
FOR ATTICUS
HMAN
OVO BAGS
"YOU COCKSUCKER!"
NAME:
BABY KING

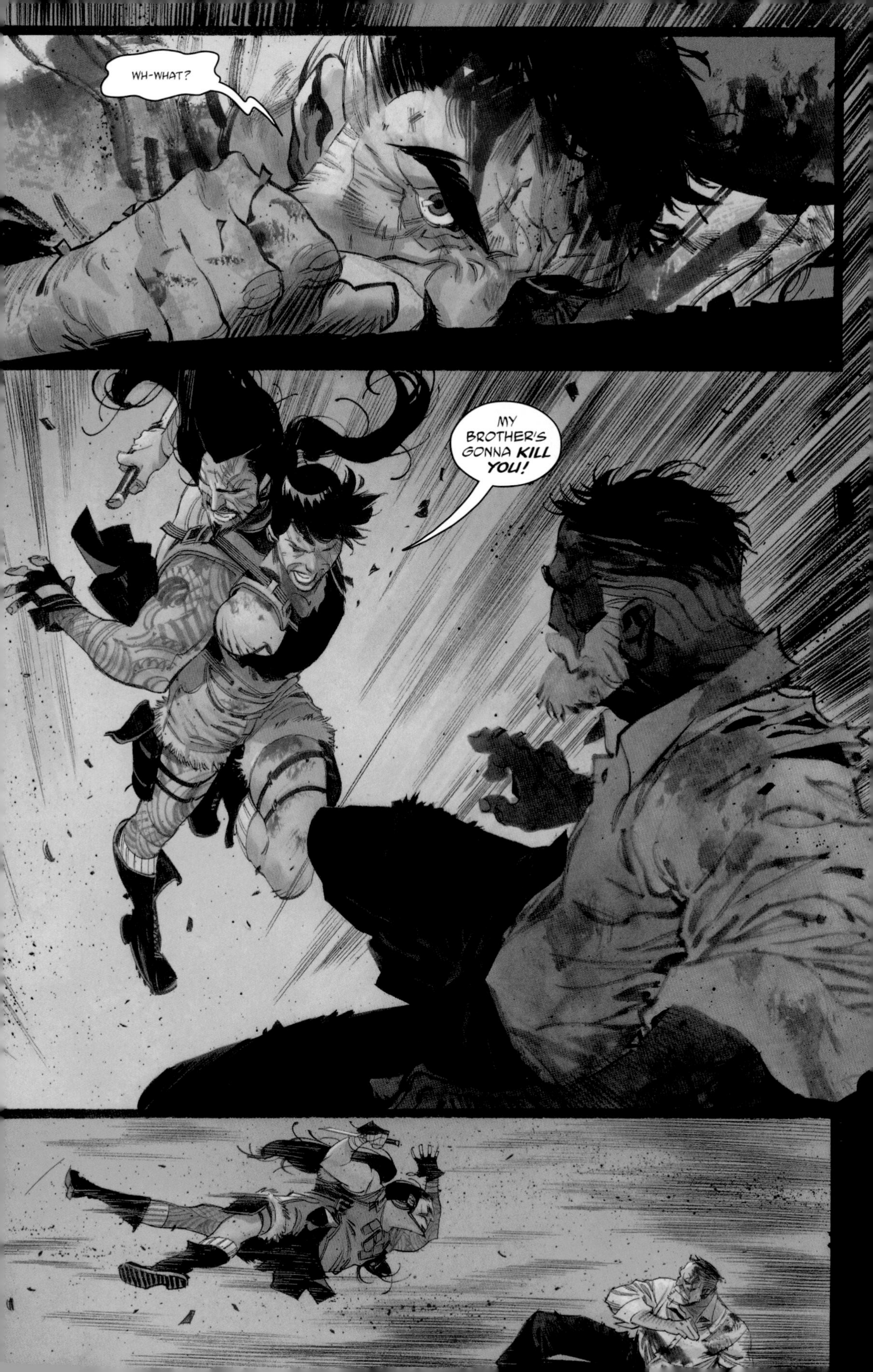
WH-WHAT?
MY BROTHER'S GONNA KILL YOU!

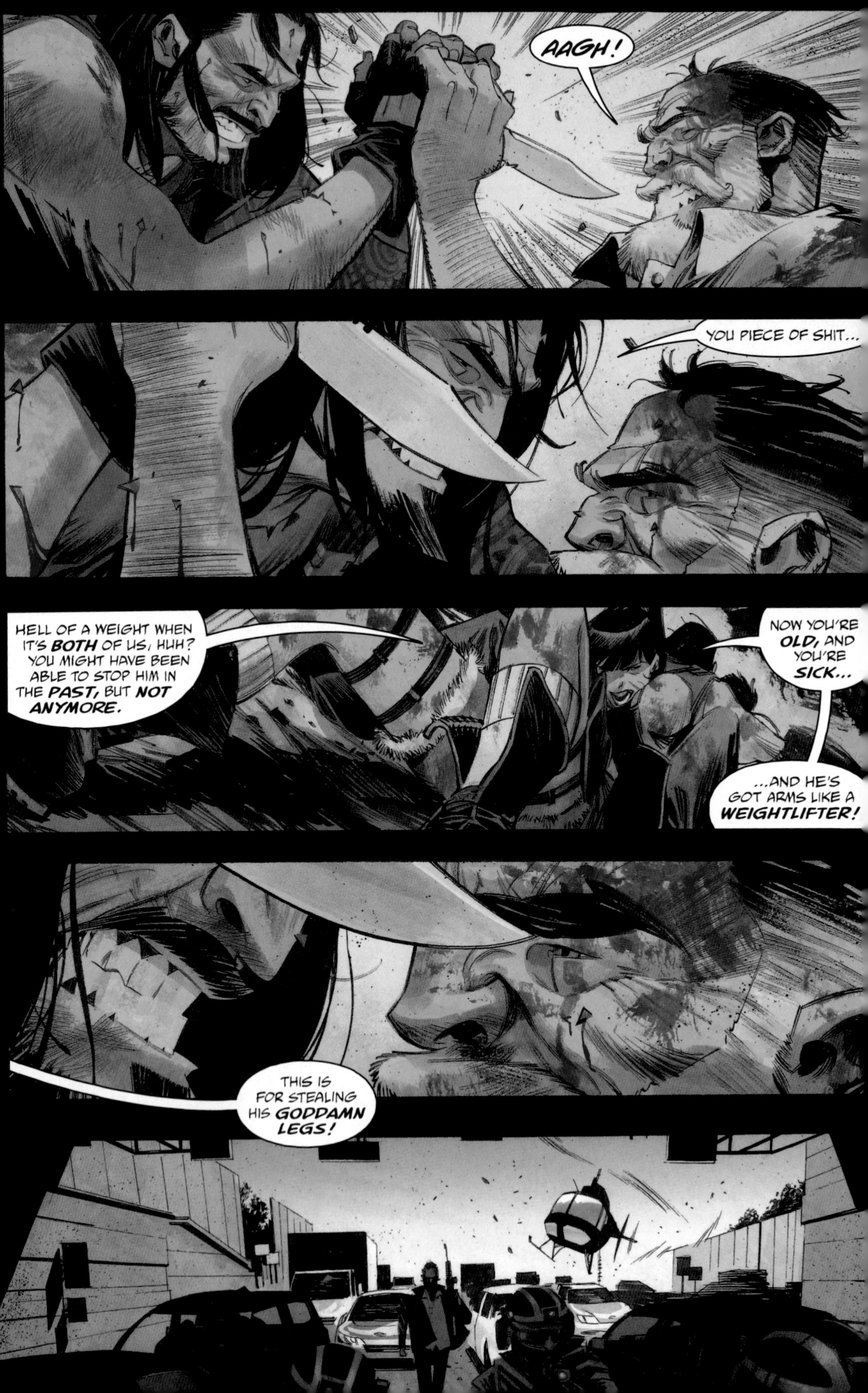
AAGH!
YOU PIECE OF SHIT...
HELL OF A WEIGHT WHEN IT'S BOTH OF US, HUH? YOU MIGHT HAVE BEEN ABLE TO STOP HIM IN THE PAST, BUT NOT ANYMORE.
NOW YOU'RE OLD, AND YOU'RE SICK...
...AND HE'S GOT ARMS LIKE A WEIGHTLIFTER!
THIS IS FOR STEALING HIS GODDAMN LEGS!

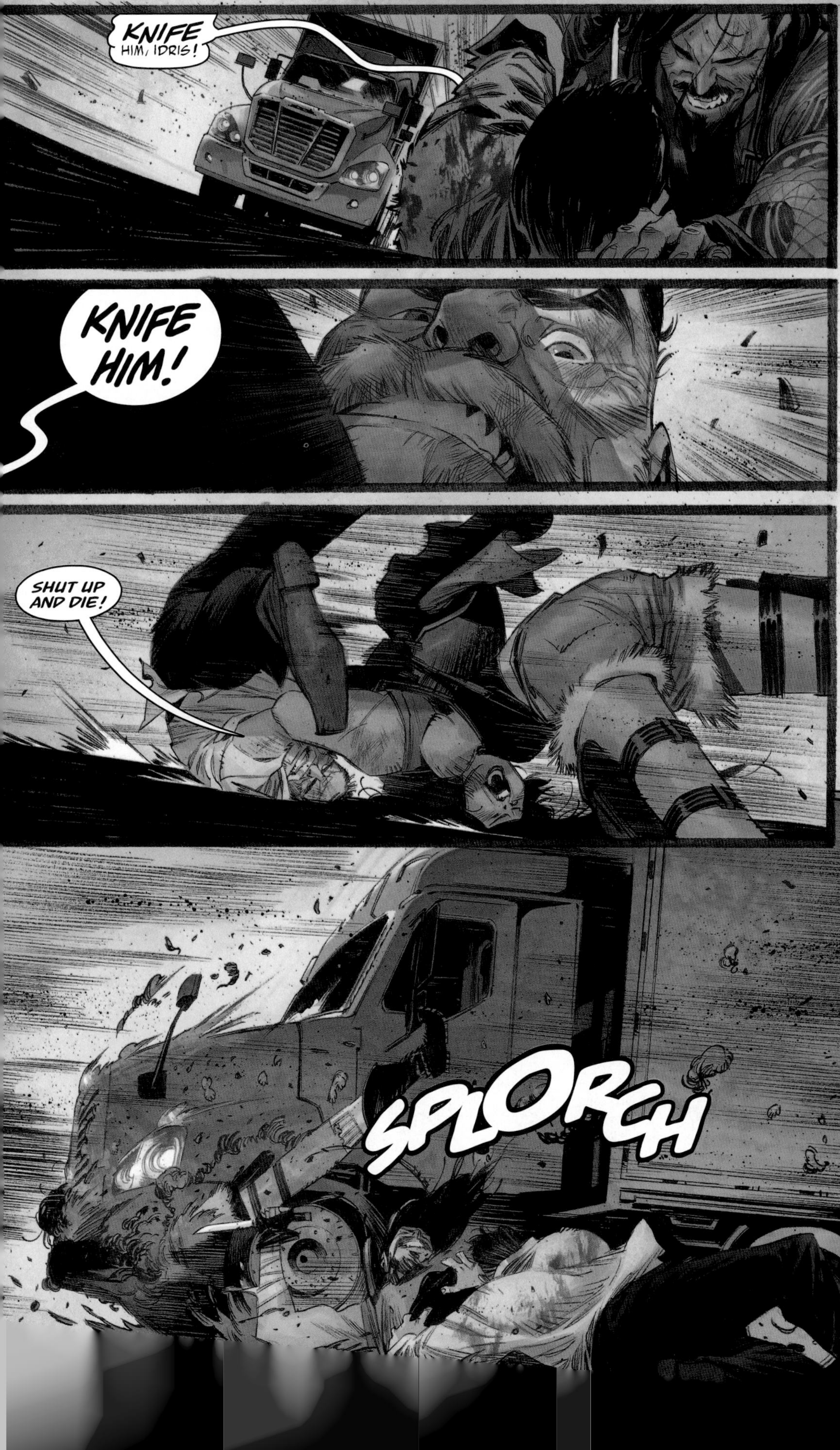
KNIFE HIM, IDRIS!
KNIFE HIM!
SHUT UP AND DIE!
SPLORCH

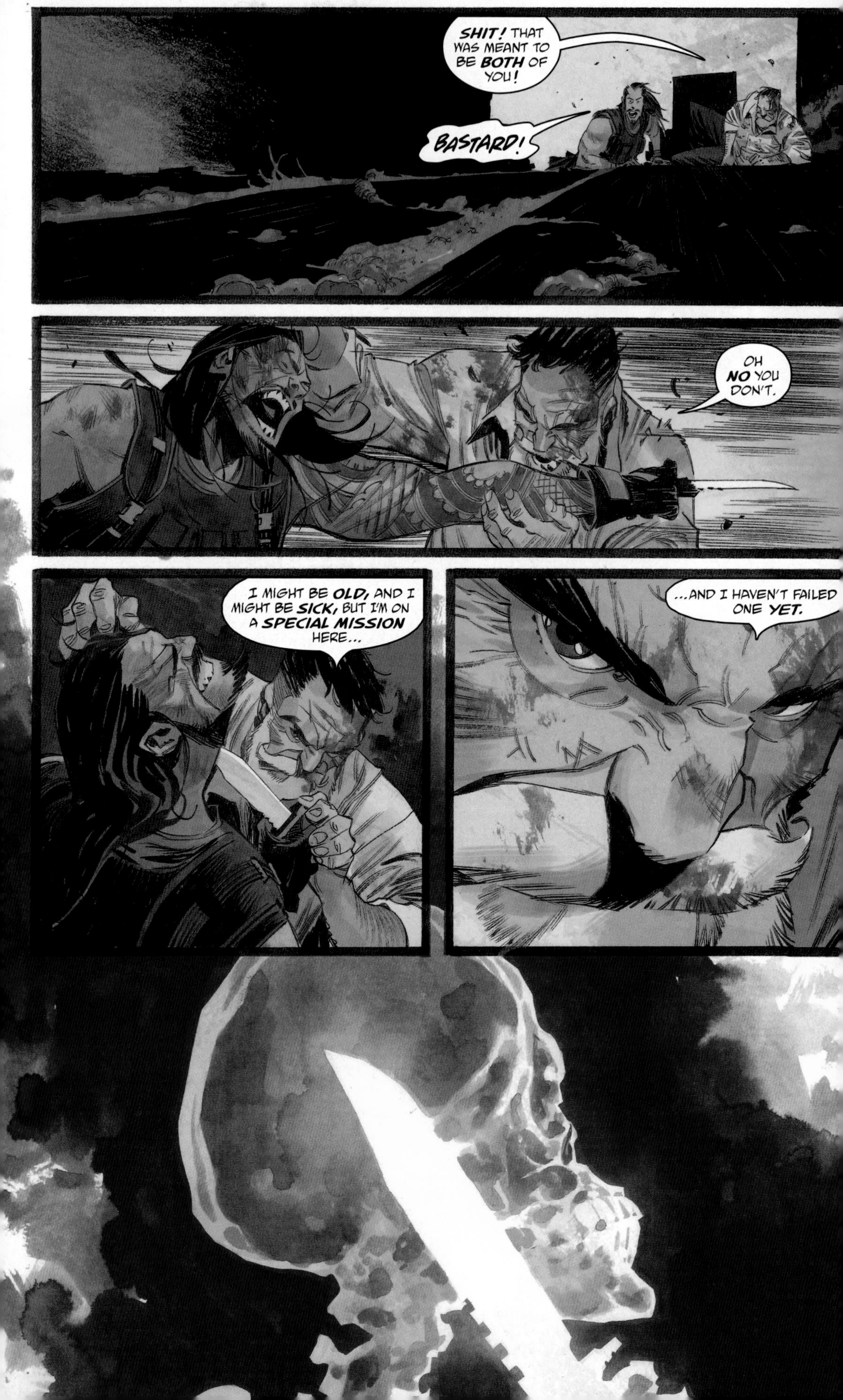
SHIT! THAT WAS MEANT TO BE BOTH OF YOU!
BASTARD!
OH NO YOU DON'T.
I MIGHT BE OLD, AND I MIGHT BE SICK, BUT I'M ON A SPECIAL MISSION HERE...
...AND I HAVEN'T FAILED ONE YET.

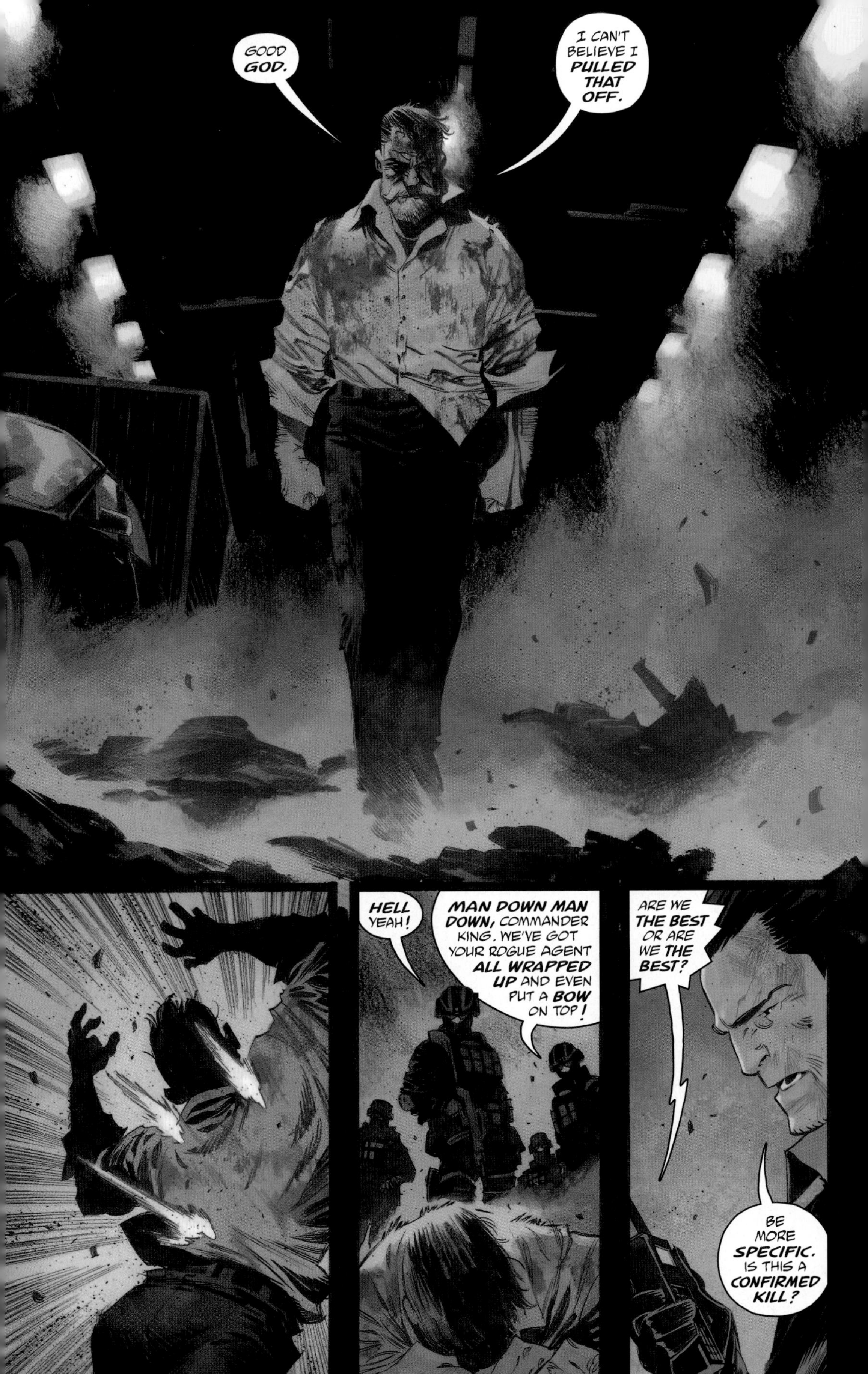
GOOD GOD.
I CAN'T BELIEVE I PULLED THAT OFF.
HELL YEAH!
MAN DOWN MAN DOWN, COMMANDER KING. WE'VE GOT YOUR ROGUE AGENT ALL WRAPPED UP AND EVEN PUT A BOW ON TOP!
ARE WE THE BEST OR ARE WE THE BEST?
BE MORE SPECIFIC. IS THIS A CONFIRMED KILL?

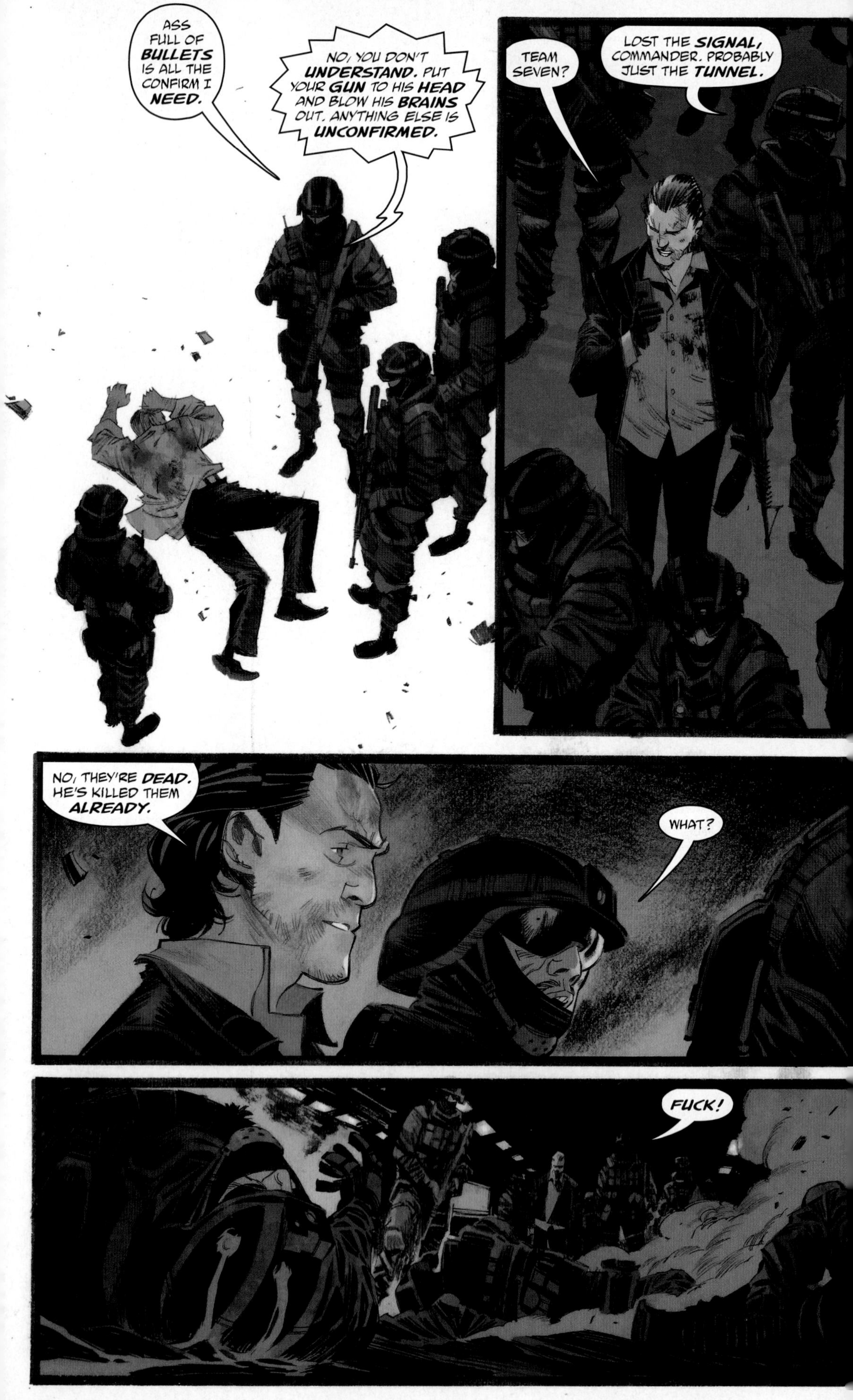
ASS FULL OF BULLETS IS ALL THE CONFIRM I NEED.
NO, YOU DON'T UNDERSTAND. PUT YOUR GUN TO HIS HEAD AND BLOW HIS BRAINS OUT. ANYTHING ELSE IS UNCONFIRMED.
TEAM SEVEN?
LOST THE SIGNAL, COMMANDER. PROBABLY JUST THE TUNNEL.
NO, THEY'RE DEAD. HE'S KILLED THEM ALREADY.
WHAT?
FUCK!

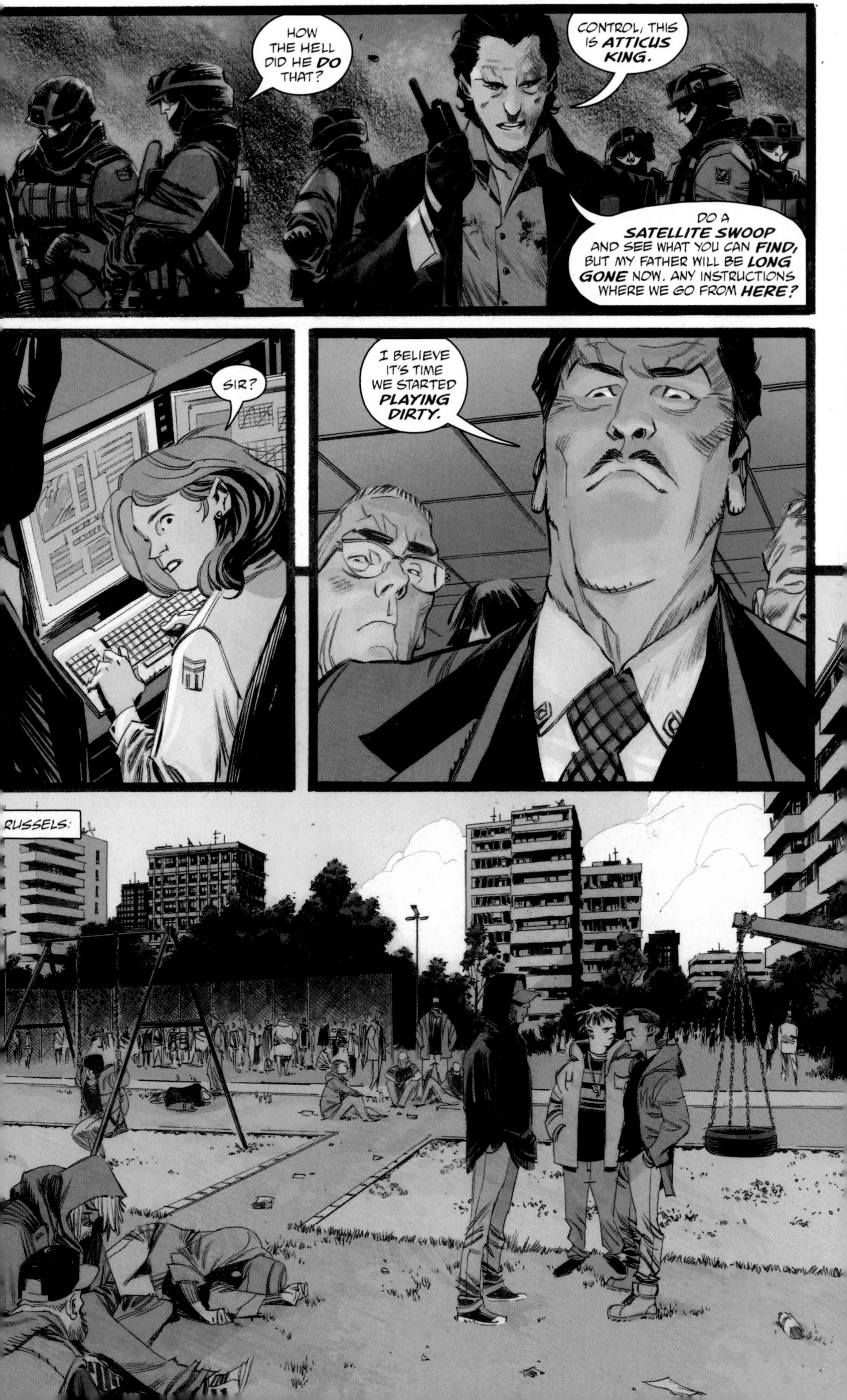
HOW THE HELL DID HE DO THAT?
CONTROL, THIS IS ATTICUS KING.
DO A SATELLITE SWOOP AND SEE WHAT YOU CAN FIND, BUT MY FATHER WILL BE LONG GONE NOW. ANY INSTRUCTIONS WHERE WE GO FROM HERE?
SIR?
I BELIEVE IT'S TIME WE STARTED PLAYING DIRTY.
RUSSELS:

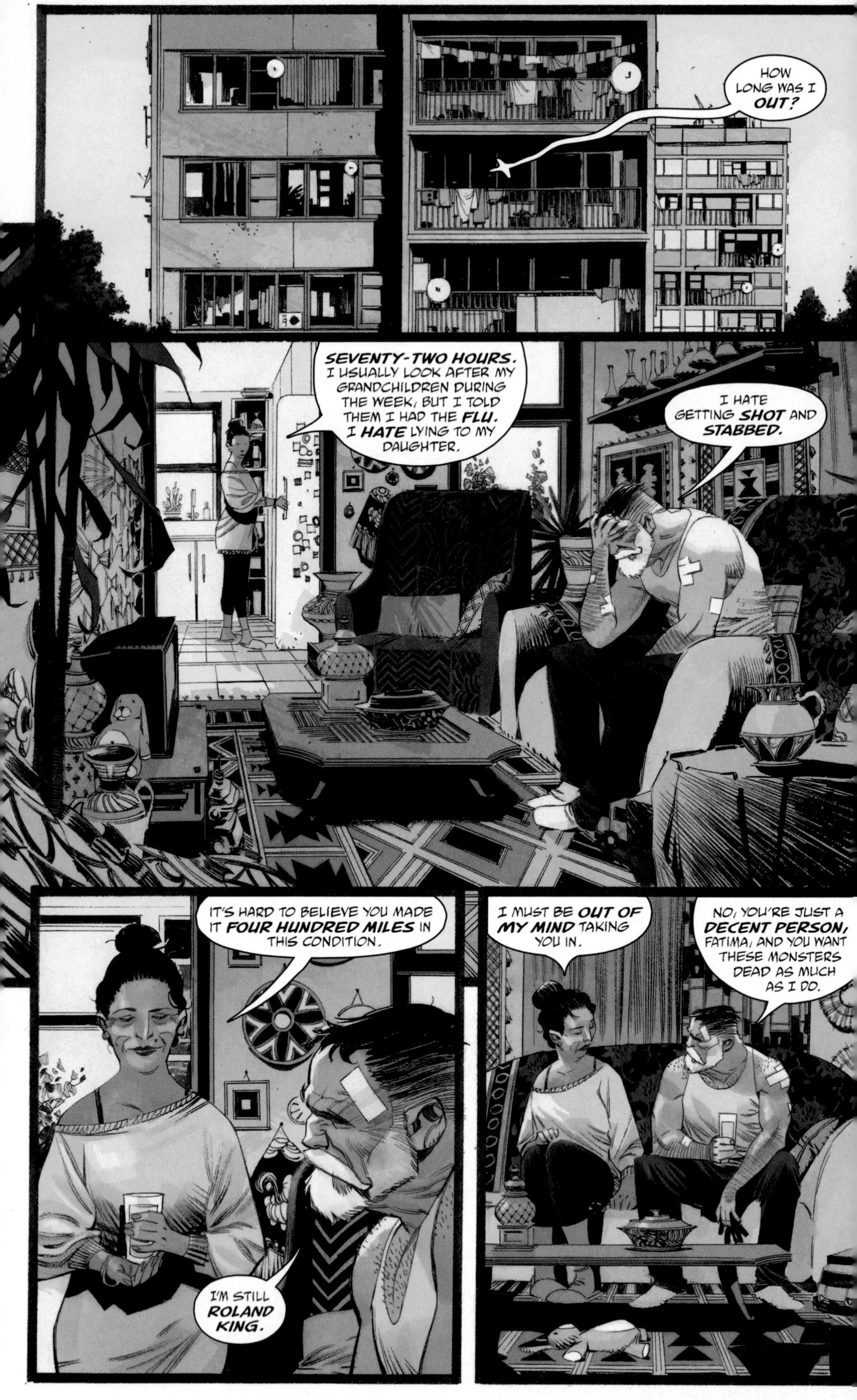
HOW LONG WAS I **OUT?**
SEVENTY-TWO HOURS. I USUALLY LOOK AFTER MY GRANDCHILDREN DURING THE WEEK, BUT I TOLD THEM I HAD THE **FLU.** I **HATE** LYING TO MY DAUGHTER.
I HATE GETTING **SHOT** AND **STABBED.**
IT'S HARD TO BELIEVE YOU MADE IT **FOUR HUNDRED MILES** IN THIS CONDITION.
I'M STILL **ROLAND KING.**
I MUST BE **OUT OF MY MIND** TAKING YOU IN.
NO, YOU'RE JUST A **DECENT PERSON,** FATIMA, AND YOU WANT THESE MONSTERS DEAD AS MUCH AS I DO.

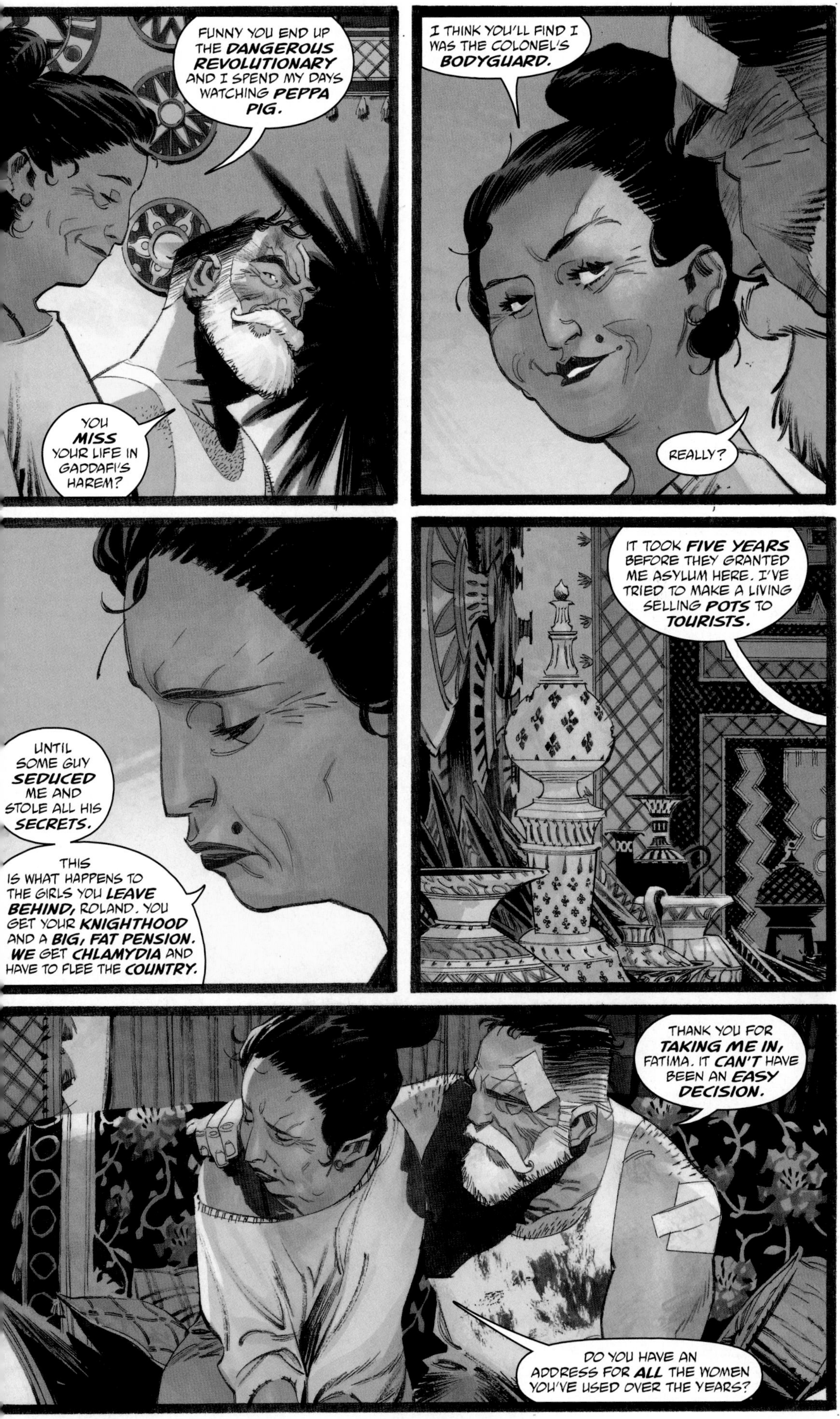
FUNNY YOU END UP THE DANGEROUS REVOLUTIONARY AND I SPEND MY DAYS WATCHING PEPPA PIG.
YOU MISS YOUR LIFE IN GADDAFI'S HAREM?
I THINK YOU'LL FIND I WAS THE COLONEL'S BODYGUARD.
REALLY?
UNTIL SOME GUY SEDUCED ME AND STOLE ALL HIS SECRETS.
THIS IS WHAT HAPPENS TO THE GIRLS YOU LEAVE BEHIND, ROLAND. YOU GET YOUR KNIGHTHOOD AND A BIG, FAT PENSION. WE GET CHLAMYDIA AND HAVE TO FLEE THE COUNTRY.
IT TOOK FIVE YEARS BEFORE THEY GRANTED ME ASYLUM HERE. I'VE TRIED TO MAKE A LIVING SELLING POTS TO TOURISTS.
THANK YOU FOR TAKING ME IN, FATIMA. IT CAN'T HAVE BEEN AN EASY DECISION.
DO YOU HAVE AN ADDRESS FOR ALL THE WOMEN YOU'VE USED OVER THE YEARS?

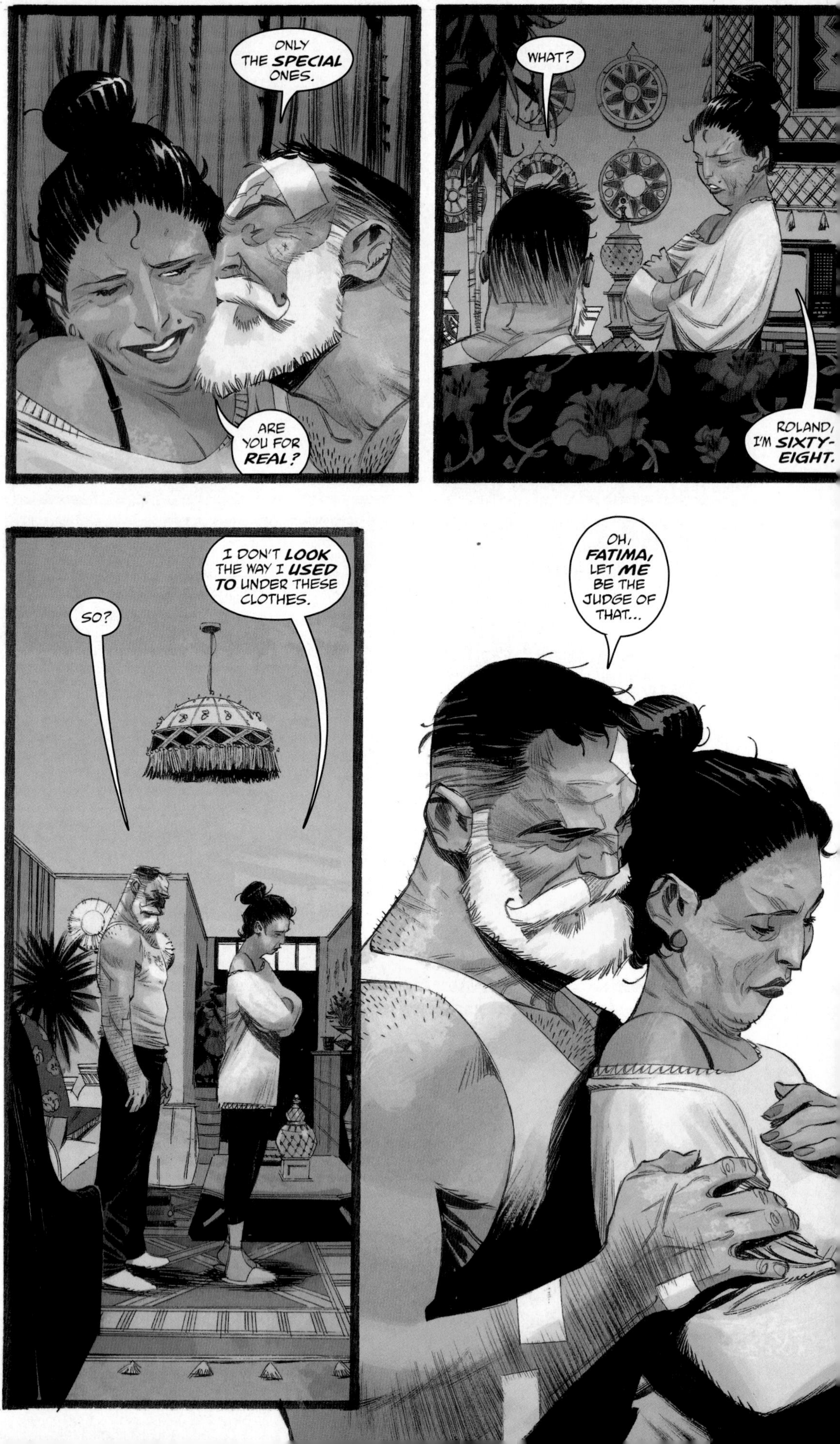
ONLY THE SPECIAL ONES.
ARE YOU FOR REAL?
WHAT?
ROLAND, I'M SIXTY-EIGHT.
I DON'T LOOK THE WAY I USED TO UNDER THESE CLOTHES.
SO?
OH, FATIMA, LET ME BE THE JUDGE OF THAT...

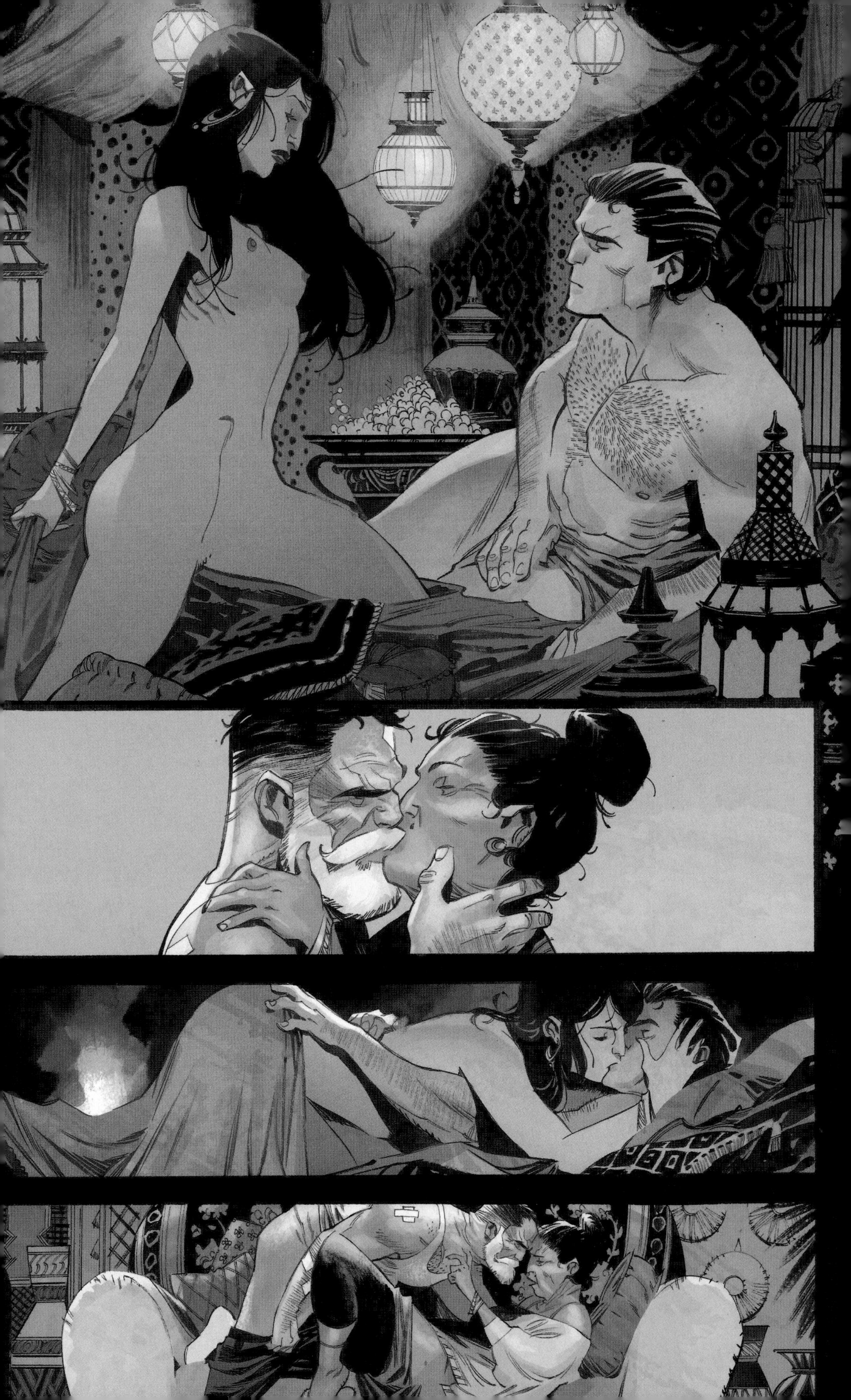

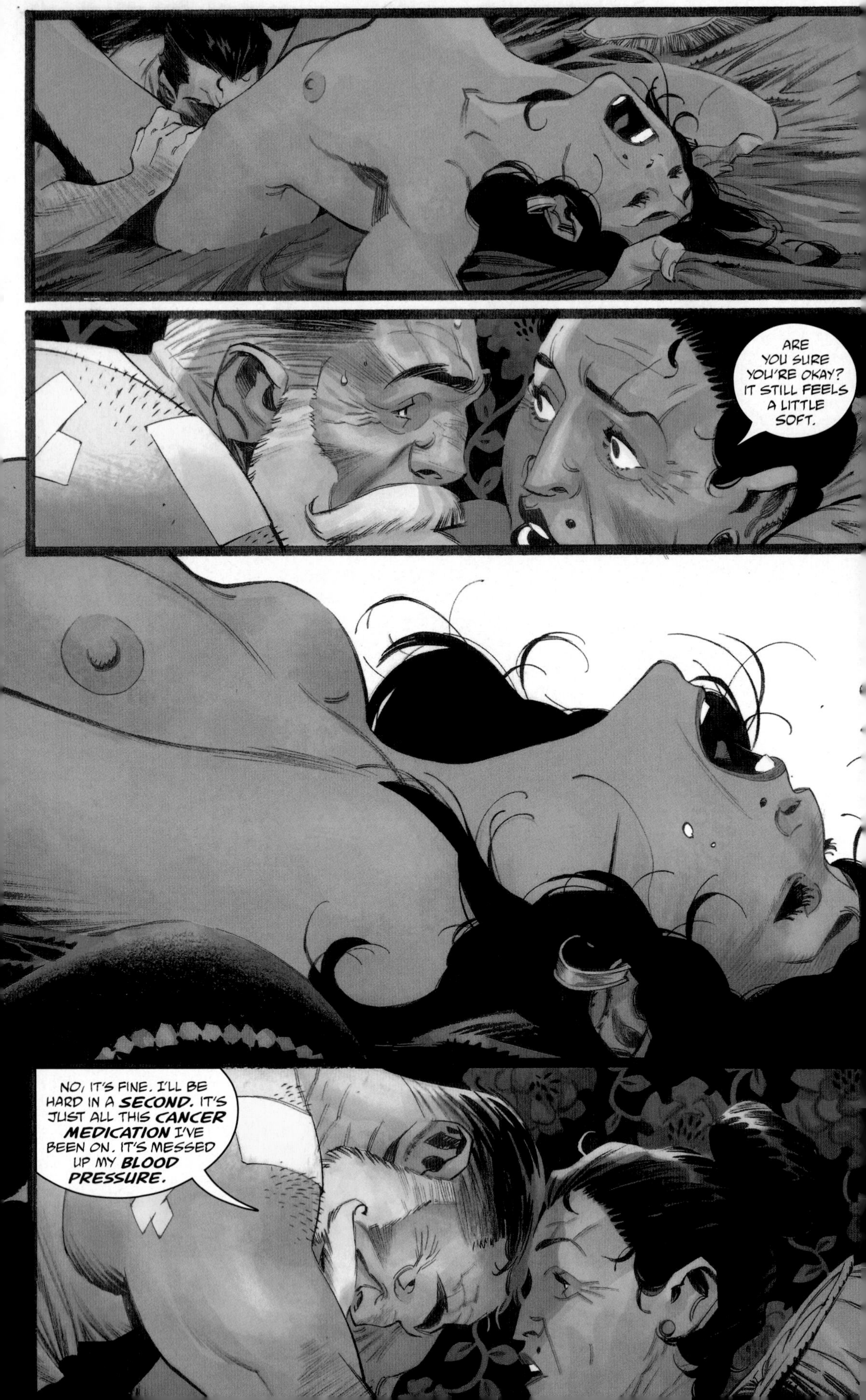
ARE YOU SURE YOU'RE OKAY? IT STILL FEELS A LITTLE SOFT.
NO, IT'S FINE. I'LL BE HARD IN A SECOND. IT'S JUST ALL THIS CANCER MEDICATION I'VE BEEN ON. IT'S MESSED UP MY BLOOD PRESSURE.

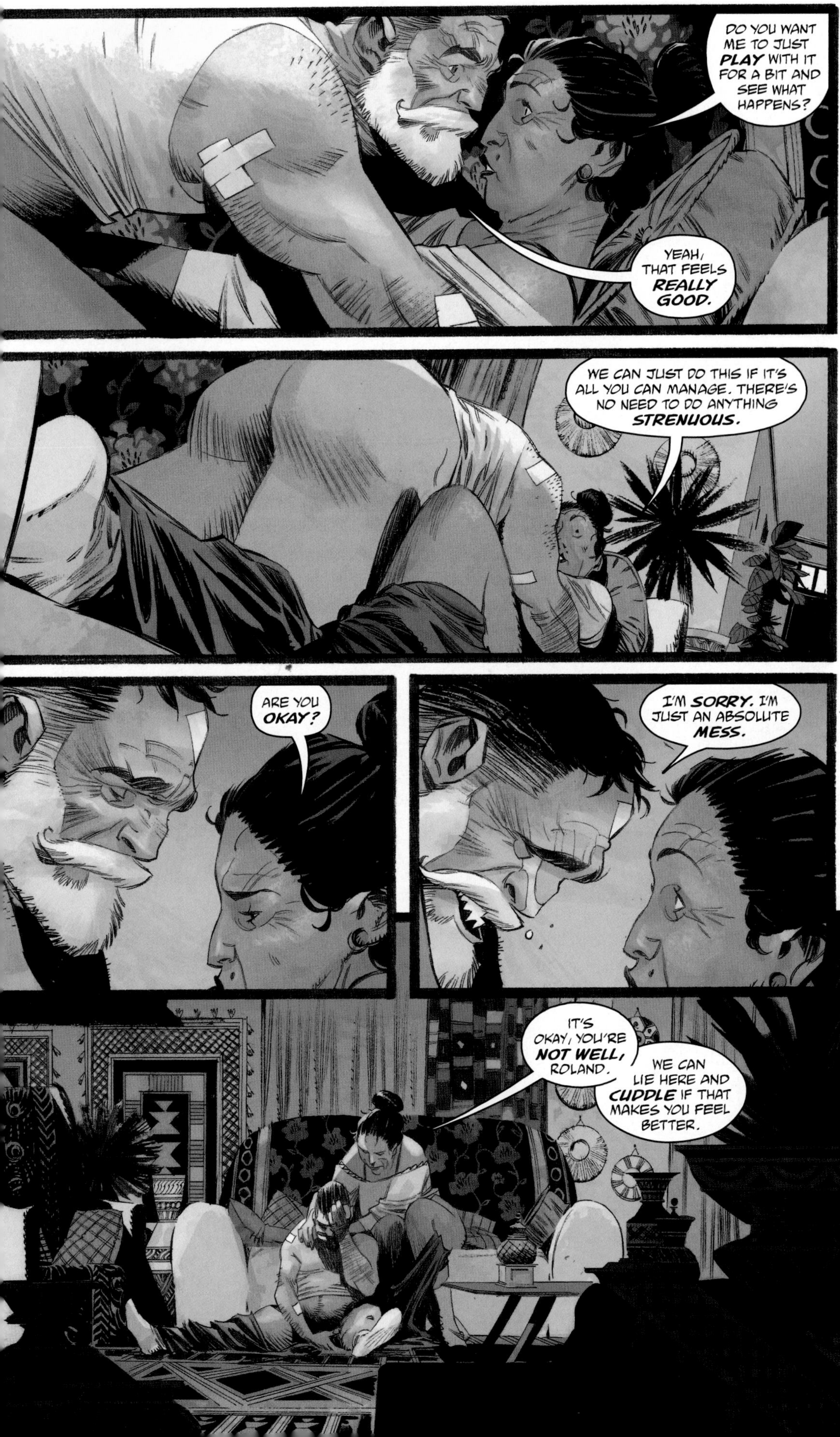

DO YOU WANT ME TO JUST PLAY WITH IT FOR A BIT AND SEE WHAT HAPPENS?
YEAH, THAT FEELS REALLY GOOD.
WE CAN JUST DO THIS IF IT'S ALL YOU CAN MANAGE. THERE'S NO NEED TO DO ANYTHING STRENUOUS.
ARE YOU OKAY?
I'M SORRY. I'M JUST AN ABSOLUTE MESS.
IT'S OKAY, YOU'RE NOT WELL, ROLAND.
WE CAN LIE HERE AND CUDDLE IF THAT MAKES YOU FEEL BETTER.

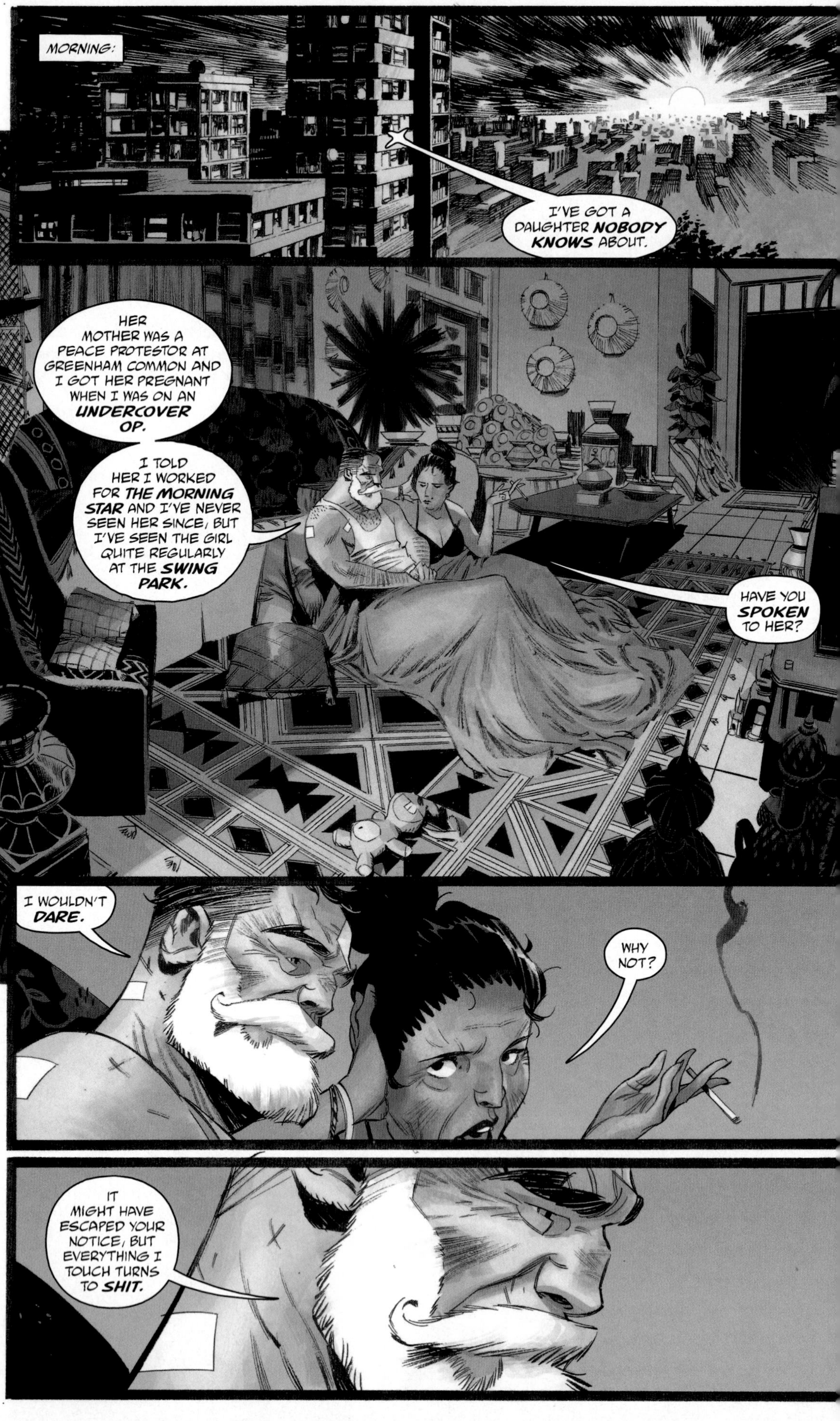
MORNING:
I'VE GOT A DAUGHTER NOBODY KNOWS ABOUT.
HER MOTHER WAS A PEACE PROTESTOR AT GREENHAM COMMON AND I GOT HER PREGNANT WHEN I WAS ON AN UNDERCOVER OP.
I TOLD HER I WORKED FOR THE MORNING STAR AND I'VE NEVER SEEN HER SINCE, BUT I'VE SEEN THE GIRL QUITE REGULARLY AT THE SWING PARK.
HAVE YOU SPOKEN TO HER?
I WOULDN'T DARE.
WHY NOT?
IT MIGHT HAVE ESCAPED YOUR NOTICE, BUT EVERYTHING I TOUCH TURNS TO SHIT.

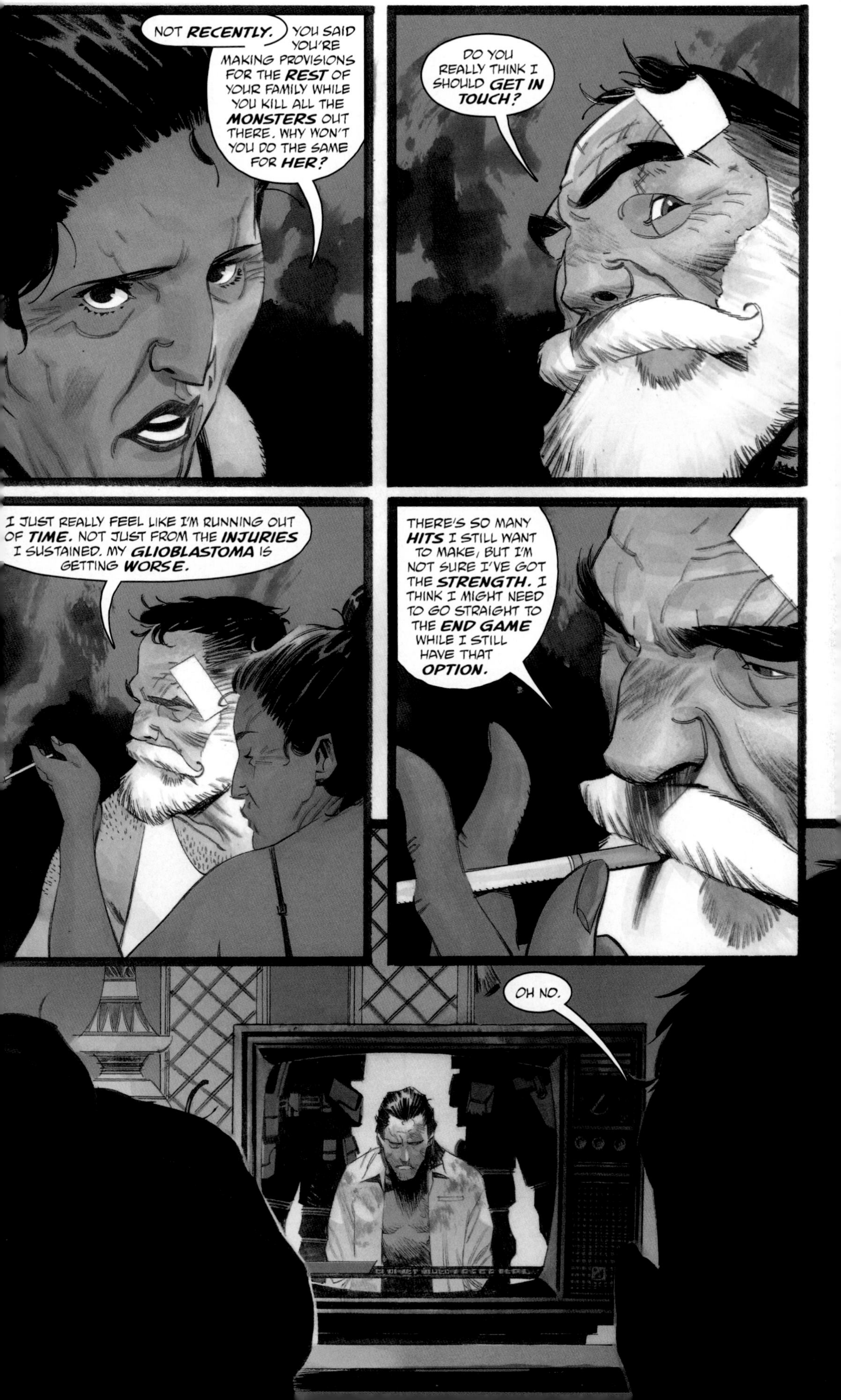
NOT **RECENTLY.**
YOU SAID YOU'RE MAKING PROVISIONS FOR THE **REST** OF YOUR FAMILY WHILE YOU KILL ALL THE **MONSTERS** OUT THERE. WHY WON'T YOU DO THE SAME FOR **HER?**
DO YOU REALLY THINK I SHOULD **GET IN TOUCH?**
I JUST REALLY FEEL LIKE I'M RUNNING OUT OF **TIME.** NOT JUST FROM THE **INJURIES** I SUSTAINED. MY **GLIOBLASTOMA** IS GETTING **WORSE.**
THERE'S SO MANY **HITS** I STILL WANT TO MAKE, BUT I'M NOT SURE I'VE GOT THE **STRENGTH.** I THINK I MIGHT NEED TO GO STRAIGHT TO THE **END GAME** WHILE I STILL HAVE THAT **OPTION.**
OH NO.

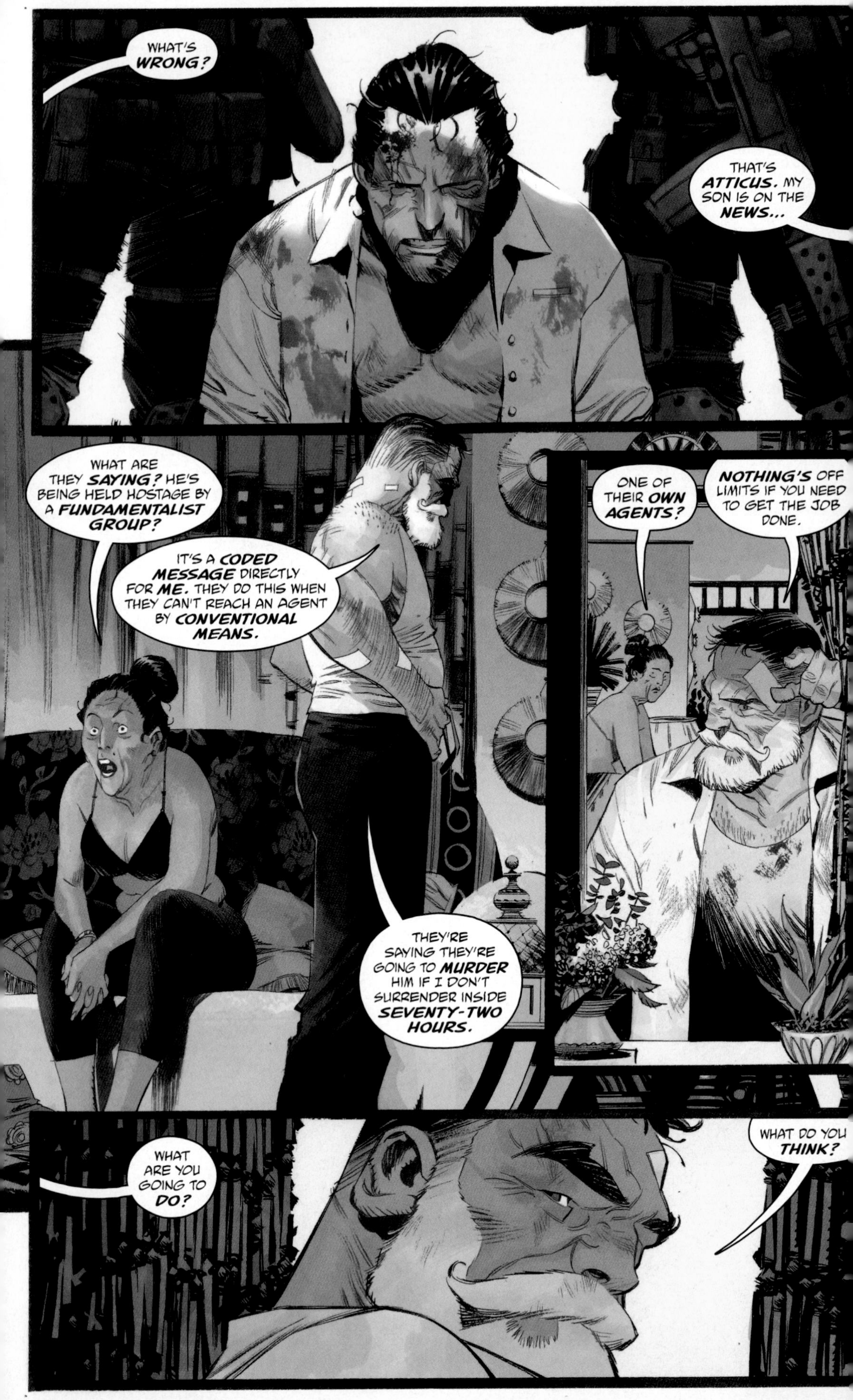
WHAT'S WRONG?
THAT'S ATTICUS. MY SON IS ON THE NEWS...
WHAT ARE THEY SAYING? HE'S BEING HELD HOSTAGE BY A FUNDAMENTALIST GROUP?
IT'S A CODED MESSAGE DIRECTLY FOR ME. THEY DO THIS WHEN THEY CAN'T REACH AN AGENT BY CONVENTIONAL MEANS.
ONE OF THEIR OWN AGENTS?
NOTHING'S OFF LIMITS IF YOU NEED TO GET THE JOB DONE.
THEY'RE SAYING THEY'RE GOING TO MURDER HIM IF I DON'T SURRENDER INSIDE SEVENTY-TWO HOURS.
WHAT ARE YOU GOING TO DO?
WHAT DO YOU THINK?

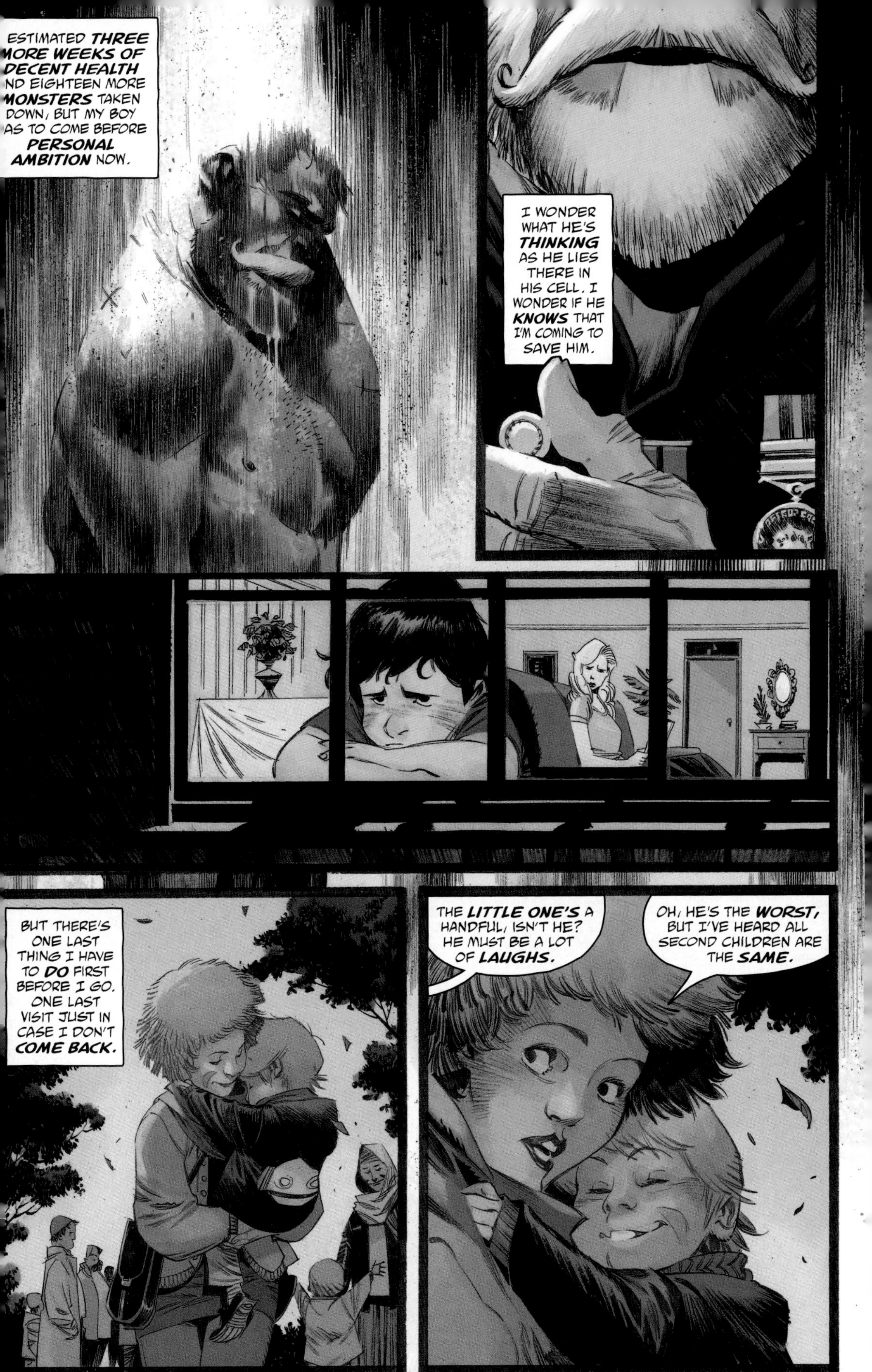
ESTIMATED THREE MORE WEEKS OF DECENT HEALTH ND EIGHTEEN MORE MONSTERS TAKEN DOWN, BUT MY BOY AS TO COME BEFORE PERSONAL AMBITION NOW.
I WONDER WHAT HE'S THINKING AS HE LIES THERE IN HIS CELL. I WONDER IF HE KNOWS THAT I'M COMING TO SAVE HIM.
BUT THERE'S ONE LAST THING I HAVE TO DO FIRST BEFORE I GO. ONE LAST VISIT JUST IN CASE I DON'T COME BACK.
THE LITTLE ONE'S A HANDFUL, ISN'T HE? HE MUST BE A LOT OF LAUGHS.
OH, HE'S THE WORST, BUT I'VE HEARD ALL SECOND CHILDREN ARE THE SAME.

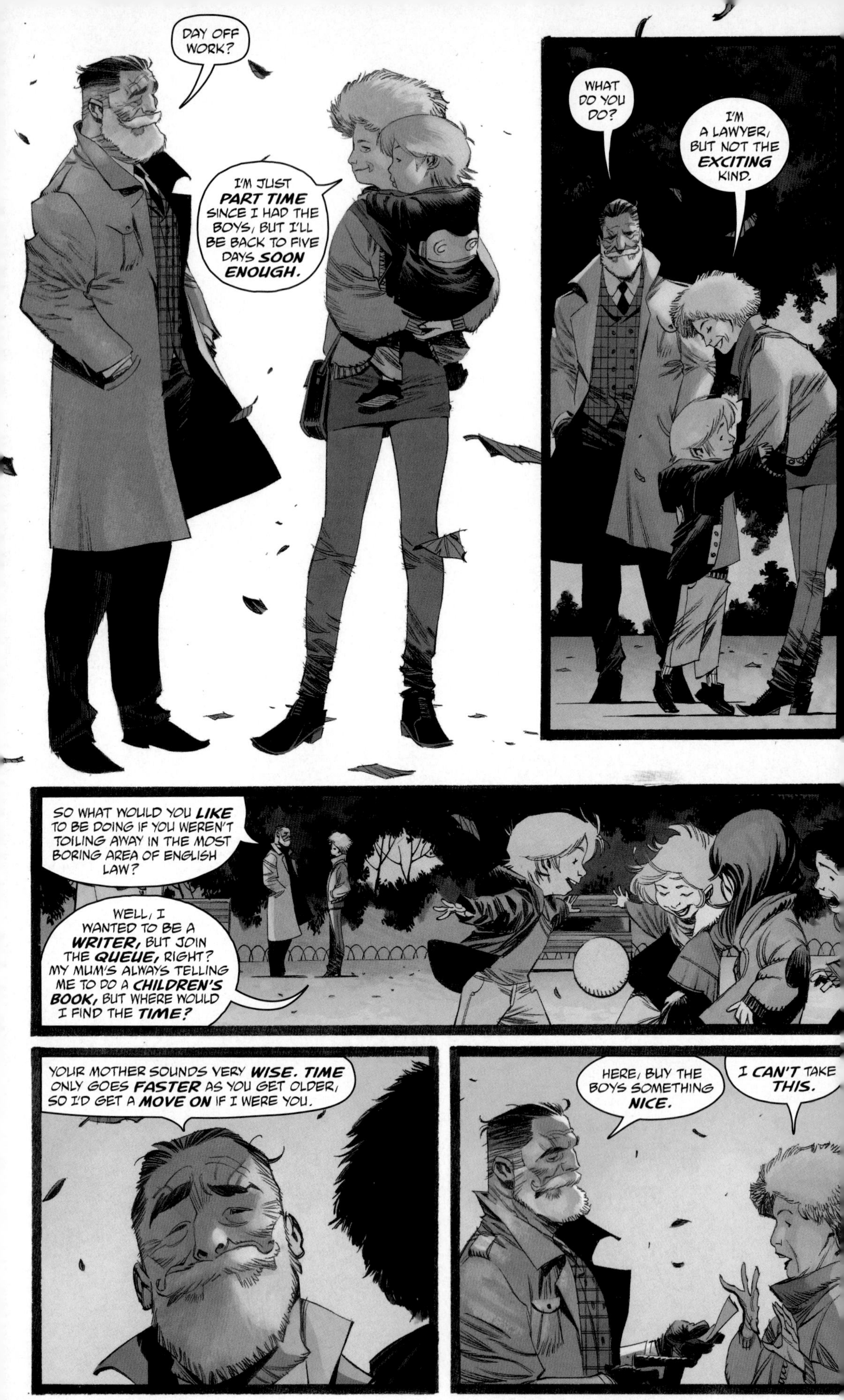
DAY OFF WORK?
I'M JUST PART TIME SINCE I HAD THE BOYS, BUT I'LL BE BACK TO FIVE DAYS SOON ENOUGH.
WHAT DO YOU DO?
I'M A LAWYER, BUT NOT THE EXCITING KIND.
SO WHAT WOULD YOU LIKE TO BE DOING IF YOU WEREN'T TOILING AWAY IN THE MOST BORING AREA OF ENGLISH LAW?
WELL, I WANTED TO BE A WRITER, BUT JOIN THE QUEUE, RIGHT? MY MUM'S ALWAYS TELLING ME TO DO A CHILDREN'S BOOK, BUT WHERE WOULD I FIND THE TIME?
YOUR MOTHER SOUNDS VERY WISE. TIME ONLY GOES FASTER AS YOU GET OLDER, SO I'D GET A MOVE ON IF I WERE YOU.
HERE, BUY THE BOYS SOMETHING NICE.
I CAN'T TAKE THIS.

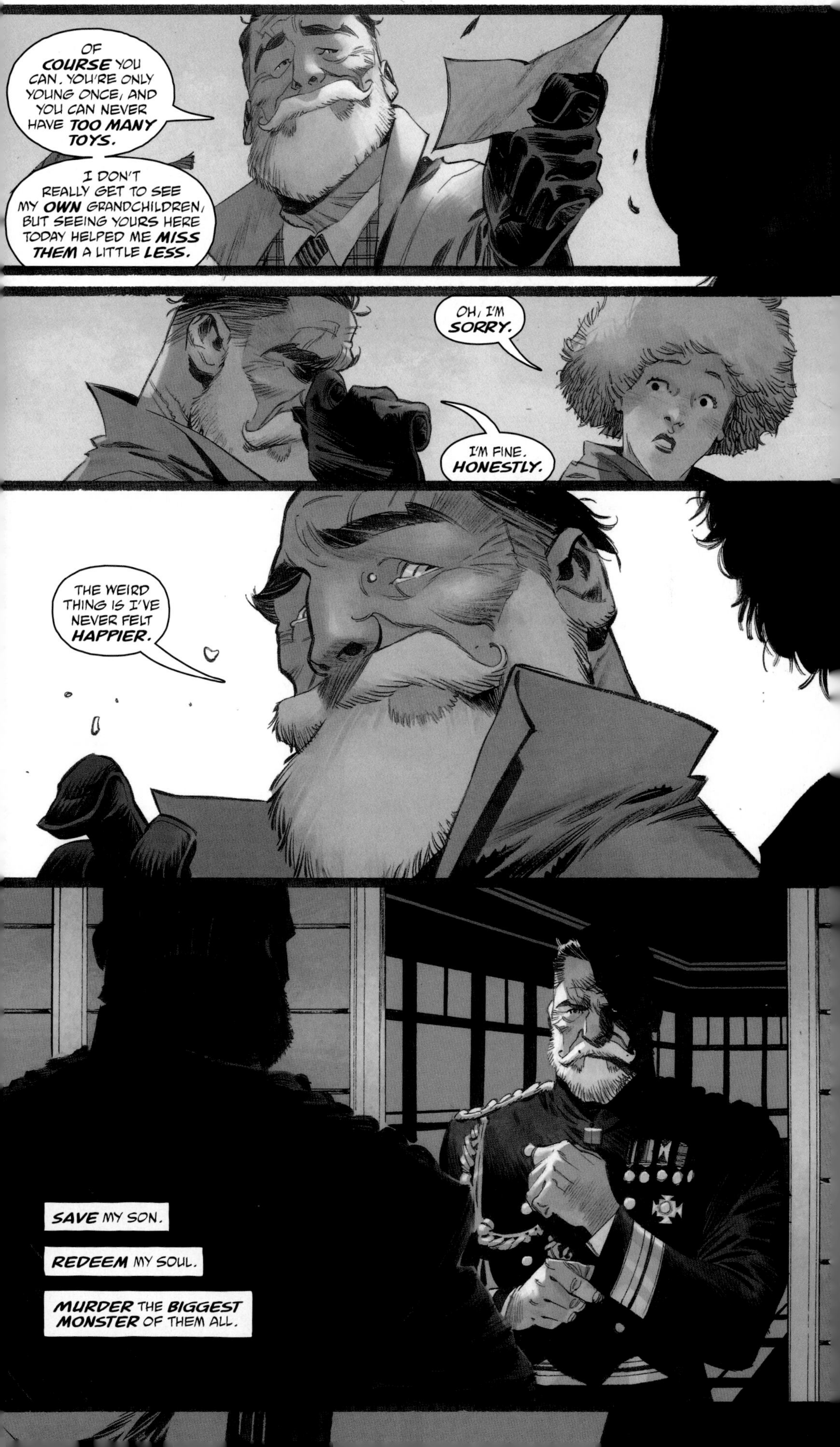
OF COURSE YOU CAN. YOU'RE ONLY YOUNG ONCE, AND YOU CAN NEVER HAVE TOO MANY TOYS.
I DON'T REALLY GET TO SEE MY OWN GRANDCHILDREN, BUT SEEING YOURS HERE TODAY HELPED ME MISS THEM A LITTLE LESS.
OH, I'M SORRY.
I'M FINE. HONESTLY.
THE WEIRD THING IS I'VE NEVER FELT HAPPIER.
SAVE MY SON.
REDEEM MY SOUL.
MURDER THE BIGGEST MONSTER OF THEM ALL.

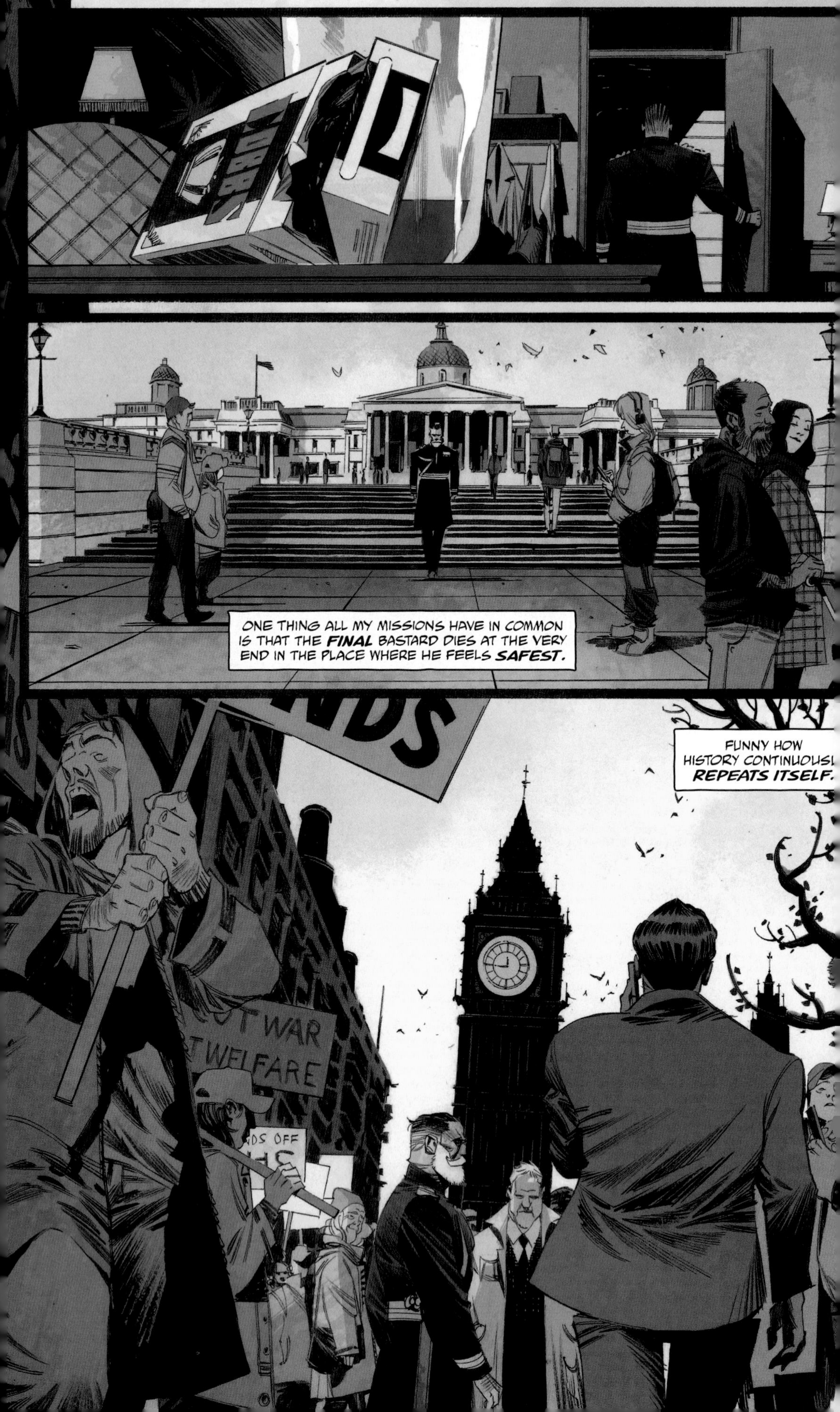
ONE THING ALL MY MISSIONS HAVE IN COMMON IS THAT THE FINAL BASTARD DIES AT THE VERY END IN THE PLACE WHERE HE FEELS SAFEST.
FUNNY HOW HISTORY CONTINUOUSL REPEATS ITSELF.
NDS
WAR
WELFARE
NDS OFF

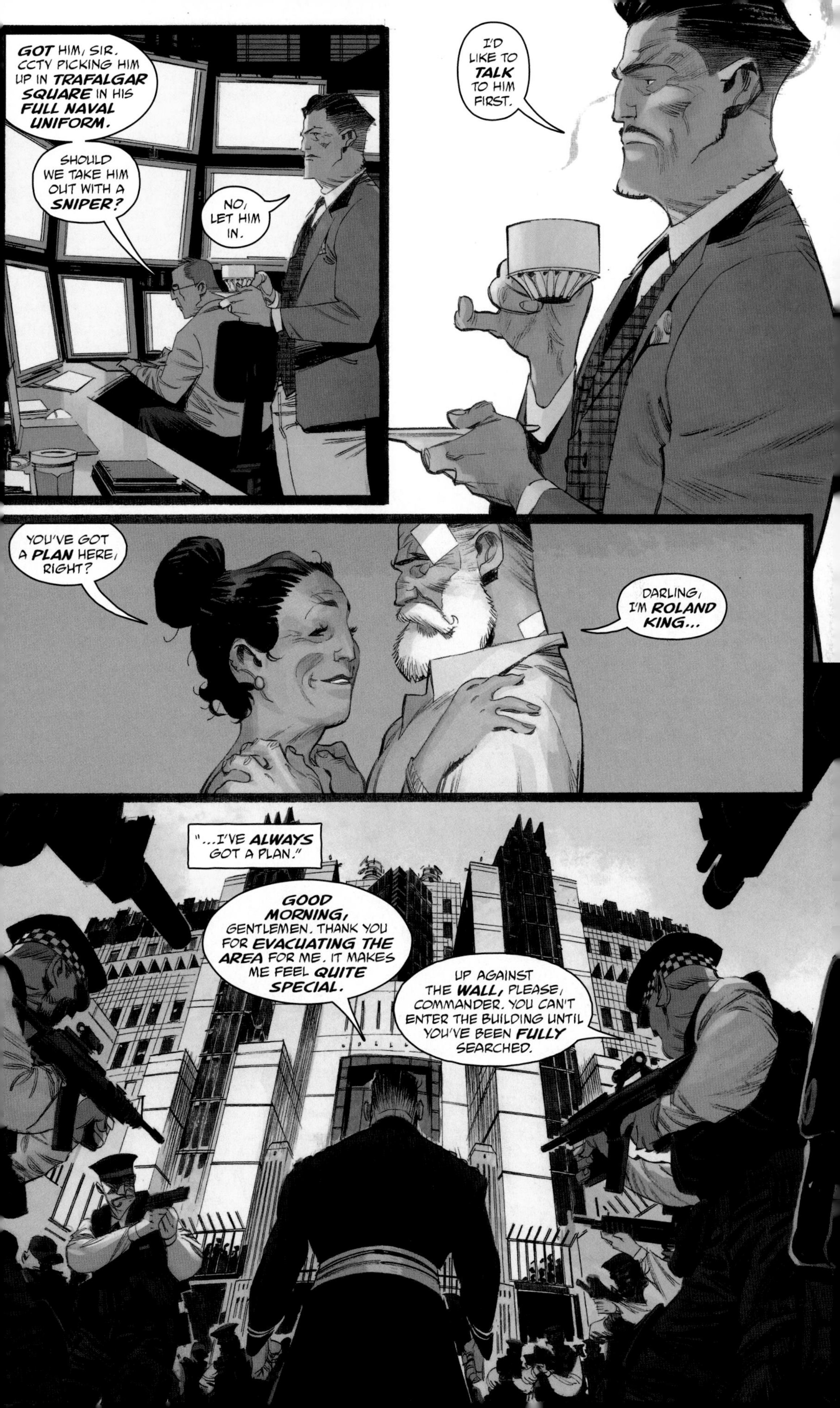
GOT HIM, SIR. CCTV PICKING HIM UP IN TRAFALGAR SQUARE IN HIS FULL NAVAL UNIFORM.
SHOULD WE TAKE HIM OUT WITH A SNIPER?
NO, LET HIM IN.
I'D LIKE TO TALK TO HIM FIRST.
YOU'VE GOT A PLAN HERE, RIGHT?
DARLING, I'M ROLAND KING...
"...I'VE ALWAYS GOT A PLAN."
GOOD MORNING, GENTLEMEN. THANK YOU FOR EVACUATING THE AREA FOR ME. IT MAKES ME FEEL QUITE SPECIAL.
UP AGAINST THE WALL, PLEASE, COMMANDER. YOU CAN'T ENTER THE BUILDING UNTIL YOU'VE BEEN FULLY SEARCHED.

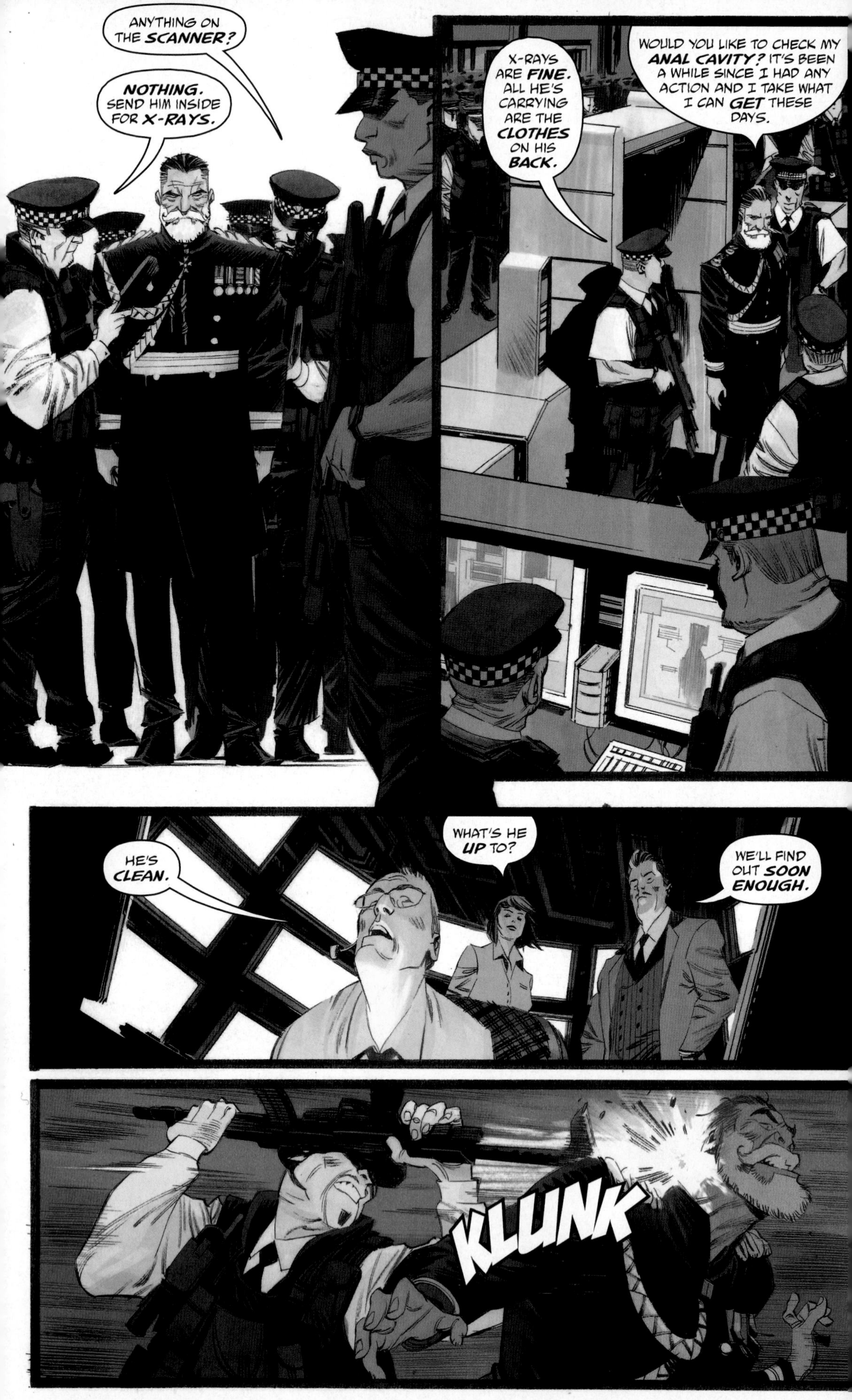
ANYTHING ON THE SCANNER?
NOTHING. SEND HIM INSIDE FOR X-RAYS.
X-RAYS ARE FINE. ALL HE'S CARRYING ARE THE CLOTHES ON HIS BACK.
WOULD YOU LIKE TO CHECK MY ANAL CAVITY? IT'S BEEN A WHILE SINCE I HAD ANY ACTION AND I TAKE WHAT I CAN GET THESE DAYS.
HE'S CLEAN.
WHAT'S HE UP TO?
WE'LL FIND OUT SOON ENOUGH.
KLUNK

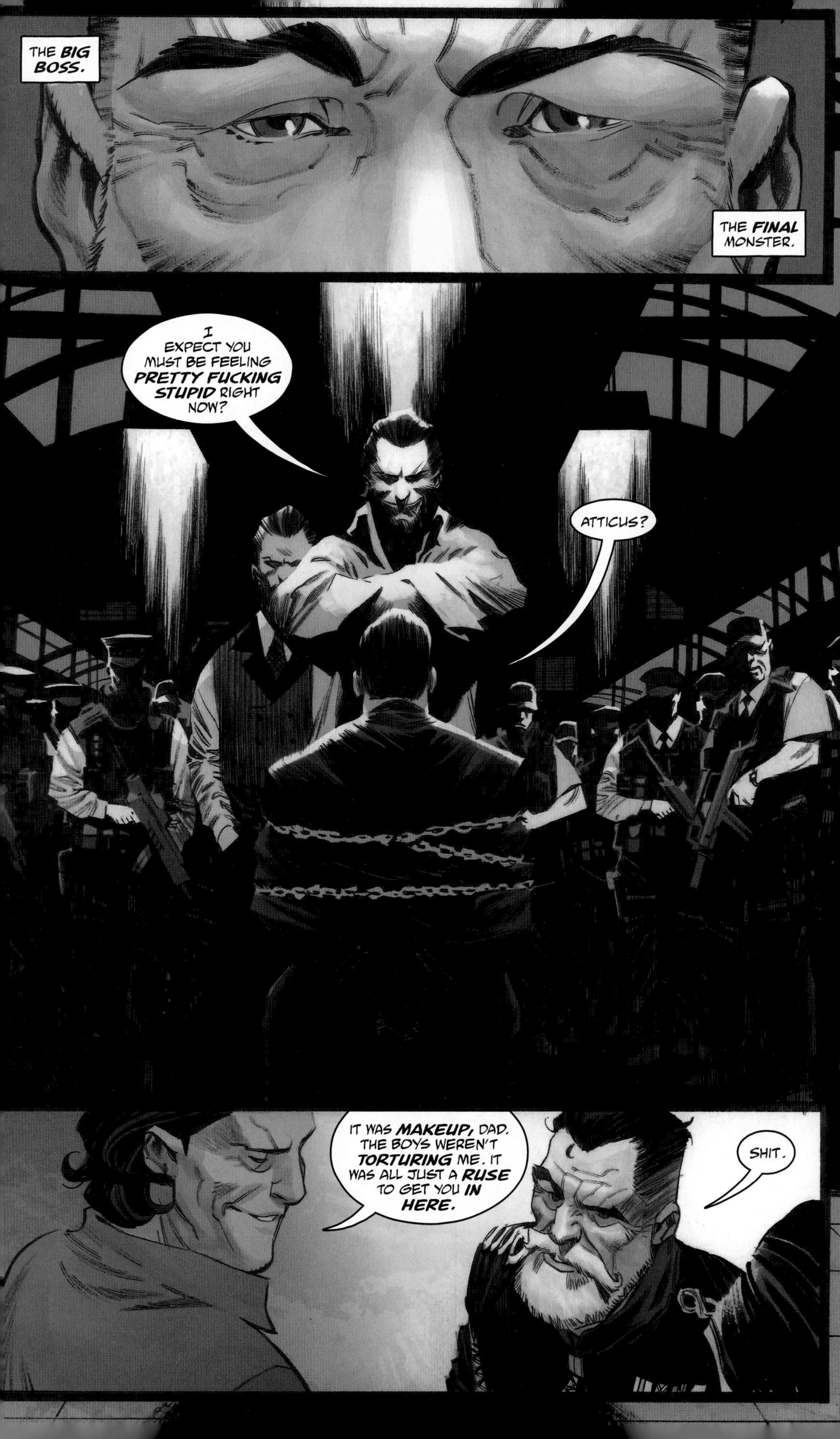
THE BIG BOSS.
THE FINAL MONSTER.
I EXPECT YOU MUST BE FEELING PRETTY FUCKING STUPID RIGHT NOW?
ATTICUS?
IT WAS MAKEUP, DAD. THE BOYS WEREN'T TORTURING ME. IT WAS ALL JUST A RUSE TO GET YOU IN HERE.
SHIT.

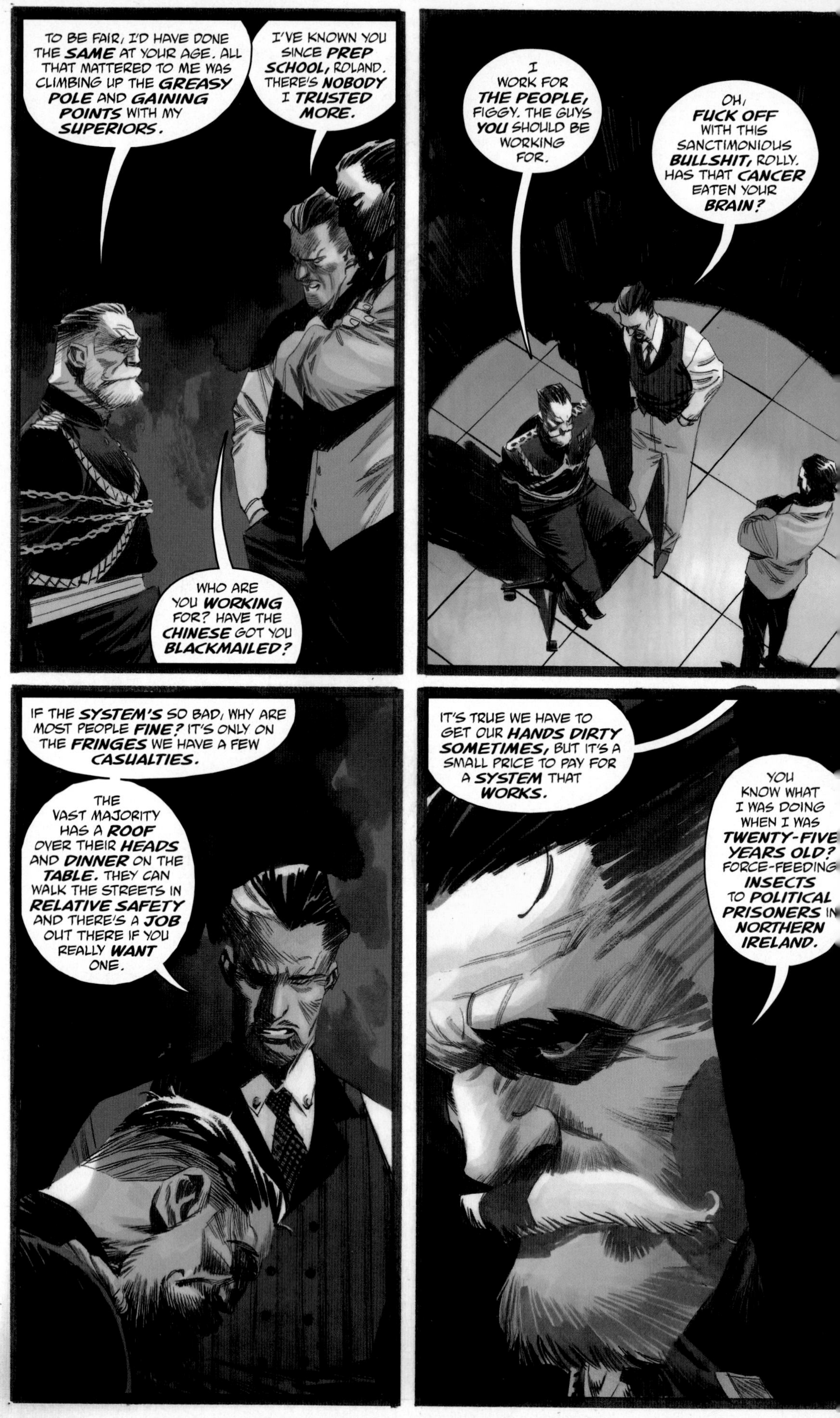
TO BE FAIR, I'D HAVE DONE THE SAME AT YOUR AGE. ALL THAT MATTERED TO ME WAS CLIMBING UP THE GREASY POLE AND GAINING POINTS WITH MY SUPERIORS.
I'VE KNOWN YOU SINCE PREP SCHOOL, ROLAND. THERE'S NOBODY I TRUSTED MORE.
WHO ARE YOU WORKING FOR? HAVE THE CHINESE GOT YOU BLACKMAILED?
I WORK FOR THE PEOPLE, FIGGY. THE GUYS YOU SHOULD BE WORKING FOR.
OH, FUCK OFF WITH THIS SANCTIMONIOUS BULLSHIT, ROLLY. HAS THAT CANCER EATEN YOUR BRAIN?
IF THE SYSTEM'S SO BAD, WHY ARE MOST PEOPLE FINE? IT'S ONLY ON THE FRINGES WE HAVE A FEW CASUALTIES.
THE VAST MAJORITY HAS A ROOF OVER THEIR HEADS AND DINNER ON THE TABLE. THEY CAN WALK THE STREETS IN RELATIVE SAFETY AND THERE'S A JOB OUT THERE IF YOU REALLY WANT ONE.
IT'S TRUE WE HAVE TO GET OUR HANDS DIRTY SOMETIMES, BUT IT'S A SMALL PRICE TO PAY FOR A SYSTEM THAT WORKS.
YOU KNOW WHAT I WAS DOING WHEN I WAS TWENTY-FIVE YEARS OLD? FORCE-FEEDING INSECTS TO POLITICAL PRISONERS IN NORTHERN IRELAND.

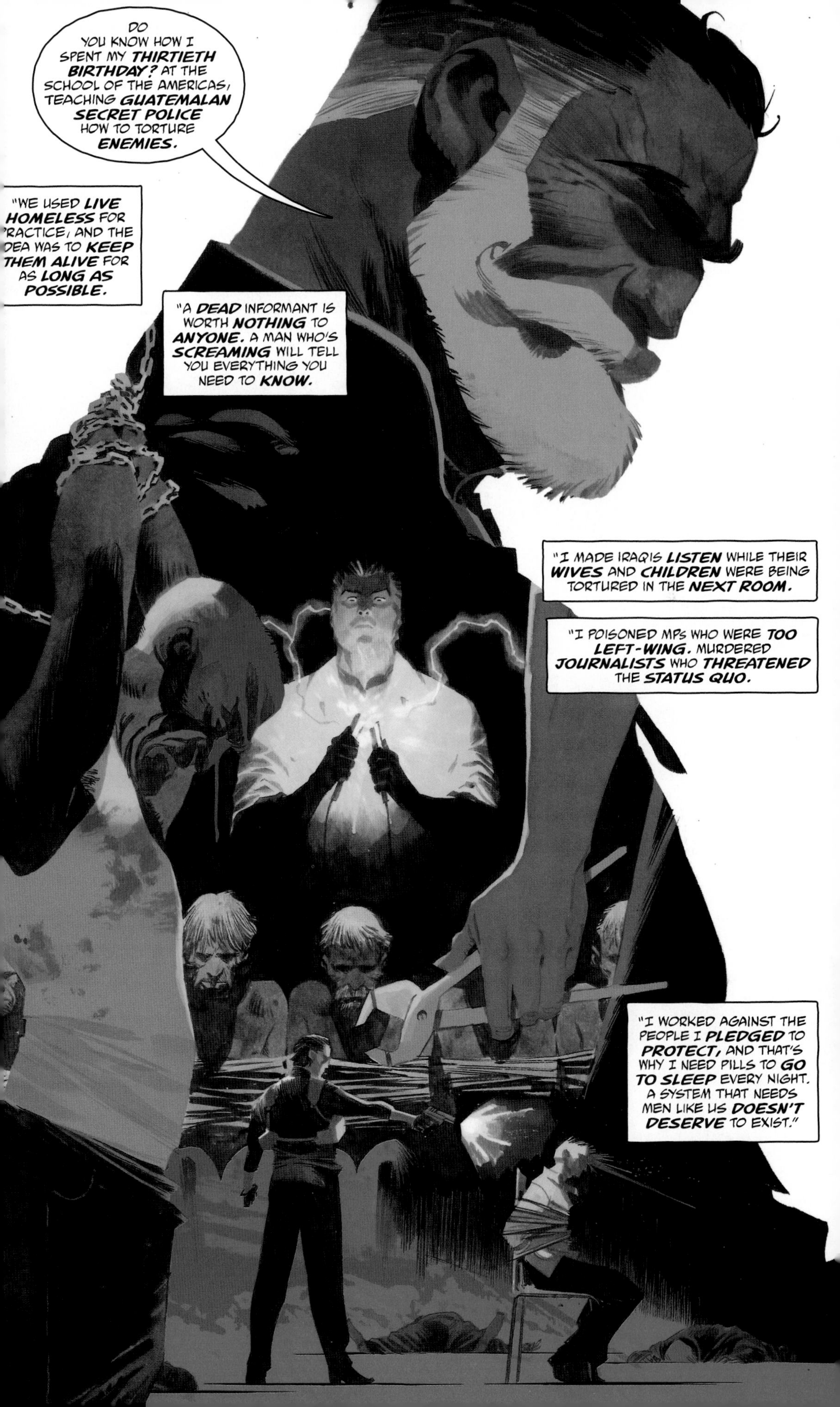
DO YOU KNOW HOW I SPENT MY THIRTIETH BIRTHDAY? AT THE SCHOOL OF THE AMERICAS, TEACHING GUATEMALAN SECRET POLICE HOW TO TORTURE ENEMIES.
"WE USED LIVE HOMELESS FOR PRACTICE, AND THE IDEA WAS TO KEEP THEM ALIVE FOR AS LONG AS POSSIBLE.
"A DEAD INFORMANT IS WORTH NOTHING TO ANYONE. A MAN WHO'S SCREAMING WILL TELL YOU EVERYTHING YOU NEED TO KNOW.
"I MADE IRAQIS LISTEN WHILE THEIR WIVES AND CHILDREN WERE BEING TORTURED IN THE NEXT ROOM.
"I POISONED MPs WHO WERE TOO LEFT-WING. MURDERED JOURNALISTS WHO THREATENED THE STATUS QUO.
"I WORKED AGAINST THE PEOPLE I PLEDGED TO PROTECT, AND THAT'S WHY I NEED PILLS TO GO TO SLEEP EVERY NIGHT. A SYSTEM THAT NEEDS MEN LIKE US DOESN'T DESERVE TO EXIST."

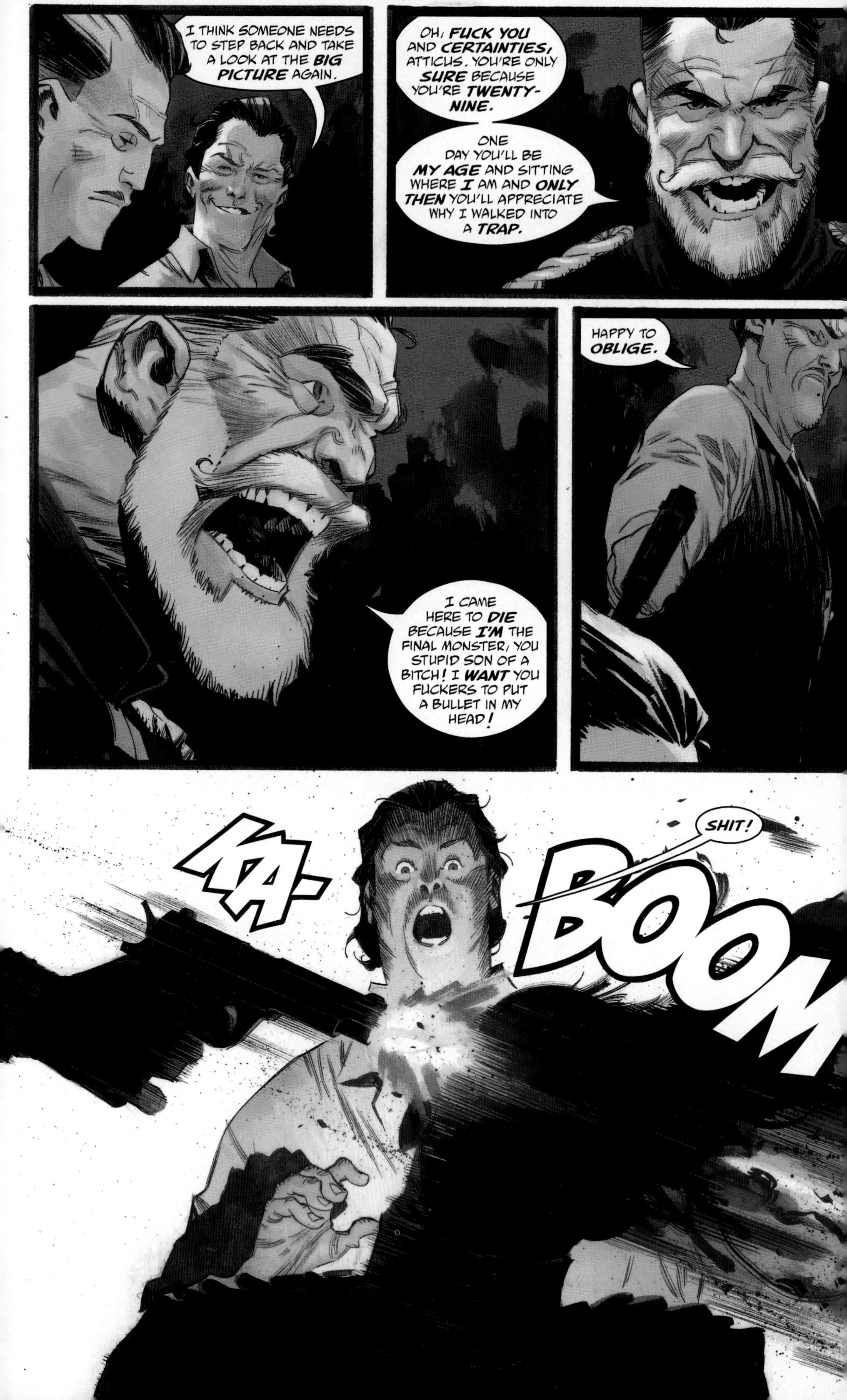
I THINK SOMEONE NEEDS TO STEP BACK AND TAKE A LOOK AT THE BIG PICTURE AGAIN.
OH, FUCK YOU AND CERTAINTIES, ATTICUS. YOU'RE ONLY SURE BECAUSE YOU'RE TWENTY-NINE.
ONE DAY YOU'LL BE MY AGE AND SITTING WHERE I AM AND ONLY THEN YOU'LL APPRECIATE WHY I WALKED INTO A TRAP.
I CAME HERE TO DIE BECAUSE I'M THE FINAL MONSTER, YOU STUPID SON OF A BITCH! I WANT YOU FUCKERS TO PUT A BULLET IN MY HEAD!
HAPPY TO OBLIGE.
KA-BOOM
SHIT!

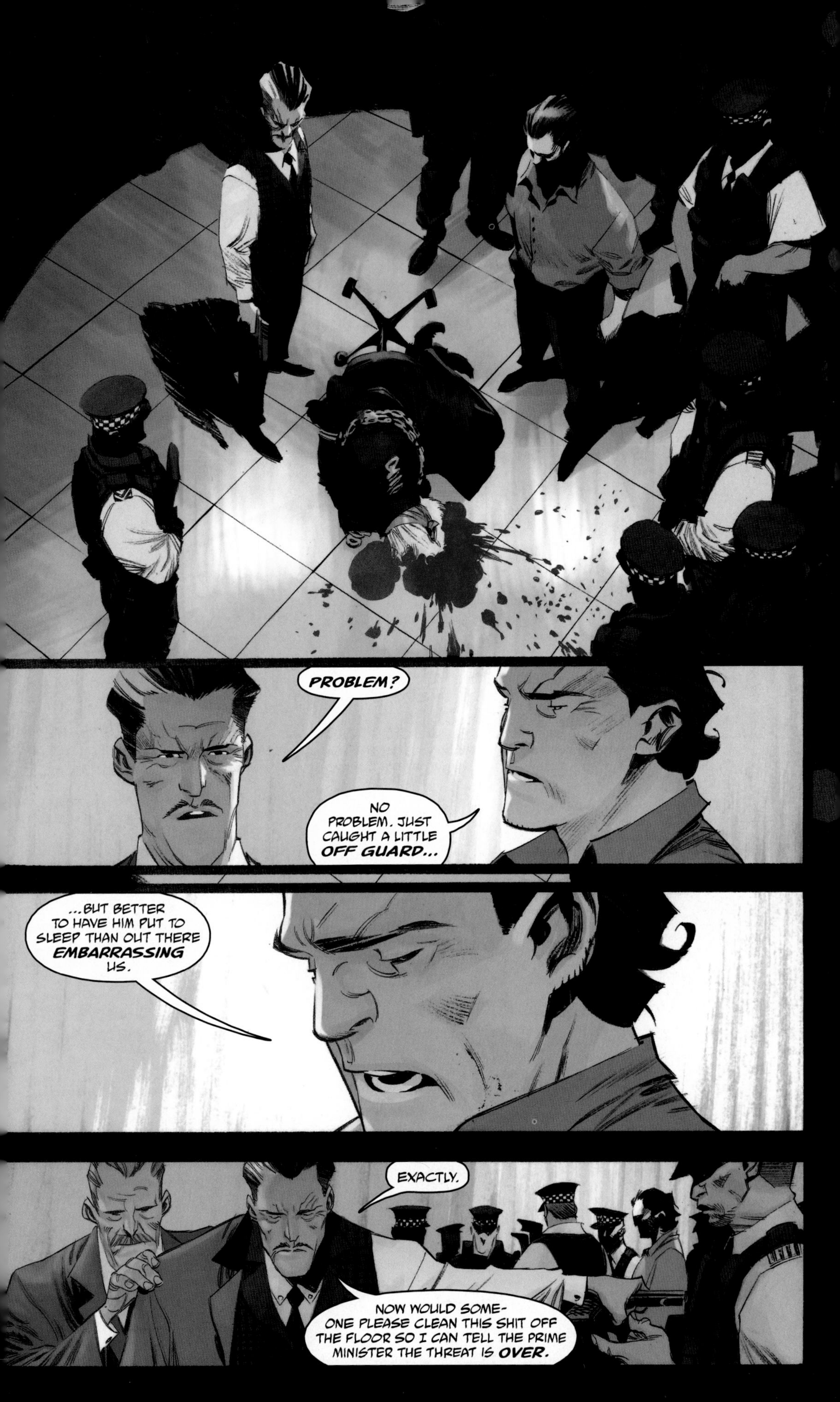
PROBLEM?
NO PROBLEM. JUST CAUGHT A LITTLE OFF GUARD...
...BUT BETTER TO HAVE HIM PUT TO SLEEP THAN OUT THERE EMBARRASSING US.
EXACTLY.
NOW WOULD SOME-ONE PLEASE CLEAN THIS SHIT OFF THE FLOOR SO I CAN TELL THE PRIME MINISTER THE THREAT IS OVER.

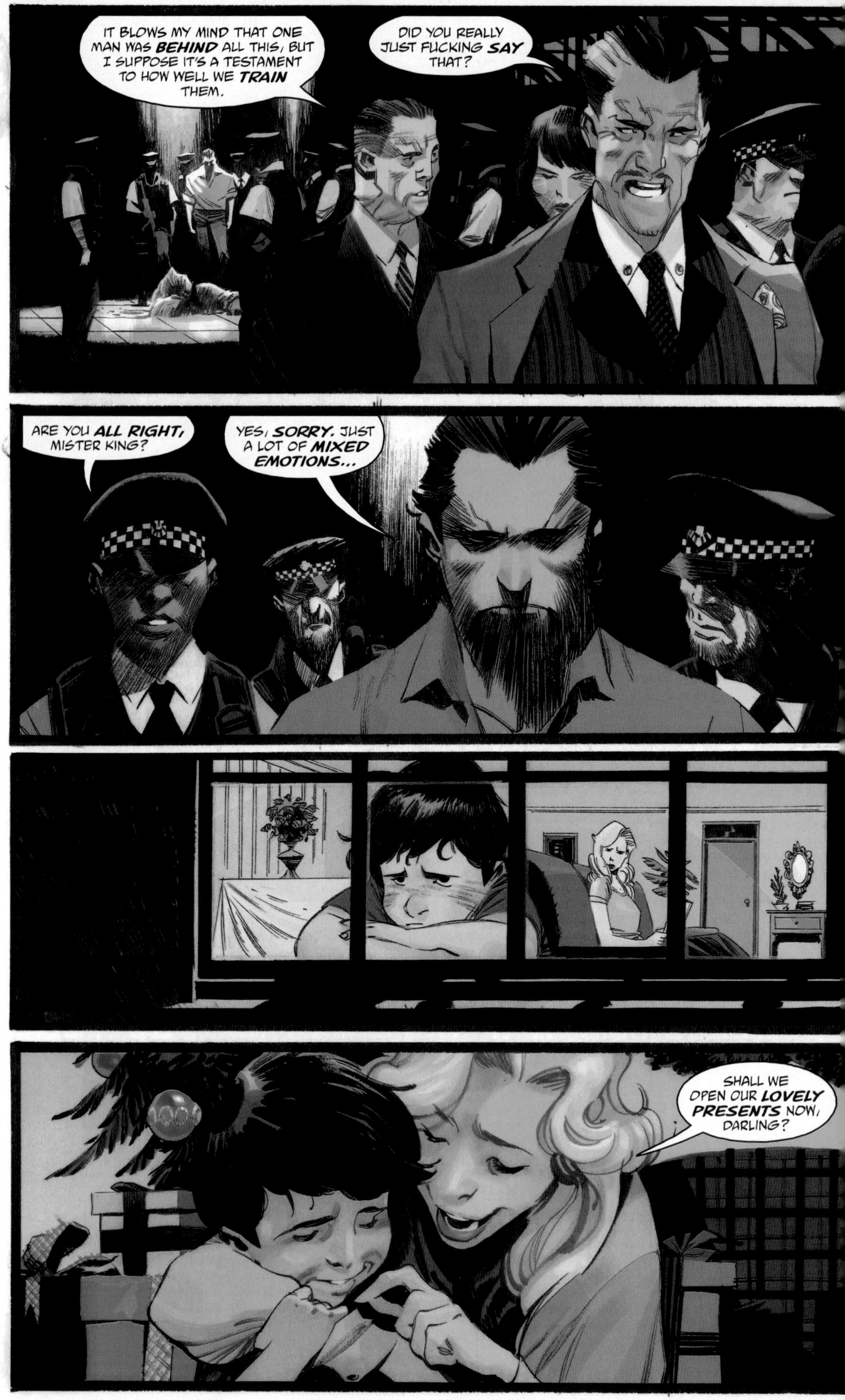

IT BLOWS MY MIND THAT ONE MAN WAS BEHIND ALL THIS, BUT I SUPPOSE IT'S A TESTAMENT TO HOW WELL WE TRAIN THEM.
DID YOU REALLY JUST FUCKING SAY THAT?
ARE YOU ALL RIGHT, MISTER KING?
YES, SORRY. JUST A LOT OF MIXED EMOTIONS...
SHALL WE OPEN OUR LOVELY PRESENTS NOW, DARLING?

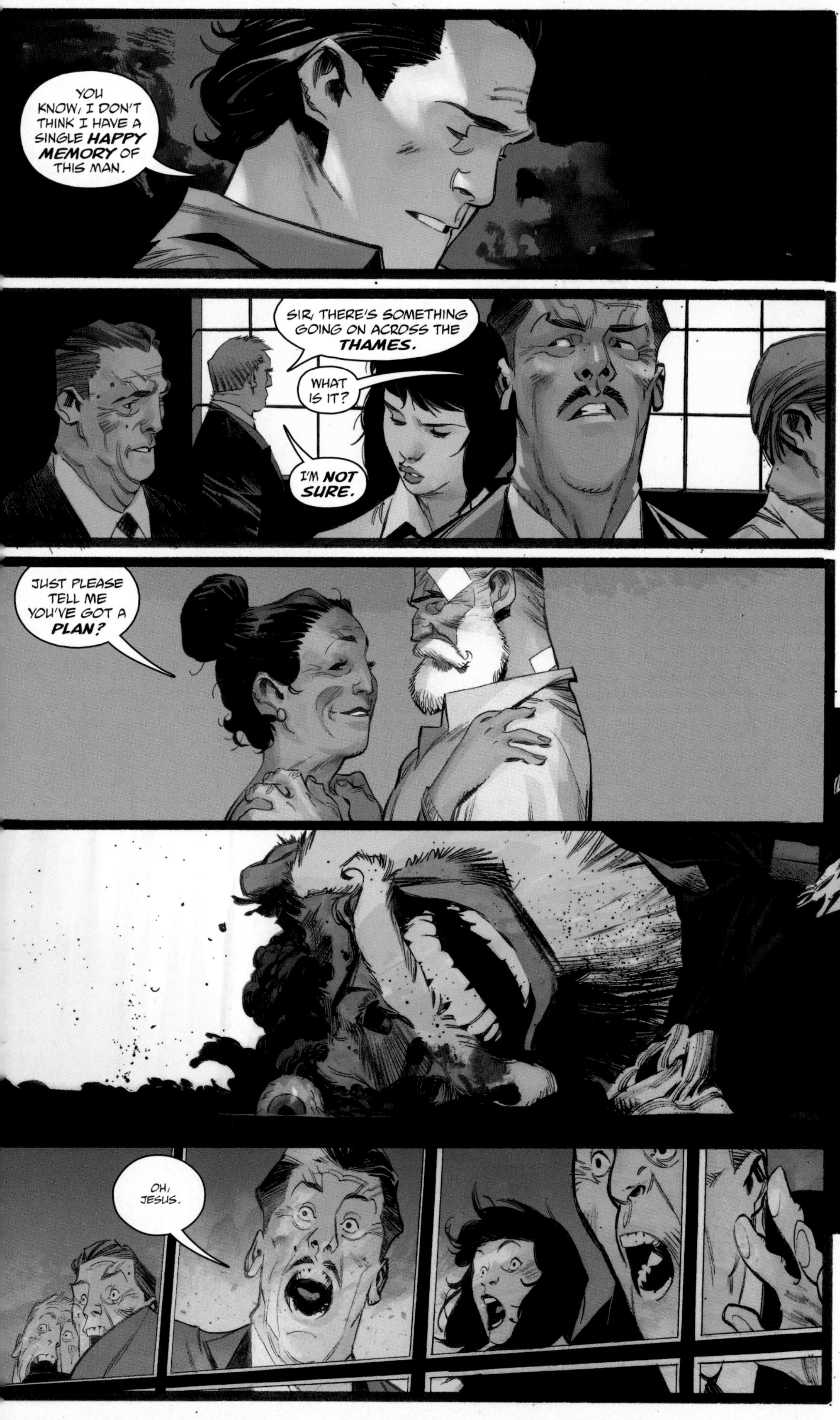
YOU KNOW, I DON'T THINK I HAVE A SINGLE **HAPPY MEMORY** OF THIS MAN.
SIR, THERE'S SOMETHING GOING ON ACROSS THE **THAMES**.
WHAT IS IT?
I'M **NOT SURE**.
JUST PLEASE TELL ME YOU'VE GOT A **PLAN**?
OH, JESUS.

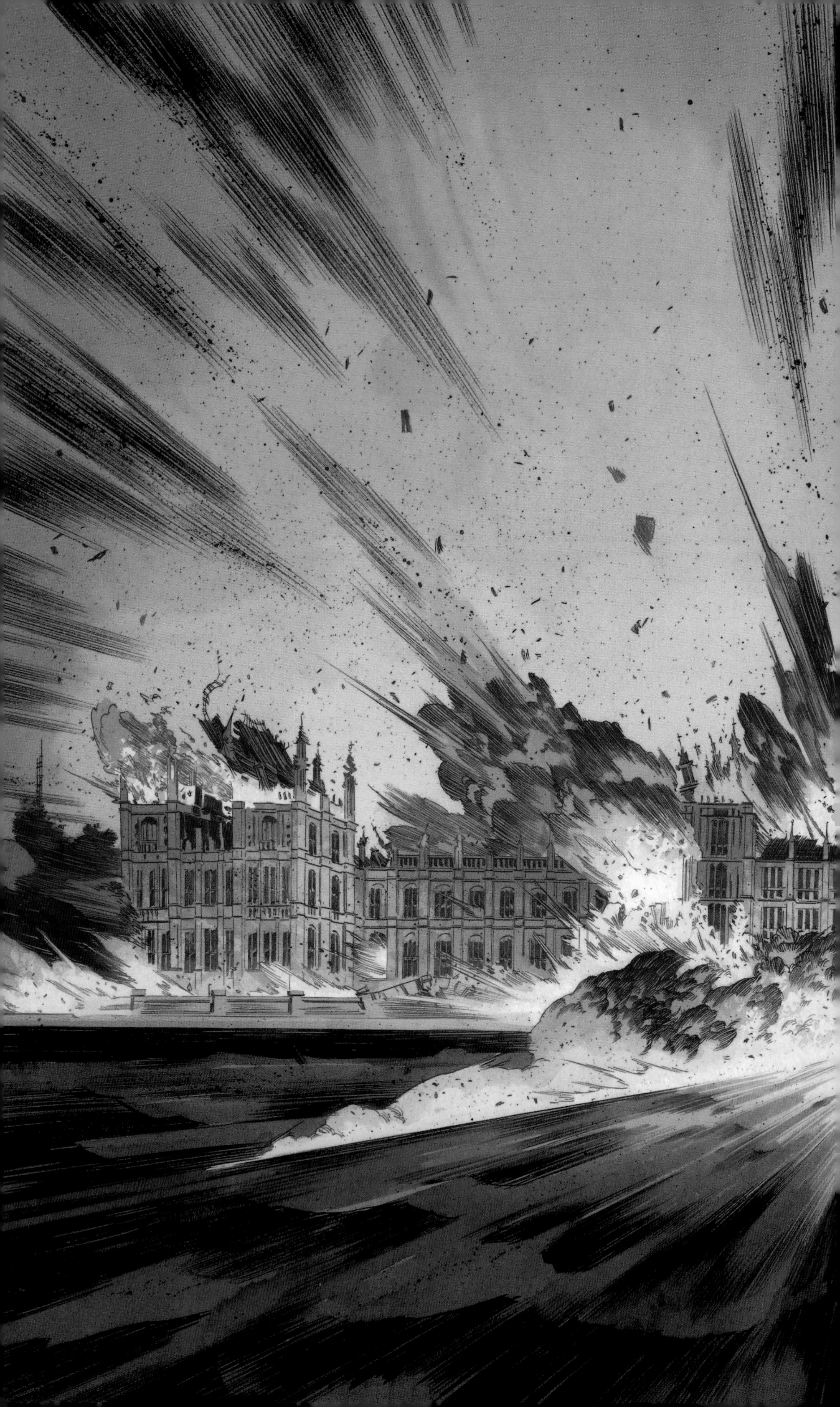

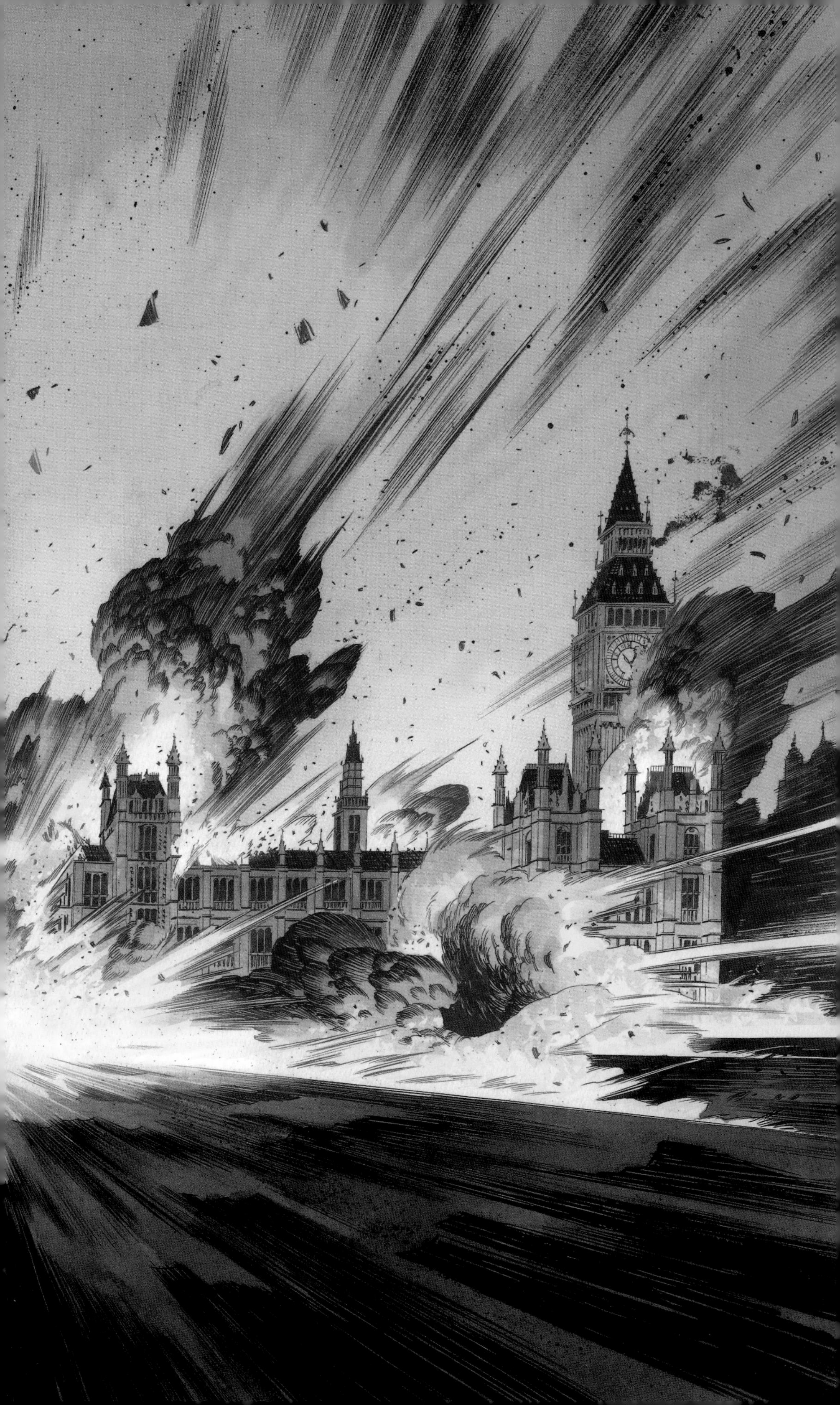

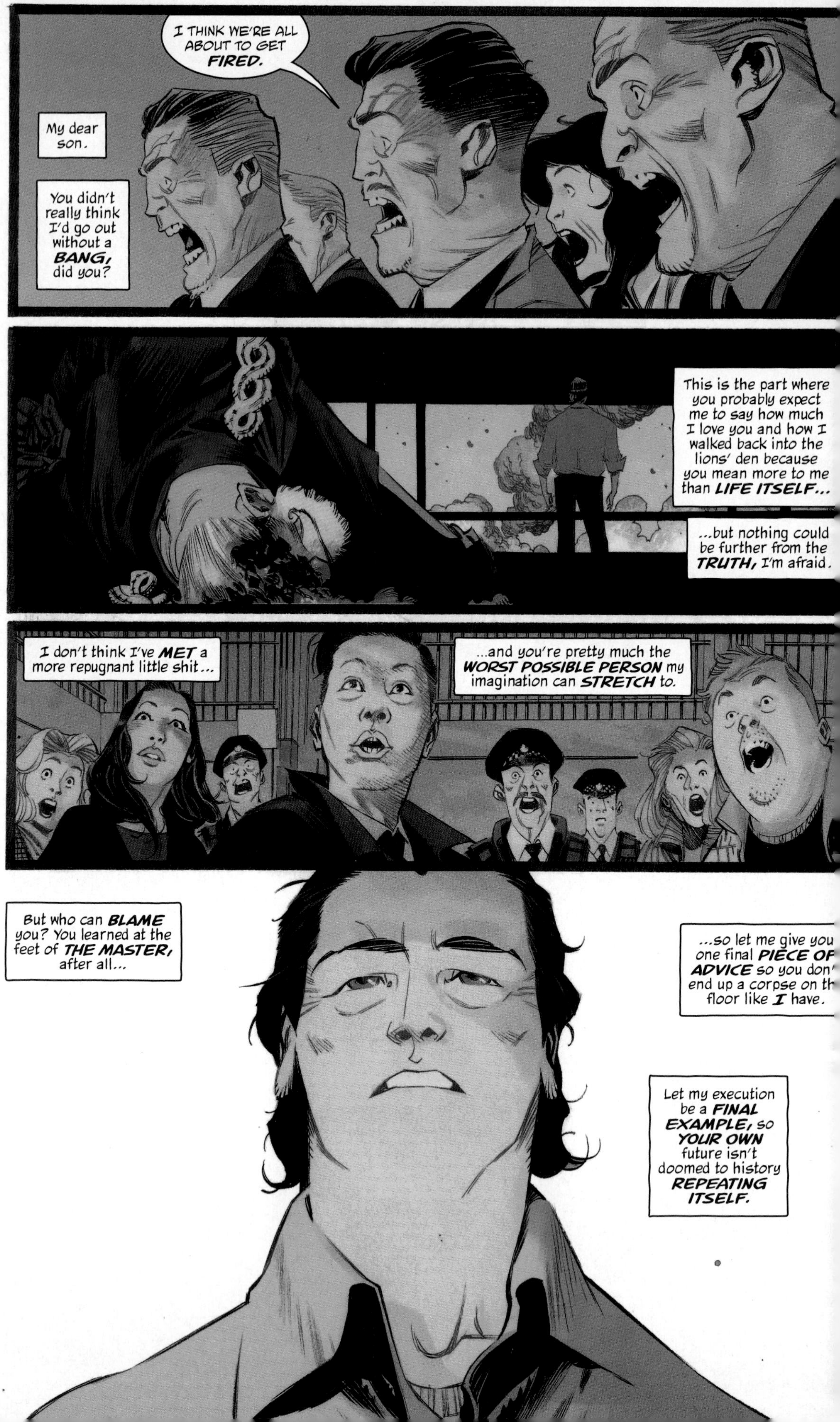
My dear son.
You didn't really think I'd go out without a BANG, did you?
I THINK WE'RE ALL ABOUT TO GET FIRED.
This is the part where you probably expect me to say how much I love you and how I walked back into the lions' den because you mean more to me than LIFE ITSELF...
...but nothing could be further from the TRUTH, I'm afraid.
I don't think I've MET a more repugnant little shit...
...and you're pretty much the WORST POSSIBLE PERSON my imagination can STRETCH to.
But who can BLAME you? You learned at the feet of THE MASTER, after all...
...so let me give you one final PIECE OF ADVICE so you don' end up a corpse on th floor like I have.
Let my execution be a FINAL EXAMPLE, so YOUR OWN future isn't doomed to history REPEATING ITSELF.

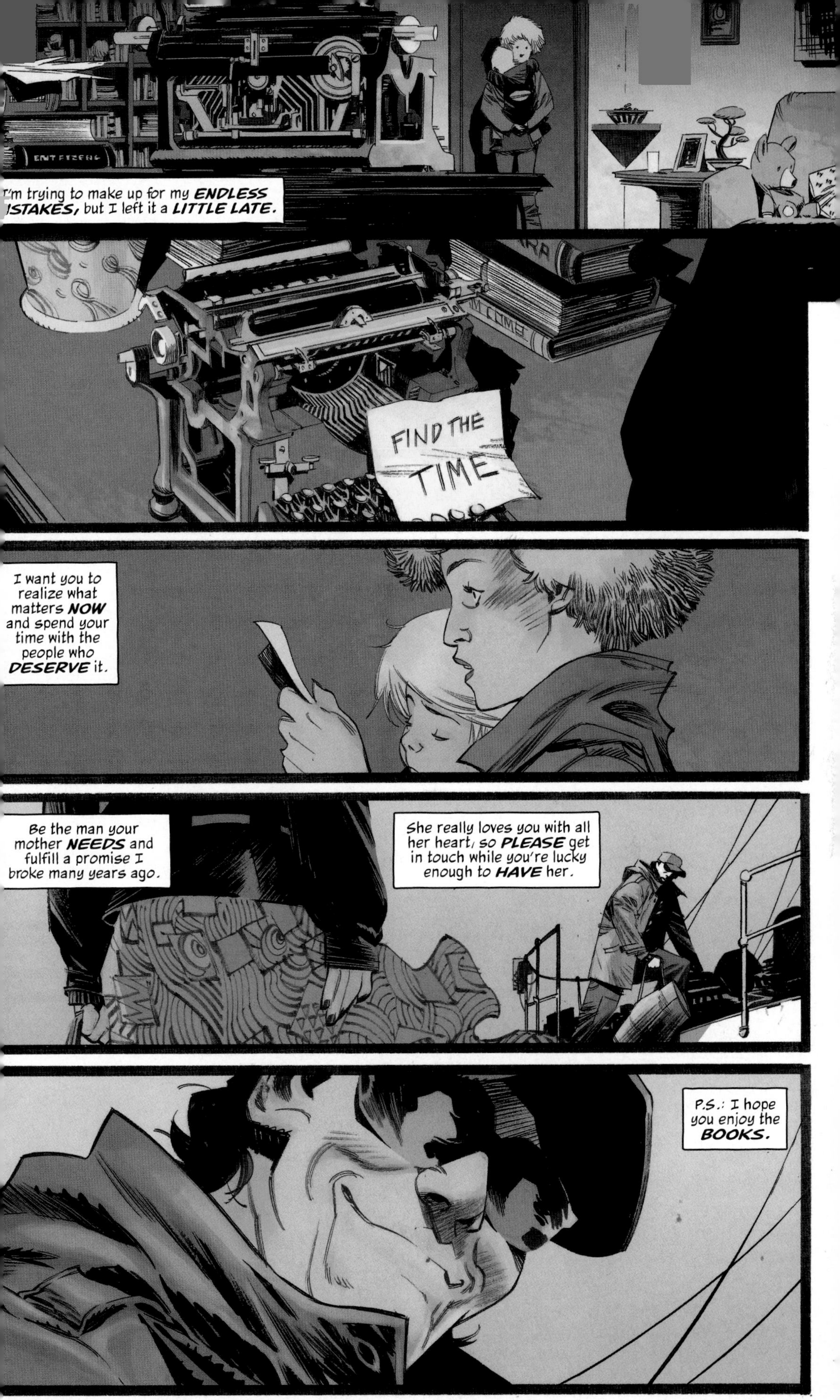

I'm trying to make up for my ENDLESS
ISTAKES, but I left it a LITTLE LATE.
FIND THE TIME
I want you to realize what matters NOW and spend your time with the people who DESERVE it.
Be the man your mother NEEDS and fulfill a promise I broke many years ago.
She really loves you with all her heart, so PLEASE get in touch while you're lucky enough to HAVE her.
P.S.: I hope you enjoy the BOOKS.

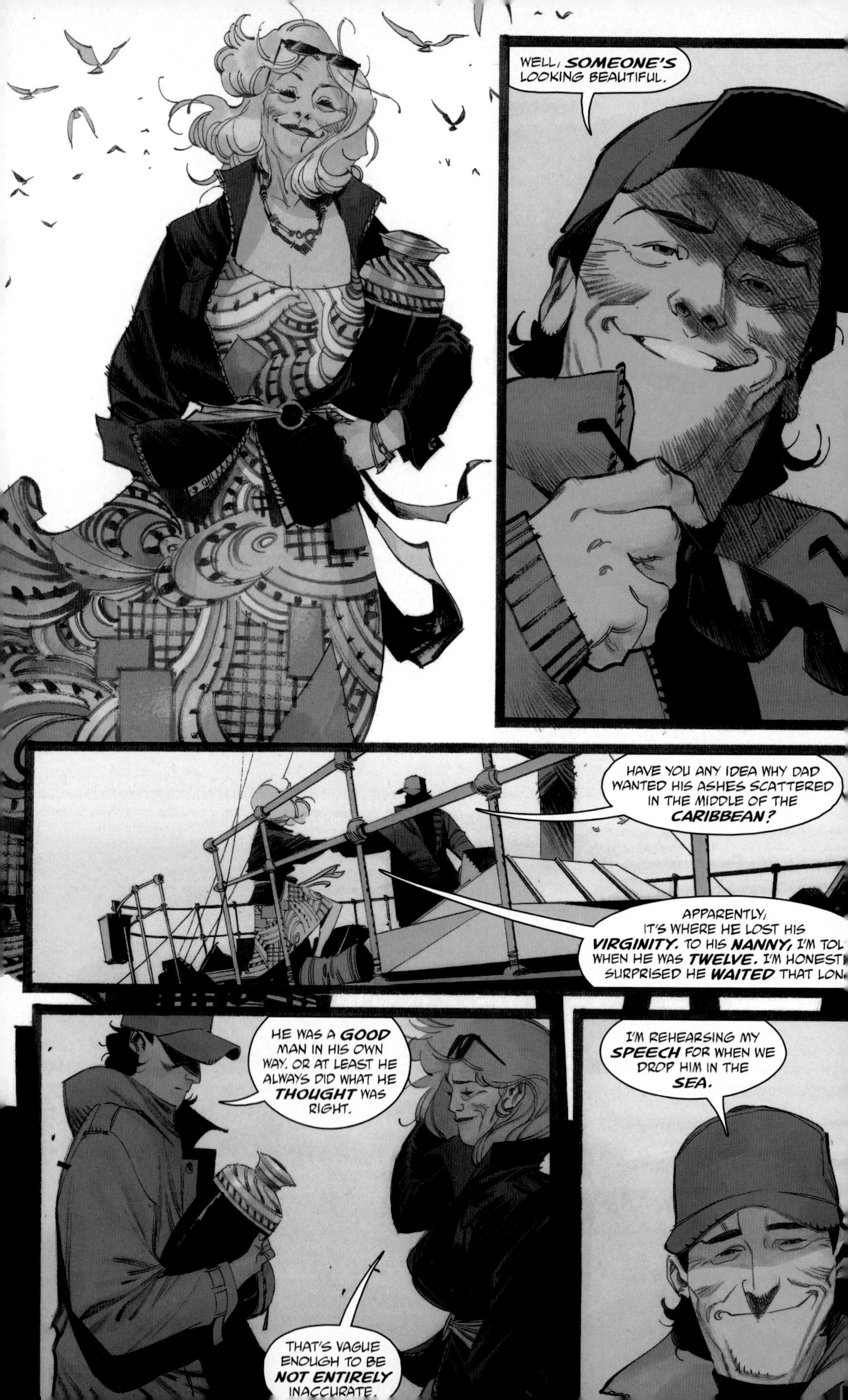
WELL, SOMEONE'S LOOKING BEAUTIFUL.
HAVE YOU ANY IDEA WHY DAD WANTED HIS ASHES SCATTERED IN THE MIDDLE OF THE CARIBBEAN?
APPARENTLY, IT'S WHERE HE LOST HIS VIRGINITY. TO HIS NANNY, I'M TOL WHEN HE WAS TWELVE. I'M HONEST SURPRISED HE WAITED THAT LON
HE WAS A GOOD MAN IN HIS OWN WAY. OR AT LEAST HE ALWAYS DID WHAT HE THOUGHT WAS RIGHT.
THAT'S VAGUE ENOUGH TO BE NOT ENTIRELY INACCURATE.
I'M REHEARSING MY SPEECH FOR WHEN WE DROP HIM IN THE SEA.

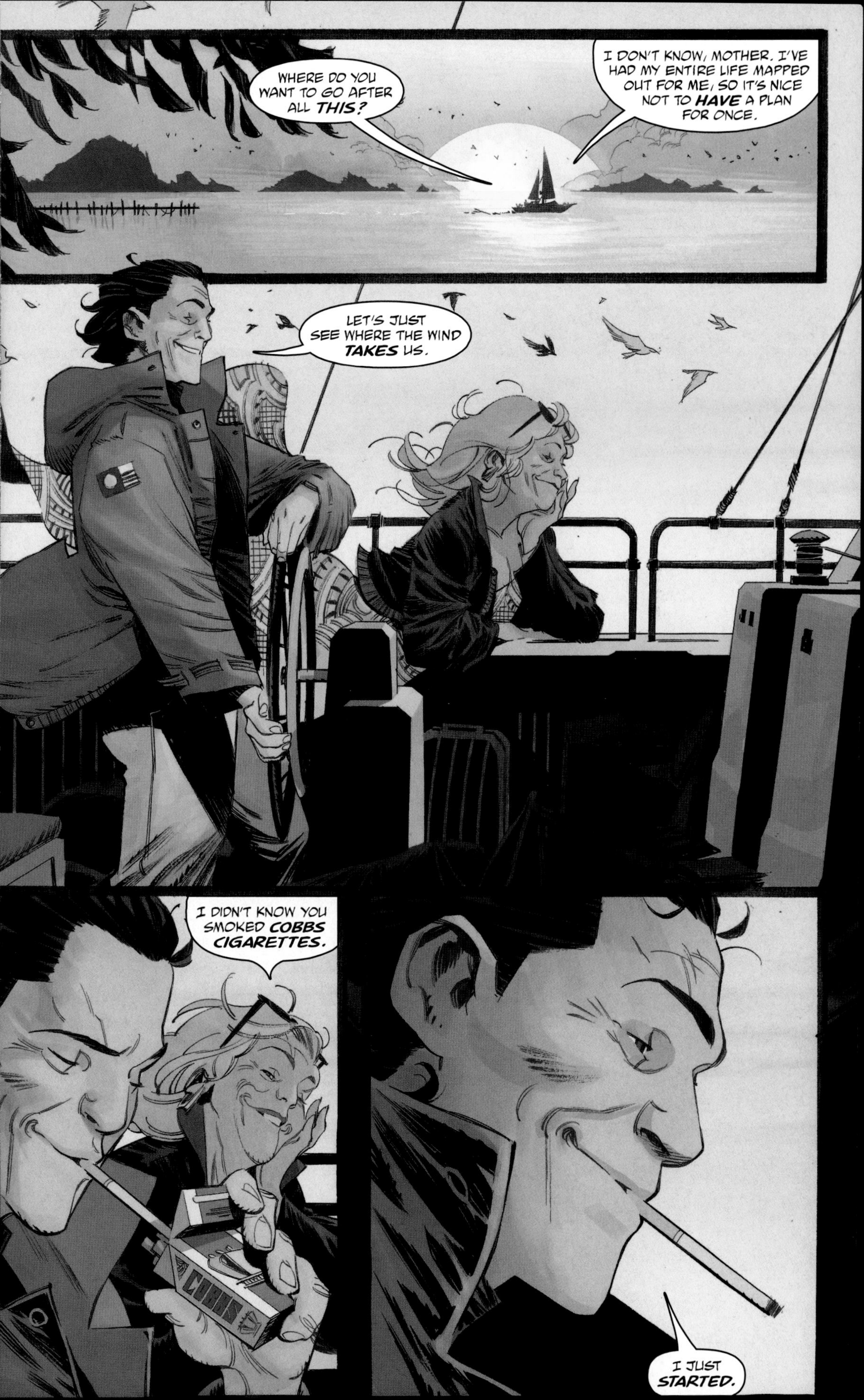
WHERE DO YOU WANT TO GO AFTER ALL THIS?
I DON'T KNOW, MOTHER. I'VE HAD MY ENTIRE LIFE MAPPED OUT FOR ME, SO IT'S NICE NOT TO HAVE A PLAN FOR ONCE.
LET'S JUST SEE WHERE THE WIND TAKES US.
I DIDN'T KNOW YOU SMOKED COBBS CIGARETTES.
COBBS
I JUST STARTED.

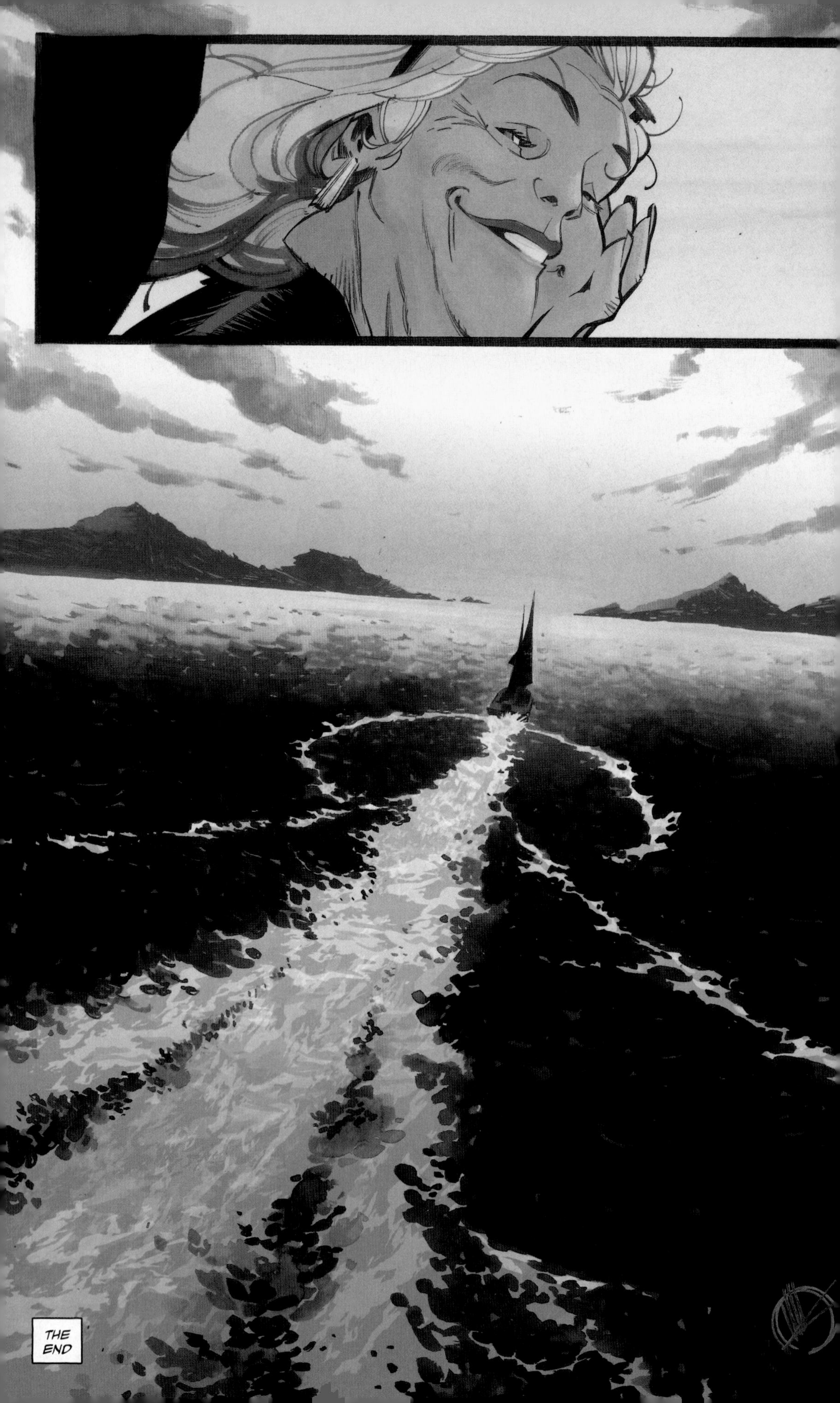
THE END

Bios

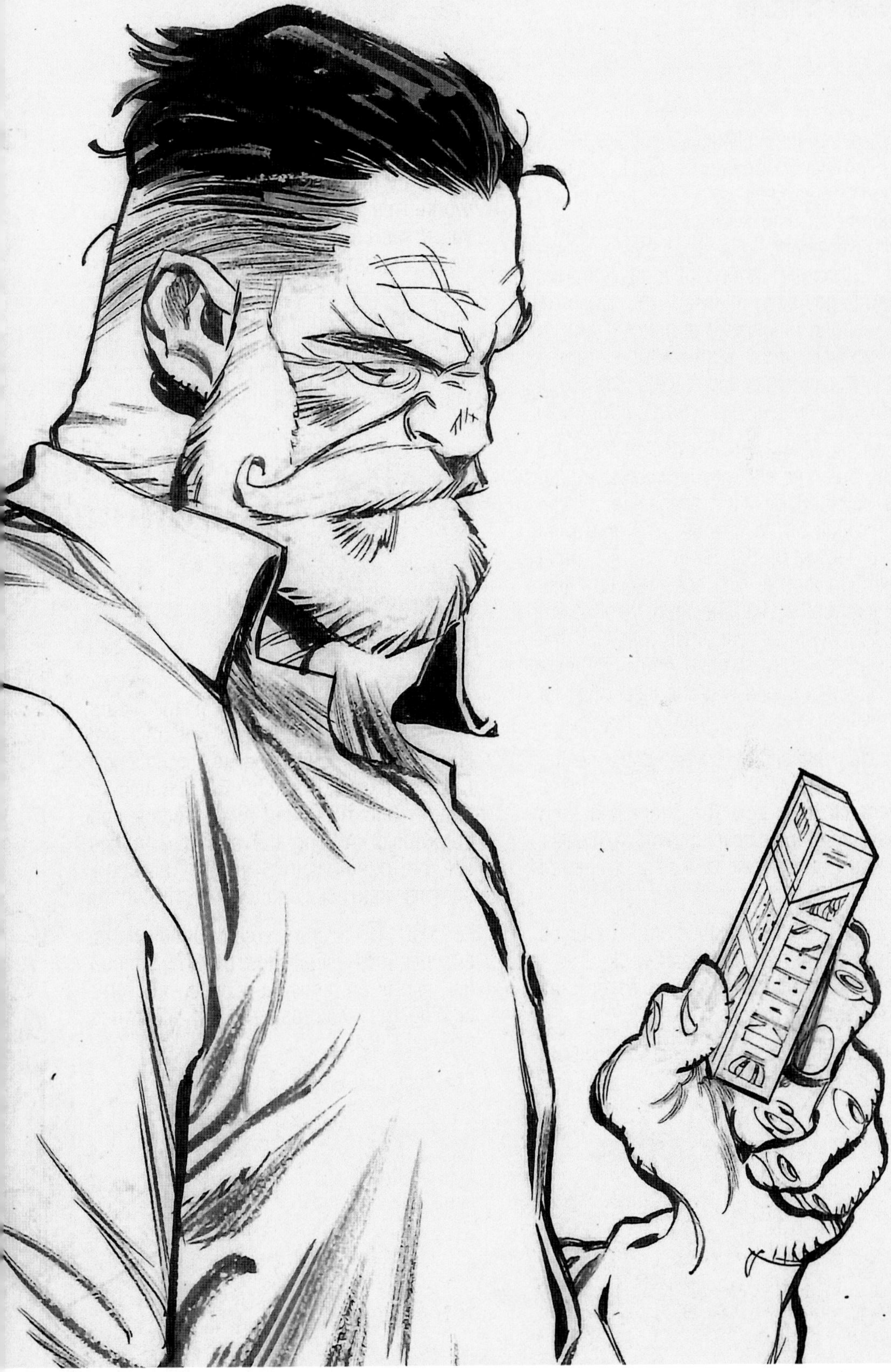

Mark Millar

Matteo Scalera

Mark Millar is a New York Times- best-selling author, Hollywood producer, and now president of his own division at Netlix after selling his publishing company to the world's biggest streamer in 2017. He also signed on to exclusively create new comics, TV series, and movies in-house as a senior executive. Adaptations of JUPITER'S LEGACY and a Japanese anime of SUPER CROOKS have already been released. THE MAGIC ORDER, REBORN, SHARKEY THE BOUNTY HUNTER, PRODIGY, AMERICAN JESUS, KING OF SPIES, EMPRESS, MPH, HUCK and a live-action SUPER CROOKS are currently being made right now.

Previously, Mark worked at Marvel comics where he created THE ULTIMATES, which was selected by Time Magazine as the comic book of the decade, and described by screenwriter Zak Penn as his major inspiration for THE AVENGERS movie. Millar also created WOLVERINE: OLD MAN LOGAN and MARVEL CIVIL WAR. CIVIL WAR was the basis of the third Captain America movie, and OLD MAN LOGAN was the inspiration for Fox's LOGAN.

CIVIL WAR remains Marvel's biggest-selling graphic novel of all time and his seminal SUPERMAN: RED SON the highest-selling Superman graphic novel in history. In 2021, RED SON was also released as an animated feature.

Mark has been an executive producer on all adaptations of his books, and worked as a creative consultant to Fox Studios on their Marvel slate of movies.

His much-anticipated autobiography, MILLAR THE GREAT, will be published next year.

Matteo Scalera was born in Parma, Italy in October 1982.

His professional career started in 2008, with the publication of HYPERKINETIC, a four-issue series by Image Comics. Since then, he's worked on INCORRUPTIBLE, IRREDEEMABLE, VALEN THE OUTCAST (Boom! Studios), DEADPOOL, SECRET AVENGERS, INDESTRUCTIBLE HULK (Marvel), BATMAN, RED HOOD AND THE OUTLAWS, BATMAN WHITE KNIGHT PRESENTS: HARLEY QUINN (DC Comics), DEAD BODY ROAD (Skybound), BLACK SCIENCE (Image Comics) and SPACE BANDITS (Netflix/Image Comics).

Giovanna Niro

Giovanna Niro has been a comic book colorist since 2006. Over the years, she has worked for Italian, American and French publishing companies: Sergio Bonelli Editore, Panini Comics, IDW Publishing, Image, Boom!Studios, Awa Studios and Futuropolis. Among the comics she has colored: ORPHANS, DYLAN DOG, THE CROW, GRENDEL: KENTUCKY and BATMAN: THE WORLD.

For Mark Millar, she colored CHRONONAUTS: FUTURESHOCK (illustrated by Eric Canete) and she is currently working on the forthcoming THE MAGIC ORDER VOL 4 (illustrated by Dike Ruan).

She lives and works in Rome.

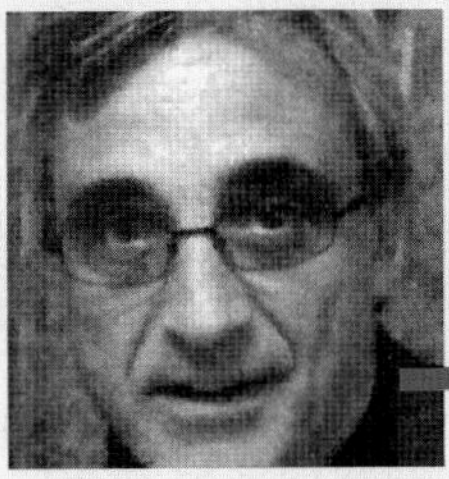

Clem Robins

Since 1977, Clem Robins has done lettering for DC, Marvel, Image, Dark Horse, and pretty much everybody else. His current projects include BATMAN: ONE DARK KNIGHT, Keanu Reeves' miniseries BRZRKR, and everything associated with HELLBOY.

His 2002 book THE ART OF FIGURE DRAWING was published by North Light Books and has since been translated into Spanish, French, Italian, German and Chinese. From 1998 through 2007 he taught figure drawing and human anatomy at the Art Academy of Cincinnati.

His paintings and drawings are in the Eisele Gallery of Fine Art in Cincinnati, and in the permanent collection of the Cincinnati Art Museum. If you're curious, you can see them at www.clemrobins.com

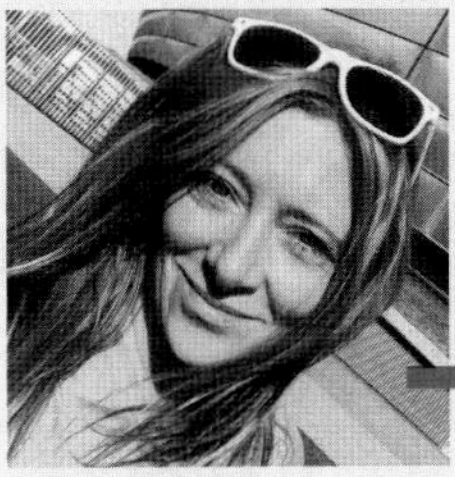

Frances Mullen

Frances ditched the corporate world and started her freelance adventure in 2014 working for a number of clients in project management roles which brought her to Millarworld in 2020 to take on a contract as Editorial Production Manager for their current titles in production.

Her portfolio of clients are mainly from the creative industries and charities.

Based in Glasgow, Scotland she can be found working from anywhere in the surrounding hills and lochs where she lives with her family.

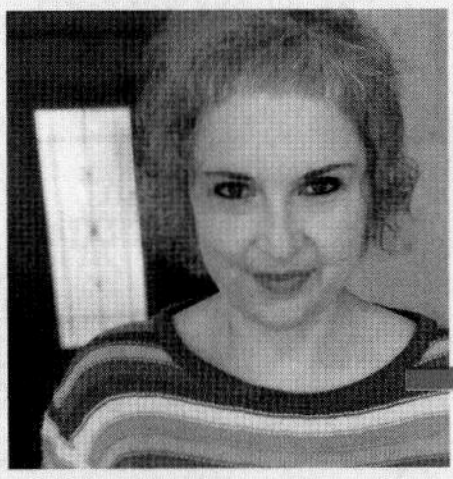

Melina Mikulic

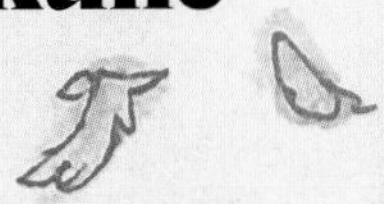

Melina is a well-known graphic designer at Croatia's comic scene: she designed many editions for all leading Croatian comic publishers.

She came on board the Millar team in 2015 to design a paperback edition of STARLIGHT and has stayed since then, working design and production on many of Millar's projects: KINGSMAN, MPH, CHRONONAUTS, HIT-GIRL, KICK-ASS, THE MAGIC ORDER, PRODIGY, SPACE BANDITS, SHARKEY: THE BOUNTY HUNTER, and JUPITER'S LEGACY.

Being curious about many art and design disciplines with a growing interest in the digital medium over the last decade, she branched out into illustration, web and UI design.

She lives happily in Rijeka, the rainiest city in Croatia.

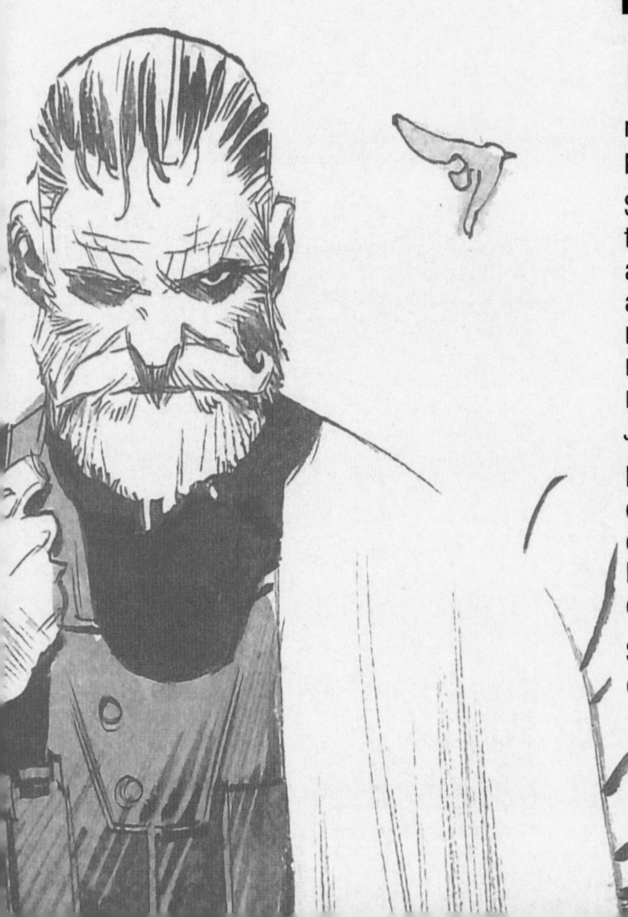

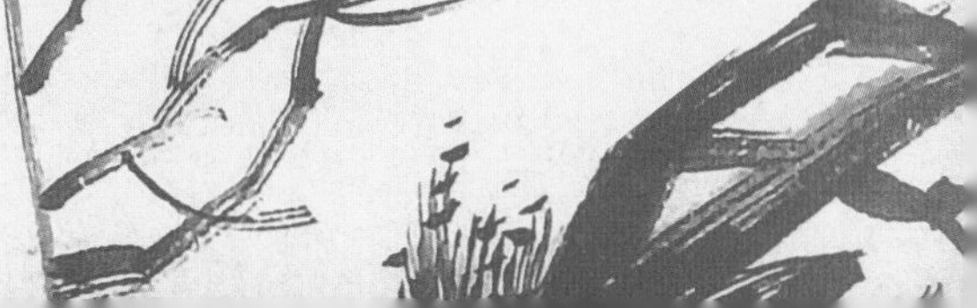

THE MARK MILLAR COLLECTION

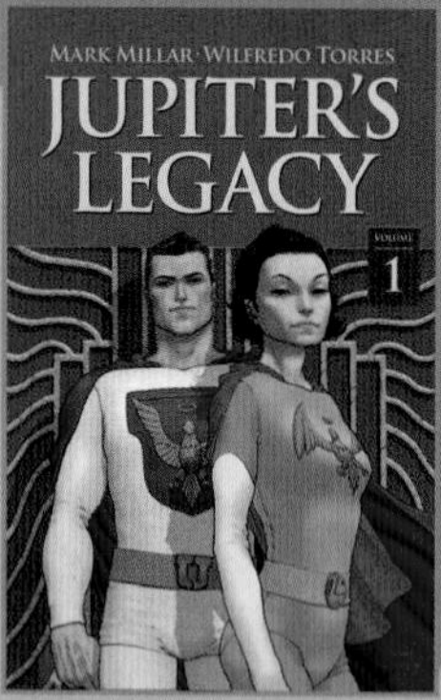
MARK MILLAR · WILFREDO TORRES
JUPITER'S LEGACY
1
Jupiter's Legacy 1-5

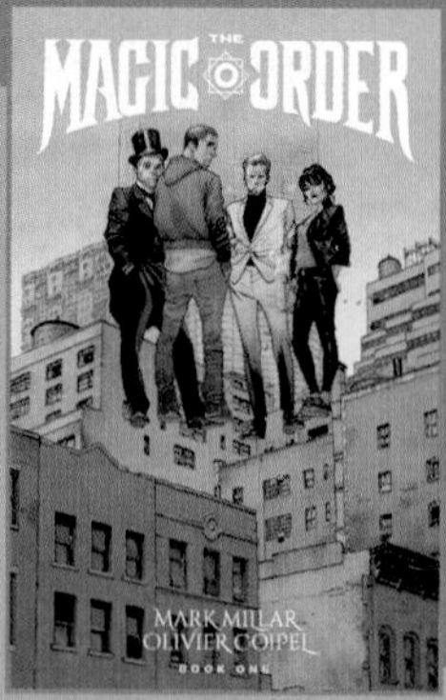
THE MAGIC ORDER
MARK MILLAR
OLIVIER COIPEL
BOOK ONE
The Magic Order

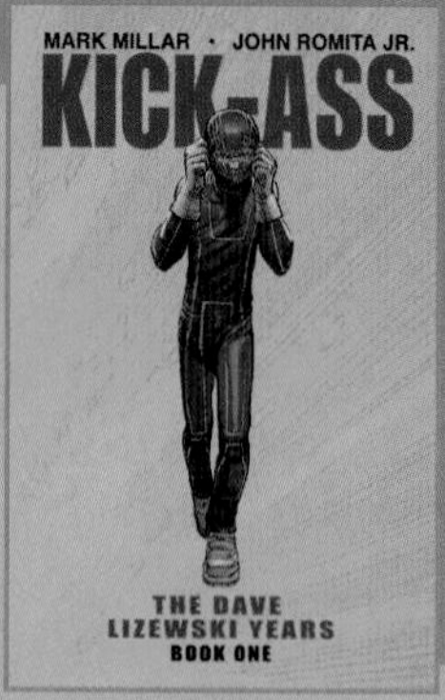
MARK MILLAR · JOHN ROMITA JR.
KICK-ASS
THE DAVE
LIZEWSKI YEARS
BOOK ONE
Kick-Ass 1-4

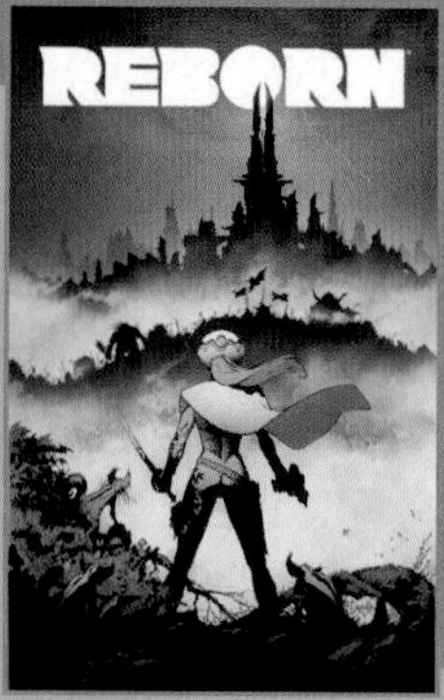
REBORN
Reborn

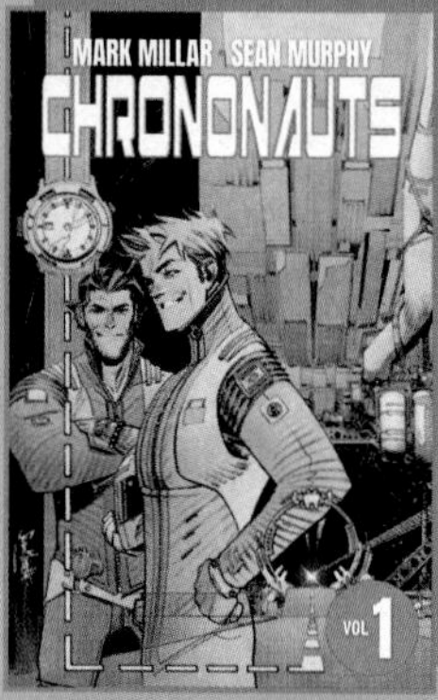
MARK MILLAR · SEAN MURPHY
CHRONONAUTS
VOL 1
Chrononauts 1-2

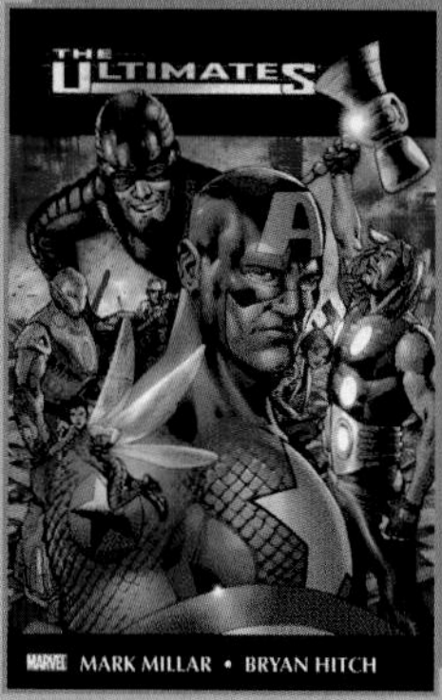
THE ULTIMATES
MARK MILLAR · BRYAN HITCH
The Ultimates 1-2

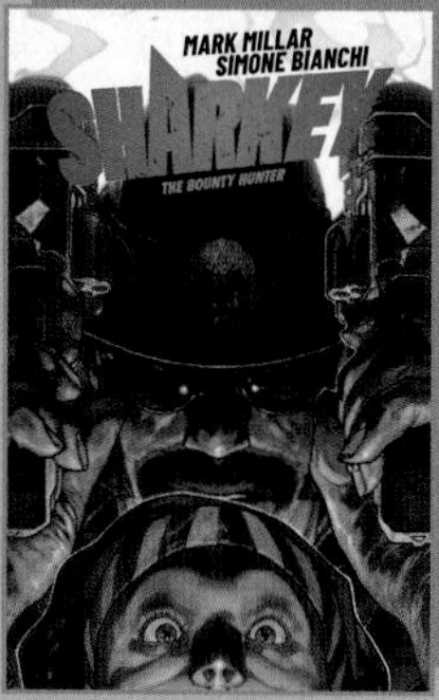
MARK MILLAR
SIMONE BIANCHI
SHARKEY
THE BOUNTY HUNTER
Sharkey The Bounty Hunter

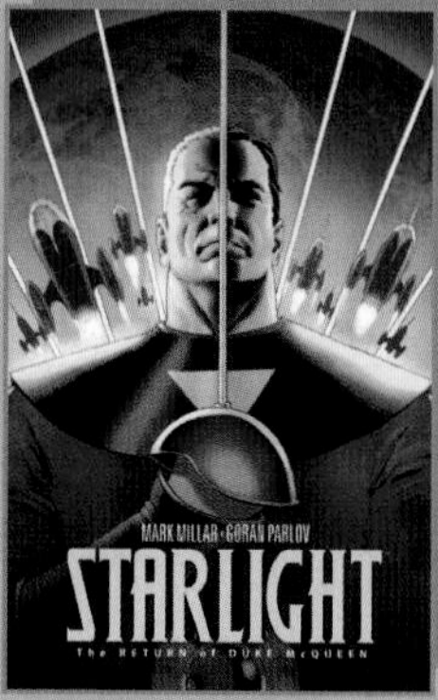
MARK MILLAR · GORAN PARLOV
STARLIGHT
Starlight

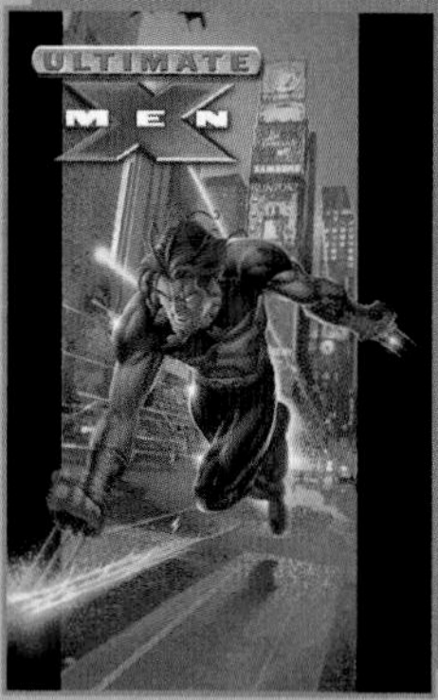
ULTIMATE
X
MEN
Ultimate X-Men 1-6

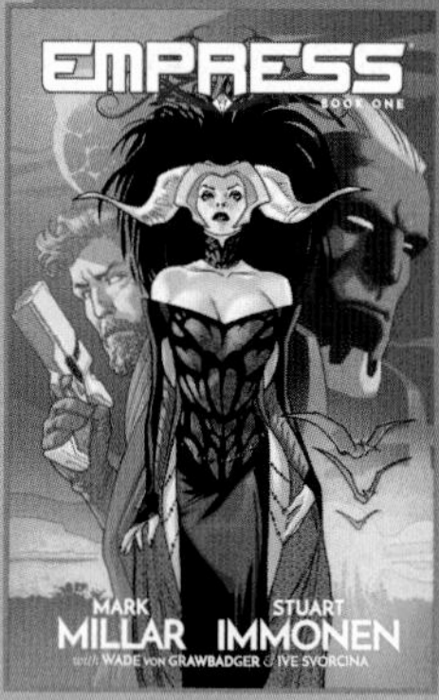
EMPRESS
BOOK ONE
MARK
MILLAR
STUART
IMMONEN
WADE VON GRAWBADGER & IVE SVORCINA
Empress

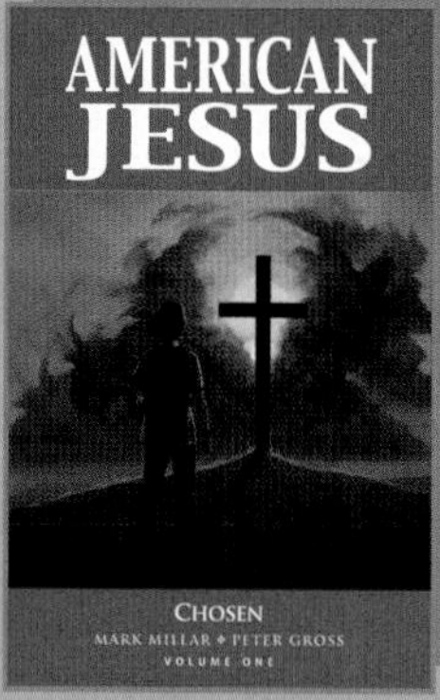
AMERICAN
JESUS
CHOSEN
MARK MILLAR ✦ PETER GROSS
VOLUME ONE
American Jesus 1-2

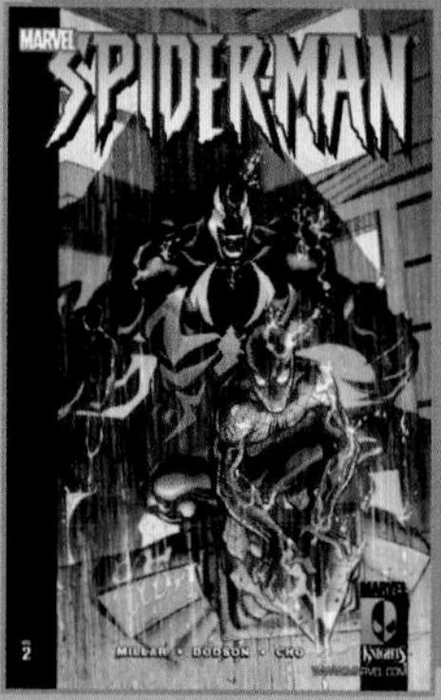
MARVEL
SPIDER-MAN
Marvel Knights Spider-Man

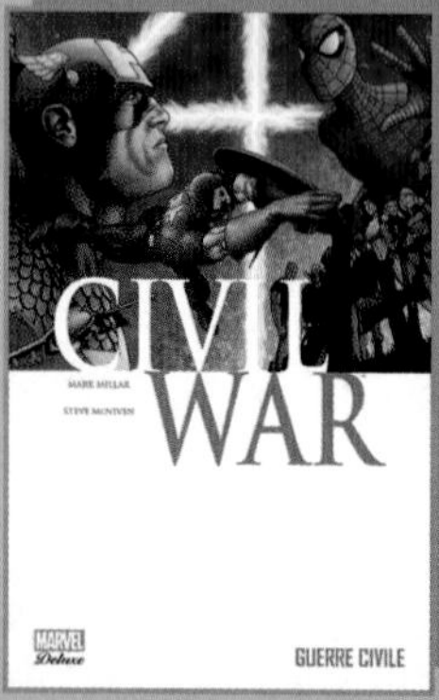
CIVIL
WAR
GUERRE CIVILE
Civil War

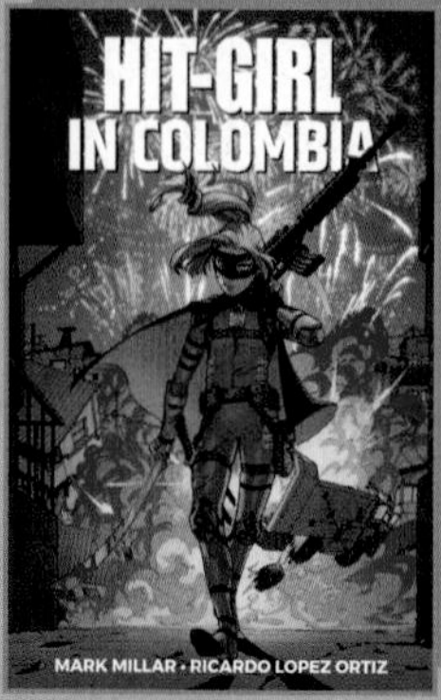
HIT-GIRL
IN COLOMBIA
MARK MILLAR · RICARDO LOPEZ ORTIZ
Hit-Girl 1-6

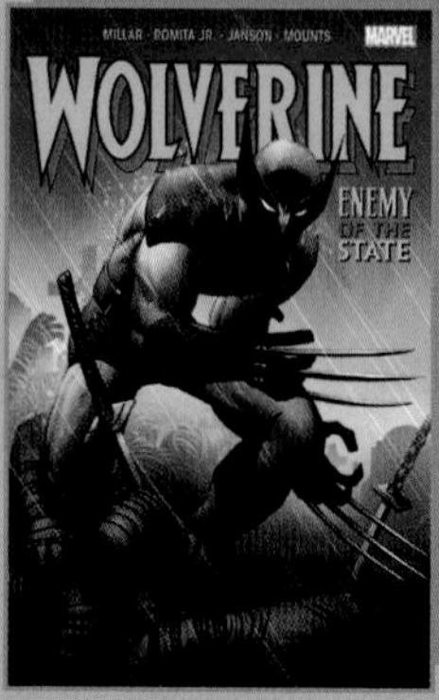
MILLAR · ROMITA JR. · JANSON · MOUNTS
WOLVERINE
ENEMY
OF THE
STATE
Wolverine: Enemy of the State 1-2

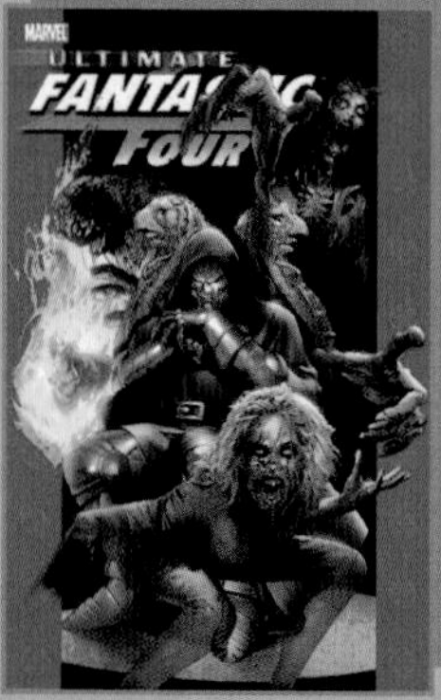
ULTIMATE
FANTASTIC
FOUR
Ultimate Fantastic Four

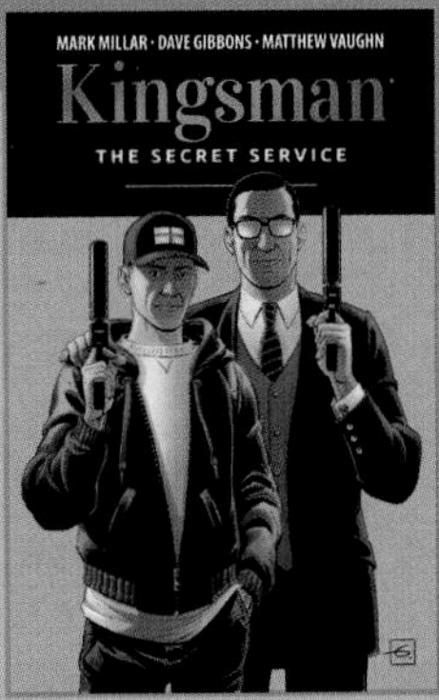
MARK MILLAR • DAVE GIBBONS • MATTHEW VAUGHN
Kingsman
THE SECRET SERVICE
Kingsman 1-2

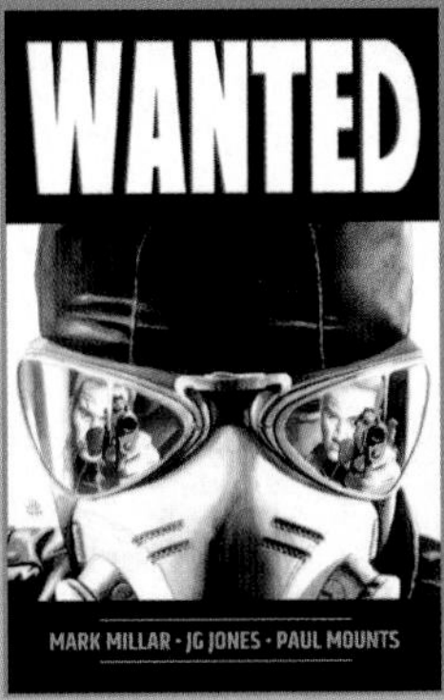
WANTED
MARK MILLAR • JG JONES • PAUL MOUNTS
Wanted

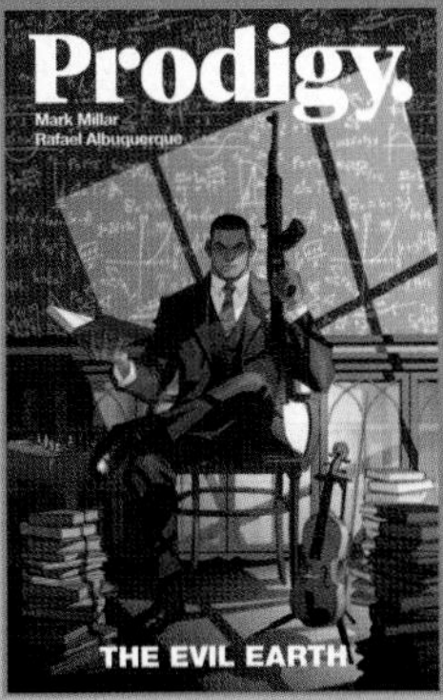
Prodigy.
Mark Millar
Rafael Albuquerque
THE EVIL EARTH
Prodigy

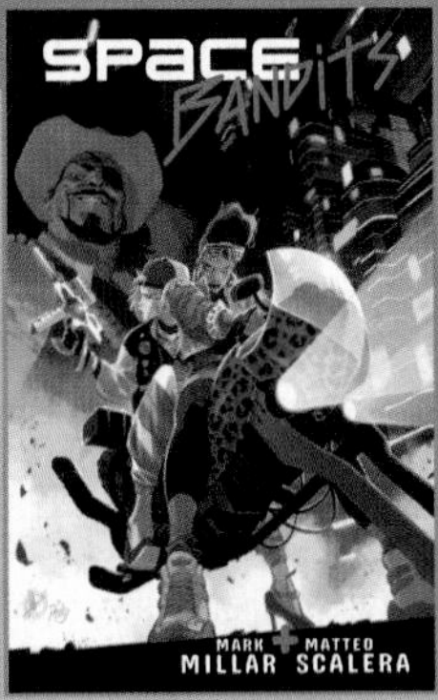
SPACE BANDITS
MARK MILLAR
MATTEO SCALERA
Space Bandits

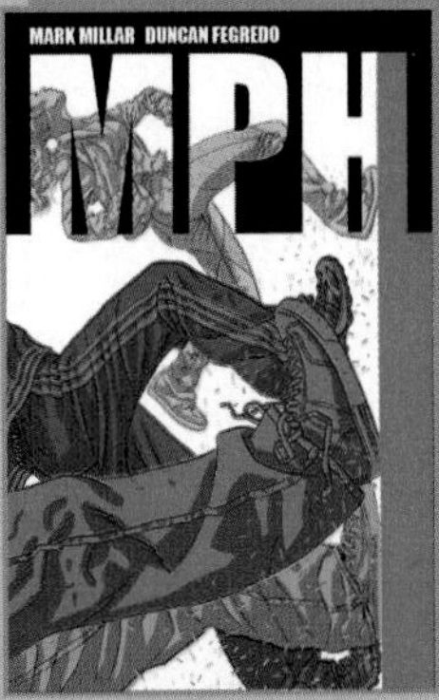
MARK MILLAR DUNCAN FEGREDO
MPH
MPH

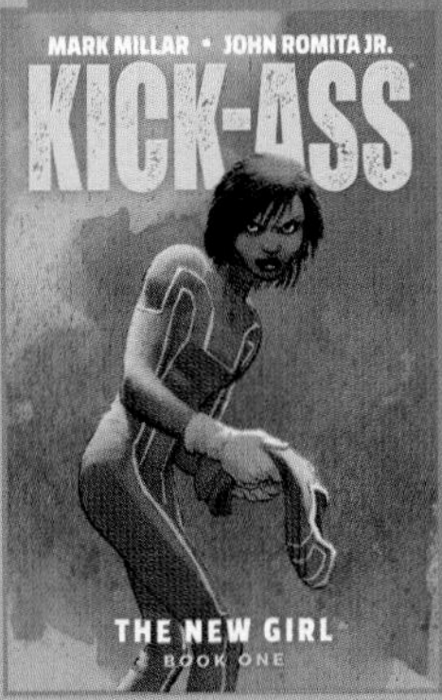
MARK MILLAR • JOHN ROMITA JR.
KICK-ASS
THE NEW GIRL
BOOK ONE
Kick-Ass: The New Girl 1-4

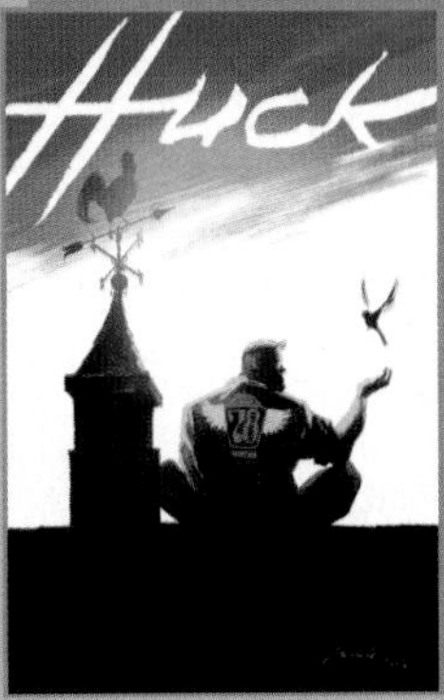
Huck
Huck

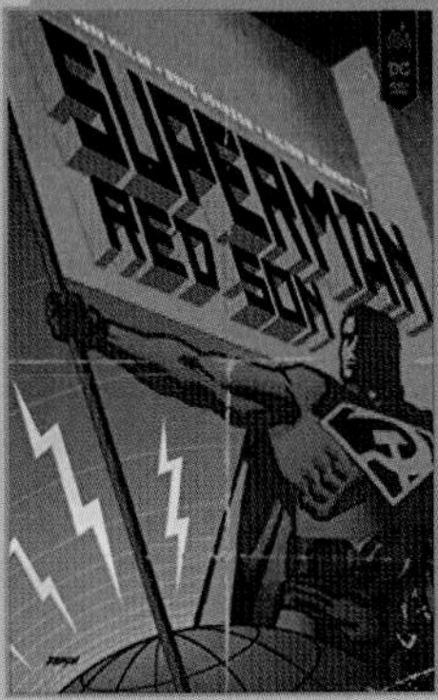
SUPERMAN
RED SON
Superman Red Son

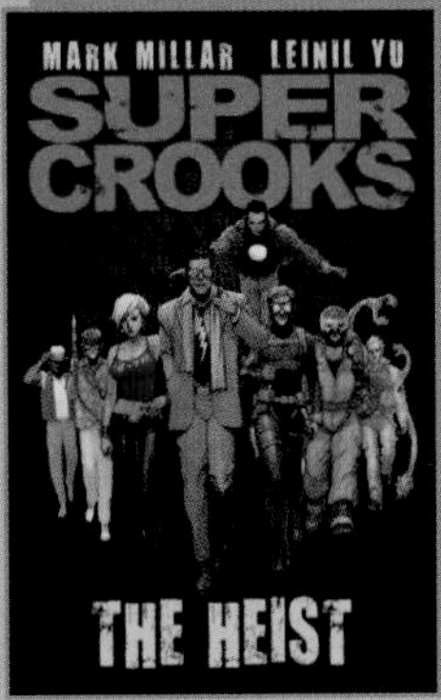
MARK MILLAR LEINIL YU
SUPER
CROOKS
THE HEIST
Super Crooks

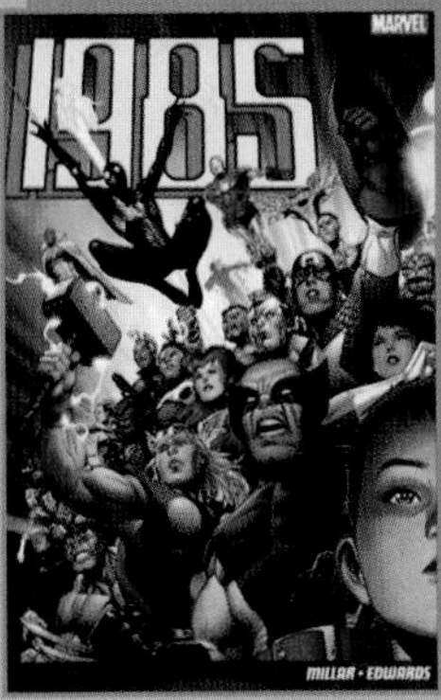
MARVEL
1985
MILLAR • EDWARDS
1985

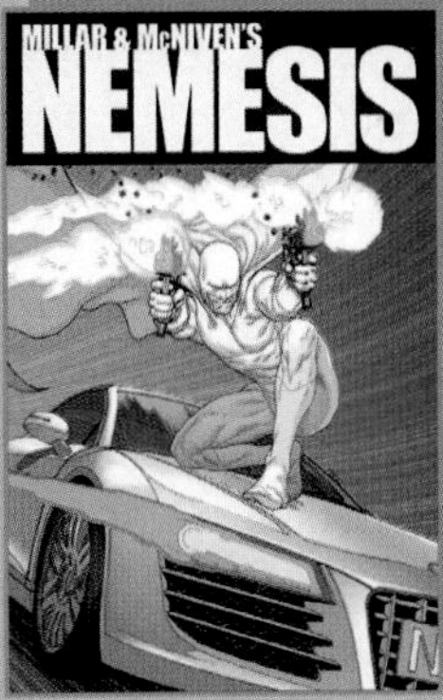
MILLAR & McNIVEN'S
NEMESIS
Nemesis

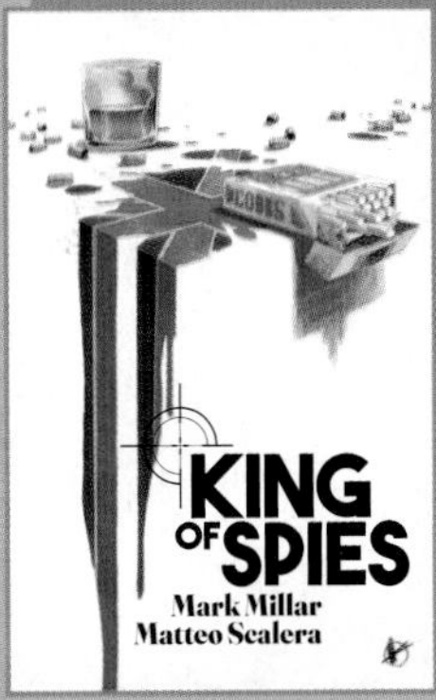
KING
OF SPIES
Mark Millar
Matteo Scalera
King of Spies

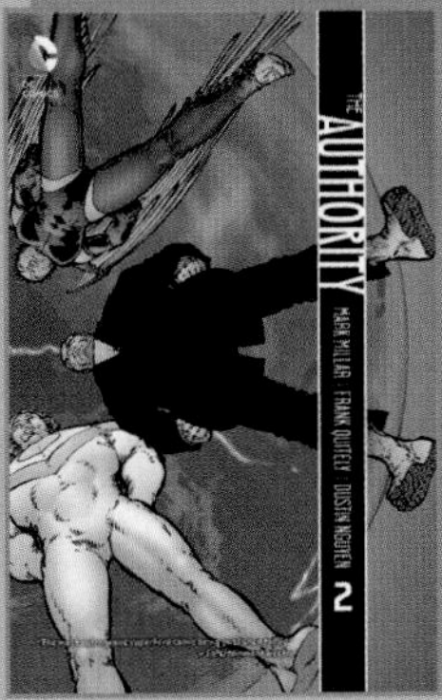
THE AUTHORITY
MARK MILLAR FRANK QUITELY DUSTIN NGUYEN
2
The Authority

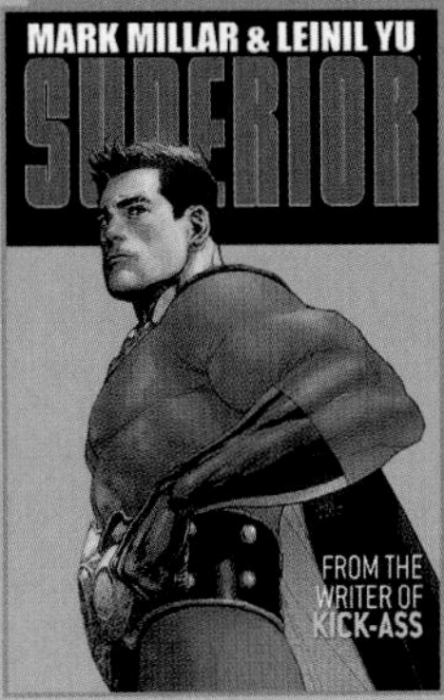
MARK MILLAR & LEINIL YU
SUPERIOR
FROM THE
WRITER OF
KICK-ASS
Superior

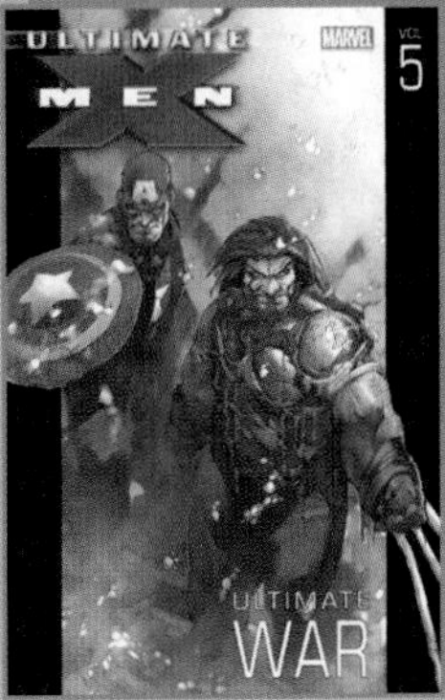
ULTIMATE
X
MEN
MARVEL
VOL.
5
ULTIMATE
WAR
Ultimate War

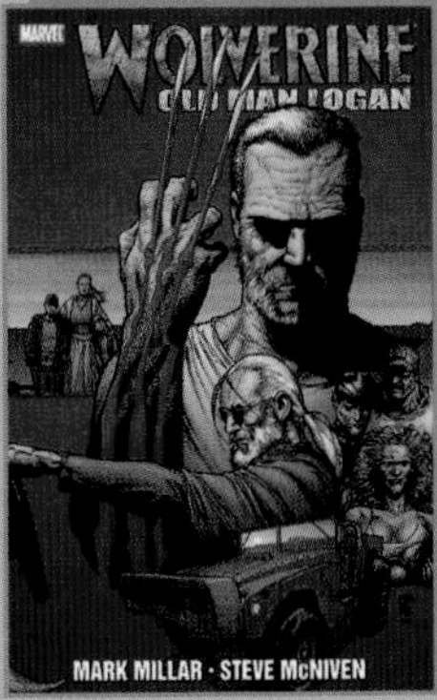
MARVEL
WOLVERINE
OLD MAN LOGAN
MARK MILLAR • STEVE McNIVEN
Wolverine: Old Man Logan

Mark Chiarello

Variant cover issue #1

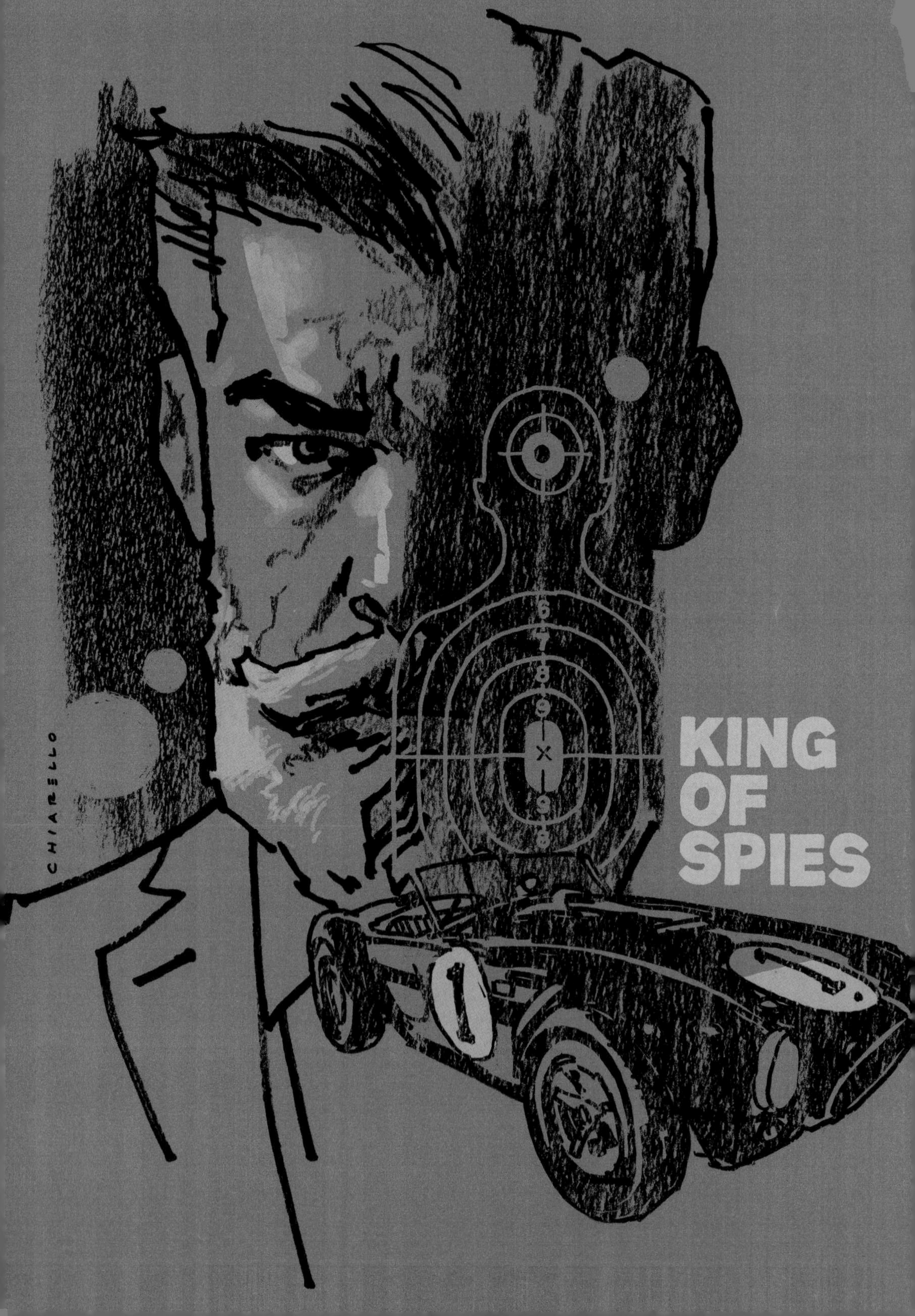
KING
OF
SPIES
CHIARELLO

Ozgur Yildirim

Variant cover issue #1

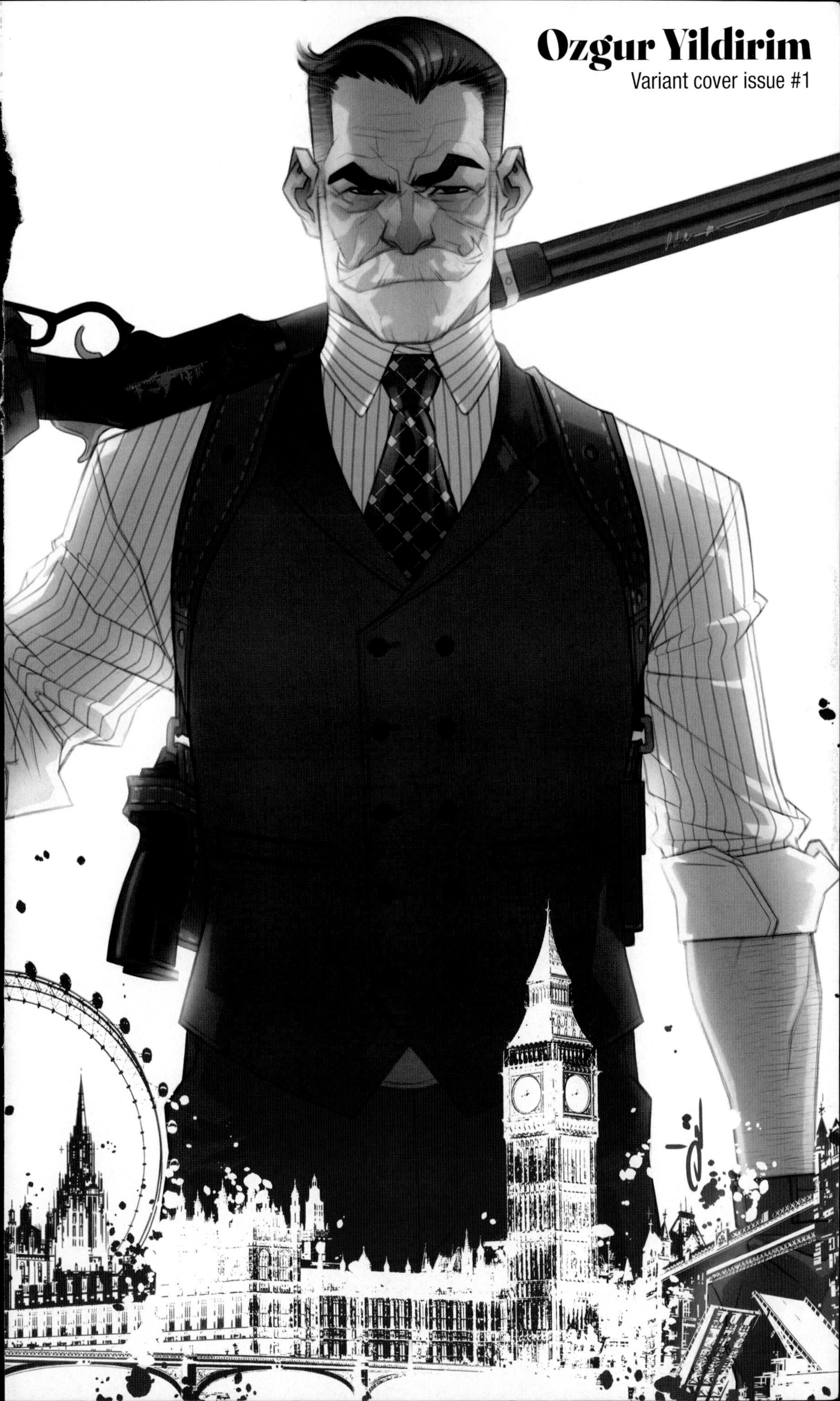

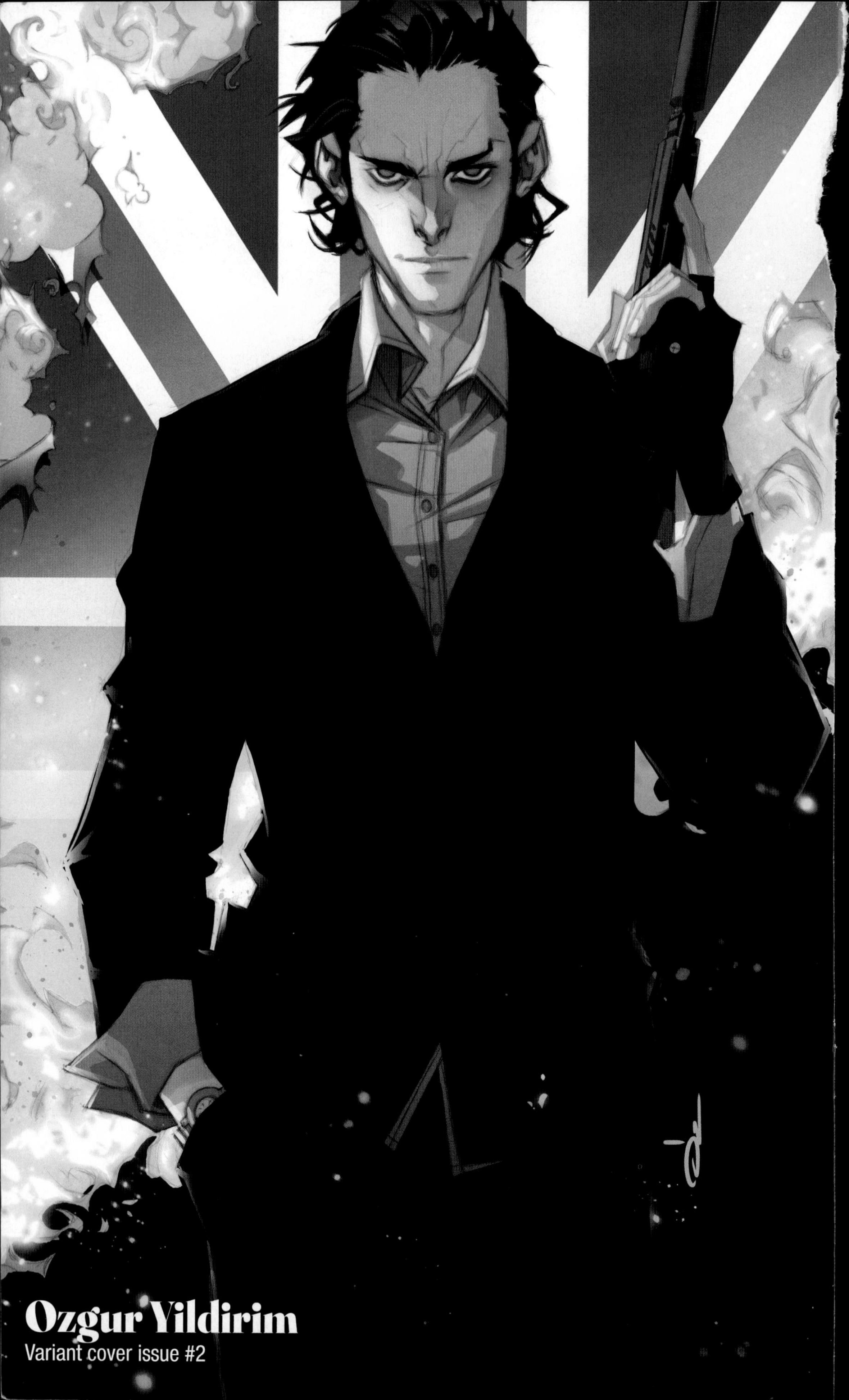

Ozgur Yildirim
Variant cover issue #2

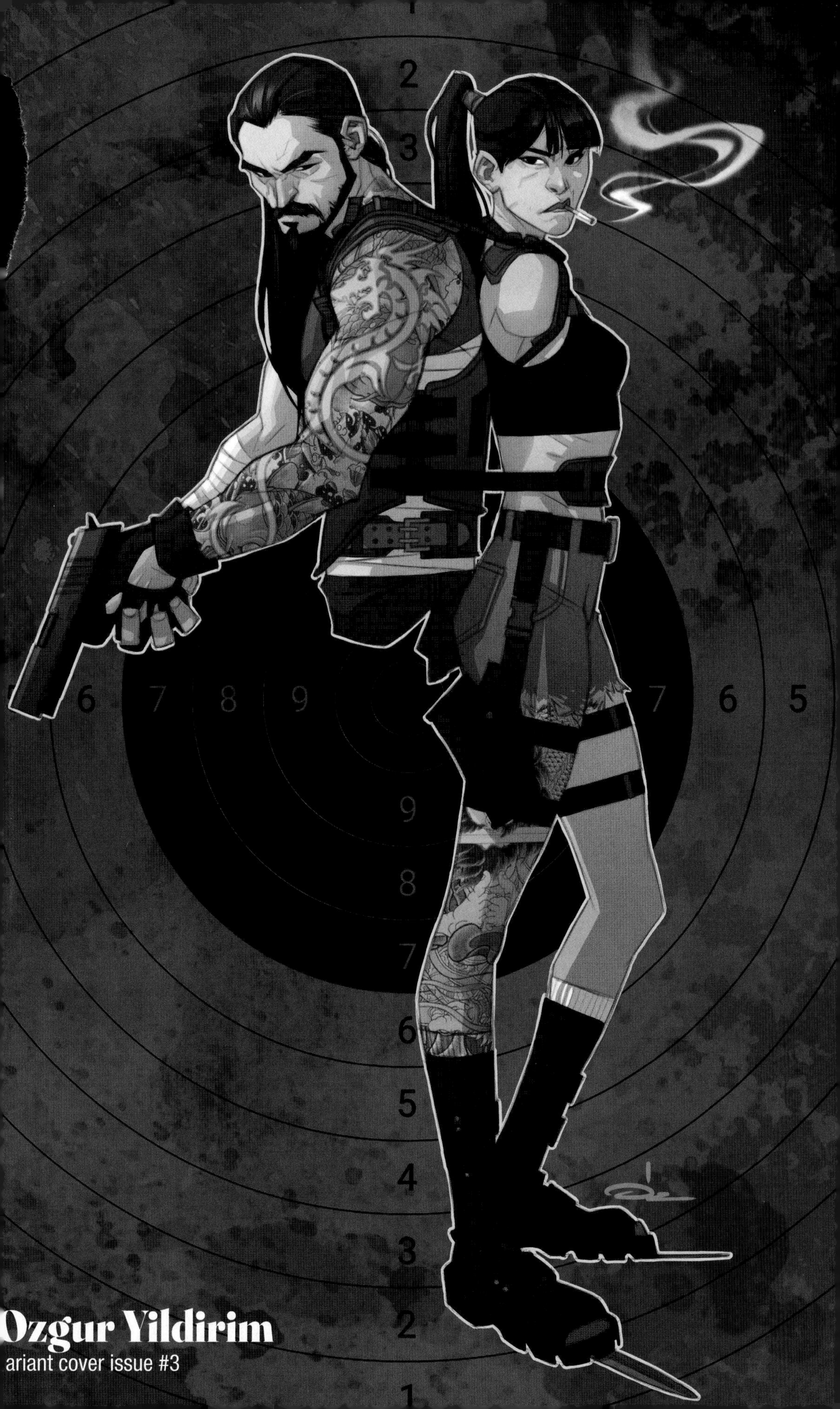

Ozgur Yildirim
ariant cover issue #3

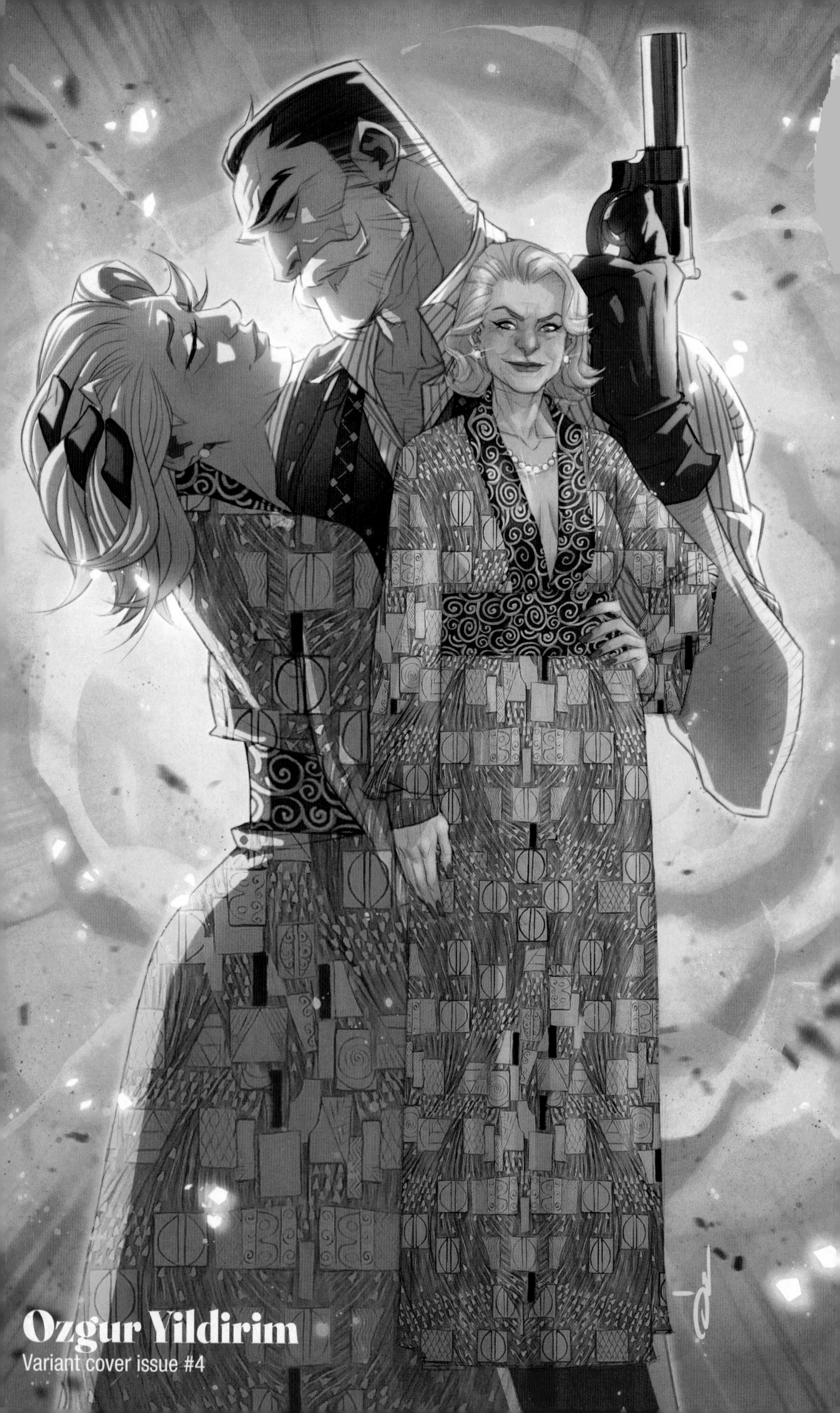

Ozgur Yildirim
Variant cover issue #4